The Best Summer of Our Lives

The Best Summer of Our Lives

RACHEL HAUCK

BETHANYHOUSE
a division of Baker Publishing Group
Minneapolis, Minnesota

© 2023 by Rachel Hauck

Published by Bethany House Publishers
Minneapolis, Minnesota 55438
www.bethanyhouse.com

Bethany House Publishers is a division of
Baker Publishing Group, Grand Rapids, Michigan

Printed in the United States of America

Library of Congress Cataloging-in-Publication Data
Names: Hauck, Rachel, author.
Title: The best summer of our lives / Rachel Hauck.
Description: Minneapolis, Minnesota : Bethany House Publishers, a division of
    Baker Publishing Group, [2023]
Identifiers: LCCN 2022060014 | ISBN 9780764240973 (paper) | ISBN 9780764241826
    (cloth) | ISBN 9781493442133 (ebook)
Subjects: LCGFT: Christian fiction. | Romance fiction. | Novels.
Classification: LCC PS3608.A866 B47 2023 | DDC 813/.6--dc23/eng/20230105
LC record available at https://lccn.loc.gov/2022060014

Cover design by Jennifer Parker

Author is represented by Chip MacGregor, MacGregor Literary.

Baker Publishing Group publications use paper produced from sustainable forestry
practices and post-consumer waste whenever possible.

23 24 25 26 27 28 29   7 6 5 4 3 2 1

To all the friends I've loved before, today, and tomorrow.
You've enriched my life. Thank you.

1

Turn, Turn, Turn

Summer

JUNE '97

The second Summer tumbled into Tumbleweed, Oklahoma, she'd arrived in the middle of the end. The beginning started three hours ago, when her manager, Clark, showed up at her Route 66 motel.

"The band left in the middle of the night," he'd said. "The Sparrows flitted. And I might as well tell you, I'm moving to LA. Got a job with the Bergman Agency. So, here." He handed her the keys to his '87 Ford F-150 as some sort of redneck consolation prize. "To get you home. And you can have it. Pink slip's in the glove box."

Sure enough, the minibus Summer had rented for her band, the Sparrows Fly, was gone, and her gear was piled up outside her Shady Rest Motor Court door.

Son of a gun. So it'd come to this? Her bandmates escaping in the night? At least her previous bands respected her enough to tell her to her face *"we're done."*

"Am I so horrible? So mean? That they sneak off in the night?" She'd tried to live "all for one, one for all," but she was really about herself. Besides, she should've let that phrase die twenty years ago. She could never recapture what had once been.

"Mean? No, I prefer terse," Clark had confessed. "Look, Summer, you *are* the show—the heart and soul of every band you've created. Why don't you just go it alone?"

Because she didn't want to go it alone. She'd grown up with best friends, the Four Seasons, and being part of a team was in her blood.

She also didn't want to be a one-hit wonder. But she was, even though technically "The Preacher" was Tracey Blue's. The country great heard the demo Summer recorded and turned it into a hit of Bobbie Gentry proportions, winning Song of the Year and Artist of the Year. Summer got a nod in the songwriter category but lost to Lori McKenna.

Four years after Tracey's release, country queen Aubrey James covered "The Preacher" because "she loved it," and the song rode Billboard's Top Ten once again.

Summer wrote fifteen new songs, formed Sparrows Fly, and hit the road again. At thirty-eight, dillydallying over *any* success was wasted success. But she failed, didn't she?

Then, as a parting gift, along with his truck keys, Clark handed her a coffee and the morning newspaper.

"Did you see the headline? Twenty years since the Girl Scouts at Camp Scott were murdered. Wasn't Tumbleweed near there? Where you were a camp counselor?"

Summer glanced at the headline and handed back the paper. Yeah, she was a camp counselor the year those girls were killed. Scared the heck out of the entire state.

After Clark said his good-byes, she sat on the edge of her bed and sipped the coffee. This was it. She quit. No more girl bands. No more this-is-my-shot-and-I-know-it business.

Face it, she couldn't make it in country music if Chet Atkins himself took her into the studio and laid down his classic Nashville Sound licks.

She'd gone eighteen years and over a million miles only to find herself driving from Tulsa to Tumbleweed. The last town she ever wanted to see again.

Up ahead, a sign came into view. *Tumbleweed. Population 2,883.* The 3 was hand-painted on the sign above a crossed-out 2. A new millennium on the horizon and the folks of Tumbleweed were still adding their newborns one by one.

Tumbleweed, what am I doing here?

Except for in the theme of "The Preacher," Summer didn't even visit Tumbleweed in her memories or dreams.

It's just that when Clark dropped all his bombs, then took a taxi to the airport, she didn't know what to do besides stand in the motor court parking lot and look pitiful.

She'd hauled her stuff inside, called Bryson at the Broken Barrel to tell him she'd be a solo act for the night's gig, and to keep occupied, she hopped into the white Ford and headed northwest. Her head did not want to return to Tumbleweed, but maybe, sort of, kind of her heart did.

Was she looking for *him*? Or the pieces of herself she left at Camp Tumbleweed on Skiatook Lake?

Arriving in town, Summer eased down the brick-laden Main Street and ached for the girl she used to be. The one who didn't need a drink to fall asleep. The one who hadn't had more lovers than she had fingers and toes. The one who didn't believe a record contract and an Academy of Country Music Award would give her life meaning. The one who didn't secretly yearn to impress people she'd left behind long, long ago.

She wanted to be the girl who loved her parents, who had three of the best friends in the world. A girl with hope, promise, and a future. A girl whose worst decision was a bad movie or crazy haircut. A girl who laughed at the memory of dumping concentrated car wash soap into the Florida State pool. A girl who spent

9

a court-mandated summer with her friends as camp counselors at Camp Tumbleweed.

She missed the girl who'd so easily, so truly, fallen in love.

But it was too late, too late, too late. The emotional effort to even remember those days cost more than she wanted to pay.

Summer angled the truck into an open parking spot on Main Street and cut the engine. In the quiet cab, she glanced down the street. Tumbleweed had not changed in twenty years, except for new signs on the storefronts and a little more color on the façades.

At eleven in the morning, the town was alive with business. The pole at the old barber shop spun red, white, and blue, and a young man walked out, settling a hat on his newly shorn hair.

The hardware store advertised a sale, and Sue's Cut-n-Curl—Sue *had* to be going on eighty—displayed a row of wigs on a sidewalk table with the sign *Free to a Good Home*.

The door to the laundromat—oh, good ol' Tumble Time—was propped open, and a woman went in with her young son.

"Wellllll, you get the soap, I'll get the washer, honey. You get the soap, I'll get the washer, babe."

The song played from way back in Summer's memories. A sound from a time gone by. Eight weeks, eight Saturdays, and the summer of '77 still defined her. Maybe because the summer of '77 had broken her.

Had broken all of them.

Maybe she should just head back to the Shady Rest, get a nap—what a luxury—and redo her set list for the Broken Barrel.

Still, she was here, wasn't she? Might as well grab some lunch from the best diner ever, O'Sullivan's Diner & Drugstore.

If God cared about her one wit, O'Sullivan's would still have the Number Five on the menu and Tank Tilly would be behind the counter. He'd be, what, in his sixties?

Summer jerked at the call of her cell phone. She'd never get used to the beck and call of a personal phone. She pulled the device from the truck's console.

It was Clark. "You okay?"

"I'm sitting in Tumbleweed. You tell me."

"Come on, Summer, it's not that bad."

"Yet here I am. After my life fell apart this morning, I thought Tumbleweed might be a step up."

"Summer, don't be so dramatic—"

"I had a hankering for a good burger, fries, and a shake. I've been all over the country, and nothing beats O'Sullivan's."

"I'm sorry, all right?" he said, his voice cracking from a weak connection. "But I had to take this opportunity with the Bergman Agency."

"And you couldn't take me with you?"

"I tried, but—"

"They don't want me."

"It's just . . ." He sighed to the soundtrack of the airport. "No one doubts your talent. Everyone I talk to tells me you should write another 'The Preacher.'"

"That song was special, Clark. The lyrics were raw and personal, birthed from a place I didn't go to often." In fact, she'd not revisited *that* place since the night she wrote "The Preacher." The tune was simple but melodic with minor-seventh chords. "But after eighteen years in the biz with nothing to show for it but one song, I'm more of a liability than a possibility. Is that right?"

"You had more than a hit, Summer. You penned a future classic."

"Never feel guilty for going for your dreams, Clark. I should've said this at the Shady Rest, but thanks for everything you did for me. You stuck around when everyone else left."

She should be used to people leaving her. But the pain of it always felt fresh and sharp.

"I talked to Lucy Carter at Music Bomb. She said to give her a call and—"

"We'd kill each other. She's lightning, and I'm thunder. She only said to call her out of pity. Or because she likes you."

"Can I give you some advice, Summer?" She teared up at the tenderness in his voice. "Find a way to fix what broke you all those years ago. I have a feeling *that* girl will know exactly what to do with her life."

"I have a feeling that girl is more confused than this one."

"Trust yourself, that's all I'm saying. You'll be all right. You've got 'The Preacher' royalties, so there's no need to rush into something else. Take the summer off. You've been touring nonstop for eons. Whatever you're looking for ain't out there, Summer. It's in you. Sit still and listen."

It wasn't like her manager and friend to wax sentimental or personal, so his words hit hard and sank deep.

"I've got to go, Clark." Summer ended the call and popped open the truck door. She'd driven to Tumbleweed for a good burger, not to rehash what went wrong in the past. She knew what went wrong. Lies and betrayal, like all good tragedies.

A car horn sounded as a late-model Cadillac pulled into a parking spot next to her. An older gentleman in a ten-gallon hat rose out of the car like a cowboy superhero. He wore a bolo tie under his button-down collar, crisp blue jeans, and a pair of dark, shiny boots that came to a sharp point at the toe. His blue gaze lingered on Summer for a nanosecond before someone called hello to him.

Levi? Levi Foley? Of course not. This man was her father's age. Without a second glance, he disappeared through a glass door labeled *Life, Health, Home, and Auto Insurance.*

Is this what you're doing here, Summer Wilde? Looking for Levi?

Because if she was, she'd best hop into the truck right now and head back to Tulsa. Besides, the cute cowboy from the summer of '77 lived in California.

Hurrying across Main, she pushed her way inside O'Sullivan's and stepped into the past. A piece of her burden lifted.

Built in the early 1900s, when the Dalton gang ran through the territory, O'Sullivan's used to be the place where cowboys gathered. The decor of saddles, saddlebags, bullhorns, worn-out boots, spurs, cowboy hats, and a row of wagon-wheel chandeliers spoke of pioneers, of courage, of people not afraid to face the unknown to make a better life. She could use a bit of their courage and blind hope.

On her left was the drugstore. In front of her were the diner's red leather booths with red-checked Formica tables and the eat-in counter with no fewer than twenty stools. Behind the counter, the kitchen.

A man in a white chef's hat, black shirt, and large apron polished the countertop while Garth Brooks sang from the jukebox about a river of dreams. Tank Tilly. He was still here. A bit of gray showed from under his beanie, and Summer hoped for her sake he still dispensed unsolicited wisdom. She needed a dose.

She picked a stool and, without looking up, the man asked, "What'll it be?"

"I'd love the Number Five, Tank." She leaned back to review the chalkboard menu suspended above her on two fat chains. It'd been a while; the order of things might have changed. But no, the Number Five was still a cheeseburger with the works, fries, and a milkshake.

Tank scribbled on a pad of paper, then gave her a quick look before turning toward the kitchen. Summer sat up. *Remember me?*

He clipped the order ticket to the wheel at the service window, then slapped the bell. "Sooner, step lively, we got a special guest. Summer Wilde, famous country singer." He greeted her with a warm smile and took her hand in his. "I knew it was you. Pretty as ever."

"Ha. I don't know about that, Tank." The road life took a toll.

"I do. Know what I see? Some wisdom, some humility in those eyes." Add stupidity and hurt and he'd have her whole number. "I bought your record when you were with Wilde, Heart, and Landon. Keep the CD in my truck for long drives. You got a voice, girl, you do."

Wilde, Heart, and Landon was her second band, the one before the Sparrows. She tried to capitalize on her first success of "The Preacher" and drove the band hard. Toured nonstop. They almost strung her up and left her for the coyotes.

"So, your friends, what'd y'all call yourselves?"

"The Four Seasons."

"That's right." He rapped the counter with his fist. "Summer, Autumn, Winter, and Spring."

"Snow. Not Winter. Margaret Snowden, but everyone called her Snow." Snow's name felt weird on her tongue. She'd not spoken of her, or any of them, in ages. Eight, ten years?

"That's right, that's right. You'd think I'd remember that one. Anyway, I remember she had pale blue eyes. Y'all keep in touch?" He turned to the service window. "Sooner, how's the Number Five coming? Don't take all day, and give this girl your best."

Sooner's frowning face appeared in the window. "What in the world are you talking about? I always give my best."

"Just checking, simmer down." Tank turned back to Summer. "Can I get you a soda while you wait?"

"Diet Coke?"

Tank grabbed a glass and filled it with ice and soda. "So, you gals still in touch?"

"Um, yes, we, um, are." So she fibbed a little. That was the least of her sins. It was what Tank wanted to hear. He seemed pleased to have remembered them. "Tumbleweed hasn't changed much," she said.

"Girl, we'll go into the new millennium same way as we went into the last. A one-horse town. Folks like it that way."

"Some things have changed from 1900. O'Sullivan's has electricity and indoor plumbing." Summer tipped her head toward the jukebox. "If I'm not mistaken, that's Trisha Yearwood singing, not Kitty Wells."

Tank's laughter caused her to drop another one of her morning burdens. She'd not felt like pleasant company in a long time. She *might* have treated the Sparrows like her employees. Or servants. It's just she—no, they—were so close to a record deal.

"You got me there, Summer. But we do like to stay the same 'round here. We only got rid of all party lines two years ago, and some folks fought that, especially those out a ways on the ranches and farms. Said listening in on other people's conversations was the only way to keep up with the news."

"More like keep up with the gossip."

"Gossip, news . . ." He shrugged his big shoulders. "Six of one."

Sooner appeared at the window. "Phone for you, Tank."

When he'd gone, Summer glanced toward the phone booth in the front left corner between the drugstore and the diner. The same one she'd ducked into twenty years ago to call Dad. His assistant, Sandy, had answered. *Sandee*, who Summer hoped snorted like a pig when she laughed. She didn't. She was beautiful, ambitious, smart, and cunning, but not the reason her parents' marriage fell apart.

"Here we are, and as they say in France, 'Good eating.'" Tank set a plate heaped with a burger and fries in front of her. The aroma was pure heaven. She shoved the soda aside for the chocolate shake, which was so thick the straw stood up and saluted.

She was three bites into her burger, five bites into the crispy golden pile of fries, and one cold, creamy, delicious sip into her shake when the bells on the front door clattered against the cloudy glass pane. Soft footsteps skipped over the hardwood toward the counter.

"Summer? Summer Wilde?" A pretty face peered around at her. The woman wore pink scrubs, and her chestnut hair was pulled back into a neat ponytail.

Summer choked down her bite. "Yes?" Did she have a fan in Tumbleweed? Tank aside.

"It is you. I can't believe it. When I called Tank to place my lunch order, he said, 'You'll never guess what the cat dragged in.'" The woman lunged at her, wrapping her in an affectionate hug. "I never thought I'd see you again. It's been twenty years."

Okay, who was this beauty from 1977?

She moved back to let Summer study her, holding her smile wide.

"Oh my gosh, Greta? Greta Henderson?" Summer grabbed her into a tight hug, as if to fill herself with everything sweet and wonderful about the girls she met that long-ago summer. "Look at you. You're a nurse or—"

"A doctor, actually." Well, that deserved a high five. "My husband and I have a general practice over on Fifth Street. We're cradle-to-grave, so we put Band-Aids on boo-boos, deliver babies, and take care of the aging. And I'm a Yeager now. My husband is Darrian."

"Girl, I'm so stinking proud of you." Summer sat back on her stool. Greta, a doctor. "Weren't you the doctor in the camp play?"

"I was, and I still have the cheap plastic stethoscope Snow found in the drugstore toy aisle. It hangs in my office."

"I knew you'd do great things, Greta. I knew it." Summer squeezed her hand and tried not to feel like a complete and utter failure. Riding the self-pity train rattled her bones.

But honestly, what had she done to help her fellow man? Written a bunch of sappy, crappy country songs so a room full of drunks could cry in their beers?

"I owe it all to the Four Seasons, Summer."

"You owe it all to Spring. She was your counselor." Greta got dropped off by her parents on their way to Europe. She was the only Camp Tumbleweed Tumbler who didn't rotate out every weekend. In fact, they'd inducted her into their unique friendship, dubbing her Baby Season.

"It was all of you." Greta's eyes brimmed with emotion. "First, you made me feel loved and accepted. Second, you showed me how to be a friend. I was a Tumbler until I was sixteen, then became a counselor. Lily did a great job running the camp. She was—"

"The best," Summer said. Mom restarted the camp she'd attended as a girl that summer of '77 and went on to run it for ten years. Summer would have to give her a call sometime. Soon.

16

"Yeah, the best." Greta held her gaze. "I'm sorry about your parents' divorce. I know how much you loved your dad."

"It was a long time ago."

The beat of silence held them for a moment, the past and present connecting with memories and affection.

"Here you go, Doctor." Tank set down two brown paper bags and a drink carrier.

"Thanks, Tank." Greta dropped a couple of bills on the counter, then turned to Summer. "I'd stay and eat with you, but I left Ned Banks on the exam table in a paper gown." She pulled a pen from her scrubs pocket and reached for a napkin. "You have to come to dinner." She scribbled her address and phone number on the napkin and slid the info to Summer. "Please. Darrian would love to meet you, and I really, really want to catch up."

A bit of dew collected in the corners of her eyes. "I can't tell you how much y'all impacted my life. I think of you all the time. Especially when I listen to your music or watch one of Snow's movies. I still hear from Spring. She's married, and a partner in a large law firm. Happy." Greta gathered her lunch. "Please, Summer, come to dinner. We have a lovely place on the lake. Tank here sold us a tract of land so we could build our dream house."

"Greta, go, you've got an important job." Summer held up the napkin. "I'll see what I can do." Lie. She was leaving town in an hour for one last gig. Then where? She didn't really know, but not here.

"Ain't it great to see her again?" Tank set another lunch box on the counter with the name *Foley* on the side. "Thanks to you gals and Camp Tumbleweed, we got two of the best doctors. Everybody says so."

"She's amazing. Seems content, happy, successful."

She and the Four Seasons had felt sorry for Greta the summer of '77 when her parents dropped her off at Camp Tumbleweed while they headed to Europe. The camp was run-down and overgrown, abandoned for twenty years. Who knew then how impactful those eight weeks would turn out to be?

"You hanging around long enough to take her up on dinner?" Tank said, giving the counter a wipe. "She's sincere in wanting to see you. I've heard her mention you girls around town. And I'm sure you know Camp Tumbleweed has taken another long nap. Going on ten years now."

"I'd heard." Summer peered up at him. She'd been here one summer twenty years ago, yet she felt like he knew her. "But I can't stay. I've got a gig in Tulsa tonight at the Broken Barrel."

"Then what? Going back to Nashville? Maybe you could come back here, hang around for a while," Tank said. "I always thought you fit with Tumbleweed. You're one of us."

"I'm not sure whether to laugh or cry, Tank."

"I know, I know. You got your dreams, your music, but life can be good here in Tumbleweed."

"And what would I do in Tumbleweed? Wait tables?"

"You could sing. I've been meaning to take out that old phone booth, put it in the front corner with the jukebox. Just never had anything put a fire under me to do it."

"Tank, I done told you to do it a thousand times." Sooner's voice boomed from the back. "If I ain't fire, don't know what is."

"Hush up, old man." Tank winked at Summer. "I could put a stage where the phone booth is now."

"Good luck with that, Tank. I mean it. It's a great idea." She pulled a twenty from her pocket. "I should get going. You still have the best burgers anywhere."

"On the house." He pushed back her money. "I'm happy to see you again."

Summer hesitated, then tucked the money into her pocket. "You reminded me life is full of good people, Tank."

He reached for her hands. "Sweet darling, I don't know what's happened between then and now, but—"

"An extreme lack of sleep."

"Then get you some rest. Tumbleweed is a good town for sleeping. Just saying . . ." He released her hands. "One more thing, Summer." Tank lowered his voice. "He's back, you know."

"Who's back?"

"Levi Foley. Took over his daddy's ranch. Mac Foley runs the insurance biz across the street."

"Levi's running the ranch? I thought he was a CPA in an air-conditioned office in LA."

"Found out he weren't built for the office, or for California. He's built for the ranch life. Ain't married, neither. And no kids."

"Well, good for him." Summer backed toward the door. "I'll see you around. Thanks for lunch. Best I've had in a long, long time."

"Should I tell him I saw you? Tell him about your show tonight?"

"No, Tank, do *not* tell Levi Foley you saw me."

Please don't tell him. She'd drown herself in someone's beer if Levi saw her at the Broken Barrel. The place was a dive. Where bands, or singers, went to die.

"Summer," Tank said, coming around the counter. "Whatever it is, you can—"

"I don't know what you mean." But her weak smile gave her away. "See ya."

Summer stepped outside and gazed west, toward the camp, to where she'd left chunks of her heart. It was amazing she had any left to live on.

What am I doing here?

The answer came, so clear, as if announced by the town crier. *Coming home.*

2

We May Never Pass This Way Again

Spring

'77

If ever a cloud needed a silver lining, it was the one hanging over Spring right now. Riding on a Greyhound bus toward Tumbleweed, Oklahoma, with sixty, no, fifty-nine strangers—the smelly guy with the watery eyes and knotted hair got off in Joplin—was not the beginning of the best summer of her life.

Nothing, *nothing* was as it should be. And Spring Duval didn't function well when life was out of whack.

She glanced at her seatmate and best friend, Summer Wilde. Behind them, Margaret "Snow" Snowden and Autumn Childe, also her best friends, slept with their heads tilted together.

Buck up, Spring. Your friends are your silver lining.

They were the only piece of the "grand" plan that remained. Weekends at the Duvals' St. George beach house? Canceled. Pool parties with friends? Nope. Sleeping in late, working on her tan, running up Daddy's charge card at Gayfers, Woolco, and Montgomery Ward? Left by the wayside. Touring Florida State's campus and preparing for her freshman year, sorority rush, and Seminole football? Going, going, gone. Backpacking through Europe for three weeks in July? Exchanged for eight weeks at a girls' camp in Tumbleweed, Oklahoma.

Their summer dreams and plans killed with one stupid, *stupid* decision. Which led to more stupid decisions. Which led to a bellyful of regret.

As the reigning Miss Springtime Tallahassee, and homecoming *and* prom queen, a feat accomplished by only one other woman— her mother—Spring once believed she could conquer anything. Just wear her proverbial crown, raise her chin, and plow ahead.

"I think I might be sick," she said more to herself than to Summer.

"What?" Summer pulled out the headphones connected to her Panasonic cassette player. "Don't puke on me." She swung her legs into the aisle, making room for Spring to exit her window seat.

But she kept her gaze on the Oklahoma dawn breaking through and battled her queasy regret. *Breathe, breathe. Just put it out of your mind.*

Everything would be all right. She was Spring Tuttle Duval, daughter of Michael Jefferson Duval and the great Judith Tuttle Duval, who was a descendant of Miami's founder, Julia Tuttle.

Greatness lived in her bones.

Summer nudged her. "Are you going to hurl or not?"

"I just need something to eat." Spring retrieved a Pop-Tart from her Granddad's WWI haversack. The army green canvas was faded, worn, and ugly, but it was one of her most treasured possessions.

"You're going places, Springroll," Granddad used to say as he

hooked the strap on her shoulder. She was what? Twelve? *"When you doubt, remember this old haversack. It was with me through the Great War. Now it'll be with you through your wars."*

Wars? She didn't want any wars. But she had a feeling a battle was coming her way.

"Any more of those?" Summer pointed to the Pop-Tart.

Spring passed over the second tart without a word. That's the way it was with her friends, the Four Seasons. Give and take. Take and give.

Come the fall, she'd be sharing a dorm suite with Summer, Snow, and Autumn. She'd signed up for cheerleading tryouts. F-L-O-R-I-D-A-S-T-A-T-E. All four were rushing sororities, but it was a lock they'd pledge Phi Mu, since her mother and grandmother were legacy. Summer played the rebel—what else is new?—claiming she might go Chi Omega with her cousin, Meg Callahan. But Spring never doubted Summie's loyalty to the Seasons. She'd be a Phi Mu with the rest of them.

Let's see, what else? Spring would spend Saturday nights at Doak Campbell Stadium, cheering on the Seminoles. Everyone had high hopes for their new coach, Bobby Bowden.

She'd study on Landis Green, and when she turned twenty-one, she'd get dunked in the Westcott Fountain.

Then there was Mal—Malcolm Oliver Smith III—whom she adored. Yet the thought of him filled her with angst and anxiety. She stared at her blueberry tart without taking a bite.

Don't think about it. Pretend it didn't happen. Forget it. It was nothing.

He was off to Duke in the fall and planned to pledge Kappa Alpha with ideas on how to maneuver a long-distance college relationship. Once a full-fledged fraternity brother, he'd make a road trip to give her his lavalier. The next year, he'd give her his pin. She'd road-trip to see him with her new sorority sisters. Being at separate universities would be nothing for people who really loved each other, he'd said. After all, they belonged together.

She'd believed his fairy tale until . . .

What she wanted now was to talk to Blaine, Snow's brother, who'd been a big brother to all the Four Seasons. Since Spring didn't have any siblings, he'd become a special confidant. If only she could talk to him . . . He'd know what to do about Mal. But he wasn't around, was he?

Forget the last six weeks. Just focus on getting through this stupid summer as a camp counselor—what exactly do camp counselors do?

She'd get to feeling better soon. Mom was right, she'd messed up her "system" from the stress of graduating, being arrested, appearing in court, and the intense week of cleaning FSU's pool every day after school with the rest of the culprits.

"Hey, stoneface, what's going on?" Spring glanced at Summer. Blaine had loved her, but she never knew . . . and never would.

"Nothing. Ready to be there." Spring tapped the tape deck. "What were you listening to?"

Summer slipped the player into her green carryall that literally bore the word *carryall* on the side.

"Mixtape of Willie Nelson, Patsy Cline, Dolly, Glen Campbell."

Summer was all about music. A whole bedroom in the Wilde house was devoted to her records, cassettes, and 8-tracks, as well as her three guitars and an upright piano.

"Think we'll get to a concert this summer?" That was another one of their *best summer* goals. Concerts in Jacksonville and Tampa.

"Haven't you heard? We're *camp counselors* this summer. Woo-hoo." Summer mimicked the cheerful, happy tone of her mother, Lily, who'd told them the judge agreed to her request to let the Seasons complete their community service at Camp Tumbleweed. What parent sends their daughter to a place named after dried-out puffballs?

"Maybe there's a concert in Tulsa. Lily said we get one night off per week, I think." Spring pulled the camp packet Lily had given them from her haversack. "Yeah, it says so right here. We're off Saturday night. Surely there's a concert in Tulsa on a Saturday night."

"Willie Nelson's Fourth of July picnic is in Tulsa," Summer said. "I'd love to go to that, but it's on the third. A Sunday."

"Maybe we could—"

"Forget it. Mom will remind us we're being punished for our stunt. So no fun allowed."

Spring laughed softly and returned the packet to her bag. "She *was* pretty funny when she was lecturing us on how serious our summer will be." Spring performed her best Lily Wilde imitation. "'You'll be swimming and hiking, playing softball, doing crafts and photography, but this is for the campers, not you girls. You're being punished.'"

Summer sat up and glanced between the seats at Autumn and Snow. "Did y'all hear that? Mom's on the bus."

"Shut up." Spring jabbed her friend. "Being a camp counselor is better than wearing an orange vest and picking up trash all over town."

When the four of them got nailed for pouring concentrated car wash soap into the FSU pool—along with thirty-two other high school friends and new FSU acquaintances (read: frat boys)—the judge was furious. Wanted to make examples of them all.

Community service for the *entire* summer and house arrest for the month of June. Insane. Even Spring's justice-loving father protested in court. Then he made a few calls. Pulled a few strings.

"Good thing Dad stepped in," Spring said.

"Only because *my* dad said, 'Mike, use your connections, man.'" Summer was right, if not a bit haughty. She believed her dad hung the moon, then turned it into cheese. Maybe he had. Jeff Wilde was pretty cool.

"You really think my dad would let his daughter be seen wearing an orange jumpsuit in public, spearing garbage?" Spring laughed. "Judith would've died on the spot, then haunted him for all eternity."

Summer turned back around and propped her knees on the back of the seat in front of her. "The look on your mom's face when she entered the police station. . . . Classic."

"What about the look on *your* mom's face?"

"My mom looked like a kid at Christmas. She saw four little helpers for her crazy idea of reopening the camp she went to as a girl."

"At least the judge sentenced us together. He could've split us apart, and the best summer of our lives would be the most rotten summer of our lives."

"The Four Seasons." Summer slapped Spring a high five. "Starting our adult lives with a criminal record."

"Hey, you two, the whole bus doesn't need to know our business." Snow poked Spring through the space between the seats. "We get it. 'My dad is better than your dad.' Some of us don't have dads."

"We *were* whispering, Grumpy." Spring peeked at her.

"We've been on a bus for thirty hours. Better believe I'm a grump." Snow made a face, then gave Spring a gentle push to her forehead.

Snow was beautiful. A winter day after the snow had fallen and a piece of the blue sky broke through. Her dark hair framed her porcelain face, the landscape over which her blue eyes glowed. She was striking, cold, and direct, yet oddly warm and insecure. She was winter on the edge of spring. Wanting to hang on but ready to let go.

"So, what were you thinking about earlier?" Summer nudged Spring, circling around to her original question. "When you look that intense, something is up."

Only a friend of twelve years could read her expression so well. Same with the two characters behind her. Best friends since kindergarten.

"I don't know. . . . I guess about the summer. How we messed it up. We've never even been to camp, let alone been camp counselors."

"I've been to camp." Autumn's sweet voice drifted between the seats. "Remember? When I was six."

"I don't remember, but you said it was a nightmare." Spring rose up on her knees to look back at Autumn. "Are you scared?"

"No, I'm not scared, you skeebie neck. I'm not six." With a laugh, she shoved Spring back down, but she popped back up.

Autumn was the brainiac of the Seasons. The daughter of FSU professors, she had a full scholarship to study nuclear science or something intense like that at Cornell, but since she was a signed-up, lifelong member of the Four Seasons, she'd remained committed to their college-together plan.

In fact, she was the one who'd started really pressing the idea. After Blaine's funeral. *"We should do something that he would do. As a way to honor him."*

"He'd want us to stick together," Snow had said. *"You're my only siblings now."*

They made a pact that night. Best summer of their lives— that's what Blaine always talked about—after high school, then live together, study together, party together at FSU. All for one, one for all.

"Here's the real question," Summer said, hanging over the back of her seat, staring down at Autumn and Snow. "Will there be any boys in this Tumbleweed town? And by boys, I mean cowboys."

"By the way your mom talks, we won't have time."

Summer grinned, a mischievous glint sparking in her tired blue eyes. "There's always time for boys. Always."

"Well, I have a boyfriend," Spring said. Which she did. And she aimed to be true.

"You didn't look like you had a boyfriend that night at the Kappa Alpha house. When we joined the stupid plot to dump soap in the FSU pool." Snow, who never hesitated to be direct, was first in line for the "pool bubble bath." She said Blaine's death proved life was fragile and, for some, very short. So she wasn't going to hold back. Now, in hindsight, she loved to vocalize her regret.

"Good point, Snowy." Summer nudged Spring again. "Who were you talking with in the shadows?"

"A friend of Billy Crumpet's." *Leave me alone. I don't want to think about it.*

"He was a hunk." The simple words from Autumn sounded so strange. She rarely went on about boys. It was a minor miracle she even went to the KA house.

"A hunk?" Spring stretched to squeeze her friend's cheek. "Did *you* want to talk to him?"

Autumn knocked her hand away. "How could I? The queen of Lincoln High had him cornered."

"Did you tell Mal you flirted with other men that night?" Snow again. The trip had definitely made her grumpier than usual.

"It was one night. No big deal. I'm sure he flirted with girls when he visited Duke's campus." Turning, Spring sat down. She'd flirted all right. Had a bit too much to drink. Got tangled up in that guy's charm.

What was his name?

"My goal for this Oklahoma trip," Summer said, "is to meet a cowboy and see if he has a friend for Fall. It's time you started dating."

"I've dated."

"A prom date doesn't count."

"Does in my book. He kissed me good-night."

Spring faded into her own thoughts as Summer and Autumn bantered. When did they start calling her Fall? Who said it first? Blaine? He was the king of nicknames. Spring was Springer. Summer was Sum-Sum, but really, to himself, he called her "the one."

Spring learned of his mad crush on Summer late one night when she slept over with Snow, who'd gone to bed early with a cold. Spring and Blaine stayed up until three, talking, listening to Fleetwood Mac's *Rumours*, Earth, Wind & Fire's *That's the Way of the World*, and America's greatest hits.

"Don't tell her, Spring, okay? Or Snow. She loves her but says

I'm too good for her. Summer's too much of a flirt. But I'm going to marry her, Springer. If I ever get her to notice me."

She'd never say it out loud, but she believed he died trying to impress Summer Wilde.

Two years later, she still missed him. What would he think about her secret dilemma? She closed her eyes and imagined him saying, *"Gotta face it, Springer."*

The laughter floating around her kept her from sinking too deep into herself. The Seasons were reminiscing about the night at FSU.

"She was so slick with soap she kept falling down." Ah, they were talking about Margo Hayes, who was a year ahead of them and already a Phi Mu sister. Spring planned to choose Margo as her big sister.

"I kept losing my shorts," Snow said.

"I lost more than my shorts." There was a blush in Autumn's confession. "It was humiliating."

"Goodness, what is this about?" The woman across the aisle couldn't stay out of it. Spring had noticed her listening to their conversation since Peoria. "Bubbles at a pool?"

Summer leaned toward her. She *loved* telling the story. "We went to a party at Florida State. Someone had the bright idea to dump soap into the pool and have a bubble bath."

"Goodness, how big was the pool? That would require a lot of soap."

"Olympic size. But one of our friends offered up her dad's concentrated car wash detergent and, well . . . we dumped in sixty gallons, then jumped in to churn it up."

"Goodness, goodness. Did it work? Did you have a giant bubble bath?"

"Not quite, but we did get arrested." Snow, straight to the punch line. "And now we're off to some Podunk town called Tumbleweed, Oklahoma, as a punishment."

"Tumbleweed?" The woman made a face. "That is quite the punishment. No one goes to Tumbleweed but . . . well, tumbleweeds."

"We'll be camp counselors for eight-, nine-, ten-, and eleven-year-old girls. The camp has the same dry, desperate name. Camp Tumbleweed."

"Summer's mother is the camp director," Autumn added. "The place has been closed for a long time. How long, Summie?"

"Twenty years."

The woman stuffed a crumbled cookie in her mouth. "Doesn't your mother love you?"

The girls laughed. "She loves all of us," Spring said. The conversation cheered her a bit. "If not for Camp Tumbleweed, we'd be picking up trash on the side of the road."

"This was supposed to be the best summer of our lives," Summer said.

The Seasons clasped their raised hands together. "Salute!" Their catchphrase since fifth grade, adapted from *Hee Haw*.

"Tell you girls what, Tumbleweed is the last place I'd go for the best summer of my life," the woman said in a slow Oklahoma drawl. "But they've got a few cowboys there. See if you can wrangle one."

"I knew it," Summer said.

"No cowboy for me. I have a boyfriend." Speaking of boyfriends and all that, Spring reached for her haversack. Her period was due any day and she'd rather not be surprised.

"Move. I'm going to the loo." Part of their "best summer" included a European backpacking trip. Now canceled, of course. But Spring figured she could still speak British now and then.

"Go for me too." Summer stayed put as she reached into her carryall and produced a Moon Pie.

"You had that and asked me for a Pop-Tart?" Spring kicked past Summer's raised knees. "I want one when I get back. I know you have a stash in there."

Summer was the opposite of Snow. Go figure. Beautiful in a wild, unmanicured sort of way, all she had to do was run a brush through her hair to be utterly striking. And she ate whatever she wanted.

"Want what?" Autumn leaned around the seat. "Moon Pie? Hand one over, Wilde."

"Me too." Snow stuck her hand over the top.

Spring smiled. See, everything righted itself with the Seasons. Twelve years of friendship couldn't be undone by a wild night of stupidity. Or by anger, fear, and misunderstanding. They were all for one, one for all on this unexpected adventure.

"Wait until I get back. We'll eat them together," Spring said. "Does anyone have a Coke we can share?"

"I do," Autumn said. "It's warm, but it'll do."

Spring started down the aisle, but the woman across the way grabbed her hand.

"Y'all are good friends, I take it?"

"The best. Since kindergarten."

"All four of you?"

"All four of us."

"Goodness." She liked that word, didn't she? "Cling to them, young lady. Good friends are hard to find. Great friends—which sounds like that's what you have—are impossible to find. Cling, cling, cling." She stuck her finger in the air to make her point.

Mrs. Parish, their third-grade teacher, used to do that all the time. Summer would mimic her on the playground, making the kids laugh.

She was the funny Season. Always ready with a quip or some sarcastic observation.

"We will. Nothing can separate the Four Seasons." Spring glanced at Summer, who reclined in the seat with her eyes closed, Moon Pie in her hand. Then at Autumn, who read a book with a penlight, and Snow, who stared out the window. Both held their Moon Pies. Waiting. They had their squabbles and nitpicky fights, but they were the Four Seasons. Friends4ever. Salute.

3

How Can You Mend
a Broken Heart?

Snow

'77

So this was Tulsa? Hot. Humid. About as bad as Tallahassee. Snow jerked her one suitcase from the belly of the Greyhound, then carefully looped the two camera bags she'd carried off the bus around her neck.

These were her treasures. Her true loves. Her Canon F5 and Paps' 8mm movie camera. She planned to document everything about this trip. It was great experience. Practice for her future.

At least what she hoped was her future.

However, if she'd listened to her mom, the stoic and independent Babs Snowden, she'd be picking up trash along Apalachee Parkway in an orange vest. Guess she could've filmed and photographed that too, but that seemed more like journalism than art. Not Snow's preferred scene.

"*Stay home,*" Mom had said. "*You'll still have evenings and weekends when you get off house arrest. Then you can go to Alligator Point or St. Marks and take pictures. We'll have time to run around, do fun things, shop for college. I'm sure the judge will—*"

"*Mom, how can I do those things without the Seasons? They'll kill me if I don't go. Besides, I'd be wondering all summer what they were doing, what I was missing. The judge said it was all of us or none of us. You heard him. This is my last summer with the Seasons. You know I won't be here in the fall. . . .*"

"Snowbird, a bit of help." Snow adjusted the camera cases and reached for Spring's trunk. The beauty queen always traveled with a trunk. Even to *Nowhere*, Oklahoma.

"Oklahoma, where the wind comes sweeping down the bus terminal, the Four Seasons are here." Summer stood by the bus arms wide, head back.

Snow grinned. As much as she loved Summer, she struggled with her. Maybe spending time with her in a remote camp atmosphere would force her to get *over* it. The *angst* she harbored.

For a moment, she tried to remember how she loved and adored her friend. For most of junior high, she'd wanted to *be* Summer. She loved her parents, Lily and Jeff Wilde, especially Jeff, who was the absolute coolest dad.

Then Blaine died, and Snow fumed over—*Stop.* Five minutes in Oklahoma and she was churning up old feelings. Summer had done nothing to provoke her. Except live and breathe.

Snow, Snow, Snow, she's one of your best friends.

See, that was the problem. Grief made it easy to give in to all the sadness and pain. For the past two years, Snow had stuffed, bottled, and hidden her broken heart. Made excuses, missed nights with the Seasons. Which only broke her heart even more. She'd lost her brother, and if she wasn't careful, she'd lose her best friends.

All for one, one for all was the thread that held them together.

Yet in some way she knew—they all knew—how precarious the thread. If one left, they'd all leave.

Snow liked being a member of a force so strong that kids at school envied them. The snooty popular girls didn't dare touch them. Even the year Autumn's now-beautiful complexion looked like pepperoni pizza. The Seasons protected her like mama bears.

"Snow, my turn for help." Autumn was tugging her fourth suitcase from the luggage compartment. She was the definition of pretty these days. Auburn hair, green eyes, light freckles on very clear skin. Besides being the brain of the Seasons, she was the athlete. Played basketball and softball all through high school.

"Geez, Autumn, did you pack the kitchen sink?" Snow set down Spring's trunk by the terminal and returned to drag a heavy suitcase across the hot asphalt.

"I had to bring all my beauty supplies. We *are* going to be at a girls' camp. I can do makeovers and maybe, if I'm lucky, cut hair." She raised her eyebrows and tipped her chin toward Snow's dark, straight, parted-down-the-middle hairstyle. "I'm telling you, I can cut your hair to look like Kate Jackson."

"Really? Tell that to Cheryl Townson. You told her the same thing, and when you were done she looked like Mick Jagger."

"I might not have known exactly what I was doing then. But I do now, Snow. Besides, can I help it that she has big lips? That wasn't my fault."

They glared at each other, then burst into laughter.

"What's the joke?" Summer walked into their circle, her carryall slung over her shoulders. She was sickeningly gorgeous. Spring was beautiful. Even striking. But Summer? Gorgeous. With exactly zero effort. Worse, she didn't know it.

"Cheryl Townson."

Summer laughed. "Remember how I had to defend her in Ellison's PE class 'cause all the boys were giving her crap about her hair? I punched Jake Pruitt."

That testimony defined Summer Wilde. How could Snow hate

someone so passionate? Who jumped to a friend's defense? It's just Summer could be so . . . What was Spring's word? *Obtuse?* No, Snow liked *selfish* better.

"Sum, are you going to let me cut your hair?" Autumn trailed after her as she headed into the bus terminal for a soda. "You would stun the world with the Farrah Fawcett hair."

"No."

"Please?"

"Get near me with scissors and you'll draw back a nub."

"How near? An inch? A foot?"

"Depends on how much you value your hand."

Autumn was the oldest of seven, so teasing and pestering were second nature to her. In fifth grade, she teased Summer so much about something—Snow couldn't even remember now—that Summer tackled her facedown in the dirt and held her head on the ground until she promised to *"Never tease Summer Wilde again. For the rest of my life."*

That lasted a day, but so went life with the Four Seasons.

Snow looked Spring's way. "Those two."

The Seasons also kept Spring from becoming one of those snooty elitists who looked down on everyone. She was a classic beauty born into a family of classic beauties. There was never a question of her becoming head cheerleader or prom queen.

"Never a dull moment around the Seasons." Spring sat on her trunk and gazed toward the street. "Lily said someone was picking us up around eleven. You want a soda?" She reached down for her grandpa's haversack. "My treat. That warm Coke almost made me sick. I need something cold."

"Sure. Thanks. You know what I like."

Most of the passengers had dispersed, but a few remained. Snow stood guard over the luggage and used the quiet to imagine the days ahead. She'd tried not to think much about it on the ride out. She'd written Mom a letter and posted it in Joplin. Then she'd written in her journal to Blaine.

*The Seasons are camp counselors. Can you believe it? This
was supposed to be the best summer of our lives! If you're
looking down on us, you know what happened, I guess.
I'm so mad at myself for going to that stupid frat party.
Then I realized you'd have been right in the thick of it all,
wouldn't you? Shoot, you wanted to pledge KA. So you'd
have been there.*

The last two passengers ducked into an Oldsmobile station
wagon, and Snow was all alone. She missed her mom. Was there a
phone around? She might call . . . Forget it. She was working. The
State of Florida Department of Energy would frown on a collect
call from Babs Snowden's daughter.

The night before the Seasons left, Mom made a final push for
Snow to stay home. *"This is our last summer together."* Come
September, Mom would be alone. *"Am I not as important as your
friends?"*

"Of course you are, but this summer is also for Blaine." Snow
pulled the ace from her sleeve.

Blaine always wanted "the best summer of my life" when he
graduated high school. It was a thing with him. *"Once I go to college, it's all work and responsibility from then on out, Snowbird.
I'll have to wear those old man pants that belt up over my waist
like you see in the movies and wear shoes that need to be polished
on the weekends. I'll buy a hat, work from nine to five, then come
home to the ol' wife and kids."*

If Summer was around, he'd always glance her way when he
said *wife.*

A knifing pain twisted through her. *Leave it.* She was too tired
to deal with the goop that lived in her inner darkness.

Mom had conceded when she mentioned Blaine. Besides their
"all for one, one for all" motto, the Four Seasons' miracle friendship worked because of their balance.

Two friends became insular. Three, a triangle, which led to

someone being left out. Four friends created a square that could contain the drama and dynamics of four young women. Remove one, and the square collapsed.

Which was exactly why Snow had jumped into Spring's car and headed to the frat party. Well, she might have been a bit tipsy too. Even more so when that cute Peter dude—or was it Paul?—enticed her to join the pool party.

"Hey, do you know the girl who can get all the soap?"

"Yeah, went to school with her."

"Cool."

And she *felt* cool. Even desirable. Not Blaine's "weirdo little sister." Which was what his friend Billy Crumpet called her. Blaine thought Billy, the star kicker on the football team, practically invented God. So ridiculous. Blaine was ten times cooler.

Anyway, back to Peter, or Paul. All she could think about was kissing his full red lips. He'd kissed her all right, in the deep end of the slick, almost-bubbly pool, and for a moment, she knew euphoria. She'd been kissed a few times, but *that* boy . . . She shivered just remembering.

Then he disappeared, and when she finally went to look for him, the cop car lights were flashing against the night.

An old green truck barreled into the parking lot with the driver tooting the horn. Snow started to call for the Seasons, but they were already walking toward her like Charlie's Angels after solving a case. Exhausted yet smiling.

The beautiful one with curves and chestnut hair. The gorgeous one with a runner's build and the wild blond mane. Then the pretty redhead with long legs and a kiss of freckles.

The driver of the truck laid on the horn again as she stepped out of the vehicle. "You must be the Four Seasons." They were. "All right, load 'em up."

She introduced herself as Moxie, the camp cook and all-wise counselor. Lean, with curly, graying hair bouncing about her face, she was tall and tan. Confident.

"She's a former army nurse with the rank of major, and she's not shy about giving orders," Lily told them just before she headed west two weeks ago. *"But you'll love her."*

"Lily didn't tell me y'all were so pretty." Moxie looked them over, hands on her hips. "Good thing we're an all-girls camp." She lifted two of Autumn's heavy beauty-supply suitcases and tossed them into the back of the truck. "My real name is Alberta Trimble. Got nicknamed Moxie in the army because there wasn't much I was scared to do." She hoisted Spring's trunk into the truck bed without a grunt or an oomph. "Served in the Pacific during the war. Got captured on Bataan and spent three years in a camp at the courtesy of the Imperial Japanese Army."

She glanced at the Seasons. "Don't worry, Camp Tumbleweed won't be a thing like Santo Tomas." She shrugged. "Well, not much." She paused right before her big laugh rang out. "Oh, come on. Don't you know a kidder? We are going to have a swell time this summer. Now, listen up. Two of you will have to ride in the back with your bags. Two can ride with me in the cab."

Snow tried to help Moxie load up the rest of the suitcases, but she had her step aside. The Seasons watched in reverent silence.

"Remind me to stay on her good side," Spring whispered.

"Salute," Snow said. "I'll ride in the bed." She set her photography bag over the side before climbing in.

"I'll ride with Snow." Summer hopped in with her carryall and surveyed Autumn's cases. "Geez, Fall, we're only here eight weeks. You'd think Spring would be the one with too much crap."

"She brought a portable beauty salon." Snow removed her camera and snapped a few pictures. Lily said something about a darkroom at camp, so she was shooting in black-and-white.

"They're preteens." Summer shoved the bags around and found a place to sit. "How much beautifying can you do?"

Autumn leaned against the side of the truck. "Braid their hair. Use very pale pink on their nails. They won't look like hussies, Summer. Besides, I can give you all manicures. I can cut your hair too if—"

"I already warned you, Autumn." Summer pointed at her with a stern expression. "Draw back a nub." She mimed cutting off Autumn's arm.

Good grief. So dramatic.

"You can cut my hair, Autumn." Snow aimed her camera at her friend. "I think short for the summer will be nice." If she happened to turn her into a Mick Jagger, she'd have time to grow it out.

"Take your life into your hands, Snowy." Summer laughed and winked.

Autumn was truly gifted with hair, makeup, and all things beauty related. She'd been cutting her mother's hair for almost a year now, and Shirl Childe always looked fashionable. Hairstyling just seemed an odd passion for a girl who loved calculus and chemistry.

Moxie fired up the truck, and Snow settled among the luggage, camera on her chest, a sense of peace coming over her.

"Wait! Nobody move." Summer jumped up. "Where's my record player? I brought a portable record player."

"Did you take it off of the bus?" Snow scanned the items in the bed. No record player.

"Of course I did. Well, maybe." Summer peered down at Spring, who'd exited the cab. "Did you get my record player?" Then, "My guitar!" Summer hopped out of the truck. "And my records. Where are my records?"

She waved and shouted as she raced toward the bus, where the next load of passengers lined up to toss their bags into the luggage hold. "My stuff, my stuff!"

Autumn glanced at Snow, grinning. "Some things never change. Come on. Let's help."

Fine, but she'd rather stay put in her comfy spot in the truck. Nevertheless, Snow stored her camera then followed Autumn. "If she cares so much about music and wants to be a singer someday, you'd think she'd get *her stuff* off the bus."

"Yes, but she's Summer."

"Don't even get me started."

See? Selfish. Obtuse. Summer had wanted a soda, so she'd left the unloading to the rest of the Seasons.

Five minutes later, with the guitar, record player, and suitcase of records safely in the back of the truck, and Moxie looking appropriately peeved—which delighted Snow—they headed up Route 20 toward Tumbleweed.

Summer made a pillow of her carryall. "Did you hear what Moxie said? She was a POW."

"I know. . . . I bet she has stories."

"You know she does. Guess what else?"

"Tell me," Snow said, drifting away under the hum of the truck motor.

"She took away every right we have had to complain about anything this summer."

Snow opened one eye to peer at Summer. "Yet somehow you'll find a way."

"Girl, don't you know it."

And she would. It was Summer's way. Heading to a place unknown on this bright, blue day, Snow knew she belonged with the Seasons this summer. Even more, she'd give her all to forgive her best friend, the one her brother loved from afar.

Just as the road lulled her the rest of the way to sleep, Snow heard Blaine's faint whisper, *"Atta girl, Snowy."*

4

Hello Muddah, Hello Fadduh

Summer

'77

At the sight of the battered Camp Tumbleweed sign, Summer rose up in the truck bed. Miles of meadows and prairie gave way to a lush oasis of trees, a crystal lake, and twenty or so shabby cabins situated among overgrown bushes.

"Snow." She kicked her sleeping friend. "You've got to see this."

Moxie drove around a stand of trees and stopped by a row of cabins, still shabby, but with their names freshly painted above the door and new screens in the windows. A bucket holding a broom and mop sat on the short steps.

"This is where we're staying?" Snow reached for her camera. "I can almost hear them begging, 'Make me alive again. Let me hold laughter in my walls.'"

"Really? I hear, wait . . ." Summer leaned forward, hand shielding her eyes from the sun. "Is that . . . yes, it is." She pointed to the first cabin. *Starlight.* "'The Texas Chainsaw Massacre Slept Here' is carved into one of the logs."

Snow snapped around, camera gripped in her hand. "Where? Where!"

Summer laughed. "You're so gullible."

Snow swung at her. "I'll show you gullible."

Summer ducked, missing Snow's fist, but tripped and fell onto her guitar.

"Serves you right," Snow said.

Summer examined the case, then grinned. "No damage, so it was worth it."

"You . . . you are . . ."

"You love me, so get over it." Summer held Snow's gaze. "I can't believe you even fell for that gag."

"I'm tired, that's all."

Sure. Whatever you say. But Snow had been weird since Blaine's death. Not that Summer blamed her, but most of it seemed directed at her. Mom said it was her imagination, and Dad suggested she either confront her or let it go.

"You don't have to be the Four Seasons forever, Summie," Dad had said.

"What are you saying? Mom, what is he saying? You're like their second dad."

"He's just joking." Mom gave Dad the eye. *"Aren't you, Jeff?"*

"Just joshing you, Summie." He'd hugged her, then asked if they wanted to go out to eat.

"This place is spooky," Spring said as she exited the truck cab. "Are we supposed to sleep in those cabins?"

"That one there is yours, Spring. Starlight. Says right on the side, 'The Texas Chainsaw Massacre Slept Here.' So you're in good company." Summer sat on the side of the truck bed and flicked Spring's ponytail.

Spring was her first real best friend. The moment she saw her in Mrs. Grant's class, she'd walked right up to her. Mrs. Grant read everyone's names, then said, *"I have the four seasons in my class-room."* Then Spring invited the three of them to her birthday party, and that day, when she turned six, they became the Four Seasons.

"Stop." Spring batted Summer's hand away.

She'd been acting weird lately too. Not for the past two years, like Snow, but for the last few weeks. Summer tried to get her to 'fess up if anything bothered her, but Spring blamed graduation, Mal going off to Duke in the fall, her parents fighting over something, the arrest and cleanup. *"I'm fine,"* she said. But Summer knew better.

Now Autumn joined Spring by the truck. Of all of them, Autumn was the true scaredy-cat.

"Hey, did you hear?" Summer pointed to Starlight. "The Texas Chainsaw Massacre slept here!" She grabbed Autumn's shoulder with a growl.

"What? Where?" Autumn jerked free of Summer's grip, fear in her voice, and reached for the truck door. "Where!"

"Dang, Fall, you and Snow are so gullible." Summer laughed. "This might be our best summer after all."

The Seasons talked at once.

"Why are you so annoying?"

"Wait until we get you, Summer."

"You'll never get me."

"Summer, come on," Spring said against the banter. "We're all tired and a bit punchy. Fall, you know there is no Texas Chainsaw Massacre unless you're sitting in the Miracle Five theater. By the way, a massacre is an event, a happening. Not a person."

Summer made a face. Killjoy and smarty-pants.

"This place is creepy enough without you adding to it, Sum." Snow scowled at her. "But listen." She raised her hand to her ear. "It's almost like you can hear Leatherface firing up his chainsaw and charging out of the woods."

42

"Now that's creepy." Summer shivered as she bent for her suitcase, shoving aside Spring's trunk, wincing when it smashed against her sneaker. "Leave it to Mom to bring her daughter and her friends—"

Summer shot up as a motor revved in the distance, sputtering and grinding. "What *is* that?"

The sound of the motor revved again and again. A chainsaw. There it was again. Only moving closer and closer until . . .

Snow screamed. "Leatherface!"

A man—*a man the size of a bear*—came around Starlight, bandana over his nose and mouth, a chainsaw in his hand, raised and poised for carving.

"Run!" Autumn was already in motion. "It's him!"

Screams, nothing but screams, cutting up the overhanging tree limbs, slicing the wind, and mowing down the tall grass.

"Go, go, go!" Summer shoved Snow over the side of the truck. "Go!" She tried to follow, but something . . . *something* . . . had her foot. "Let go! Let go!"

"Summer, come on!" Spring reached for her hand. "Summer!"

She jerked and pulled, but her foot wouldn't break free. "Forget about me! *Saavvve* yourselves."

She collapsed in the truck bed, tucked into a ball, and waited for the first pangs of death by chainsaw. *Just let me go quickly.*

Her rapid, hot breath billowed against her chest, and sweat beaded along her brow, down her neck and back.

"Hey! You—" Summer screamed as someone touched her back. Moxie's laugh melded with the buzz of the chainsaw. "Get out of there. Lily and lunch are waiting for you at the Lodge." She shoved aside the truck and freed Summer's long shoelace. "You should've seen your face." Moxie chuckled. "'*Saavvve* yourselves.'"

Summer jumped up and glanced toward the sound of the saw. The man was cutting bushes and low-hanging tree limbs. Another man—a boy, really, with startling blue eyes and a bandana over his nose and mouth—pushed a lawn mower.

"It's not funny." She tied her shoelace before jumping over the side.

"Oh, it's funny. I wished I had a camera. I can't wait to tell Lily this one." Moxie motioned toward a large log building about fifty yards away. The word *Lodge* was painted across the top log. "Go on, she's waiting for you. I'll unload your gear and put it in your cabins."

"How do you know whose suitcase is whose?"

"I was in the army, gal. I read people like a book."

"Oh yeah? Read me." Summer leaned against the truck, arms crossed, her adrenaline still flowing.

"All right. . . . You're a leader, but you're a bit scared. You're a rebel but without a cause. You're cautious but willing to take a risk. You skirt the lines but don't go over. Even at that pool bubble party, you wanted to quit just as the cops showed up."

"I was covered with soap. It was in my ears and my eyes, and my shorts kept sliding off."

"You're beautiful, but you're sloppy about it. You ask yourself, 'What if I really tried but the boy I want don't take a shine to me?'"

Ha. What does Moxie know? "I have a lot of boys who take a shine to me."

"I'm sure. But the one you want?" Moxie lowered the truck gate and reached for the record player. "You brought all this music stuff, so I'm guessing that's a passion. Or maybe hobby. You want to be a musician but can't commit all the way. 'What if I fail?'"

"I'm not afraid to fail."

"You left all your music gear on the bus, gal."

"I forgot, that's all."

"That's all?"

"Golly mo, you ask a lot of questions. I was tired. You ride thirty-six hours on a bus and . . ." Yeah, Moxie's moniker as a former POW was going to take all the fun out of complaining this summer.

"I know a bit about you from Lily. Only child. Adored by your parents. Adored by your father, who adopted you when you were three."

"The loser who contributed to my existence walked out on us. Before I was even born."

Mom didn't talk much about the man she loved before Dad, which never mattered to Summer since Jeff Wilde was the grooviest, coolest, handsomest, kindest, and sweetest father on planet earth. She'd do nothing to hurt him or risk their affection.

It was enough to bear the tension rising between her parents. If they didn't think she could hear their muffled, closed-door arguments at night, they should think again.

There'd been little bouts and arguments between them over the years, especially when Dad started his engineering business, of which Mom was the vice president. But none of those lasted more than an hour or so. But something happened this past spring that changed the tone of the Wilde household. Changed Mom. Next thing Summer knew, she'd accepted a position as a camp director in Oklahoma.

As far as Summer could make out, it had something to do with Dad, before he met Mom. Summer had tried to offer her two cents by telling Mom to chill out about whatever Dad did in the past.

"It wasn't murder, was it?"

"Honestly, Summer, you can be so ridiculous at times. Of course it wasn't murder."

"Then what?"

"Leave it. Now, do you want to order pizza from Barnaby's? I don't feel like cooking."

"You're a star, Summer." Moxie removed the last of the gear off the truck. "Don't be afraid to shine. Don't be afraid to try and fail."

She picked up Summer's suitcase and guitar and headed for Moonglow. "By the way, the fella with the chainsaw? Skip, maintenance man and groundskeeper. He's bigger than a barn but sweeter than honey. The kid with the mower is his nephew, Levi. They're getting this place in shape for the Tumblers."

"Tumblers?" Summer looked toward Levi as he came around with the mower again.

"That's what we call the campers. I camped here as a girl in the twenties, if you can believe it." Summer could. No stretch for anyone's imagination. If Moxie was a nurse in the war, she had to be in her late fifties or early sixties. "I treasure those days. Had the time of my life." Her deep chuckle vibrated as she headed inside Moonglow. "'Forget about me. *Saavvve* yourselves.'"

Summer pictured the scene, heard herself calling to the Seasons. "*Saavvve yourselves.*" Okay, fine. It *was* funny.

Inside the Lodge, the air was cool under the pitched, beamed ceiling, and it pinged with mystery and magic, as if the laughter, love, and lore of campers past hovered there, waiting and dreaming for the camp to come alive again.

The Seasons sat at a table with sandwiches, chips, and sodas, talking with Mom. They were talking in stereo while waving their arms. "Forget about me. *Saavvve yourselves.*"

"She did not," Mom said. "Summer? Afraid?" She chuckled and popped a potato chip into her mouth. "Are you going to tell her?"

The Seasons laughed again, stopping when Summer asked, "Tell me what?"

Instant silence. Snow stood with her camera and snapped Summer's picture. "Isn't this place amazing?"

"Don't change the subject, Snowy. Tell me what?"

"I mean, look . . . high beamed ceilings. Stone floor and fireplace. And a loft with chairs and lamps for reading." Summer glanced toward the loft, then around the Lodge. The walls were large timbers held together by a thick gray plaster. Two of them had floor-to-ceiling windows. "And, Sum, did you see the Memory Wall back there?" Snow pointed to the far wall peppered with framed photographs.

"Tumblers from every year since 1910," Mom said. "Minus the silent years, but we're changing that now."

"Why was it silent for twenty years?" Snow snapped a photo of Mom.

At least she looked like Mom. But a woman with wild, untamed curls and no makeup, wearing a T-shirt over hiking shorts and boots, had swallowed her manicured, expertly dressed, and made-up mother of 1680 Killarney Way, Tallahassee, Florida.

"The owners died, and their kids tried to make it a money machine. They stopped investing in the girls and the property. By the mid-fifties, no one wanted to come. They held on to it because their parents loved it but finally sold it to my old Camp Tumbleweed bunkmate, Josie. She married into a Ponca City oil family and bought this with her 'mad' money. Summer, grab some lunch."

With a sandwich and a bag of Cheetos, she joined her mother and the Seasons.

"So, what are you not telling me?" Summer glared at Autumn. If she kept a secret too long, she broke out in hives.

"Nothing."

"Autumn . . ."

"Okay, fine. I saw the dude with the chainsaw coming around the cabin."

"So did I," Snow said.

"Me too." Spring's laugh set them off again. "Now who's gullible?"

"You're a regular riot, Alice. A regular riot." Summer harrumphed and munched on a Cheeto. "At least you know I care. Y'all left me."

"All right, all right. Let's not argue. We have eight long weeks of camp ahead of us." Mom passed a clipboard to each Season. "Camp Tumbleweed counselors, let's go over exactly what we do here."

The eight weeks of camp had just filled up, with Josie scholar-shipping half of the registered campers. Twenty-four girls each week, arriving on Sunday afternoon and leaving Saturday morning.

"Since you four, along with me, Moxie, and Skip, whom you all have met"—the snickers started again—"are the sum of our staff, we have to do all the cleaning between camps. I'm putting the four of you in charge of laundry. Tumble Time promised to reserve five washers and dryers for us on Saturday afternoons so you can go in, load up the machines, then hang around town if you want. There's the diner and drugstore, O'Sullivan's. A fabric store, a secondhand shop, a clothes and furniture store. A hair salon." Mom glanced at Autumn. "Well, you'll see when you go into town. Oh, and there's a park with a carousel. Beautiful place with lots of trees and a little stream." Her expression waxed sentimental. "When I was a Tumbler, we went into town every Friday afternoon, bought ice cream and candy, then rode the carousel until dusk. After that, we roasted hot dogs and marshmallows at the firepit."

"Can we do that this year?" Snow said. "That sounds romantic and fun."

"What is it with you and romance, Snowbird?" Summer wasn't quite over being laughed at. Give her a minute. Or an hour. Okay, a day. "You hate romance."

"Hate romance?" Autumn said. "Do you not remember her wall of romance novels?"

"Girls! Focus." Mom tapped her clipboard. "Friday carousel ride and firepit is on the schedule. We couldn't get real horses this year, so the carousel will be a solid substitute."

This year? Was Mom planning on doing this *again*?

Wake-up bell was at seven. Breakfast at eight. Lunch at noon. Dinner at five. Campfire at eight with snacks. Bedtime at ten. And in between?

"Swimming, archery, photography . . ." A "Yay" came from Snow. "Spring, I'd like you to be in charge of crafts." Mom pointed to the loft. "There's material, yarn, construction paper, you name it, and a sewing machine in one corner. Summer, in the other corner will be music."

48

Music. All right, Mom. "There's a guitar and a banjo, and a flutophone, but I'm not sure it's sanitary. Moxie bought new guitar strings, so between the camp guitar and yours, you should be able to teach some music lessons. Snow, you'll handle photography, of course. There's a darkroom right over there." She pointed to a closed door by the kitchen. "Autumn, our scholar and athlete, you're in charge of sports—swimming, archery, and softball. We have new equipment for archery and softball, and I've ordered floats and life jackets for the lake.

"Oh, girls, the lake is so beautiful. There's a big rock about fifty yards out, and when I was a Tumbler, the strong swimmers always raced out. Whoever got there first would climb up and be queen of the rock. We had a blue team and a white team in my day, with all sorts of competitions. Capture the Flag was the best. Josie and I were captains of the opposite teams and—"

Mom stopped as if realizing she'd gone to a different place. She stared down at her clipboard.

"Tell us, Mom." Summer liked hearing her stories, but she didn't talk much about her past. Dad said all her memories got bottled up with "the man who gave her you" and walked away.

"Well, it was the best fun," Mom said. "That's the goal of camp, right? Have fun. Make lifelong friendships. Which, of course, you girls are the supreme example. So, let's have fun. Let the girls run around, scream, play, hike, swim. I do think you should have some sort of softball tournament, Autumn. We should be a little organized."

"What about a play?" Snow said. "I could write and direct. Summer could do the music. Spring could make the costumes, and—"

"I could do all the hair and makeup." Autumn had sort of wilted when Mom put her in charge of sports. While she loved sports—she was a top athlete at Lincoln High—she'd turned a bit green when Mom mentioned swimming.

Listening to Mom go on about camp with one side of her brain,

Summer considered the weirdness among the Seasons with the other side.

First Snow, though she'd been weird for a while, ever since Blaine died. Since April, Spring had been quiet, often cutting their evening phone calls short. Now Autumn and water. She'd not jumped into Spring or Summer's pool in ages—except for the night at FSU. Come to think of it, the last time they went to St. George Island, she'd stayed inside reading.

"A play? What a great idea, Snow." Mom shuffled through the pages on her clipboard. Summer could hear the cogs of her mental wheel grinding. *This is not what I had planned.* "I'm not sure when we could fit it in." Mom gave her a broad smile. "Let me review the schedule and see what we could do. Where would we have it?"

"How about the old barn?" Autumn said.

"Yes, the old barn." Mom stared at her clipboard.

Summer wanted to laugh. No one messed with Lil's schedule. It tipped her sideways. Maybe that's what she and Dad had been fussing about lately. Dad's business was growing, and he liked to make quick decisions. Yet how would that have anything to do with his past?

Mom continued talking. "You'll have two pairs of shorts, and shirts with the camp logo. There will be two T-shirts for all Tumblers. Over here on the wall are the old camp rules. I think they hung that sign when I was a Tumbler."

Camp Tumbleweed Rules
June 1947

1. Tumblers must follow all the rules.
2. Obey the bell!
3. Listen to the counselors.
4. Be kind.
5. Be courteous.

6. Be modest. It's a virtue.

7. Look out for your fellow Tumblers.

8. Use the buddy system.

9. All pranks must be kind.

10. No food fights. Ever.

"No food fights ever?" Summer said. "I don't think I can stay at this camp if I can't throw mashed taters at Snowy."

Snow snarled at her. The mashed potato bit *was* getting old. Yet it was one of their best shared memories.

"Let's not bring that up," Mom said. "You two had the whole lunchroom slinging food. The principal was furious."

Snow and Summer had sat in the principal's office, covered in bits of potatoes and macaroni, trembling in fear. Principal Norton had a really big paddle. But Mom and Babs charmed him out of corporal punishment, and he agreed to let them apologize to their lunchroom crowd instead.

"The bell is everything," Mom said. "We live by the bell. It wakes us up, puts us to bed, clangs for meals and when it's time to change to a different activity. If a storm rolls in, the bell clangs and clangs and clangs."

"We are in Tornado Alley, so please listen to and obey the bell." Mom looked to Summer. "Last but not least, the camp song. I want you to learn it on the guitar. We'll sing it every night at the campfire."

Camp Tumbleweed Song

Oh come and let us sing,
the joy of Camp Tumbleweed.
Of the laughter and fun we've had here.
All our memories to remain dear.
Day and night, sun and rain,
you are the melody of our youthful refrain.

Camp Tumbleweed, Camp Tumbleweed, to you we'll
   always be true.
Camp Tumbleweed, Camp Tumbleweed, we will never
   forget you.

Snow snapped a photo of Mom singing, eyes closed, chin raised, lost in days gone by. Summer leaned into the haunting, sentimental melody, chording the song in her head.

Maybe she was tired from the long journey—not the one from Tallahassee to Tumbleweed—but from the tension between her parents, from growing up, from graduation where she said good-bye to her childhood, from the FSU pool party, from being arrested and spending a night in the police station to her sentence in the judge's chambers, to the tense final week of school, where she and the others scrubbed dry concentrated soap off the pool's cement walls and floor. Suddenly she wanted to cry.

Buck up. Hold on. Her emotions started to wane just as Spring looped her arm through hers. Summer rested her cheek on her friend's shoulder and brushed away her tears with the back of her hand. Spring reached for Snow, who put her camera down and drew Autumn to her side.

Mom started the song again, and Summer felt like the words and melody were a part of her.

"Always be true . . . never forget you."

Her life spent with Snow, Spring, and Autumn finally had words. Finally had a melody. The Four Seasons finally had a song.

5

Yes We Can Can

Spring

'77

Spring was more than happy with this place. Run-down, abandoned-looking, who cared? For the first time since she loaded the Greyhound and headed west on I-10, she felt normal. Almost normal, anyway.

She'd consumed an unholy amount of junk food on the trip. No wonder she felt like she'd been punted over a goalpost, then hit by a Mack truck.

Grabbing the last set of stiff white sheets Moxie dropped off at her cabin, she made the top and final bunk for her first set of Tumblers. Her cabin, Starlight, was bare, except for four sets of bunk beds and the counselor's corner with a bed, a lamp, and a cubby with a door and no lock.

Still, the place, with the deep screened windows, had a cozy quality, especially with the beds made. Tomorrow, Lily promised to run them into the Five & Dime, where she'd give each counselor twenty dollars to "spruce up" her cabin.

"We still have a lot to do, like clean up the grounds and the barn . . . so no dillydallying. You can go to O'Sullivan's and ride the carousel when the work is done."

Spring decided to write Mal tonight, tell him she'd been thinking about their relationship and suggest, *"We should break up."*

Hearing the words in her head, she wanted to scream. But she couldn't tell him the truth. He had to go to Duke. Besides, they were missing the best part of summer together. Might as well free him now.

They needed to be practical about their relationship. He'd be ten hours and six hundred miles away come fall. And if she broke up with him, set him free, she no longer needed to consider his feelings. She could make something of this unusual summer.

A memory from the FSU pool party popped up, but she shoved it aside. *Nothing to see here.*

The screen door creaked open. "You still working?" Summer crashed on the first bottom bunk and stretched out.

"Hey, skeebie." Spring slapped her feet. "I just made that bed. Square corners and everything. Get up."

Summer rolled onto her side and propped her head in her hands. "I'll fix it. Snow's Paps taught *all* of us to make those military corners."

"I miss him."

"Me too." Summer flopped over again, her long legs crossed at the ankles, her hands clasped behind her head. "And Blaine."

"If I were you, I'd not bring him up."

Summer raised up. "Why not? Is there something you're not telling me?"

"Of course not. It's just, you know, Snow still misses him something fierce."

Summer thought a moment, then plopped down on the pillow.

Spring finished making her bed and arranging her alarm clock, mirror, and toiletries on the open shelves and in her cubby while Summer hummed the camp song.

"Did you get the chords worked out on your guitar?" Spring crawled in beside Summer and stretched out next to her.

"What do you think? It's a pretty simple melody."

"I wish I loved something the way you love music."

Summer glanced at her. "I do love it, Spring. No, more than love it. . . . I'm the me I'm meant to be when I play."

"I'm jealous." Spring wrapped her hand around Summer's. "Remember me when you're rich and famous."

"Who said anything about rich and famous?" Summer squeezed Spring's hand. "You'd tell me if there was anything wrong, wouldn't you?"

"With Snow? Of course," Spring said, her words a bit rushed. Summer was zeroing in on her.

"No, I mean you."

"Me? What makes you think anything is wrong?"

"Spring, I know you better than anyone. You've not been yourself. Where'd you get off to the night of the pool party? I saw you with that hunk, according to Autumn, and—"

"He kissed me."

"Really?" Summer rolled onto her side and stared down at her. "Did you tell Mal?"

"No, never, and I feel horrible about it. After going to the movies with Craig Emmitt, I said I'd never stray again. I blame all the Miller Lite—"

"You don't think he's kissed a girl or two without telling you? Remember Jay Westmark's graduation party?"

"He swears he didn't."

"That's not what Jenny Reed says." Summer flopped back down on the cot.

"I trust him, Summer."

"I know. You two are solid. Just don't feel bad if you kissed a cute guy at a party. Geez."

"Who'd you kiss?"

"Who said I kissed anyone?"

"Summer—"

"Okay, Billy Crumpet, but if you ever tell—"

"Wait, what? You kissed Billy 'The Lothario' Crumpet?" Spring laughed. If a guy could have a sullied reputation, it'd be Billy Crumpet.

"That's when I knew the night had gotten out of hand. He probably told the whole FSU football team he did *it* with me among the so-called bubbles in the pool."

"'So-called' is right." Once she started laughing, it was hard to stop. "It took me two hours to get the dried soap off my skin and out of my hair."

"I think I still have some in my hair," Summer said.

Laughing together was good, healing, almost like a pledge that the summer would be better than they imagined. Then they fell silent for a few minutes, listening to the wind in the trees, the hum of a chainsaw in the distance.

"*Saavvve* yourselves," Spring said softly, crying out when Summer squeezed her hand too tight. "Let's make it a great summer," she said.

"The best."

Beyond the walls of Starlight, they could hear Autumn and Snow talking and singing Elton John and Kiki Dee's "Don't Go Breaking My Heart" as they tidied up Sunglow and Twilight.

Summer sang along with her rich and smoky voice. When the song ended, the birds on the limbs picked up their melodies again.

The camp bell clanged over and over. Spring and Summer scrambled off the bunk and out the door to see Lily, waving, telling them they had an hour of free time.

"Go to the lake!" she called.

Summer sprinted to Moonglow. "Last one in is a rotten egg."

Spring pulled on the Jantzen one-piece Lily required for Camp Tumbleweed, tied up her hair and pinned back her Farrah Fawcett layers, and darted out of the cabin.

Summer was ten yards ahead, with her hair flapping behind her, a towel in one hand, her radio in the other. Snow was on her heels.

Spring stopped short as a wave of nausea hit. She paused by a tree, breathed deep, and battled another wave. What was this? The long, hot trip was over. She was here now, ready for the best summer of her life.

"Spring?" Autumn bent to see her face. Her long, pale, freckled legs begged for a touch of sun. "You okay?"

"Yeah, just . . . I think the egg salad I had for lunch was bad." A hot bead of perspiration ran down her neck.

Autumn's green eyes popped wide. "I hope not. I had two sandwiches."

"No queasiness?" Spring said.

"Spring, why don't you let me cut your hair? Get it off your neck and out of your face." Autumn tugged on Spring's ponytail. "You must have twenty bobby pins holding back these layers. Judith isn't here to give you heck. What do you say? I'm giving Snow a Kate Jackson cut tonight."

"Well . . ." It would be nice to have a wash-and-go style, not mess with bobby pins, hair ties, and flyaways. "Maybe something cute? Like Dorothy Hamill."

Mom would be furious, but so what? Spring was an adult now. A woman. She could cut her hair if she wanted.

"I love her hair. Done. My cabin. After dinner."

"But first, you have to race me to the lake. You heard Summer. Last one in is a rotten egg."

Blech, don't say *egg*.

Spring raced with Autumn stride for stride, but when they arrived at the dock, and Spring dropped her towel to the boards, kicked out of her flip-flops, and sailed off the end into the water, Autumn remained standing on the beach.

"Fall, get in!" Summer's splash didn't even hit the sandy shore, let alone Autumn. "You're the rotten egg."

"I think I'll sunbathe." She held up a book. "And read."

"Read? We're at a lake on a beautiful *hot* day. Get in, have some fun." Splash, splash, splash.

"Summer, the water is missing me by a country mile." Still, Autumn backed up toward the grass. "I'll get in later."

"It's not the monthly curse, is it?"

"Leave her alone, Summer." Snow shoved a wave of water toward Summer. "Let's race to the rock."

Spring floated on the cool, slick surface, watching Summer and Snow compete, then glanced at Autumn. She'd known for a long time something bothered her about water. But she thought she'd get over it.

As for her monthly, Spring wished that was her problem. When it came, it'd be a blessing. A very welcome blessing.

Summer and Snow raced back, laughing. They got along best when competing. Of the four of them, they acted the most like real sisters—arguing, then loving on each other. It was a weird dynamic.

Summer hauled her lean self out of the water and turned up the Pointer Sisters' "Yes We Can Can." She started a jig with Snow, who broke free to draw Autumn into the fun. Maybe it was a reflection off the water, but Autumn looked like Spring felt fifteen minutes ago. Sick.

"Wait for me." Spring hoisted herself onto the dock.

Just as she started dancing, Summer wrapped her arms around Autumn's legs and hoisted her up. "You're going in the water, Esther Williams."

"No, no. Come on, Summer, put me down." Autumn kicked and struggled to be free while the Pointer Sisters sang, "Yes, we can, can . . ."

"Summer, she said put her down." Snow grabbed at Summer's arm.

"Why? She's the best swimmer of all of us. Spring, help me out."

"Summer, no, stop. Let her go in when she's ready. You're being obtuse."

"Obtuse? Look, camp starts Sunday, and Fall better be ready for the swim test."

Autumn kicked free and stumbled away from Summer, her expression pure terror.

"Don't you ever listen, you freak?" Autumn came at Summer with a hard shove. "The whole world doesn't revolve around your sick sense of fun. You once shoved me in the dirt for teasing, and now you're the worst one."

"Take a chill pill, Fall." Summer stepped closer and motioned to the lake. "It's just water."

"Summer, enough," Spring said.

"Come on. In you go." Summer inched Autumn to the edge of the dock.

"Summer," Spring said. If she didn't back off, she'd tell Autumn to charge her, knock her down. Or was Autumn still the girl who got her faced shoved in the dirt?

"Stand aside, Summer." Autumn stretched one leg toward the radio. "I'm warning you."

"You wouldn't dare."

Oh, Autumn dared. With a flick of her foot, the radio splashed into the lake.

"Fall, hey, what they heck?" Summer dropped to her belly and reached over the dock for the handle.

"Blame yourself, Summie." Snow aligned with Autumn. "She told you to leave her alone."

"If my radio is ruined, you're going in, Fall. Face-first." Water dripped from the box as Summer set it on the dry boards. "And you owe me a new one."

"Like heck I do."

"You know, I always thought Snow was the oddball Season, but it's really you, isn't it?" Summer faced Autumn, hands on her hips, jaw set.

"Summer Wilde! Take that back," Spring said. "What's wrong with you?"

"Wrong with *me*? What's wrong with *her*? She's the camp counselor in charge of swimming." Summer jabbed Autumn's shoulder. "But she won't even get wet. What's up, chick? Spill."

"Get out of my face, Summer."

"Ooh, fighting words." Summer danced around, lightly punching the air like Rocky Balboa.

"Okay, okay, y'all. Settle down." Spring stepped between Summer and Autumn. "We're all on edge from the trip, never mind being stuck in this godforsaken place. Summer, try your radio and—"

At the same time, Summer swooped forward, scooped up Autumn by one arm and one leg, and without a pause or by-your-leave, hurled her into the lake. She was a wee bit too close to the dock, and Autumn's arm hit with a loud thud.

"Summer! You jerk! . . . Autumn, are you okay? Did you hit your head?" A pale-faced Snow shoved Summer with such a force she tumbled backward and over the side, then dove in to rescue Autumn. But she'd already sputtered to the surface and was swimming to the shore as if her life depended on it.

"Summer Wilde." Autumn's voice was low and mangled. "You go too far." Her legs and arms shook as she reached for her towel. "You're a brute, and I hate you. I really do. Stay away from me. What I want to know is why *you're* a Season. As for you, Spring, thanks for *not* helping."

"Me? I was trying. I told Summer to stop. But, girl, she's got a point. If you're in charge of swimming, how are you going to help the girls from the dock? What's the big deal?"

"The big deal is I told her to stop. The big deal is she thinks I shouldn't be a Season." Autumn shot Summer a quiver of daggers.

"She was just kidding." Spring again. This argument churned her already upset stomach. "Summer, tell her. We can't be Four Seasons without each other. All for one, one for all, right?"

"Forget it, Spring," Autumn said, turning to Summer. "I don't have to do everything you do all the time. I know my own mind. I'm a National Merit Scholar, for crying out loud." She worked the towel over her hair. "Look at my arm. I'll have a bruise."

Summer winced at the bright red mark on Autumn's forearm. "All I want to know is why you're scared of the water, brainiac."

"I'm not."

"Then why won't you get in? Not just here but at home too."

"Because I don't feel like it. Man alive, we're not conjoined quadruplets. And I did get in at the pool party, sad to say."

"Fine, gee whiz." Summer backed away, hands raised. "Will it help if I let you cut my hair?" Spring grinned at Summer's way of saying sorry.

"Oh you will?" Autumn scoffed. "If you let me near you, you'll walk away with a flat top." She snatched up her book and spun away.

"She'll cool off." Spring handed Summer her radio, and watched Autumn head toward the cabins.

"You should listen to her, Summer." Snow reached for her towel. "Don't be such a bully. Tell her you didn't mean what you said. About being a Season." Snow's request sounded half like a question. "Otherwise, it's going to be a long summer."

"She knows I didn't mean it."

"Does she?" Snow glanced toward Autumn. "I'm going to check on her."

Summer opened the radio's battery compartment and water spilled out. "Great, this is ruined."

This was not how Spring wanted to start the first day of camp. With new tension added to the old, she wasn't sure how much more she could handle. She hated feeling so . . . fragile. If she were alone, she'd let loose and cry.

Instead, she breathed in and said, "Summer, you're one of the coolest people I know, but when it comes to reading other people, you're a dolt. Pay attention, will you? Think before opening your big bazoo. Why would you even think Fall's not a Season, let alone say it?"

"I don't know. . . . She just ticked me off. She's been avoiding swimming since Blaine died. Snow's been acting odd too. Especially toward me." Summer snapped up her towel to dry the radio. "I'm not the dolt you think I am. I threw her in on purpose. I wanted her to tell us why she won't swim." Summer collected the radio parts. "I'm going to see if I can dry this out with a blow dryer."

So, Summer had noticed Snow's attitude too. "I'll come with you."

Tomorrow *had* to be a better day. Just like the Pointer Sisters sang, "We can work it out, oh yes we can, yes we can can."

6

We Can Work It Out

Summer

'77

"How do you like your cabin?" Mom peered through Moonglow's screen door. "It's a bit hot now, but things will cool off this evening." It was after dinner, and Summer was gathering her things for a shower. She and the Seasons, along with the soon-coming Tumblers, had to trek a good thirty yards to the latrine.

"It's fine. I sort of like it."

"What happened with Autumn?"

"I threw her in the lake, and I might have told her she was the oddball Season."

Mom sighed, and the screen door's hinges moaned as she stepped inside. "Did you apologize?"

"I told her she could cut my hair."

"You think that's enough, do you?"

"Somewhere between trimming bushes and cleaning out the barn this afternoon, she told a joke and I laughed really hard and extra loud."

The Seasons had spent the afternoon doing yardwork and hauling off tree limbs and debris to a burn pile. Mom had miraculously reworked her clipboard schedule so carousel night was Thursday, which left Friday for Snow's play.

"Keep it simple, Snow. Use the barn as the playhouse, but hear me, I don't want them rehearsing more than a half hour a day. I know, I know, it's not much, but that's all you get."

The barn wasn't in bad shape. All they had to do was move hay bales and muck out empty stalls. Then Spring discovered three snakes napping in the loft under a stream of sunlight and nearly passed out.

"Black snakes," Skip said, picking them up one by one and dropping them into a gunnysack. *"Keep the rats away."* Still, he hauled them out to the far corner of the meadow.

By the time Moxie rang the dinner bell, Summer was exhausted. Almost fell asleep face-first in her sloppy joe and corn on the cob.

"I don't get it, Mom. Autumn wanted to be Esther Williams when we were kids. Ever since Blaine died, she and Snow—"

"Do you blame them? Blaine was Snow's big brother. Her hero. Autumn is close to Snow. Blaine was like her big brother."

"She has six siblings. Why would she want another? And he was a big brother to *all* of us."

"Summer, come on." Mom remained by the cabin door. "You know Autumn liked him with more than sisterly affection. Blaine was a handsome, charming kid."

"He was? I hadn't noticed." At this, Mom laughed. Everyone noticed Blaine Snowden.

Summer had a huge crush on him in ninth grade, but he was so intense around her that she started feeling trapped. She knew why he asked her to run to the store with him or to listen to music in his room. He liked her. But he was too much, and she had this sense if she ever gave in to him, he'd suffocate her.

"If you all are going to endure this summer . . ." Mom inched down the narrow center aisle and sat on the edge of Summer's cot. "If it's going to be a *good* summer for the Seasons and the Tumblers, you're going to have to pay attention, baby. Listen. Check your tongue. You can't walk over people."

"Walk over? Is that what I do? I was goading Fall into telling the truth." Summer rolled a pair of fresh underwear, shorts, and a top into her towel. "Besides, we all got in. I thought she should too. She *is* in charge of swimming."

"How'd you like it if I forced you to do something you didn't want to do?"

"I'm here, aren't I?"

Mom laughed. "That was your own doing."

"Don't worry about Autumn and me. This wasn't our first fight. Probably won't be our last."

"No, I guess not. How did you like the lake otherwise?" Mom raised her face to feel the breeze coming through the screen. "Moxie added fans to our list. That'll help keep things cool."

"I love the lake. Snow and I raced to the rock."

"Josie and I used to do that too. The rock was part of the team competition," Mom said. "It's supposed to be named for the winning team, Blue Rock or White Rock. Last I knew, it was Blue Rock. We'll have to get teams going next year, though. It doesn't make sense for a weekly camp."

Summer tucked her towel roll under her arm and sat next to Mom. "Are you coming back next year?"

Mom shrugged. "Maybe. I loved camp as a kid. I still have friends from those days."

"You never talked much about it when I was growing up. Why didn't you send me to camp?"

"I don't know. . . ." Her voice and attention faded away. "I lost some zeal for it when Tumbleweed closed. It felt like part of my past died."

"Mom, is everything okay with you and Dad? Is that why you left him?"

"Being a camp director for two months is not *leaving* your father."

"Then why all this?" Summer pointed to Mom's hair and hiking boots. "Why the Euell Gibbons imitation? Did you leave your brush and curlers at home?"

Mom made a face. "I brought my brush, and I don't need any judgment from you, thank you very much."

"Is everything okay at Wilde Engineering?"

"I guess you've heard us arguing." Mom stared out the window, then focused on brushing barn dirt from her khaki shorts and white Camp Tumbleweed pullover. "Marriages go through rough patches. We'll get through it."

"I know it has something to do with the past. Is it me?" She'd never told Mom her secret. What she'd heard Dad say to his friend Ralph Morgan eleven years ago during their first Fourth of July bash, a party that had become legendary among friends, family, and acquaintances. The *Tallahassee Democrat* even ran a feature about it: "A Wilde Kind of Fourth." "Did I do something?"

"Besides filling a university pool with sixty gallons of concentrated soap?" Mom smiled and squeezed her hand. "I'm not supposed to tell you, but Dad's quietly proud of you for that one. He said it took him back to his college days."

That was a look of pride? Not from where she sat in a holding cell, shivering, her clothes and hair stiff with concentrated soap.

"Really?" Summer warmed with her mother's confession. "Well, I *am* his daughter." She loved being Jeff Wilde's kid. He chose her, along with Mom, to be his family. "He loves to brag how he put Limburger on the high school's furnace one winter." Dad grew up in Portsmouth, Ohio, a cozy town along the Ohio River.

"I must've heard that story a thousand times." Mom squeezed Summer's hand. "Don't worry about your dad and me. Just have fun this summer. I think you're going to love the Tumblers. Oh, hey, I wanted to ask, is everything okay with Spring?"

"I guess so. She didn't feel good on the bus ride out, but you know how she is. . . . She *messed* up by being part of the pool party. She kissed some dude at the frat house too. She broke the rules, proved to the world she's not Miss Perfect. She probably has knots in her stomach for each gallon of soap she helped pour into the pool."

"Does Mal know about this other boy?" Mom said. "Is everything okay with them?"

"She didn't tell him, so yes, everything is okay with them."

"I should go. There's work to do." Mom pointed to Summer's shower roll. "You might want to wait. Skip is setting up the campfire. Moxie is bringing out the graham crackers, marshmallows, and Hershey bars. You'll get all smoky. Did you learn the camp song?"

"Got it all worked out." Summer tucked her towel roll by her pillow. While she was tired and longed for a shower, the idea of playing her guitar by a campfire and munching on s'mores revived her.

"Good." Mom moved down the aisle. "Let the other Seasons know. Campfire at nine o'clock. We'll keep it short. We're all exhausted." She paused at the door. "But do keep an eye on Spring. She seems off to me."

"She's fine, Mom." If you asked Summer, they were all a bit *off*.

"And maybe officially apologize to Autumn."

Summer made a cutting motion toward her long blond hair. Close enough in her book.

"Summie, I know you don't like when I say things like this, but you're the leader of the Seasons and—"

"I am? Don't tell Spring."

"Yes, she's a leader, but you have a way of moving the needle the others don't. So be careful with your words. Be careful with Autumn and Snow."

"What about me? Who's careful with me?"

"You're stronger than you know. Set an example, give your all to these young girls. Some may never get a chance to come to camp again." Mom returned to the bunk and brushed her hand over Summer's hair. "Maybe the best summer of your life is giving these girls the best summer of theirs."

Mom's tone stirred Summer's tears, and she hated crying in front of her. "Okay, fine, fine, rah, rah, we'll have a bee-last."

"After today, it seems you girls need a Truth Night." Ah, the infamous Truth Night, where they could confess anything they wanted without fear or shame, without consequences. Well, unless someone confessed to robbing a bank or to murder, then all bets were off. "As I recall, those unearthed a few dark secrets in the past."

"I'll think about it."

When Mom left, Summer shouted the evening plans across the yard to Autumn in Sunglow. "Campfire at nine with s'mores."

"Since when?" Autumn peered out of the window. "I'm cutting hair tonight."

"Since Mom just told me. So cut hair now."

"Want to come? I'm dying to try out my new clippers."

"I bet you are." Summer grinned. "Um, Autumn, you know I didn't—"

"I know." Through the window screens, and across the thin grassy space between their cabins, the lake event was mended. "Just don't throw me in again."

"Deal, but you have to tell me why—"

Autumn was gone, hollering for Spring and Snow. Summer returned to her cot and reached for her guitar. She played through the camp song, singing her devotion to a camp she barely knew while sorting through her feelings, admitting that nothing felt right the summer after high school. Nothing at all.

Autumn

'77

Autumn batted away the smoke from the campfire, took a bite of her second s'more, and stared across the circle at Summer, who played a melody on her guitar.

Why was she so . . . so . . . ignorant? How did she miss signs like *I love you* written all over a guy's face, or *I don't want to go into the lake, egghead* from her best friend?

A twist of anger made her want to toss the last of her sticky dessert at her face, but they'd spoken their final words on the subject. A food fight would only bring it all up again and break a sacred camp rule.

She hated that about herself—how easily she let stuff go and forgave. Autumn blamed Granny Childe for telling her grudges only hurt the person holding on. But, man, couldn't she be ticked for a day? Or even a week?

Granny, never meet Summer.

Seriously, if Summer really ever allowed her to cut her hair . . .

Snow and Spring looked adorable with their new haircuts, even though Spring had a bit of an emotional conniption when she saw her beautiful chestnut hair lying on the floor.

But when Autumn dried and styled it, Spring had a fresh light in her eyes, and Autumn knew once again that hair was her life's calling. Snow loved her new bob, and now as she leaned toward the fire, she brushed aside her new bangs.

Lily had told Moxie, *"Autumn can do anything. Sports, math, science, art, composition. If she doesn't know how, give her a few days or weeks and she'll figure it out."*

But she couldn't do "anything," could she? Pools and lakes had become her enemy. She only went in the lake by brute force. She'd been full of beer when she jumped into the FSU pool—which in hindsight made her quiver. But she'd wanted to have fun, be an almost-college girl. If only for one night. Then some drunken hoodlum tried to pull her under.

She was climbing the fence to escape when the cops showed up.

"How are you, Fall?" Lily joined her on her log. "Everything good?"

"Everything's good." Shoot, now she was choked up. "I miss home. Miss my brothers and sisters. Ridley's none too happy with me now that he has to look after the kids when my parents are teaching, which thankfully is only two days a week for the summer quarter." Ridley was the oldest boy, a year younger than Autumn. "He'll feed them junk food all day, let the twins get into Mom's makeup, and probably forget to change Chris's diaper."

Lily laughed softly and bumped Autumn's shoulder. "Admit it, it's nice to be on your own. Not be a second mom."

"I'm not, Lily, I promise. Mom tells me all the time to go out, do stuff. But I don't know, I like my brothers and sisters. One day we'll all be grown and out of the house, only seeing one another every couple of years. Ridley's a bit of a pain, but—" She stared across the fire at Summer. "He's also fun."

Rid had a huge crush on Summer. She had no idea, of course. If she knew, she played it off. Same with Blaine and Autumn. If he knew how she felt, he never let on.

"I'll be gone in September, anyway. Living in the dorms." Autumn hadn't been raised to tell lies, but until she made her announcement, she went along with the grand plan.

"Did you meet anyone at the big pool party?" Lily asked.

"Not really. Talked to a guy named Eric who had great Robert Redford hair."

"Speaking of hair, Spring and Snow look really cute. You have a gift." Across the way, the two of them swayed side to side as

Summer sang "The Candy Man." Lily moved on to camp issues. "Did you inspect the sports equipment? Do we have everything we need for two softball teams and for the archery course?"

"I gave a list to Moxie at dinner." She was going into Tulsa tomorrow to get everything the Seasons needed for the specialty areas.

Summer needed more strings for the guitars. Spring wanted thread and yarn. Snow had a whole list of supplies for developing photos.

"Autumn, if you need anything, tell me, okay?" Lily gave her a mama hug, then moved to the middle of the circle, batted away a plume of smoke, and called her counselors to attention. She reviewed the camp rules, then instructed Summer to lead them in the camp song.

> Oh come and let us sing,
> the joy of Camp Tumbleweed.
> Of the laughter and fun we've had here.

Laughter? Joy and fun? Were the words prophetic or hopeful? Were they true? Did past Camp Tumbleweed Tumblers think of this place with fondness? Autumn went to camp once as a six-year-old, and the counselors told them ghost stories. She didn't sleep for a week and had nightmares when she got home.

She had nightmares once again. About the day Blaine died. Not every night, not every week, but when they came, she woke up gasping for air. She *should* tell someone. She caught Summer's gaze. *No, not her.* But when she smiled, Autumn couldn't help but smile back.

If she stayed mad at Summer, Snow and Spring would pester her. Lily would ask what was wrong, and Autumn felt sure she'd burst with everything she'd been keeping inside.

When Summer ended the song, Lily whispered, "Again."

This time, Autumn closed her eyes and tried to live in the lyrics.

71

Willed herself to make her one and only summer at Camp Tumble-weed special. For her friends and for the little Tumblers. She'd never come back here, but it might be good to think of this place fondly in the years to come. To try for the best summer of her life.

7

Staying Alive

Spring

'77

"Are we ready?" Standing on the back of the dock with the six girls from her cabin, Spring glanced down the line. "Last jump into the lake, then we have to get ready for play rehearsal."

In two days, on Friday, the inaugural performance of the Camp Tumbleweed Players would hit the barn stage. Snow's script, *You Can Do Anything*, inspired the girls to go for their dreams. This afternoon, Moxie had taken their handcrafted flyers into town to advertise their little musical drama. Lily received quite a few calls from locals planning to attend. They might actually have a standing barn only.

"We're ready." The girls echoed one after another.

Greta, Marianne, Connie, Lisa, Michele, and Vicki. Ages nine, ten, and eleven. They were amazing. Lily had assigned her *the best* Tumblers for week one.

Spring loved them so much she almost forgot her troubles. But in the evening, when all was quiet, the weight of her predicament, of her decisions, haunted her sleep.

"Spring? Aren't we going?" Greta, the camp's permanent summer Tumbler, crouched in the race position, ready to charge down the dock and into the water. She was eleven going on twenty, and pretty much the boss of Starlight cabin. Maybe the whole camp, except Lily and Moxie. All the Tumblers adored her.

"Go!" Spring shouted, racing down the dock, screaming, then flying off the edge with arms high, legs wide.

Breaking the surface, Spring sank through the blue-green waters toward the dark. She exhaled and drifted lower. Could she drown her guilt and shame? Let them lie on the lake floor?

I was sinking deep in sin . . .

The hope she had when she first arrived at camp, when the queasiness faded, was short-lived. On Sunday morning, she woke up from a sound sleep, nauseous. She'd slipped out of the cabin and through the silky night to throw up behind a tree. Then she'd tiptoed back inside, crawled into bed, and pulled out the sleeve of saltines she'd *borrowed* from Moxie's kitchen.

All she needed was her period. One single, stupid period. Never in her life had she hoped for her monthly. Then yesterday, after lunch, she'd felt a twinge, a cramp of good times to come, but so far, nothing.

Letting out another breath, she sank down, down, down.

Drown, shame, drown. She wanted to be the Spring she was before that April night. *Please, God, please.*

She stretched her legs through the cold, searching for the bottom, even though she knew the lake was too deep. But if she could touch down, then everything would be all right. *Everything.*

She wouldn't have to tell Daddy and Mom, Malcolm, or the Four Seasons. She could go on living according to *the* plan. The plan was important. Very important. If she'd learned anything from Mom and Grandma, it was the importance of any plan.

"Duvals and Tuttles do not fly by the seat of their pants."

The splashes above jostled her about in her watery hideaway.

. . . far from the peaceful shore.

She was out of air. Her lungs burned and demanded, *Breathe. Breathe!* Still, she did not kick her way to the top. The burning became a fire, and her pulse drummed in her ears.

Very deeply stained within . . .

Another splash, and someone almost landed on top of her. Her pulse was a runaway train. *Breathe!* If she could only bury her secret in the lake.

. . . sinking to rise no more.

A hand grabbed her hair and tried to tug her up, but after a moment, let go. Then someone hooked onto her bathing suit straps and pulled.

Love lifted me . . .

Air! She wanted air. Desperately. What had she been thinking? Spring kicked and fought her way to the surface. When she broke through the top, she gulped and gasped, struggling to fill herself with life.

"Spring, you idiot." Summer hauled her toward the shore with one arm around her waist. "You scared the crap out of us. What were you doing?"

"Sorry." Spring fell to the beach, her entire body shivering. "I was, um, just . . . just . . . seeing how long I could hold my breath."

"You lost that contest in eighth grade," Snow called from the dock, where her legs dangled over the side, swinging above the ripples of Spring's rescue.

"Don't do it again." Summer dropped down beside her. "If anything happens to you, Judith will kill Lils. Never mind what it'll do to Snow, Autumn, and me. Gee whiz—"

"You weren't going to lose me. Geez." *So why'd you do it?*

Spring reached for her towel, still apologizing to her lungs with large grabs of air. She looked past Snow and Autumn to her Tumblers. Greta stood with one arm around her waist, head down and fingers pressed to her lips. Gone was the laughing girl who led the camp cheer every morning.

"Tumblers, time to get ready for play practice, then ice cream floats." Autumn blew her whistle. "All Tumblers out. Let's go. Moonglow and Starlight, fall in with Sunglow and Twilight."

Ice cream floats usually elicited a cheer, but not this afternoon.

Spring stood to escort with her Tumblers, but Summer tugged her back down. When they were alone, she let loose. "Greta thought you were drowning. That she'd done something to you when y'all jumped together. Snow turned more pale than usual, which I didn't think was possible. She was back there with Blaine all over again. Dang it, Spring. Everyone says I'm selfish and unaware, but you're no better. What's going on with you? Do you know Mom asked me if you were okay? Tell me, are you?"

"Leave me alone." Spring wrapped her towel around her shoulders. Maybe it wasn't rational, but she somehow believed if she put words to her fears, they'd become true. "You're making a mountain out of a molehill. Plenty of people hold their breath underwater. We should go." She reached for her sandals. "Play practice was rough yesterday."

"Greta dove in to save you," Summer said. "She got your hair but couldn't hang on. She almost drowned herself trying to save your big butt."

Oh, Greta. "I'll talk to her."

"Talk to her? Apologize to her." Summer's expression softened, and Spring realized fear fueled her friend's temper. "Come on, it's me. What's going on?"

"I broke up with Mal." There, that should satisfy Summer for now. And she had called to break up when Lily took them to town on Saturday, but he wasn't home. She decided to write to him. Or call again later. Or perhaps disappear in the lake.

"What?" Summer made a face. "Girl, as your future maid of

honor, why didn't you tell me? I thought you loved him. You two are perfect for each other."

"Perfect? We're only eighteen." Spring's lungs had finally stopped burning. But she was shaking inside. "What do we know about life? About love? A mere five years ago you thought you were going to marry Bobby Sherman because the president of his fan club answered your letter."

"That's not the same and you know it."

"Can we just go? We have camp counselor stuff to do. Look, Mal and I have four years of college ahead of us. Who knows how we'll change? We need to be free to date other people. If I have a boyfriend, I won't be able to flirt with anyone in class or at a frat party."

"Are you telling me you won't mind if he flirts with girls at a party or in class?"

Spring raised her chin. "Nope. 'Cause he won't be my boy-friend."

"You are such a liar. Duval women don't cotton for second place." Summer started for the Lodge, then turned back. "You coming?"

"Yes, of course." *Wait, Summer, there's one more thing. I think I'm pregnant.*

8

I'm a Believer

Snow

'77

Midnight Thursday. Snow was exhausted, but the final set hadn't been painted for *You Can Do Anything*. Skip had built the stage with old pallets and plywood and wired the barn's crossbeam with a string of naked white bulbs. They weren't pretty, but they did the job.

The Seasons had gathered tonight after the campfire to paint the plywood backdrop. The first Camp Tumbleweed play opened tomorrow night. However, everyone was tired and punchy, complaining and goofing around so much Snow sent them packing. Man, they could be such pains in the—

A clatter outside the barn door caused her to look up. Holding her paintbrush like a weapon, Snow peered through the shadows.

"Hello?" She leaned forward as if to see through the closed

barn door. "Summer? Spring? Don't mess with me. I'm sick of your shenanigans."

Snow wouldn't put anything past Summer. Besides being mischievous to the core, she had a way of swaying the Seasons to do what she wanted. Even Autumn, who'd been ready to chop Summer's head off a few days ago, joined the goofing-around bandwagon. As far as Snow was concerned, Autumn had forgiven Summer for throwing her into the lake too easily. And for calling her the "oddball Season."

Still, the way Summer could bring them together and smooth things out and turn a fight into fun was a trait Snow loathed and admired.

Snow listened another second for a sound outside the barn, then returned to painting a backdrop of white clouds in a blue sky.

Lily called the play a new Camp Tumbleweed tradition, and Snow coined them the Camp Tumbleweed Players. She'd written a script. Designed a set that Skip built. For the life of her, she didn't think he'd heard a word of her description, but when she'd corralled the Players into their first rehearsal Tuesday after dinner, the barn was set up exactly as she'd described.

They rehearsed every afternoon for about a half hour. Summer wrote a couple of little ditties to the tune of "Anything You Can Do, I Can Do Better." A few of the lines were hilarious and made the girls crack up. The play ended with the camp song, followed by one Summer wrote.

Autumn was in charge of hair and makeup with a couple of Tumblers too shy to be on stage. Spring and her helpers took on costumes. With Lily, she raided the secondhand shop in town, Main Street Thrift, and came away with doctor, cowgirl, lawyer, artist, and housewife outfits.

The actresses ranged from eight to eleven, from shy to bold. Greta played the doctor, and Snow believed she had a future actress on her hands.

Their first play was tomorrow night, and tonight the Players succumbed to nerves. They forgot their lines and missed their marks. Two of them melted into tears, but the final product was pretty darn good. Even funny.

Tomorrow night, the curtain, which Moxie was still making, would go up at seven for locals and nearby parents. The production was small-time no doubt, but Snow considered this her first Snow Snowden production, and she didn't care one wit if it was in a barn in the middle of nowhere.

She'd dedicated the play to Blaine. *"To my big brother, Blaine, who told me to shoot for the stars."* If he could see her from wherever he'd landed in the afterlife, he'd be smiling.

Snow painted the last cloud, then stood back to admire her work. She was a better writer than artist. She'd run out of room with the final cloud, so it ended up *floating* through one of the treetops. But it would do.

She carried the paint pan and brush to the water spigot as another thump resounded beyond the walls. Dropping the brush and pan, she grabbed the broom they'd used to sweep out the stalls.

"Summer? This isn't funny." Snow gripped the chipped red handle like a samurai sword and tiptoed down the center aisle, ready to swing and then duck into one of the stalls. Unless a spider sat down beside her, then she'd scream like a banshee, intruder or not.

Tossed in the front corner was a pair of worn leather boots Summer found in the loft earlier that week. She braved putting them on and sauntered around the barn singing "Desperado" at the top of her lungs.

"Hey, desperado," Snow said. *"Come to your senses and help us set up our theater."* Just saying "our theater" made her warm-happy. She had a *theater*. One day she was going to be "in the pictures," as Paps used to say.

Summer had ignored her—so what else is new—and continued her song. Love her or hate her, she was her own girl. And her voice was magic.

Snow just about decided the thump was a tree branch falling against the barn when she heard a loud bang-clank. *Okay, that's it.* She grabbed her flashlight.

"Who's there? I've got a broom! I'm not afraid to use it." She hated feeling afraid, and the small glow from her flashlight gave her no courage.

She glanced behind her. Should she lock the side door? There was no way to bar the front. The rusted lock had crumbled in Skip's hands.

She startled at another bang-clank. "Seasons, come out wherever you are. You got me. I'm terrified. Ha ha, joke's on me."

The scent of a cigarette drifted past. Menthol. Like Paps used to smoke.

"Skip, is that you? Moxie? Show yourself 'cause if I have to come out there"—Bravado was almost as good as the real thing. Almost. No, not at all—"you'll get a walloping."

A tin can echoed as if being kicked down the road, and the scent of menthol faded. Snow dropped against the nearest stall, her trembling hand losing its grip on the broom. Now she had a different problem—walking back to Twilight alone.

What if whoever was behind the sounds and smoke waited outside?

Snow clicked off her flashlight. There was no one outside the barn. No one waiting to get her. She was just tired, and exhaustion caused her to imagine things.

The first week of camp had been . . . well . . . a blast. Laughter-fueled fun at a hundred miles an hour. However, after lights out, Snow worked on the play. Sleep was last on her to-do list. But next week should be easier. And the one after that.

At tonight's campfire, her Twilight Tumblers had challenged Autumn's Sunglows to a relay first thing in the morning. A cold swim to the rock and back. Not all the girls were strong swimmers, but they were competitors and had eagerly accepted the challenge. Snow needed to be alert and strong in case anyone needed help, so she'd best get some shut-eye. As it stood now, Autumn would be no good to a struggling swimmer. She'd not jumped in the lake all week.

Fall, what are you not telling us?

Snow washed out the paintbrush, then dumped the water out the side door. The camp was quiet. Serene.

With a final tidy-up and a glance around the barn, she flipped off the lights and snapped on her flashlight, then grabbed the broom and rehearsed her dark path to Twilight, the broom poised for striking.

With only the glow of her flashlight, the barn seemed extra dark, and Snow sensed a foreboding. Like the July morning Blaine died when she'd tried to talk him out of going to Wakulla Springs.

"Let's go to Alligator Point instead."

He argued that everyone, which really meant Summer, was going to the Springs. Their friends, his football teammates, Billy Crumpet, who Blaine adored for some dumb reason. He was a whole year younger.

She tried to convince Summer that Alligator Point was better, but she was all in for the Springs too.

"Everyone is going to be there." Which really meant Mitch Conroy, who Blaine loathed.

Snow hated the love-drama of being a teenager. Blaine said his friends thought she was a stone-cold fox. Emphasis on *stone* and *cold*, thank you very much. She had dreams to achieve. Boys were a distraction.

"Why not be nice to one of them? You might get asked out on a date."

"Why would I want to spend an evening with some random boy when I have you, dear brother?"

Nothing in the Snowden household had been the same after Blaine died. Mom wore black for a year, slept a lot, rarely cooked, signed Snow's report card without even checking her grades, watched *Leave It to Beaver* on TBS and endless reruns of *M*A*S*H* with a box of tissues in her lap.

Then one day, she snapped out of her grief, and life almost seemed normal.

The barn door rattled and creaked open. "Stop right there." Snow blinded the would-be assailant with the flashlight beam.

"Don't shoot." Autumn raised her hands, laughing.

"Jive turkey, you scared me." Snow lowered the light and set the broom against one of the stalls.

"Why's it so dark in here?" Autumn grabbed Snow's flashlight and walked over to the barn's light switch. In the bare bulbs' glow, she inspected the scenery. "I'm sorry we abandoned you, Snowy."

"It's okay. Say, did you see or hear anything out there?"

"Out where?"

"There." Snow pointed to the barn door and sniffed the air. There was no hint of cigarette smoke. Just the slight scent of manure on the passing breeze. "What time is it? Why are you up?"

"About one. Had to pee. Drank too much lemonade at the campfire." Autumn wore shorty pajamas and pink fuzzy slippers. Her freckled legs were a rosy hue from her first week in the sun. "Did I show you the pictures Jenna and Janna sent me? They found Dad's Polaroid and went nuts. There must have been ten shots of the dog." Jenna and Janna were Autumn's younger twin sisters.

"You did. Rover is so cute . . . even if his name is cliché," Snow said. "So, Autumn, did you see anyone or hear anything when you went to the latrine?"

"No, why?"

"I thought I heard something."

"Like what?"

"Noises. A thump. A kicked can. Smell of menthol."

"You think someone was out there?"

"I don't know." Snow reached for the broom and motioned for Autumn to click off the barn light. "We should go. Our Tumblers are competing in the morning."

"I'm sorry, you know, that we got caught with the soap and everything." Autumn sat on a nearby hay bale. "But I'm not sorry we got stuck here. I like this camp."

"Me too. It's dark and creepy at times, but I like helping the girls. Makes me feel like I'm giving back instead of taking for once. Blaine would be proud." Snow leaned against the barn wall, broom still in hand. "He'd have loved the pool party too."

Autumn laughed. "So we shouldn't feel too guilty."

"Guess not." In the peaceful lull, Snow considered telling Autumn her secret. She'd have to tell the Seasons sooner or later.

"Hey, Autumn—"

"Hey, Snow—"

"Jacks, you owe me a coke," Snow said. "What were you going to say?"

"What were you going to say?"

"Nothing."

"Me too. Nothing."

Okay, they were both lying, but they had the rest of the summer to tell the truth.

"We should get some shut-eye." Snow pulled Autumn from her straw perch.

At the barn door, lightning cut through a black sky, and the breeze was scented with rain. In the distance, thunder rumbled.

"This beats a cigarette smell." Snow breathed deep and the eeriness from before faded. The banging probably was the wind shoving a tree branch and an empty can against the barn.

"You know Oklahoma is Tornado Alley," Autumn said as another bolt of lightning lit up the campground. "We should run for it." With that, she took off, her pink feet flying, her arms pumping.

"Wait for me." Snow started after her but stopped cold as her flashlight beam landed on the large fresh footprint of a man's work boot.

Summer

'77

Week one of Camp Tumbleweed in the can. Summer loved the Tumblers, loved being a counselor.

The play last night was a hoot. Rough, unpolished, and filled with memorable gaffes, like Tumblers asking, "What's my line?" in the middle of the show. One of a kind. The cows and sheep mooed and bleated when they were supposed to be singing. One of the Tumblers noted with a loud declaration, "Cows and sheep *don't have lips.*" That got the small audience of twelve—eight towns-people and two sets of local parents—rolling with a good laugh.

The best faux pas was when the horse costume Mom found at the thrift shop fell apart, and the Tumblers playing the horse stayed in character as if nothing had happened. The horse got a standing O.

As the Seasons loaded up the laundry for their first trip to Tumble Time Laundromat—Mom dubiously handing Summer the truck keys—Snow prattled nonstop about next week's improvements.

Fine, fine, but hey, Seasons, it's Saturday! Their day off. Technically, they didn't have to return to camp until tomorrow at two. Never mind that Mom warned them a half dozen times, *"Do not go gallivanting all over eastern Oklahoma."*

Killjoy.

Mom had taken Greta to Skip's place to ride horses. *She* wasn't being punished for vandalizing public property, so *she* didn't have to do laundry. Mom charged Spring with Greta's washing and handed Autumn a canvas bag of coins.

"This is for laundry, not the candy or soda machine, or tips at the diner."

So, on their first free day since boarding the Greyhound, the

Four Seasons piled into the rattling blue camp pickup and headed to Tumble Time, a long and narrow establishment that was hotter than blazes, despite the large oscillating fans suspended from the four corners.

And, like he'd promised, the owner, Marv, reserved five washers and five dryers for Camp Tumbleweed.

Once the first round of laundry was loaded, Spring and Snow headed down Main Street to the fabric store. Summer sat on top of an empty washer and played music until the heat made her fingers fat and sticky.

"Let's go to the diner, Fall." She set her guitar in the case. "It's too hot in here."

Autumn looked up from where she penned postcards home. If she held any resentment toward Summer, it didn't show. But Autumn was cool that way. She got over things easy.

"I should stay with our stuff. I don't mind the heat. Besides, I want to finish these and drop them at the post office on our way out."

Summer flopped down in the chair next to Autumn and pulled her into a side squeeze. "You know we don't deserve you." And she meant it. "Especially Snow."

"Oh, I'm not the oddball now? The one who really shouldn't be a Season?"

"Okay, I'm sorry. I have a big mouth, and I say things before I think."

Autumn gave her a green-eyed look. "You know I could never stay mad at you. Even if you deserve it sometimes." She finished the postcard she was writing. "I love you, Summer. I really do."

"I love you too." Summer hesitated a second, then hopped up and headed for the door. "Want me to bring you anything?"

Autumn motioned to the cold orange soda she'd just bought from the machine. "I'm good for now. Let me know how the menu looks at O'Sullivan's."

"Will do." Out the door, Summer headed down the sidewalk,

squinting through the afternoon sun. Save for the breeze, it was hotter outside than inside.

Waiting on the curb for a car and a truck to pass, she noticed a boy leaning against an ancient, beat-up red truck, chewing on a straw, all cowboyed-up in a hat, jeans, and boots, watching a group of local girls walking down the sidewalk.

"What are you looking at?" Summer called as she dashed across the brick street.

Slowly, he turned her way with a smile that could melt the sun. "Seems I'm looking at you."

Hey, the same blue eyes as the boy mowing down three feet of rough prairie grass.

"It's you," she said.

"And I see it's you. Did you ever make it out of the truck?"

Well, that's embarrassing. "I'm here, aren't I?" She laughed, tossed her hair, and walked straight into the *Two Hours Only* parking sign.

Stumbling, she caught herself with one hand on the hood of a parked Pinto, and willed herself not to look back. If he was laughing, she didn't want to see it. She could be such a jive turkey.

In the cool air of the drugstore and diner, she rubbed the spot where her forehead met the metal sign and thanked the Lord she'd never see that hunk of a cowboy again.

She wasn't sure what she expected of O'Sullivan's, but it was something from another era with saddles and saddlebags on the wall, bullhorns, worn cowboy boots, spurs, and hats. A wagon-wheel chandelier. Red leather booths and red-checked Formica tables. And a wide plank floor scarred with bootheels and spurs of days gone by. This was an outright homage to the old Wild West, and she loved it.

She gave a quick glance inside the drugstore—which was pretty modern, considering the rest of Tumbleweed. The magazine rack at the cash register sported *People, Cosmopolitan, Newsweek,* and *Ebony* magazines, and rows of romance novels.

Back in the diner, a man in a white chef's hat, black shirt, and large apron polished the countertop while a classic country song twanged from the jukebox.

"What can I get you?" he said without looking up.

"Um, I don't know." Summer scanned the chalkboard menu suspended from the ceiling by two chains. "What's good?" She chose a stool at the middle of the counter.

"Everything." He tossed his towel over his shoulder and approached with order pad in hand. *Tank* was etched over his heart in white thread.

"I'll have the Number Five. Cheeseburger with fries and a chocolate shake." She should wait for the others, but she was starving. Entertaining everyone while doing laundry was hard work.

The man scribbled on an order pad and stuck it in the window. "Number Five, Elsie." Then he looked at Summer. "Ain't seen you in here before."

"I'm a counselor at Camp Tumbleweed. My mom, Lily, re-opened it this summer." Was that a pay phone in the corner? She could call Dad.

"Lily . . . great gal. We sure were excited when the camp re-opened. It was a staple around these parts for decades." He offered Summer a handshake. "Name's Tank. Will we be seeing you in here every Saturday?"

She shook his hand while giving him the once-over. He appeared to be Mom's age but definitely not her type. So she didn't come to Tumbleweed for him.

"Probably. O'Sullivan's is our reward for spending hours at Tumble Time. That place is an oven."

"I've been telling Marv to install an air conditioner. The man's a skinflint. Say, last I knew, Lily didn't have any counselors. How'd you land the job, other than being her daughter?"

Summer recounted the FSU pool party, to which Tank laughed heartily. "If that don't beat all. A proper-looking beauty pulling a prank like that."

"Me? I'm not proper beauty. Wait until you see my friends. And you should know, we were a complete failure. All that soap did was make everyone slick and sticky." Summer nodded toward the booth. "Does the phone work?"

"Since nineteen thirty-two. Hold the receiver to your ear, speak into the mouthpiece. If you want the operator, dial zero."

"Nineteen thirty-two?"

"Yessiree Bob. It was the *only* phone in town for almost thirty years."

Summer squeezed into the phone booth, which felt like a trip back in time. She dialed zero and asked the operator to make a collect call home.

As the phone rang, she rehearsed what to say. That she missed him. That Mom missed him. She could tell a little white lie, couldn't she?

We're having a good time. The Tumblers are really sweet.

Hey, Dad, is, um, everything good? . . . I mean . . . Mom being out here and all . . .

Do you really love me? As your daughter?

That question had nagged her for years, fading for long seasons, but never completely going away. She needed to grow up and put it to rest. But why did he call her "Lily's kid" at the first Fourth of July party?

After six, maybe seven, rings, she was about to hang up when Dad picked up.

"Hello?" The voice was feminine and unfamiliar. When the operator asked if she'd accept the charges, the woman said, "Charges? Who's calling?"

Summer slammed down the receiver. Darn operator punched in the wrong number. She called again, overpronouncing the digits. Dad answered on the first ring.

"Hello?"

"Dad, hey, it's me. The operator called the wrong number and some woman answered." In the background, Summer heard ice clink against a glass. And voices.

"Well, how's it going?" Dad sounded extra exuberant.

"Good. Better than—" More clinks in the background. A woman's laugh. "Who's there, Dad?"

"Some colleagues. We finished a big job this week, and I'm hosting a team cookout."

Without Mom? The hostess. The best in Tallahassee.

"First time I've used the pool all summer," he said.

A flirtatious voice asked, "Jeff, where's your utensils?"

"In there, Sandy, yeah. Oops . . ." Dad laughed. "Don't fall. There you go . . . okay."

"Who's Sandy?"

"You know her, Summie. She's my new secretary."

"What happened to Evie?"

"We promoted her to office manager. We hired Sandy a few months ago."

"Does Mom know?" Sandy sounded a bit too sexy for Summer's taste. She knew flirting when she heard it.

"Summie, what's this? Of course Mom knows. Tell me, how was the first week?"

"Are you having the Fourth of July party?"

"With everyone calling and writing to say they're coming, even Uncle Earl, I guess I have no choice. You know Uncle Earl isn't doing well. This could be his last time to see everyone."

Uncle Earl isn't doing well? "I won't get to see him. Neither will Mom."

"We'll go home at Christmas. Everyone says to tell you and Mom hi. Sandy, here, let me help." Dad's tone and chuckle sounded foreign. "Hey, kiddo, I should . . ." The doorbell chimed. "Sandy, honey, can you get the door?"

Honey? Mom was honey. Mom answered the door. Mom was the *hostess*. She was *honey*!

Summer listened to the muffled noises at home as Dad and *Saandeee* directed the guests who brought side dishes. Her attention landed on the initials *TH loves RH* carved into the booth's wall.

Who are you, TH? Do you still love RH?

Does JW still love LW?

"Okay, Summer, I'm back. So, camp is good?"

"You called Sandy *honey*."

"What?"

"You called Sandy *honey*."

"I did?" His low chuckle sounded guilty. "Force of habit. I'm so used to your mom being here."

"Dad, is everything okay? With you and Mom?" She didn't think she had the courage to ask but—

"Me and . . ." She could almost picture him staring out the window toward the patio and pool, smoke rising from the grill, someone setting up croquet in the yard. "Did she say something to you?"

"Mom? No, why?"

"Summie, this is your summer of fun. You're with your Seasons. Best summer of your lives, right? Don't ruin it with worry. Hey, Dave, you made it. . . . Great, give that to Sandy."

Sandy, Sandy, Sannndeeeee!

"Listen, sweetheart, I've got to go. I'll write, I promise."

"You said that before I left."

"Sorry, I've been busy." *With Sandy?* "I'll write this weekend."

"Do you want me to tell Mom anything?"

"Tell her I said hi." Just hi? That's it? What kind of loving husband gives his adoring wife the greeting of strangers? *"Hi."*

Tank tapped on the door as Summer hung up. A heaping plate of burger and fries waited for her, along with the rest of the Seasons.

"I called Dad," she said when she emerged, and they knew exactly what Summer needed. The four of them huddled in the group hug they'd perfected over the years.

"Everything okay?" Spring said.

"He says so. But he's having a party, and *Saaannddeee*, his new secretary, is acting as hostess. He called her *honey*. I hope she snorts like a pig when she laughs." Summer stared at her heaping plate of food. Ten minutes ago, she was starved. Now she was full of angst. "Autumn, who's watching our stuff?"

"Marv came by, let us lock our stuff in the office." She held up the key hanging around her neck. "He said to keep this for the summer."

"Are you sure you're all right, Summie?" Spring settled her hand over Summer's. "About your dad and *Saaannddeee*?"

"I guess so. He told me to have fun, and I can't do that if I'm worried."

"You know we're here for you." Spring glanced up at Tank. "I'll have the Number Four, please."

"Your parents love each other," Autumn said. "They're Jeff and Lily, the couple we all want to be someday. I'll have the Number Five, please." She peered at Tank. "The Number Two looks good, but there's no way I'm ordering a Number Two."

Tank's bellowing laugh cracked the ice forming around Summer. "First time I've ever heard that one, I tell you the truth, no lie."

On that note, Summer exhaled and bit into her burger, and the Seasons fell into their practiced pattern of chatter. Until the food arrived, and then it was nothing but hums and murmurs of "so good."

With her plate cleaned, Summer worked on the last drops of her chocolate shake.

"Your dad wouldn't cheat on your mom, Summer." Snow leaned in close. "He's a good guy. Like a hip Ward Cleaver. I wanted him to be *my* dad, remember? Even asked Mom if he could adopt me."

"Really? I don't remember." Summer tried to imagine Snow as her real sister and . . . Nope. She liked having Dad all to herself.

"I like Ward Cleaver," Autumn said.

"That's because your father *is* Ward Cleaver." Spring tossed her wadded-up napkin at Autumn. "Someone in Hollywood met Robert Childe and modeled a whole TV character after him."

Autumn tossed the napkin back. "Now you made me miss him."

She hopped off her stool and started for the phone booth. "What'd you do, Summer, call collect?"

Summer repeated Tank's instructions and considered how lucky she was to have three best friends who understood her, loved her, and above all, patiently endured her.

So what they weren't touring London or the Louvre or the old churches in Toledo, where chains hung on the wall in remembrance of the persecuted Christians? They were *together*. And in some small way, they were making one week of a little girl's summer full of memories.

Autumn emerged from the phone booth, smiling. "They all say hello."

Tank cleared away their dishes, and the girls settled up the bill. Snow needed to acquire one more thing from the fabric store, and Autumn handed the office key to Summer, then headed to the drugstore for nail polish and candy.

"All right, but hurry up, you two," Spring said. "We'll save some of the folding for you."

Crossing Main toward Tumble Time, Summer scanned Main Street for signs of the cowboy. But the red truck and the boy were gone.

Inside the laundromat, Summer unlocked the office, grabbed the change bag and a wire basket, and moved to her washer. "We need a Truth Night."

"Do we?" Spring pulled a basket to her machine. "I don't know. . . ."

"We never really debriefed after the pool party." Summer dumped a pile of damp linens in the basket and pushed it over to the first dryer.

"Why? It's pretty clear what happened."

"Is it?" Summer dropped two dimes into the slot. "We lost you for the better part of two hours." She had a lot of linens. Better drop in two more dimes.

"I told you what happened." Spring pushed her basket to a

dryer on the other end. Summer passed her the coin sack. "Let's finish the laundry, then go ride the carousel."

"Snow and Autumn don't know." Summer eyed her friend with suspicion. "And you're not the only one hiding something."

"I'm not hiding anything. Neither are the others. You're paranoid 'cause you think your *parents* are hiding something." Spring dropped four dimes into her machine and turned the knob. "I haven't been on a merry-go-round in forever."

Summer moved her basket to Snow's washer and began unloading. "I did see a cute cowboy outside of O'Sullivan's."

"Now you're talking." Spring laughed. "Tell me more."

9

What Becomes of the Brokenhearted?

Summer

'77

Someone shook Summer awake from a sweet dream. One where the blue-eyed cowboy was about to kiss her.

"Wake up." Mom's husky whisper was warm against Summer's ear.

"Why? I didn't hear the bell ring." She burrowed under her pillow. "It's still dark outside."

"Summer Elizabeth, get up now." She sat up. Mom never used her middle name. "Come with me."

"What's going on?" Summer fumbled for the shorts and T-shirt she'd dropped to the floor last night as she fell into bed. After laundry duty, they'd ridden the carousel, which was a blast, then inspected all of the shops and businesses in downtown Tumbleweed, and Summer picked up new batteries for her dried-out radio.

When they got back to camp, Snow convinced them to join her in the barn to paint a new set. They were up past midnight.

"Is there a tornado?" The bell was supposed to ring a million times if there was a tornado.

"Just follow me."

Slipping on her sneakers, Summer stepped out under the orange light of the sunrise and into a sheriff's deputy with a 12-gauge cradled in his arm. There was a deputy posted at Starlight, Twilight, and Sunglow.

"Mom? What—"

But she'd disappeared into the next cabin and exited with a groggy Autumn. She did the same with Spring in Starlight and Snow in Twilight.

"What's going on?" Autumn glanced between the deputies and Summer as she pulled her hair into a ponytail.

"I don't know, but I don't like it." Sheriff's deputies with shotguns. At a little girls' camp? Something was wrong.

"What in the world?" Spring looped her arm through Summer's. "Did Lily tell you—"

"No." Summer leaned toward the deputy guarding Moonglow. "What's happened?"

"She'll tell you." He jutted his chin toward Mom.

"I'm scared, y'all." Autumn snuggled between Summer and Spring, then waved to Snow as she exited Twilight, scanning the scene with her wide eyes. "Over here."

Week two Tumblers had arrived yesterday afternoon, rambunctious and ready to go. The Seasons, Mom, and Moxie had a time getting them organized.

They'd shouted and talked all through Mom's greeting. Ran and shouted, pushed and shoved, during the camp tour. Summer had hoped the swim test would calm them down, but the water only seemed to fuel their energy.

They used their roasting sticks as ballistae and launched burned marshmallows at one another. Forget teaching them the camp song. Mom, poor Mom, tried to be Camp Tumbleweed cheerleader and spell the girls toward good behavior. "Let's be G-O-O-D and L-I-S-T-E-N."

It was Greta who put the whole scene right. She zeroed in on the ringleader, Belinda, grabbed her by her hair, and dragged her into a dark stand of trees. When they returned a few minutes later, Belinda sat quietly on her log bench, and Greta pointed to Summer. "Sing the camp song."

But now in the predawn, Mom wasn't the frustrated camp director but . . . a terrified woman.

"My office. Now." She walked past the Seasons, breaking into a jog. Two sheriff cruisers were parked by the Lodge, and two deputies stood by the door with their hands resting on their holsters.

"What in the world?" Spring whispered.

Two more deputies with rifles guarded Mom's office. The Seasons hovered outside the door as yet another deputy talked with Mom.

"Are you sure?" Mom looked scared, pale and visibly shaking.

"Yes, but we *are* taking precautions."

From the kitchen, Moxie clanked and clattered about, getting breakfast started.

"Girls, come in." Mom motioned to the uniformed man in front of her. "This is Sergeant Cody Dover. He's . . . um . . . he's with the Osage County Sheriff's Department." Her voice faltered, and the hostess with the mostest collapsed into her desk chair. "I-I can't believe I'm about to say this, but—"

Spring grabbed Summer's hand. Autumn grabbed Snow's. *What, Mom, what?* "Th-this morning . . . at the Girl Scout camp, Camp Scott, in Locust Grove . . ." She put her fist to her mouth. "One of the counselors found . . ." Mom covered her face with her hands and sobbed.

"Counselors." Sergeant Dover took over in a deep, controlled tone. "They found the bodies of three girls. They were taken from their tent, raped, and murdered."

"What?" Autumn took Spring's hand, closing the gap between them. "When? How? Why? Three little girls?"

"Sometime in the night, and that's all the details you need. Why? We don't know, other than he's a sick, vile individual. The girls were eight, nine, and ten. Every law enforcement agency in the state is organizing for a manhunt. The Feds are in on it as well."

"Are you saying this *person* might come here?" Spring gripped Summer's hand so hard her bones cracked.

"We don't know. Right now, the hunt is localized to Locust Grove, outside of Tulsa, but our Osage County sheriff has ordered security at all summer camps, schools, and playgrounds. Not that parents will let their kids out to play, but we want to make sure people are safe."

"Where were their counselors?" Summer said.

"The girls slept alone in a tent on the edge of the camp."

"Oh my gosh . . ." Snow drew her hand from Autumn's and faced the high, wide windows overlooking the western edge of their little camp. The one that was starting to feel like home.

She had to be thinking of Blaine. Any tragedy, near or far, sent her right back to that sunny day at Wakulla Springs.

"W-what does that mean for us?" Summer turned to Mom, who wiped her cheeks with a tissue. "How far away is Locust Grove?"

"About eighty miles." The deputy moved to the framed map of the Sooner State hanging on the wall. "We think the initial search radius will be six miles around Camp Scott. But we want to make sure nothing happens here. We're setting up security around the clock. I've deputized some local men for just this sort of occasion. Hoped I'd never have to use them, but . . ."

Mom's grief gave way to a taut expression. "As of right now, we're on lockdown. No one comes or goes. As people wake up and hear the news, parents will be calling. Sergeant Dover and I will institute the camp security plan so the parents know their girls are safe. However, I've no doubt some will arrive this afternoon to take their babies home." She glanced at Summer, took a breath, and went on. "I called Josie to see what she wants to do. She's going to check with her lawyer, see if we should close. Until then—"

"Close? Mom, we just got here." Okay, that sounded a bit selfish, but she truly wanted the Tumblers to have a terrific summer. At least one week of it.

"What do we tell the Tumblers?" Autumn said.

"What about Greta?" Spring had already become somewhat of a big sister to her. "Her parents are still in Europe for six weeks. If we close—"

"Seasons." Mom held up her hands. "We'll tell the Tumblers nothing. They won't know the difference."

"They'll see the rent-a-cops," Summer said. "Greta will notice something different."

"Tell them someone spotted a bear. Or mountain lion."

"Mountain lion?" Summer again. "On the Oklahoma plains?"

"Tell them it's protocol, Summer. Just don't say three little girls exactly like them were murdered a mere . . ." Mom's voice pitched and faded. "A mere eighty miles away. It could've been us." She gathered herself and continued in a stronger voice. "No Tumbler goes anywhere alone. Not to the latrine, to the lake, to the kitchen for seconds. High noon or midnight, they are escorted everywhere."

"Last week, two of my Tumblers got up in the middle of the night and trekked off to the bathroom alone," Spring said.

"Tell them to wake you."

"Won't we have security on hand?" Summer said. "If they sneak off, the rent-a-fuzz can watch over them."

"I don't care. No Tumbler goes anywhere alone, and I mean it, Summer. Do not challenge me. Do not let the girls out of your sight." Fear and anger flashed in her blue eyes.

"I've talked to the mayor, and Tumbleweed will shut down pretty tight." This from the Sergeant. "The park and carousel will close as well as the school playground. While this particular perpetrator may be done for now, we don't know if he worked alone or with someone. We don't know if there'll be copycats. We are on high alert."

"I say we stay open." Summer's opinion didn't matter, but she wanted to voice it anyway. "Why should a perverted lunatic ruin the best summer of our lives?"

"Summer," Autumn said. "What is wrong with you? Three little girls were murdered. We can't go on swimming and shouting, having fun. It's callous. It could've as easily been us. It could've been Jenna or Janna. They're nine."

"But it wasn't, Autumn."

"Lily, if Josie wants to close," Autumn went on, cutting Summer a hard glance, "she should. We'll go home and pick up trash."

"Thank you, Autumn. We'll see how the parents respond. See what the lawyers say."

"Who cares?" Snow turned from the window. "Who cares what lawyers say? What do *we* say? Three children were *murdered*. Don't we owe it to them to shut down and mourn?"

"Or go on living and let that psycho know we're not afraid." Summer mourned Blaine every bit as much as Snow, but in the end, he wasn't her brother. She'd mourn for these girls and their families, but in the end, they were not her sisters. "What about the little girls who are still with us? Do they not get a fun week at camp because of a tragedy eighty miles away? They won't even know it happened unless someone tells them."

"Gah, Summer, you can be so, so cold." Snow bolted from the office. "I'm going to check on my Twilights."

"What'd I say? Spring, Mom, am I not right? Why punish our Tumblers because—"

"Summer," Spring said. "Give Snow a break. You know why she's acting that way. Lily, we'll watch out for the Tumblers. What else do we need to do?"

"Be alert. If you see anything suspicious, say something. I'm even concerned for you girls. This man went after little girls, but there's that madman killing girls your age out West. What's his name?"

"Bundy," Dover said. "Ted Bundy."

"Right, so we are on lockdown. Twenty-four-seven."

"What about laundry day?" Summer said.

"You go straight there and back."

"There will be security in town," Dover said. "But it's good not to talk to anyone you don't know, especially men."

"We don't know the rent-a-cops." Summer's sarcasm earned her the Mom-eye. *Well, they don't.*

"We trust Sergeant Dover's selection of men. Summer, ring the bell, get the morning started."

Sergeant Dover instructed the deputies by the fireplace to walk out with the Seasons, then check the camp perimeter.

"Remember," Mom said, "be as normal as—" The desk phone rang, and she answered with a quaver in her voice. "Mrs. Dalrymple, hello. Yes, we've heard. Horrible, *horrible* news. Beyond tragic. No, no, please, do not worry. We are all fine. I understand . . . if you want to get her, yes, of course. We have security in place. . . . Um-hmmm, right." Mom looked at the sergeant. "Armed deputies."

"Can y'all check my girls for me?" Autumn said as they exited the office. "I want to see if Lily will let me call home real quick."

"Autumn, Jenna and Janna are fine," Summer said. "So is Tabitha."

"I know, I know. I just want to hear their voices."

"I'll check on Sunglow for you," Spring said.

"Thanks. And, Summer, I'm sorry—"

"Hey, let's just say we're sorry now for whatever we do the rest of the summer, okay?"

Autumn smiled softly and took a seat at the nearest table. "Deal."

"Come on, Spring, let's get the day started."

In the shadow of the guards with guns, Summer rang the bell and started week two at Camp Tumbleweed.

Three clangs usually meant "Good, good morning!" But today, the clangs were for the three Camp Scott girls who would not see the sunrise.

Clang. Clang. Clang. Summer repeated the series three times, and as the last bell resounded in the warm air, she started for Moonglow.

Stepping over a low area where Thursday night's thunderstorm had left a small puddle, she paused when she saw a boot print in the drying mud. The sole was ridged like a work boot. Not smooth like Skip's cowboy boots.

She glanced at the deputies who worked the perimeter of the camp. It could be one of theirs, but this imprint had partially dried.

She chilled as she glanced back at the Lodge and the fear in Mom's voice sank through her.

"No one goes anywhere alone."

10

Hello Old Friend

Spring

JUNE '97
TALLAHASSEE

There were days, months, even years when Spring didn't think about the summer of '77 or her childhood friends formerly known as the Four Seasons.

Memories were useless. They made her melancholy and sentimental and wish for things long gone. For a practical lawyer like Spring Duval Smith, the past wasn't worth the emotional effort.

Then, last week, her old friend Autumn Childe emailed. Spring knew the contents of the link before she even opened it. The twentieth anniversary of the Camp Scott murders.

Spring,

Long time no write. I debated sending this link to you but since I'm typing this email, I guess I've decided. You've probably already seen the article. All these years later, it still feels like a part of our story. We told ourselves we'd remember those girls, and since you're the only Season I talk to these days, I thought I'd send this along. On the off chance, I wonder if you'd like to have lunch sometime?

Autumn

The invitation came as a surprise. Spring hit reply without pausing to consider all sides. She was sick of doing that. Thus the reason she was trying a new profession. For a few months, anyway.

Name the day and place.

The date was today, and the place was the Melting Pot.

Spring clicked the story link again. The headline said it all.

Still No Justice After 20 Years. Slain Girl Scouts' Parents Haunted by Murders.

She skimmed the familiar details of the June night in '77. How the accused, Gene Hart, was captured, tried, and acquitted, thus moving the Camp Scott murders into the dark pit of cold cases. The more time passed, the colder it became, and the families of Lori Farmer, Denise Milner, and Michelle Guse still had no justice.

With the wisdom of hindsight, Spring understood how the summer of '77 formed her life. The night at the Kappa Alpha house, being shipped off to Camp Tumbleweed, the murders, the baby, the fight at the dock, the truth, the failure of the grand plan.

Even why she chose the law as her passion. Why she said yes when Malcolm Smith III called one Saturday night twelve years ago to say, "I still love you." And why they'd just celebrated their tenth wedding anniversary.

"You're lost in thought." Mal entered the kitchen, dressed for work in a button-down Oxford and khakis, his cologne a subtle, clean cloud around him. His brown loafers skipped in a soft rhythm over the kitchen tile as he made his way to the coffee maker. "What's your day like, Ms. Lawyer-Turned-Writer?"

She smiled at him. "Writing a great novel. After all, that's why I took the sabbatical."

Or was it really to make sense of a long-ago season? Spring stared out the window toward the pool. She was lucky, blessed, to live in this beautiful house, with the neat, well-kept lawn and gardens and the grand pool filled with perfectly blue water. (Not concentrated car wash soap. She'd be so angry if someone dumped soap in her pool.)

And she shared it all with Mal—who loved this house. Who loved her.

They'd been married for about three years when he drove past the new community on the south side of Killearn Estates, the suburb where they'd both grown up.

"*Plenty of room for children,*" Mal had said. "*And with a pool, we'll be the hangout house.*"

Mal wanted to fill up the five bedrooms with children ASAP, but she'd put him off for the sake of her all-hallowed, all-important career. She wanted to be the youngest partner at Case and Turner. Which she achieved two years ago.

And really, if they'd started the family right away, he'd never have risked going into business with his brother, Dan, a tech genius. They'd attended a conference in 1989 and Mal came home raving about something called "the world wide web."

"*By the early 2000s, babe, every home will have a computer. This is a great opportunity to get in on the ground floor of something big.*"

Since she made more than enough to support them, the subject of children dropped until Mal and Dan got their business off the ground. In the meantime, Mal and Spring worked hard and lived well. Young and aspiring, with a gorgeous house and nice cars, they bought a place at St. George and went every weekend in the summer with friends, unless she had a pressing case.

In the winter, they skied Colorado and Vermont, or spent evenings at home in front of the fire. They hosted family barbecues. They'd vacationed in Europe, the Caribbean, and the South Pacific.

Then she took a pro bono case for a friend of Turner's—a man looking for his child. A man who never knew he'd been a teenage father, or that his son had been put up for adoption, and he wanted to find him.

Piece of cake, right? Just do her job, work the case. But in doing so, the dam holding back Spring's own secret and memories broke open.

She found the adoptive family and rejoiced with her client when they agreed to a meeting.

Case closed, she tried to move on, only to find she could not. A nagging little voice developed in the back of her mind.

Tell him.

How? If it was easy, she'd have told him a decade ago. But walking with her client through his pain made her realize all the more what she'd put her husband through and she just couldn't—

He'd hate her for keeping such a secret.

Then, one restless night, she'd sat at her old typewriter and started a fifty-two-thousand-word love story. It was so sweet the darn thing almost gave her a cavity. Yet so much of it was true, a picture of her life—*if* her story didn't involve lies and secrets.

"Spring?" Mal sat at the table. "Did you hear me?"

"Yes." *No, not a word.* "You're doing something today with Dan."

He made a face. "Good guess, counselor. I said I'm having lunch with the governor. Your dad finally finagled it."

"You could've told him no." Dad was eager to have Malcolm join him in the Duval family business—politics. He'd tried and failed to get Spring tangled up with the governor's legal team, so he'd turned to his son-in-law.

"It's just about the state technology advisory board. Plus, you never know, a connection with the governor's office might come in handy someday. As Dan keeps saying, 'Network, network, network.'" Mal took a big gulp of coffee. Hot or cold, he always drank in the same way. With gusto.

Which was also how he loved her, and she prayed to God that would never change.

"What about the deal you're working on for Smith Technologies?" she asked. Dan had recently connected with a guy he claimed would change how the world did business.

"Still chugging away. I tell you, this guy Jeff Bezos is a genius's genius. His company, Amazon, is revolutionary. We're meeting with him in Atlanta next week to talk about the code Dan is writing. Speaking of which, Dan wants to work on our golf game this afternoon in case Bezos plays. Don't hold dinner for me."

Spring scooted back from the table. "Do you want breakfast? Eggs and toast?"

Mal watched her over the rim of his cup. "Are you offering to make me breakfast?"

"I kind of like the role of Carol Brady." She retrieved the iron skillet from the stove drawer, but when she glanced at her husband, she saw passion vibrating in his eyes.

That man . . . goodness.

"Are you talking to me in code, Mrs. Smith?" Mal slipped his arm around her waist. "Are you *nesting*?"

"Nesting? Mal, who says *nesting*? Plus, I'm not a bird." She should watch her wording next time, as all good lawyers must. "I'm not pregnant. But these few months of being home, not rushing out to the office, have been nice. I can do all our shopping and errands while you're at work. Dinner is ready when you come home. I'm not preoccupied with a case." She turned to kiss him. "You know I love you."

"I do." He drew her close and kissed her until she was a bit breathless.

"Um, do you, still want breakfast?"

"I'd like to sweep you into my arms and carry you to the couch, but we have a call with Bezos at ten and I need to go over our notes. As soon as I'm done with that call, I'm off to lunch with the governor, then golf. Speaking of . . ." He trailed off. "I need my membership card to the club. Do you know where—"

"Nope. That's all you, babe. Where'd you put it last?"

"I don't know. It was with a pile of stuff I threw in a box when the bathroom pipes flooded."

Ugh, what a disaster. They'd meant to go through those boxes, throw away the items they'd been hanging on to for no reason, and organize the things they loved—pictures, mementos from college, movie tickets from their very first date when they saw *The Outlaw Josey Wales*.

Spring considered the frying pan for another second before returning it to the cabinet and retrieving Pop-Tarts from the pantry. Mal would take forever looking for his club card. Besides, Pop-Tarts were his favorite. She placed them in the toaster and pulled the butter from the fridge and a napkin from the holder.

She'd just finished buttering the pastries and wrapping them in the napkin when Mal returned, his briefcase in one hand, a photo in the other.

"This fell on the floor when I was going through the boxes." He handed her the picture. "I've never seen this baby before. Who is it?"

Spring tucked the picture into her robe pocket without looking at it. "She's, um, the daughter of a friend. Someone I knew in Oklahoma." She shouldn't even have such contraband. But Moxie had sent it. Said she couldn't help herself.

"Do I know this friend in Oklahoma?" He collected the napkin-wrapped Pop-Tarts and nodded at her pocket. "She's beautiful. Could've been a Gerber baby."

"Yep, a Gerber baby."

Mal slung his messenger bag over his shoulder and took a bite of both Pop-Tarts. "Thanks for breakfast, wife." He kissed her with his sweet, buttery lips.

"You're welcome, husband. But be careful. I don't want to hear how you stained the Porsche seats with butter." With a smile, she pushed him toward the door. "Go make us rich and famous."

"Rich, maybe, but the fame is up to you." Mal disappeared through the garage door, but after a second, he came back in. "Can we talk about kids sometime? Like tonight? That picture . . . I don't know, hit me here." He pumped his fist against his chest. "I want kids when I'm young enough to play ball without pulling a muscle or breaking my back." He stared at her for a long, hopeful moment.

"Yeah, me too." The picture felt like a brick in her thin pink pocket.

"So tonight? I'll bring home some steaks. We can grill out."

"Sounds . . . perfect." She waved him off. "Have a good day."

After he'd gone, Spring sat at the table, pulled the picture from her pocket, and stared at the face of a child who had her eyes and his nose.

Mom said she'd have to tell Mal one day, but Spring didn't see why. It was the past. The place she never visited.

11

You Can Go
Your Own Way

Autumn

'77

"Autumn, watch this." Her Sunglow girl Ellie balanced on one of the many inner tubes populating the lake. With a quick bounce, she launched into the water, sending the inner tube skimming over the surface.

Autumn tensed, her hands in fists until Ellie came back up. Okay, good. She smiled and gave her a thumbs-up.

She didn't want to be here by the water watching Tumblers, but the big sister in her refused to do anything less. But more? No. Though she'd managed to put on her Jantzen and pretend she was ready to dive in.

She touched the fading bruise on her arm from when Summer threw her in.

As a matter of routine, camp was the same this week as last week. Except there was an invisible yet tangible fear waiting to chain them because of something that happened eighty miles away.

Autumn couldn't shake Monday's news. She'd slept between fitful dreams, waking only to feel homesick, then crawl out of bed to check every Tumbler in her bunk.

During the day and into the evening campfire, she jumped at little sounds like a twig snapping or a squirrel scampering. The slam of a cabin's screen door had her in jitters. She hated it. She hated death.

Ellie and the other Tumblers jumped from the dock, from the inner tubes, laughing, splashing, screaming. It looked really fun, and a small part of her wished to join them, but Autumn would not—could not—go in.

What she really wanted was a nap this Thursday afternoon. She was exhausted from the lack of sleep, from the constant vigilance.

Then there was her *new* secret. She didn't mean to have this particular secret, but she'd overheard Lily talking to the sergeant as she waited outside her office to call home.

In between the calls from frantic parents, Lily began sharing her story with Sergeant Dover as if they were long-lost friends.

Autumn tried not to listen, told herself to get up, move, but she'd remained anchored in her chair.

So, on top of fear and guilt, she carried Lily's mind-blowing, world-crushing secret while having her own secrets to manage, thank you.

"Autumn, aren't you ever going to swim with us?" Mallory, her youngest Tumbler, floated by on a raft. "It's fun."

"I'm standing guard on the shore while Snow watches you in the water."

She envied Mallory's innocence. She had no idea what had

happened in the wee hours between Sunday night and Monday morning. Her fears were pint-sized and easily explained away. Hopefully she knew nothing of death, which was a thief, acting as its own judge and jury, answering to nothing and no one.

The parents of those three Girl Scouts had no idea when they dropped their daughters off for a fun week at camp that they'd never see them again.

Just like Blaine had no idea a beautiful day at Wakulla Springs with his friends would be his last. Autumn had watched his rescue from the shore, willing him to breathe.

She'd not been in the water since. About a year ago, she'd tried to talk to Mom about it in between herding the twins into the bath, changing the baby's diaper, and answering a call from her college dean.

"It's just grief, baby. It's hard to lose a close friend at your age. Here, make sure the twins dry off."

"Boo." Snow grabbed her from behind, laughing. "Didn't you see me waving to you when I got out of the water?"

"Sorry, lost in thought."

"You've been lost in thought all week. Talk to me, Fall." Water ran from Snow's bathing suit, down her lean legs. "The murders?"

Autumn glanced toward the cluster of thick trees. "If he snuck up on them, then he could sneak up on us."

"I know, but we're safe. We have around-the-clock armed guards."

Behind the cabins and through the trees sat the local, deputized men, talking around a low, smoldering fire, rising every thirty minutes to check the perimeter.

In the distance, the camp bell rang, calling the girls to snack time. Snow and Autumn whistled their Tumblers out of the water. Twelve girls, glowing and rosy, lined up. Autumn had been a stickler about order this week, about lining up, going together.

Walking with Snow and the girls to their cabins, she reminded them of the plans for the afternoon ahead. "Dry off and change for snack and play practice. Hang your bathing suits on the line to dry. They don't belong in a heap on the cabin floor."

"You heard her, Twilight Tumblers. Hang up your suits." Snow bumped Autumn's arm. "You're such a big sister."

"That's because I am a big sister. Heather, that's not what we do with our towel. On the line, sugar. Hang it on the line."

"Thanks for helping me jump off the dock." Sally, one of Snow's Tumblers, wrapped her in a big, wet hug. "Tish and I decided to be best friends, like you and Autumn."

"Good for you." The girl's big brown eyes consumed her small face, and her thick, unruly brown hair needed taming. But she'd found something more valuable. A friend. "That's what camp is all about," Snow said. "Now, get changed, and I'll see if Autumn will braid your hair."

Autumn peered at Snow as Sally scampered away. "Moments like these and I'm glad we poured soap into the pool."

"Almost makes me forget what happened at Camp Scott."

She was about to head into the cabin when Lily came toward them.

"Sally's parents are coming to get her. Her mother tried to let it go, but she said she's not slept a wink all week. She trusts us, but of course having her girl at home leaves no doubt."

"But it's Thursday. There's only two more nights," Snow said. "She just jumped off the dock for the first time. Never mind that she and Tish decided to be best friends. She'll be crushed."

"I tried to tell them she'd bonded with her cabinmates, but her parents were adamant. They're taking her to Six Flags Over Texas with some of her cousins as a consolation prize. Apparently that's what she wanted in the first place, but they insisted on camp."

"What reason will they give for picking her up early?" Autumn said.

"That they missed her too much and changed their minds about Six Flags."

There it was again. The kind of fear that led to lying.

Sunglow and Twilight Tumblers rushed from their cabins, swimsuits and towels in hand, and dutifully hung them on the line. Autumn went inside to change from her dry swimsuit into shorts, a T-shirt, and a pair of Converse. "Wait for me, girls."

The screen door banged behind her as Summer entered. "Mail call!" She passed a thick envelope to Autumn, then a dozen smaller ones.

"Looks like everyone in the family wrote to you."

Autumn reviewed the return addresses. Mom and Dad, Grandpa and Grandma, brother Devon and the twins, even Tabitha, who was three. Mom wrote a note on the back of Tabitha's letter.

Just sending this off and saw a letter from the Young Scientist Fellowship. You got it, A. You got the fellowship! The money is generous. Look and see. We're so proud. Mom.

Autumn crushed the letter to her chest.

"What is it?" Summer said.

"The Young Scientist Fellowship. I won."

"Fall, so cool." Summer slapped her a high five. "A full ride to FSU and now extra cash for mad money. Pays to have brains."

But she didn't want to go to grad school. She'd only applied for the fellowship because her parents insisted. It was supposed to be a long shot. A long, *long* shot.

Snow popped inside. "I'll take the girls to the Lodge."

"Thanks. I'll be just a minute." The big envelope was from Ridley. He'd written TOP SECRET on the side. She was anxious to open it.

"Can I ask you something, Autumn?" Summer leaned against the nearest bunk frame and opened a snack bag of chips.

"Why this says TOP SECRET?" She laughed. "Ridley being Ridley."

"Are you having fun?"

"That's a weird question." Autumn stacked the letters in her cubby. They'd be perfect bedtime reading. "Yeah, I am. Are you? D-did your dad write?"

Summer's smile was wide and white, perfect. "To my surprise, he did. Sent me some money too."

"So you're buying lunch on Saturday?" Autumn paused. "We are going, right? To do laundry? Even if we can't talk to a flipping soul?"

"Yes, we're going. Mom is scared and going overboard, if you ask me. We're not little girls, and the sergeant said there'd be security all over town." Summer munched on a couple of chips as she asked her next question. "Fall, are you not swimming because of Blaine?"

"What? No." But bull's-eye. How did she do that? "The lake water is bad for my hair."

Summer made a sound like a game show buzzer. "Try again."

"Snow watches them in the water. I watch them from the shore."

"What if something happens and Snow's too far away? Will you go in?"

The question alone was enough to drown her. She hoped that moment never came. "Of course I will."

Summer regarded her for a second, exuding confidence, as if nothing could ever rattle her. Though Autumn knew her parents' recent arguing bothered her.

"I keep checking the lock on our door at night." Summer tipped the bag up, dumping the crumbs into her mouth. "I jerk awake at the smallest sound and reach for my mini bat."

"Mini bat? The one we got at the Braves game?"

"Yeah, I tucked it in my suitcase. I'd like to hit that creep in the head with it."

"Me after you."

"Hey, we should go to a Braves game when we get home since we won't be in Europe. Create a few more Four Seasons memories."

"I'm not sorry we didn't go to Europe, Summer." Autumn grabbed her brush and a hair tie and motioned for Summer to sit on her bunk. "What a difference we're making here."

"As much as it pains me to say it, I think you're right."

"What if the best summer of our lives isn't about parties or shopping or backpacking through Europe but giving these girls a summer they'll never forget?" Autumn worked Summer's thick hair into a French braid.

"That's what we're doing, right?" Summer winced. "Easy there, Trigger."

"Do you think we'll still be best friends in four years?" *In four weeks?*

Summer twisted around to look up at her. "What kind of question is that, Fall?"

"Hey, you made me mess up. Face forward. I just wondered what you thought." She tied off the braid, then reached into her beauty case for a red ribbon. Summer was not a ribbon sort of girl, but what the heck. Give it a try.

"If you're asking me this question, we need a Truth Night." Summer frowned at the ribbon but didn't stop her. "After the Tumblers are in bed."

"You think we can? Lily said not to let them out of our sight." Autumn reached for two mirrors—yes, she had two—so Summer could approve the braid. "The ribbon is perfect."

"Yeah, it's okay." Summer wadded up the chip bag and banked it off the side of the cabin into the trash can. "Let's tell the others it's Truth Night. On the dock. Mom can alert the rent-a-dudes." She walked to the door. "You coming?"

"In a minute. I want to braid my hair too. Save me a seat?"

"Yeah, okay." Summer hesitated. "Autumn, I know I'm a pain sometimes, but you can trust me, honest. And yes, we'll be best friends in four years. In ten years. Forever."

"Salute. And Summer, you're not a pain."

She laughed. "Lie to me. I like it."

Alone again, Autumn tore open the TOP SECRET envelope from Ridley. A thick letter fell out, along with a ripped piece of notebook paper.

Thought you'd want to read this. Geez, A, do the folks know? Tell Summer hi for me. Rid

Poor Rid. When it came to Summer, he was solidly stuck in the little-brother zone.

But never mind him. . . . Autumn unfolded the pages.

Tallahassee School of Cosmetology
*   Dear Autumn,*
*   Welcome to the Class of 1977–78. We are excited to have you as part of the growing field of cosmetology. Classes begin . . .*

She'd been accepted. She'd feared her eleventh-hour submission was too late, but she'd told God, or fate, or whoever made cosmic decisions, that if beauty was her future, make a way.

The Young Scientist Fellowship was almost too on the nose. Of course, she excelled in science. Had a scientist for a mother. But cosmetology? That's where she came alive.

She was going to beauty school, and Truth Night was the perfect time to rid herself of one secret, making room for a new and much, *much* bigger one.

Which, if it ever got out, the Seasons would never survive.

12

One More for the Road

Snow

'77

Mom's letter was short and to the point. She had an idea.

> *Let's sell the Camaro, tune up Paps' old Mercedes, buy new tires, get the cute guy at Al's Garage to wash and wax it, then drive out to California together. The Mercedes is a much safer car than the Camaro. I'll sleep better knowing you're not broken down and stranded on a busy LA highway. We'll use the cash from the sale, plus I've been saving a lot. I'm desperate for a vacation. We can go to the Hollywood Walk of Fame, and I'll kiss Cary Grant's star. What do you think?*

What did she think? That it was really happening. She was going to leave Tallahassee, leave her best friends, her mom, everyone she'd known as family, for UCLA film school.

But sell her Camaro? She loved her car, a gift from *Anonymous* on her seventeenth birthday. Mom swore up and down she didn't know who'd left the dark blue car in their driveway with a bow on the windshield and a sign that said, *Happy birthday, Snow.*

Still, she liked the idea of driving Paps' Mercedes out west.

Also, I paid your first year's tuition, room and board. You're on your way, sweetie. Living the dream. I've saved up some spending money for you so you can get used to things in LA before looking for a job.

How's camp? I miss you. No one to share pizza night.

Love, Mom

Snow folded the letter. Leaving home meant leaving Blaine behind. Mom offered to give her some of his ashes in a little jar, but Snow feared it'd get knocked over or lost, and pieces of Blaine would end up in the wind or, worse, a vacuum cleaner bag.

Yet the Mercedes was quintessential Paps. He bought the car new in 1966, when his business was booming. Then his partner embezzled everything. In the end, all he had was the car, his house, and Grandma. She was the best part, he'd said. When she died of cancer, Paps moved in with Mom, Blaine, and Snow.

Snow tucked the letter into her pocket. Summer had called a Truth Night, so she might as well tell them. Not everything but something. *Mom's selling the Camaro.* That would be the first hurdle of telling them she was skipping out on their plan and going to UCLA.

Mom came alive when Snow's acceptance letter arrived. Almost as if she were the one going away to college. Then came the fees and tuition, living cost details. Gulp! How could she afford it? Snow left the letter on the dining room table for Mom and crawled into bed.

She'd resigned herself then and there to go to FSU with the rest of the Seasons. Big deal. They were her best friends. Still, she'd come *this* close to UCLA film school. . . .

After Mom read the letter, she barged into Snow's room. *"I'll take care of it. Get up, let's go out to eat, celebrate. I'm starved."*

Within the week, Mom had the money for Snow's first year. Where did she get it? Snow didn't ask.

It was on that high Snow let herself be talked into dumping gallons upon gallons of industrial car wash soap into a university pool.

Stretching out on her bunk, she listened to the lullaby of sleeping Tumblers while waiting for the appointed hour for Truth Night. She sat up when voices tangled outside her cabin. Summer? Lily? Snow tiptoed quietly out of Twilight.

"We're just going down to the dock, Mom. For Truth Night."

"You absolutely *cannot* leave your Tumblers. I promised Josie and *every* parent the counselors would *remain* in their cabins all night. *All night.*" Lily was down to her last straw.

"So we're prisoners?"

"Don't be ridiculous."

"If we can't leave, then we're prisoners. Mom, the cabins have locks."

"What if there's a fire? Hmmm, what then? Camp Tumbleweed is on *lockdown*, which means from nightfall to sunrise, then from sunrise to sunset, you're *on* the premises *with* your Tumblers. It's not hard to grasp, Summer."

"We lock it if we have to take a Tumbler to the latrine."

"That's different."

Snow locked Twilight's door with the key Skip had handed her Monday night. Each cabin must be locked at night and any time they were away. Lily's rules.

"I'm on lockdown because you're living in Fear Town. Mom, we can't live in fear."

"Summer, I will not debate you on this. If you can't live by my rules, then I'll call your probation officer and tell her to find you an orange vest."

Snow held back, beyond the edge of their voices. The night was pleasant and the stars were making a pale debut against the last of the daylight.

She was all for one, one for all, except when it came to a Wilde woman fight. She also thought Lily was right. The murders had just happened. Who's to say that a psychopath hadn't made his way to their camp?

"This is better than TV." Autumn's flashlight beam waved across the well-worn path.

"I should get my movie camera."

Autumn snickered and propped her arm on Snow's shoulder. They were the two peas next to each other in the Season pod. Autumn was the one she'd miss the most.

"We're going to be a hundred yards away at the dock," Summer pressed on. "Not Timbuktu. Seasons, help me out. They won't even know we're gone, and the rent-a-fuzz are right over there."

"What's this?" Spring came alongside Snow. "A Wilde fight?"

"Lily doesn't want us to go to the dock." Snow tapped the letter in her pocket, the urge to make her UCLA confession bubbling up. *Just say it!*

"Girls, go back inside," Lily said. "No Truth Night. Maybe Saturday, but when the Tumblers are here, you are on guard in your cabins."

"We're prisoners, Seasons," Summer said. "Chained by the fear of one man's actions."

"We don't know if it's one man," Snow said.

"Okay, then the actions of men. What if some Brownshirt Nazi walked in here and told us to give up Dani because she has dark skin? Do we cower in fear?"

Lily stepped closer to Summer. "If a Brownshirt comes in here demanding we surrender Dani or any other Tumbler, I'll shoot him where he stands. Unfortunately, a psychopath wanting to bludgeon little girls doesn't usually announce himself."

Lily raised her flashlight to Snow, Autumn, and Spring. "We're living on lockdown until this perpetrator is caught." She kept her voice low. "Sergeant Dover just told me the Camp Scott leaders dismissed a break-in where they found a note saying the girls in tent one would die. So, if you see or hear *anything* unusual, find any notes, or discover something missing or out of place, let me know immediately. Also, gently tell the Tumblers to let you know if they see any strangers or something unusual. But don't scare them."

"Wait, they ignored the note saying the girls would die?" Spring said.

"They thought it was a prank."

Snow flashed back to last Thursday night. To the boot print, to the cigarette smoke, to the clank of the tin can.

"I'm sorry it has to be this way, Seasons, but—"

"I saw a boot print." Snow heard herself after she said it. "Outside the barn. Thursday night."

"What?" Lily stood in front of her.

"There were sounds too, like a branch hitting the barn and a kicked tin can. And I smelled cigarette smoke."

"You're just now telling me?" Lily swung her light down the path toward the barn. "Let's go. Show me. Seasons, you stay put."

"Wait," Summer said. "Me too. I saw a boot print Monday morning after I rang the wake-up bell."

"I'm astounded." The strain in Lily's voice was deep. "We told y'all to keep watch, to be on your guard, and you leave out something as critical as boot prints. Here I thought y'all had grown up a little this summer. Spring, Autumn, keep watch. Summer, Snow, come with me."

The boot print Summer saw had faded, but it looked exactly like Snow's, which had faded even more. But the ridges were evident. Lily covered both prints with sticks, told Summer and Snow to return to their cabins, and went to call Sergeant Dover.

"You didn't say you saw a boot print," Summer muttered.

"Neither did you."

Back with Spring and Autumn, no one said anything.

"Anyone scared?" Autumn said.

"No, yes, maybe. Hard to tell," Summer said.

"Were they the same boot print?" Spring asked.

"Looked similar, like a work boot." Snow wanted to check her cabin door, make sure it was locked. "But the prints were drying up."

"Spring, you out there?" Greta's small voice crept from Starlight.

"Yeah, sugar. What do you need?" Spring aimed her flashlight at the screened window.

"Some of us have to pee."

"All right, come on, hurry." She unlocked the cabin door, and three Tumblers tumbled out of the cabin. "Hold hands."

"Why is our door locked, Spring?"

"Um, well, to keep, um—" Spring forced a laugh. "Old habit, I guess. I always lock the door at home."

Good answer, Spring. Snow was impressed.

"Autumn?" Ellie called from Sunglow. "We have to go too."

So a latrine hike was on. Spring and Autumn led the line while Summer and Snow stood guard, and a rent-a-fuzz made his way over from the fire.

"Everything okay here?" Shazam. It was the blue-eyed boy who was mowing with Skip, the chainsaw hacker, when they arrived. Maybe Snow imagined it, but it seemed to her his attention was glued to Summer.

"Some of the Tumblers went to the bathroom." Summer pointed to the six-shooter in his holster. "They didn't tell us boys were allowed to carry guns."

Good grief. She was flirting. *Run, cowboy, run.*

"I'm eighteen. All legal. Didn't I see you in town Saturday? Running into a parking sign?"

Snow aimed her flashlight at Summer. "You ran into a parking sign?"

"It was his fault."

"Oh sure, you were probably flipping your hair and flirting."

"Yep, she sure was," he said.

Okay, Snow liked this guy. "I'm Snow, and you are?"

"Levi Foley. Skip's nephew and part-time deputy." He turned to Summer. "I never got your name."

"Summer. Summer Wilde."

"Snow? Summer?" He glanced between them.

"Before you ask, the other two are Autumn and Spring. Yes, we were named after seasons. That's how we became friends. So, what do you do?" Snow said.

"Work the ranch with my dad. Going to OU in the fall." He answered Snow's question, but his attention remained on Summer.

"We're all going to Florida State," Summer said.

Levi frowned. "Oh, I'm sorry. If you want to go to a good university—"

Summer popped him on the arm with her flashlight. Levi tried to grab the flashlight but got her hand, and in an instant, Snow was in her living room with a bowl of popcorn in her lap watching *Donny & Marie* by herself while her supposed best friend flirted with her brother in the kitchen.

"Hey, leave her alone, Blaine. She came to watch TV with me."

"Take a chill pill, Snow. We're just goofing around."

Levi and Summer had moved to the steps of Moonglow while Snow remained a stump in the middle of the path. After a moment, she said, "I'm going to bed. Careful, Levi, there are a lot of boys back home trapped in Summer's solstice, looking for a way out."

"That's not true."

"I have no doubt it is," he said.

Stretched out on her bed, Snow pulled Mom's letter from her pocket and tucked it under her pillow. Eyes closed, she tried to drift off, but the sound of Summer and Levi's flirting carried on the breeze.

A coal ignited deep, deep down and Snow's anger simmered. If she could tell Summer what she thought of her before she left for California, it'd be one of the greatest days on earth.

More laughter. More flirting. Thank goodness camp ended in six weeks and Levi would be free from her spell. Blaine never had the luxury.

Because Summer Wilde killed him.

13

Just the Way You Are

Summer

'97

Perched on a stool center stage under a solo spotlight at the Broken Barrel, Summer Wilde sang songs that could make the most hardened trucker cry in his beer. Songs from the bottom of her own broken barrel. Songs about love and loss, about longing for the old days, about returning home when all the roads were closed. About regret.

The crowd applauded softly as she finished her song. It was after midnight, long past the time for her to end the set, but she kept playing. The music was healing.

"I want to thank you all for coming out." She set the capo on the second fret. "I know the sign says Sparrows Fly, but gosh darn if three of my sparrows didn't fly the coop." That got a small laugh. "So it's just me." She strummed the opening of her last song, tuned the E string, then picked the melody to "The Preacher." The audience applauded.

"I love Tracey Blue," someone shouted.

"Hark, a voice from the dark." Summer squinted between the lights toward the sound of the voice. "I wrote this song eighteen years ago, trying to figure out a few things. I never thought anyone would hear it, but my manager asked me to lay down some tracks. Two years later, Tracey cut it, and you know the rest of the story."

Summer played through the chorus again. The words and melody were so much a part of her that no matter where she was, how high or how low her road, she always had "The Preacher."

> Where was the Preacher when we needed Him?
> Where was the bulwark, the strong tower to run in?
> Couldn't He see, couldn't He be, where and when we
>   needed Him?
> The summer of '77 was supposed to be
> The best summer of our lives for my friends and me.

Singing with her eyes closed, she wasn't bothered by the tear that settled on her lashes. Last song. Last show. Let the tears flow.

When she sang the chorus again and opened her eyes, Levi Foley sat at table one between the stage lights and the bar shadows.

"What are you looking at?"

"Seems I'm looking at you."

He was nothing like the eighteen-year-old she'd crushed on way back when. Even in the dim bar light, she could see he was taller and broader, muscled, and wearing a light scruff on his cheeks.

What was he doing here? Her heart thumped a bit too hard for someone like her, and her nervous fingers slipped off the strings. Darn that Tank. She'd told him *not* to tell. Not!

She gave him a half smile, and the tears brimming in her eyes spilled over. She pressed her cheek to her sleeve and finished the song.

"Thank you again, everyone, I'm Summer Wilde, and—"

The bar bell rang. "Got a request, Summer." Bryson waved a bill, then dropped it in the tip jar. "This gentleman wants to hear 'If You Can't Go Country, Just Go On Home.'" He pointed to Levi.

"'If You Can't Go Country' . . . wow." Why did he want to hear that song? Summer fished for the opening chords and lyrics. "I didn't think anyone beside my goldfish ever heard that tune."

"If You Can't Go Country" was to be her first big break. The studio released a single in the fall of '85 and had her in the studio fast-tracking an album. But the song didn't even hit the country Top 100, and the label escorted her from the studio two months later.

"If You Can't" was the soundtrack of her first failure. But the melody was fun, fast, and chompy, and Summer sat a little taller as she sang.

"Now listen here, what I'm telling you, there's only one way to go, only one way to be, and that's country." She held out country with a pronounced twang.

Bryson rang the bell as she finished, waving a bill and shouting out another request. Levi tipped his hat.

Then again, and again, and again.

At two in the morning, Summer played his last request. The three bleary-eyed drunks at the far table stamped their empty mugs on the table.

"Them happy songs was a might better than them 'I wanna kill myself' songs."

Good point. Good point. She felt a little brighter herself. "Thanks for hanging out with me. Good night." Summer walked her guitar backstage with a glance toward table one. Levi had gone.

Bryson cut the stage lights and shooed the stragglers out the front door. "You got way more show than I paid her for, so go on. Git."

Collapsing in the battered chair outside the ladies' room, also known as the green room, Summer downed a tall bottle of water.

"Hope you don't mind cash." Bryson handed her a thick envelope. "The tips were abysmal until that one cowboy started making requests."

"He made me sing for my money." Summer peered inside. Bills, lots of one-hundred-dollar bills. "Bryson, what is this?"

"The five hundred from the Barrel and five hundred from the dude calling the songs."

"I can't take this." She headed to the front of house. "Is he still here?"

"He left when you were talking to the drunks. How do you know him?"

"I don't really. We met twenty years ago, exchanged a few letters that faded to the occasional Christmas card." Summer held up the envelope. "I can't take his money."

"Why not? You earned it."

"Fifty dollars a song?"

"That is rich money for these parts. Most acts get a hundred-buck tip for the whole night. He must have money."

"Maybe. His dad owns a ranch."

"What's his name?"

"Levi Foley."

"Of Foley Ranch? Over by Tumbleweed? Darling, everyone in these parts knows the Foleys. They own six hundred acres of prime Oklahoma ranching land."

She had no idea. "Still, I can't take his money." Pity money.

"Now I have to drive to Tumbleweed to give it back. Wait until I see Tank."

"Summer, you earned it fair and square." Bryson took the envelope from her and stuffed it into her backpack. "Would you accept it if you didn't know this dude?"

"No. Well, I don't know. If I could find him, I might return it."

Bryson chuckled. "Girl, are you in love with Foley? 'Cause it sure seems to me you're putting up a useless fight. Now, go on, I want to close up." He exited through the kitchen door, singing, "If you can't go country . . ."

"I'm not in love with Foley," Summer called after him. "Bryson, you hear me?"

In love with Levi? She barely knew the guy. Which was why she had to return his money. Seriously, who walked into the Broken Barrel with that much cash?

Out the side door, she locked her things in the truck cab, then ran around front, hoping to find him. The parking lot was empty, except for the blueish-green hue of the Broken Barrel's neon lights. "Levi?" She walked toward Route 66. "Levi Foley!"

Dang it, she did not want to backtrack to Tumbleweed, but it looked like she had no choice. She'd just returned to her truck when she heard, "I loved the show."

He was tall like she'd imagined, thick and well-built and sporting a smile that still rivaled the sun.

"Why'd you pay five hundred dollars to hear a bunch of old songs?" She jerked open the passenger-side door and pulled the envelope from her backpack. "I can't take this, Levi."

"Then give it away 'cause I'm not taking it back."

"It's too much."

"Who says? I made a request, you sang the song, I tipped what I felt it was worth. Seems to me that's how business works."

"But fifty dollars a song?"

"I'd pay more than five hundred dollars if I went to your concerts."

She laughed. "State fair admission is only ten bucks. You'd have to attend fifty fairs."

"I've attended one to two fairs a year most of my life, so—" He stepped closer. "I loved watching you up there. It was worth every penny to hear you sing. Finally."

Her eyes blurred. "Th-thank you."

He leaned against Clark's blue Ford and hooked his thumbs in his pockets. He wore a tight, torso-fitting T-shirt, jeans, boots, and his ever-present hat. "I looked for you at the '80 Orange Bowl when FSU played OU for the National Championship."

"I left school in '78 after Ted Bundy murdered my sorority sisters. It was Camp Scott all over again. I'd just been initiated, but I couldn't stick around." Especially without the Seasons. "I'd almost picked one of them to be my big sister."

"Wow, Summer, I didn't know," he said. "I'm sorry."

"Wasn't your fault." She almost didn't rush a sorority, but her cousin convinced her to go through and pledge Chi Omega with her.

"I wrote you before the game," he said. "Told you I had end-zone tickets, but the letter was returned. I still looked for you."

"I'd already gone to Nashville. My parents sold the Tallahassee house."

"Is Music City good to you?"

"Not really, but I'm heading back there."

"What if I came along?"

"To Nashville? Why?"

"Hang out with you."

"I hear you're running your daddy's ranch. And what happened to your girlfriend? Weren't you almost engaged?" She did remember some things from their letters and Christmas cards.

"We broke up when I discovered California wasn't for me. I missed being outdoors, missed the meadows, missed the bulls and cows. Missed my family. Dad wanted to retire and open an insurance agency. My brother had his father-in-law's ranch, so Dad asked me to take the Circle F. I couldn't say yes fast enough. I have everything I want except . . ." He moved closer, and she inhaled the prairie, the wind and rain, the clean scent of his skin. "A wife."

Summer laughed. "I hope you're not saying that in my direction."

"What if I am?"

"Levi." What was he doing talking like this? "You don't know me. You remember the fun, innocent, semi-wild girl from '77." She pulled away from him. "But that girl is long, *long* gone. I've spent eighteen years on the road trying to build a career. I've broken up bands and relationships. I've broken men's hearts. Broken my own stinking heart. I've had more lovers than I care to remember." Talking against the early morning darkness gave her a bold honesty. "You deserve better. Look, I'm not trying to throw a pity party. I'm not some sad sack who can't get her chin off her chest. But Levi . . . you and me? No. You deserve a woman who—"

"Loves me back. That's all I want. I'm not innocent or naïve." If she moved, he moved. He was so close she could feel the heat of his skin. "I get what life might have been like on the road."

"I'm not sure you do." She brushed her hand over his thick chest and battled a wild desire to kiss him. He was Levi Foley . . . the cowboy who'd captured her with a glance.

"Summer, forget your past, my past. We're here right now and I can't let you go."

"Levi," she whispered. "It's been twenty years. You couldn't have pined for me all this time. I write country songs. I don't live them."

"Can I have your number?" He pulled a cocktail napkin from his pocket. "I don't have a pen, but—"

"You can't have my number."

"Your email, then?"

"Summer at AOL dot com. But, Levi—"

"Here's my number and email." He handed her a second napkin. "And my home address." When she didn't take it, he stuffed it into her pocket. "Call me anytime."

He was messing with her. Making her feel things. "I won't. I need you to know that, Levi."

"Then can I please have your number?" He held up the blank napkin.

"I don't have a pen either."

"Just tell me. I'll remember. I was a CPA in my previous life. Numbers are my thing."

Summer fired off her number while he was still talking. But he repeated it back perfectly.

"You're going to be exhausted tomorrow," she said. "Don't you get up at five?"

"I have cowboys to help."

"You said your brother had his father-in-law's ranch?"

"He does. Caleb just turned forty and has four daughters who are excellent cowgirls. The oldest is a junior in high school and a kick-butt basketball player. Colleges are looking at her."

"And your parents?"

"You saw Dad in town, hawking insurance. Mom still cooks and paints, plants gardens, dotes on her granddaughters. I told her you were at O'Sullivan's. Know what she said?"

"'Summer Wilde? Who's she? Son, what about that nice girl you were engaged to in LA?'"

"She said, 'Well, are you just going to sit there staring at your dessert, or are you going to find her and marry her?'"

"Don't." Summer stepped away. "You're mocking me."

"Do I look like I'm mocking?"

"You can't want to—" She sighed and checked her words. "I'm not the marrying kind." *Please don't offer me what my heart wants, because in the end, you'll have to take it all back.* "Your mother doesn't know me. If she did, she'd tell you to hightail it the other way."

"It's not her business. All she sees is a girl her son can love and can love him back." Was he born with all this confidence?

"Levi, I'm telling you, you can do way, *way* better than me. It's late and dark, so I'll just say it. I'm a broken mess." She could only see half of his expression under the shadow of his hat, but by his silence, she guessed he was weighing his options. And it was time to go.

"Thanks for coming tonight. It was fun to play the old songs." She offered him her hand, then, for old times' sake, said, "Just know, I'm kissing you in my mind right now with everything I've got."

Levi tipped back his head and laughed. "Um, I do believe that's my line, Ms. Wilde."

"Maybe . . ." In so many ways she wanted to fall into his arms and drop every burden on his shoulders. Yet she remained steadfast. "I've never forgotten it. It's the hook to an unfinished song, lost in a box in my friend's garage."

"I've never forgotten you. Not in the least." He flipped off his hat, hooked his finger in her belt loop, and roped her in his arms and kissed her. Kissed her as if he'd done it a thousand times. As if his full, warm mouth knew how to find hers.

Summer resisted for half a second before giving in to the tenderness of the moment, surprised how the feel of him awakened her dull, used-and-abused passions.

When he shifted his position and held her closer, she was eighteen again, standing by Skiatook Lake, scared to love him, scared not to love him. How could she fall in love over a short summer when she had her whole life ahead of her?

Too soon he broke away and smiled. "Summer, I—"

She pressed her finger to his lips, unwilling to add his name to her graveyard of one-night stands and short-term lovers. For once, just once, she'd like to put someone else ahead of herself.

Even so, she kissed him one last time. She only meant for a taste, but he gripped her waist and kissed her until she held on to his shirt to stay upright.

"Would you stay if I asked you?" His husky voice had her attention.

"Is that a proposal?"

He laughed softly and traced her jaw down her neck to the top of her blouse. "Not yet, but it's an invitation to find out. Will you stay in Tumbleweed?"

"And do what?" But oh, she was tempted. What kind of life could they have? Could she wipe her past clean? "I have a career in Nashville, Levi." A career she could not make work, but . . . "Sparrows Fly just broke up, and I need to figure out my next move."

"Will you do me a favor?" His question was low and almost shy. "Factor me in?"

"Levi, do us *both* a favor and stop this craziness. I can't believe you have any intentions whatsoever about me after all these years. It's nuts. Loony."

"I fell in love with you the first time I saw you."

"That day in Tumbleweed? When I ran into the parking sign?"

"No, when you were stretched over the side of the camp truck, yelling for the Seasons to, 'Forget about me. *Saavvve* yourselves.'"

She burst out laughing. "Oh my gosh . . . 'The Texas Chainsaw Massacre Slept Here.' I thought I was *so* clever, freaking Snow out, until your uncle came around the cabin with a running chainsaw in his hand."

They laughed together until Summer felt something break off of her. "How is your Uncle Skip?"

"Still going strong. He got married for the first time at fifty-five. She was a widow with grandchildren, and he took right to the papaw life."

"Good for him."

"But what about me, Summer? Will you give me a chance? I know it's been a lot of years, and I'm not the kind of guy who hangs on to the past or how I imagined life would turn out, but all my years in college, then grad school, and in my time in Southern Cal, I never forgot you. I tried. I met some amazing women. Smart, fun, beautiful. I wanted to marry one of them, but when I got down to it, Summer, she wasn't you."

"I'm so broken, Levi," she whispered, tears coming to the surface. "I need you to see that, please. I can't be the woman you want."

"Do you think I have some pie-in-the-sky idea of you, of marriage? Because I don't."

"Do you know I've barely talked to the Seasons in the last twenty years? I missed Spring's wedding. I wasn't even invited to Snow's. After my parents' divorce, I went on the road and worked hard to never go home. I've missed holidays and birthdays. I've mended things with Mom, but Dad and I . . . He remarried, which complicates things more than you can imagine. I was so driven for success with some wild desire to prove myself that my bandmates hated me. I'm harsh and mean. Impatient." The tears began to overflow. The cover of night *was* a powerful confessor. "I wanted *him* to be proud of me."

"Your dad?"

"Forget it." She wiped her tears with her hands. "You should get home."

"I don't care if you're broken." He reached for her again, kissing her easy and slow. "I like broken things. Besides, we *are* standing beside the Broken Barrel." He rested his forehead against hers. "Think about it, please, before you close and lock this door. I just want a chance."

He kissed her once more, set his hat back on his head, and said good-night. She watched him until his truck's red taillights folded into the bend in the road.

"Think about it, please . . ."

It was laughable. A life with Levi? He'd have to build a storage unit for all her proverbial baggage. He had no idea. . . .

Yet she wanted it. What he offered. Love, marriage, the white picket fence, the kiddos.

But that wasn't her life, was it? As she backed away from the Broken Barrel's lonely shadows, her cellular phone rang from the pocket of her backpack. Summer fumbled to flip it open, and before she even said hello, Levi's voice came through loud and clear.

"See, I told you I'd remember."

14

Bridge over Troubled Waters

Spring

'77

"I'm going to the diner, y'all. Want to call home." Spring folded up the style section of the five-day-old *Tulsa World* to hide where she'd torn out the bottom corner. An ad offered her a solution to her little problem. "Anyone want the front page?" She tucked the ripped newsprint into her pocket and glanced again at the bold headline.

Three Tulsa-Area Girl Scouts Slain; Child Molester Sought.

The murders investigation continued, and she was homesick for the sound of her parents' voices. She planned to call them today, hoping a touch of home would make her feel better. Take her mind off how she'd woken up every day this week before the bell and bolted out of Starlight to find a place to puke.

Then, to her surprise, she slept in this morning, waking up with her usual Spring Duval energy. Ta-da. She was back.

Until she hit the breakfast line, then it was a fake smile and a dash to the latrine. When she returned to the Lodge, Moxie watched her with dark, questioning eyes.

Move on, nothing to see here.

Autumn looked up from her book and pointed to the newspaper. "What'd the article say?"

"Still looking for the guy who did it. Parents aren't even letting their kids camp out in the backyard." Spring made her way down the narrow laundromat aisle. Summer sat on the last washing machine, strumming her guitar. "Two of the three search-and-rescue dogs died."

The music stopped. "Dogs have died?"

"One of them got hit by a car, and the other died of heat exhaustion." Now Spring was homesick for their dog, Spike. "The play was good last night, Snow. The week two Tumblers really gave it their all."

Snow sat in the corner on the opposite side, scribbling in her notebook. "I'm learning so much." She had the brightest smile. "Greta gave me a list of ideas this morning."

"She'll be directing all of us before the end of summer," Spring said.

The Tumblers played to an audience of five: Lily, Moxie, and Skip sitting on hay bales, and two rental deputies leaning against the open barn door. Lily had closed the camp to the public.

This morning, they all said a tearful good-bye to their new favorite Tumblers, loaded up the laundry, and headed to town.

Meanwhile, Lily drove Greta to her grandparents in Oklahoma City. After the news of the murders hit, they wanted to hug their girl.

Before leaving, she gave the Seasons a stern and serious reminder of the lockdown. *"Be careful. Don't go anywhere alone."*

Then she suggested Moxie do all the laundry so the Seasons

could stay in camp. Idea, meet lead balloon. Moxie's expression still made Spring laugh.

Sergeant Dover assured Lily that town was safer than camp with Tumbleweed PD walking the street—all five of them—so she relented. In fact, two officers walked past Tumble Time right now.

"Okay, y'all, I got a song. Listen." Summer started the melody of "You Get a Line, I'll Get a Pole." The guitar's rhythm kept time with the hum of the machine.

"*Wellllll*, you get the soap, I'll get the washer, honey. You get the soap, I'll get the washer, babe. You get the soap, and I'll get the washer, we'll go washing at the Tumble Time laundry, honey, oh *babe*, be mine." She ended with a grand strum, then laughed. "Who would marry a man who took her to the laundromat for a good time?"

"You never know where love will take you," Snow said, still bent over her notebook.

Spring whispered a soft "Salute" to herself. Love had taken her to a strange place.

Her plan to break it off with Mal weakened by the day. She should call him, but she couldn't bring herself to say the words. She knew, *just knew*, the moment she said it, her monthly friend would pay a visit.

And she couldn't break up with him in a letter. Never mind he wasn't even home. He'd gone to the Outer Banks with his family.

"I thought you were going to make a call." Summer slid off the washer and aimed for the soda machine. "Autumn, Snow, you want a coke?"

"I am . . . going to make a call," Spring said, then ran smack-dab into Summer's cowboy, who strolled into the laundromat like Clint Eastwood in *Josey Wales*, hat low on his brow and a piece of straw jutting from his lips. Sweet magnolia, he was a hunk and a half.

"I came to see if y'all were okay." He had his deputy badge pinned to his chest.

Summer stood by the soda machine, looking like a goof, cradling three soda cans, her eyes fixed on Levi.

Levi's smile could jump-start a girl's heart. Any girl, ages one to ninety-two. From her corner, Snow watched with an unblinking stare.

"We're good, Levi," Spring said. "Summer, Autumn, Snow, are we good?"

"Yes."

"Of course."

"I was wondering if Summer would like to go mudding. Got my truck outside and—"

"I'd love to go mudding." Summer passed out the sodas, then huddled up with Levi. "I'll see y'all back at the camp. Spring, the truck keys are in my guitar case. Oh, bring my guitar back, will you?"

"Wait a doggone second." Spring stepped in front of Summer. "We're on laundry duty."

"And lockdown," Autumn said. "You can't go off with him. Lily's rules. Spring, you really shouldn't go to the diner alone either. And we have to be back at camp by four."

Her recall of Lily's speech was uncanny.

"I'm not with just anybody, Fall. I'll be with Deputy Foley." Summer patted his chest, which he seemed to enjoy. "What could be safer?" She shoved around Spring and backed toward the door with Levi.

"We're not doing your laundry, Summer." Snow blocked her exit this time. "Your new Tumblers will wonder why they got the cabin with no sheets, and why their counselor wears the same smelly, tattered cutoffs and the same *Have a Coke and a smile* T-shirt. If you walk out that door, that'll be all you own by tonight."

Summer scoffed. "You're going to destroy my clothes?"

"No, but we're not drying and folding them. So whoever comes in here after us . . ."

Spring folded her arms with a huff and leaned against the doorframe. Fire and ice, as the Seasons called any standoff between Summer and Snow.

"We moved Truth Night to tonight," Autumn said. "We're going to pop popcorn, paint our nails. You actually asked me to trim your hair, Summer. And, in case you forgot, there's a murderer out there." She pointed to Levi. "For all we know, it could be him."

Spring made a face, trying not to laugh. Oh, Autumn. So smart. So naïve.

Summer glanced at Levi. "Are you the murderer?"

"Absolutely not."

"Happy now?" Summer shoved Snow aside. "Levi, let's go. Spring, will you bring home my guitar?"

"No, she won't," Snow barked like a junkyard dog as she pulled Summer back by the hair. "You're not going anywhere."

"Lily will be mad, Summer," Autumn said. "You've already been in two fights with her. Are you going to butt heads all camp?"

"You should ask her. Snow, let me go." Summer spun around, swinging. Snow released her and ducked.

"Hold up, hold up." Levi held his hat in his hand. "I didn't mean to start a ruckus." He touched Summer's arm. "Another time?" He flipped a glance at the rest of the Seasons. "There was supposed to be a dance in town tonight, but it's been canceled 'cause of, well, everything. Maybe they'll have one before y'all head home. They're usually pretty fun. I know some of the boys would love to dance with y'all."

The Seasons gathered at the window, watching him go, sighing in harmony as he disappeared down the street.

"Well, thank you very much." With a huff, Summer hopped onto her washing machine perch. "What happened to all for one, one for all? Did you see him? He's a fox. Spring, who covered for you when you snuck out with Mal after prom? Me. Snow, who helped you with math all junior high? Me. Autumn, who helped you babysit a thousand and one times? Me. Y'all couldn't have backed me up this once?"

"*Once?* Ho boy, that's rich."

"We've covered for you a bazillion times."

"Let's start with you and Candace Richmond spending the night at Alligator Point in ninth grade?"

"Okay, okay." Spring stepped in to bring peace. It was her role with the Seasons. Unless she was fighting with Summer, and then it was a free-for-all. "Let's not pile it on. Summer knows." By her expression, she *more* than knew.

"Fine, I'll finish laundry duty, but before I blow this Popsicle stand, I'm getting some alone time with that hunk-of-burning-love." She tried to sound harsh, but there was a laugh in her eyes. She picked up her guitar and started singing the Elvis classic.

Spring started for the door. "Back to my original mission. I'm calling home."

"Wait, I should go with you." Snow shoved her notebook into her backpack. "I can call Babs after you call Judy, Judy, Judy."

"Um, okay." Spring had hoped to make her twofold journey alone, so . . . "Why don't you call your mom while I dash into the drugstore?"

"Ooh, I want to go to the drugstore too." Dang, Spring couldn't catch a break here. "I want to look at the magazines."

Spring hurried across the street with Snow, weaving between cars backed up from the town's one traffic light. If Snow planted herself by the magazines, Spring would have time to inspect the package she'd spotted last week. The *e.p.t. Early Pregnancy Test.*

Outside of O'Sullivan's, a man passed out flyers. "If you see anyone suspicious, call the hotline." He pointed to the 1-800 number in bold black print as he handed one to Spring, then Snow.

Spring tucked the flyer into her pocket next to her secret slip of newsprint and faked a need for nail polish while Snow went around to the magazines.

Walk past the polish . . . to the feminine products aisle. With a glance to see if the coast was clear, Spring picked up the home pregnancy test.

"You married?" She spun around to see the woman at the counter, watching. "Just got those in. For the married gals."

Shhh. Geez, lady, the man with the flyers can hear you. She glanced to see if Snow heard. Hopefully not. Spring shoved the box back onto the shelf. Should she lie to the woman? She didn't have a ring, but lots of women didn't have rings. Spring glanced at the box. "I am—"

"One of the gals working the camp this year?"

Spring regarded her for a moment. "Yes." The woman was Granny's age, with beehive hair and '60s-blue eyeshadow all the way up to her eyebrows.

"I knew Lily when she was your age, coming to camp. You her daughter?"

"Summer is her daughter. I'm Spring." She motioned in the direction of the magazines. "Snow is here too."

"Ah yes, the Four Seasons. Lily told me about y'all."

"Did she? Wow. . . . " The woman had her rattled. How was she going to get a kit with Eagle Eye watching? Wait, how was she going to buy it? She'd not factored the checkout lady into her plan. "I'm going to call my mom," she whispered to Snow, who had a stack of magazines on her lap.

"Get me when you're done." She never looked up from the issue of *People* with Liza Minnelli and Liz Taylor on the cover.

In the diner, Tank polished the counter, took a second to recognize Spring, then nodded.

She tucked into the phone booth, reversed the long-distance charges, and teared up when Mom answered.

Oh, Mama, I might be in trouble.

"Springy, sweetheart, I just hung up with Leona Buckwalter. We were trying to arrange for you and Susan to room together this fall. It'd be nice to stretch out your wings—"

"Mom, I'm not rooming with Susan Buckwalter."

"Well, I know that now. Guess what Leona told me?"

"Hi, Mom, I'm fine. Thank you. Camp Tumbleweed is great. Although there's a murderer on the loose."

143

"Spring Tuttle Duval, what in the world? A murderer?" That got her attention.

"Three Girl Scouts were abducted from their tent Sunday night and murdered." Spring recounted the details. "We're on lockdown, or as Summer calls it, prison."

"Lily kept the camp open?"

"The owner felt it was safe after Lily and Moxie—she's the cook and a former army nurse—and a local sheriff sergeant set up security. One set of parents came for their daughter and she'd just made a best friend."

"Of all the things I thought you might say when you called, a murderer being on the loose was not one of them."

Except what Spring really wanted to tell her would rattle her ten times more. "Mom, I, um, want to tell you that—" Her eyes filled, stalling her confession.

"So you're all right?"

Spring choked out a yes. "Mom, there's something I—"

"We sure do miss you." *Mom, would you just listen?* "We're going to the beach house next week, and I'm not sure we'll stay long. It's never the same without you. Now listen, don't tell the rest of the Seasons, but Susan Buckwalter is pregnant."

"W-what?" Spring jerked up, slamming her knee into the booth's phone book shelf. "Susan Buckwalter? She what? No, Mom, no. Susan is so . . . *good.*" She had a light about her. Not the fake kind like Danielle Stark, who smiled as she stabbed you in the back. Susan had a true light.

"Apparently she fell for some Wakulla County biker."

"You're making that up." Susan Buckwalter and a biker?

"She met him at one of those parties y'all snuck off to every weekend in the spring."

"Snuck off? Mom, what are you—"

"You're eighteen, an adult. I can't tell you what to do, but I hope you kept your head about you, Springy. One wrong decision and your whole life changes. In my day, there was always the one girl who suddenly disappeared and came back a year later with some story about visiting relatives in Georgia or Indiana."

"It's 1977, Mom. Things have changed. An unwed mother doesn't have to leave town."

"Tell that to the Buckwalters. Her daddy is a deacon at church and Leona sings in the choir. You can bet your bottom dollar Susan's going away. Leona is so upset. Susan was an Alpha Delta Pi legacy. As for you, I hope you're ready for rush. Keep an open mind, Spring, about the Seasons. They don't have to do everything you do or vice versa. I heard Summer say she might go Chi Omega. I'm lunching with Leggy Martin to get intel on FSU's homecoming court. It's changed since my day."

Spring rested her head on the side of the phone booth. Mom had it all mapped out, didn't she? What she didn't count on was her daughter joining the same sorority as Susan Buckwalter.

"What does Susan want to do, Mom? What about the guy?"

"Something crazy like marry the hoodlum. Leona and Simon are flat devastated. Susan's going to family in Ohio for the duration, where she'll be the *wife* of a young man working on the oil rigs. Leona's talking to an adoption agency. She's terrified Susan won't go to school after the baby's born. Why don't I see if Susan will talk to you, sweetie? She's always admired you."

The sides of the old phone booth seemed to cave in, and the air became very, very cold. "Mom, I need to help fold laundry. I just wanted to say hi and tell you that I miss you."

"I love you, sugar lump. Can't wait to see you. Wait, your dad's hollering at me. What, Mike? Your father says, 'Thank goodness we raised a smart girl who knows better than to get herself knocked up.' Mike, be nice."

"Yep, she sure does." Trembling, she hung up and pulled the ad for the Tulsa Women's Clinic from her pocket and stared at the telephone number.

But first . . . Spring exited the booth, rounded back to the drugstore, snuck past Snow, who remained on the floor with a pile of magazines, and returned to the feminine products aisle. The nosy cashier was gossiping on the phone, her back to the store. It was now or never.

Spring snatched an e.p.t. box, tucked it into her haversack, and walked out of the front door, never looking back.

15

Always on My Mind

Summary

Summer

'77

Under the night sky, the crickets talked more than the Seasons. No one felt like popcorn after their late lunch at O'Sullivan's. Moxie set out snacks for dinner, but even then, they didn't eat much.

So, they gathered the battery-powered lanterns and headed to the dock for Truth Night.

Summer and Spring powered them on, and Autumn broke out the pink nail polish.

"Pink? Come on, Fall. Don't you have a burnt orange or hunter green?" Summer held the bottle up to the lantern light. "Pink is for the Tumblers."

"Spring, didn't you say you were getting a new color?" Snow said. "I saw an ad for Colorado Colors nail lacquer in *People*. It was like a deep purple. I loved it." Snow sat on the dock and pulled her knees to her chest.

"Like purple mountain majesty?" Summer said. "Above the fruited plains?"

Snow laughed. "Leave it to you to find a song in nail polish. Hey, Spring, what did you buy at the drugstore?"

"What?" She glanced back from where she stared out over the water. "Oh right. Nothing."

"Spring . . ." Summer tugged the end of Spring's hair. "Come on, what'd you buy?"

"Nothing." She moved out of her reach.

Hmmm . . . didn't sound like nothing. Spring had been more than a million miles away since she called home.

"Truth Night." Autumn's soft voice stirred the air. "Is anyone scared?"

"Of what? Truth Night?" Summer stretched on the dock, folded her hands over her middle, and looked for the Milky Way. "Just think, y'all, we'd be headed to London soon, touring the pubs, kissing boys we don't know."

"Kissing boys we don't know?" Autumn sounded appalled and also a little intrigued. "I missed that detail. I'm asking if y'all are afraid because a murderer is on the loose."

"Murderers are cowards. Especially ones who kidnap and tor-ture little girls."

"If I think about it, I'm a little scared," Snow said softly. "Not about the same fate as those three little girls but how anything can happen. Their poor parents had no idea when they sent their daughters to camp, they'd die the first night. And we never talked about kissing boys we don't know. Summie is making it up, Fall."

"I have a question," Summer said. "Why did it happen? Where was God? Why those three of all the girls at the camp? Why that camp?" Summer poked at Spring. "You're the churched Season. Where was God?"

"You're asking me why bad things happen?" Spring moved to the edge of the dock. "How should I know? Ask Him."

"Hey, God." Summer sat up and shouted to the stars. "Where were you that night? I want to know. You don't know me, but Summer Wilde is asking."

She had a few more questions if He cared to listen. Like where was He when her biological dad walked out on Mom? Where was He when Blaine and Snow's dad died testing a plane for the air force? And where the blazes was He when Blaine's head crashed against the diving platform?

Everyone in the park that Saturday heard him hit.

"Well," Spring said, "did He answer?"

"Nope. Must be getting ready for Sunday morning." Summer stretched out on the dock again, hoping a drop of bird poop wasn't her pillow.

"I refuse to believe in a God who won't prevent such evil," Snow said. "Who lets an eighteen-year-old with his life ahead of him die? Or looks on as three little girls suffer at the hands of a psycho?"

"Salute," Autumn whispered.

"Lord? Big Guy? Still waiting," Summer shouted, and the Seasons snickered.

"He's busy, Sum," Snow said. "Too busy for the likes of us."

"Guess so. Still . . ." Summer thought for a moment. "He supposedly parted a sea, so why not do a miracle or two for me. Hellooouuu, God?"

"Remember when Mom gave me the book *Are You There God? It's Me, Margaret*?" Spring sat next to Summer. "We dog-eared that thing, searching for the secrets of getting our periods, love and sex, even faith."

"I was just thinking of that book." Snow reached over Summer to slap Spring a high five. "Mom gave me a copy for Christmas, and Blaine stole it. He said he didn't, but I found it under his bed."

"The Four Seasons," Summer said. "Reading about the Four PTSs."

"The Four PTSs," Spring said. "I'd totally forgotten. Wow, we're not as original as I thought."

"We are completely original," Summer said. "We're real. They were made up."

"Salute!"

Summer had not thought about that book in ages. She wasn't so curious about periods and love anymore. Sex, yes, but the rest of growing into womanhood sort of fell into place.

Truth Night fell silent again, except for the breeze rushing through the trees, shushing the heat of the day. The crescent moon's silver light barely cut the night. The "mourning moon" seemed fitting to Summer.

"I'm still mad at y'all for stopping my fun with Levi," she finally said.

"Get over yourself, Sum." Man, who wound Snow up? "You have a job to do here because technically we're being punished for destruction of property. Never mind the lockdown."

"I'm just trying to salvage some of this summer. You get your play. I get me a cowboy."

Spring laughed, drawing in Autumn and Snow, and just like that, Summer wasn't mad at them anymore. "Who else has a truth?" Summer said. "Y'all know mine. I'd like to make out with Levi."

"Aren't you worried about your parents' relationship?"

"Snow—" Spring whispered. "Shush."

"Mom's here. Dad's in Tally. They say they're fine. Guess I have to believe them. Enough about me. Springy, you're next. Spill."

"Susan Buckwalter is pregnant." The confession was low and rushed.

Summer bolted upright. "Beg pardon, but what?"

"Susan Buckwalter is pregnant." Spring sat on the edge of the dock, legs dangling above the water. "Mom told me not to tell you, but I did, so there. Mrs. Buckwalter is beside herself."

"Susie Buckwalter? Talk about kissing a boy you don't know." Summer scooted over next to Spring. "Who's the father?"

Susan was their class salutatorian, a model student, the girl most likely to succeed. Autumn, as valedictorian, was the girl most likely to invent a cure.

"Some biker dude from Wakulla County. Susie wants to marry him."

Summer's laugh echoed over the water. "Let this be a lesson to us all, Seasons. The second smartest girl at Lincoln High got pregnant. Don't tell me she didn't know about birth control? It's 1977. What a moron."

"She's not a moron, Summer. Gah, have some compassion." Spring jumped up and started pacing. "She made a mistake, and she'll pay for it well enough. Hey, maybe she wanted a baby?"

"At eighteen, when she had a full-ride scholarship? I doubt it. Don't you remember her graduation speech? 'So we strive to go farther, do more, the ceiling of our parents has become our floor.'"

"Those little girls from Camp Scott will never have babies." Autumn was a broken record when it came to those girls.

"We should remember them," Spring said, "before we leave. Float candles on the water or something."

"We have to remember Blaine in July," Snow said.

"Definitely."

"We won't forget."

"Snowy, we'll never forget Blaine."

"I know, I know. Hey, y'all, newsflash. Mom's giving me Paps' Mercedes." Snow sort of blurted that out. "She says it's safer to drive. She won't worry about me being stranded anywhere."

"Stranded? At FSU?" A branch dropped onto the dock from a low swinging branch and Summer tossed it into the water. "We'd come and get you if you were stranded. What about your Camaro? I'll take it if you don't want it. Dad bought me that used Pinto, which stalls all over town. Wish I had a mysterious benefactor."

"Ah, Summer, the Pinto is cute. We don't mind pushing you for a jump start." Snow laughed softly against the night.

"I'm going to cosmetology school."

What? Summer swiveled to face Autumn.

"I don't want to be a scientist unless I'm concocting a new hair color or my own makeup line. I know everyone thinks I have this brain to cure some heinous disease or invent a new sports drink for overexercised jocks, but helping women look and feel beautiful is just as worthwhile."

"Wait, Autumn." Spring shed her previous preoccupation. "Florida State doesn't have a cosmetology school."

"Nope. I'm going to Tallahassee Cosmetology. I want to own a salon someday."

"You have to go to FSU," Summer said. "You're Snow's roommate."

"Ah, don't worry about me," Snow said.

Summer cast a side look at her, but in the light of the mourning moon and the battery-powered lanterns, she could only see shadows on Snow's complexion. "Of course I worry. You're our suitemate. Autumn, that's not the plan."

"I'm not going to waste time and money at school when I know I want to do something else," Autumn said.

"Your parents must not know yet, because they were alive and well at the bus depot. Fall, you won the Young Scientist Fellowship. Beaucoup money," Summer said. "Spring, Snow, help me out here."

"I support her." Snow stood. "If she wants to do hair, let her. Why do we always have to do everything together? Shouldn't friends cheer each other on? Autumn's right. Why waste time and money on school if she's not interested?"

"Who knows where the future will take us," Spring said. "Locust Grove showed us how short, how precious, life can be, how one decision can change lives—" The glow of headlights bounced through the trees. "Lily's back with Greta. I'll go get her settled. Night, all."

Spring left the dock without another word.

"I guess Truth Night is over then?" Summer called after her.

"She shouldn't go alone." Snow started to follow her.

"Summer, we should go too." Autumn extended her hand to help her up.

"Go on." She reached for her flashlight. "I'll be right behind you. Fall, you're really going to cosmetology school?"

"I'd hate being a scientist the rest of my life, Summer. I want my parents to be proud of me, but—"

"I hear you there. Not Mom so much but Dad."

"Your dad is proud of you, Summer. Your relationship with him is special."

"I know but . . ." She got up and dusted debris from her shorts. "It feels like everything is changing, breaking up."

"Hey, can I ask you something? Do you ever wonder about your real dad?"

"Jeff is my real dad."

"I mean, the man who sired you."

"Sired? He's not a horse, Fall. Who cares about him? He left. *Sayonara. Adios. Au revoir. Auf Wiedersehen.*" Summer had watched too many episodes of *The Lawrence Welk Show* with Granny. "Come on, let's raid the kitchen before Moxie locks everything up. I'm hungry."

"You'll still see me, Summer." Autumn helped collect the remaining lanterns. "I'll come over all the time, get football tickets through my parents. You'll hardly miss me."

"But you're not coming with us, and it changes everything."

"Summer!"

Summer woke with a start, blinking through the darkness of Moonglow, kicking off the thin sheet. The oscillating fan stirred the night air, which carried the hum of conversation from the deputies' firepit.

Who called her? Or was she dreaming?

She glanced at the glow-in-the-dark hands of her bedside clock—one in the morning—then listened for another moment before flopping back down on her pillow, arms wide, one leg dangling over the side of the cot.

Truth Night had been a bust, save Autumn's big announcement. Not going to FSU? For Summer, the initial shock faded into some sort of I-knew-it sensation. Autumn only got good grades in science because she was a genius. Not because it was her passion.

Wonder who'd they get to share their suite? Maybe her cousin, Meg. The motor of the fan lulled her back to sleep, and as she drifted, Summer's thoughts wandered through the scattered conversations on the dock.

Babs selling the Camaro. Driving the Mercedes. Safer.

Summer demanding answers from God.

Mom and Greta returning from Oklahoma City.

"Summer, come!"

She sat up, heart thumping. "Who's there?" She'd not been all the way asleep, so the voice was not in a dream.

Wait, she heard music. Scrambling from the cot, Summer leaned against the windowsill. Yes, someone played the guitar while a girl sang.

Who, where? Grabbing her flashlight, she slipped on her sneakers and stepped outside, inching between Autumn's cabin and hers toward the sound. The deputies must have a radio.

The music faded, giving way to the deep voices of the deputies. They were talking football. Oklahoma versus Oklahoma State.

A twig broke under her foot, and the debate stalled. "Who's there?"

She recognized the voice of rent-a-fuzz Jim. "It's just me, Summer." She aimed her flashlight on her face. "Did you call me?"

"No, why?"

"I don't know. . . . Hey, I thought I heard music."

"Music? There's no music out here," Jim said. "Cam, you hear music?"

"I wish. You know Dover won't let us have a radio."

"Y'all didn't hear anything?"

154

"Only the sound of our gums flapping. What'd you hear, Summer?"

"My name, then someone playing the guitar and a girl singing."

"You must've been dreaming," Jim said. No, she'd not been dreaming. "Want me to walk you back to your cabin?"

"I'm fine." She raised her flashlight as if to make her point. "Thanks."

"Holler at me when you're tucked inside." Jim returned to the fire and football. "Oh hey, Summer"—there was a chuckle in his voice—"next time you hear your name in the night, say, 'Here I am, Lord.' You know, like Samuel."

"Who?"

"Samuel, in the Bible."

"Yeah, okay." They didn't cover that character in VBS.

Summer started back, but no, she'd *heard* music. Now she saw lights in the meadow just beyond the campfire.

She moved quietly between the trees. Was there a concert in the meadow? How? And at this hour?

"Summer, go back."

"Who's there?" She aimed her light behind her. The voice was different. Deeper. Darker. Earlier her name sounded like the actual season—warm, bright, fragrant.

"Summer, come!" She whirled around to the vibrant voice. What was happening?

Glancing back toward the cabins, she debated. Mom would freak if she knew she'd trekked through the woods alone. Even though the deputies were one scream away.

But the lights coming from the other side of the trees . . . She had to see. Pushing on, Summer came to an opening. A large tent, set with chairs and a stage, consumed the meadow. A girl with long blond hair, wearing jeans, a peasant blouse, and a red headband, stood in front of a microphone, strumming her guitar. Behind her, a guy with Andy Gibb hair sat at the drums and another thumped an upright bass.

"Summer, go back!" The dark voice tugged on her.

"Jim?" she whispered, though she knew it wasn't him.

Under the tent, the girl played and sang a new song, and Summer felt as if she'd known her forever.

"Summer, go back." Two voices? One calling her back.

"Summer, come!" One calling her to the tent and lights, stage and music.

I'm coming. But as she took a step forward, a twig snapped. A branch fell. She ran toward the cabins. Fear was a powerful force.

Tripping, stumbling, she burst into the quiet space between Sunglow and Moonglow. The music faded. The tent lights dimmed. Even Jim and Cam had stopped talking, and for a moment, Summer felt completely alone in darkness.

16

Reminiscing

Spring

'97

Spring sat across from Autumn, feeling only slightly less uncomfortable than she did at their first lunch last week at the Melting Pot, where they gave the highlights of their lives and then raised a glass to remember the Camp Scott girls Lori, Michelle, and Denise.

Spring learned that Autumn's salon, the Kitchen, had sixteen chairs and appointments were booked out six months. *"Our stylists work long hours, but they're making a mint, so they don't complain."*

Adding fame to her name, Autumn recently met the governor's wife, who hired her for a private appointment, loved what she'd done with her graying locks, and mentioned her by name when interviewed by the *Tallahassee Democrat*.

Spring gave Autumn a brief update on her law career, most of which she already knew from Lincoln High's alumni newsletter, then mentioned her recent sabbatical to write. *"Maybe I was promoted too fast, but I feel like I've accomplished everything I wanted already."*

"You always were a bit of an overachiever." Autumn spoke frankly, intimately, and Spring soaked it up. Their friendship may have lapsed over the last two decades, but the Four Seasons were in her blood, part of her very being. How had she lived all this time, save her friendship with Mal, without her besties? Without those who knew her thoughts before she formed them?

After the Melting Pot, they had no plans to reunite anytime soon, but fate intervened. A week later, they ran into each other at the Killearn Publix.

Autumn had popped in for a few things after checking out a second shop location where she might include a cosmetology school, and Spring was running errands to avoid the pain of the blank page.

They walked out together, talking, paused by their twin silver Mercedes S-Class, and laughed. And that's how they found themselves dining at a Wendy's.

"I think the last time I had a burger with you, it was at O'Sullivan's," Spring said.

"Now that takes me back." Autumn took a big bite of her sandwich. "God bless Wendy's, but nothing beats an O'Sullivan's burger."

"Salute."

Autumn choked down her bite. "Gosh if that doesn't take me back."

"I've not said 'Salute' in a long, *long* time."

"Well, we've not been the Four Seasons for a long, long time."

Spring wondered which one of them would bring up the past first. Or would they just leave it?

"Mind if I ask you something?" Autumn stirred the ice in her soda cup. "Why novel writing? Even if you rose to the top fast at the firm, isn't the satisfaction of the law enough? I know you make a lot of money."

Spring sat back with a fry in her hand. She liked this question. She'd been wondering the same thing. Did she speak as an old friend, or as a lawyer and redirect the conversation?

"You're hesitating," Autumn said.

"I am." Spring laughed. No point denying it. "I always wanted to write a novel. The sound of it satisfies the bohemian in me."

"The part Judy, Judy, Judy never let you explore?"

"Not in a million years." How fun to talk to someone who *knew* her. All of her. There was no preamble with Autumn.

"Are you trying to have kids?"

No preamble and apparently no barriers. "We're talking about it. What about you? Do you want to get married and have kids?"

Autumn sipped her drink. "One day, I guess. I'm too busy to date anyone. Apparently, there's some new dating website, Match or something, and Chris signed me up."

"What?" Little brother Chris was in junior high the last time Spring saw him.

"I had no idea why I started getting emails from men asking to meet for coffee or drinks. He fessed up at dinner one night. I could've killed him." Yet she was laughing. "You know Chris and Tabitha live with me." The youngest Childe siblings. "Mom and Dad are still teaching at DePauw University in Indiana. Ridley has three kids, Jenna and Janna have toddlers. Devon isn't married either and lives in Jacksonville. We compete with the nieces and nephews for the most fun house. We both have big yards and pools. But Dev just put a basketball court in at his place. Rid is so jealous."

"You should put in a tennis court."

"Don't tempt me."

So there they were, two of the Four Seasons, reminiscing and laughing as if this was how it should be.

"Proud of you, Fall," Spring said. "Then again, we were the Mary Tyler Moore generation, weren't we? Career and independence, living in a cute apartment, hanging with our friends."

"All well and good until your friends get married." Autumn stared toward the parking lot. "Or don't talk to you for twenty years." When she faced Spring again, tears sat in her eyes.

"For thirteen years, I've been all about the law." Spring leaned in, resting her arms on the table. "When I cooked or cleaned, when I stood in the shower, my thoughts were on a case. Going through details, formulating an argument. Now that I'm on sabbatical, my thoughts are on, what? The past and all the things I can't change. Truth is, novel writing is way harder than I ever imagined. It requires heart and emotion, digging inside and pulling out a story. The law is facts and making a case.'

"I know you, Spring," Autumn said in that familiar way. "If you set your mind to it, you have to try. And you'll do well."

Spring held onto the encouragement. "Mom thinks I'm crazy for risking the partnership to write a *romance*. 'You and every other living soul trying to be the next Danielle Steel.' Dad says it's good to mix things up, but he's being nice because he hopes Mal and I will fall in love with politics."

"One thing I always knew about you, Spring. You followed your heart. Did what was right."

"I'm not so sure." She wadded up her burger wrapper into a tight ball. "I, um, didn't tell him. Mal. Was that right? Lately, I think about it every day."

"Mal?" Autumn thought for a moment. "Spring, you never . . . Wait, you married him without telling him? Why?"

"That's the million-dollar question. I'm not sure. He was so, *so* in love with me. I was so in love with him. He told me all the time how he'd never loved anyone like me. Even more than the girl he dated in college for two years. I couldn't believe he called me again, you know? I thought, *God, you must love me a little to have Mal call.* I was so scared of rocking the boat. Mom was staunchly on the side of letting the past be the past. And to be honest, Autumn, I didn't know *how* to tell him. Still don't."

"But you do, Spring. You've just said it a couple of times. He loves you. We all knew you two would end up together. Do you really believe he'd walk away now if you told him you had his baby nineteen years ago?"

"Deep down, no. But I'm afraid it will change how he sees me. Destroy his trust."

"Just because you've never told him doesn't mean the truth isn't playing a part in your relationship. *You* know, and I bet it's impacting you in some way, in how you relate to him. Never mind he played a part in you getting pregnant."

"That doesn't make it any easier to confess. 'Hey babe, did you like dinner? By the way, we had a baby in February of 1978. Do you want ice cream for dessert?'" Spring shifted, changed her posture, tried to get comfortable.

"Well, you don't have to be so casual about it, Spring. Geez."

"I know, but, Autumn, so much time has passed."

"The summer of '77," Autumn said, matter-of-factly, without any hint of sentiment. "What we didn't know when we boarded that Greyhound bus."

"You got the worst end of the deal." Spring's confession was long overdue. "Maybe it's twenty years too late, but I'm sorry. I really am. I should've stood up for you."

"Don't. You had bigger worries. Though I wonder if Summer still hates me. Do you want more to drink?"

Spring handed Autumn her soda cup. "Tab, please." When she returned to the table, she said, "She doesn't hate you. You know Summer. Talks a big game but is a powder puff inside."

"Powder puff or powder keg?"

"Depends on the day." The two of them laughed, and Spring realized how much she needed this conversation. "The business with Lily and Jeff really messed her up. I got a postcard from her about six years ago. She was on the road with her band. Snow sends a Christmas card every now and then. Greta writes two, three times a year. She's a doctor married to a doctor."

"She writes me too." Autumn leaned forward and considered her words. "I'm not sentimental, Spring. I don't live in the past. I've moved on from the Four Seasons, though Snow and I exchange Christmas cards. And having lunch with you feels sort of healing. But when Summer skipped your wedding, she broke us permanently. And I was done."

"She might have come if it hadn't been for Jeff and—"

"Too bad. Grow up. She let her emotions, her pity party, keep her from *your* wedding. From being *your* maid of honor. I was willing to put everything aside, and so was Snow, for you to have your day. And she didn't even bother to show up. Didn't even call. We always said she was selfish and obtuse, but cruel? I didn't think she had it in her."

"I don't think she meant to be cruel. I had you and Snow with me."

"You know I believed deep down your wedding would bring back the Four Seasons. But she never gave us a chance. And if she lumped all of us in with Lily and Jeff's divorce, then there's no hope."

The passion of Autumn's confession gave her cheeks a rosy hue, and Spring felt the truth of every word.

"Summer was right about one thing," Spring said. "It took all four of us to make our friendship work. We were a square, and if one side collapsed, all sides collapsed." She reached across for Autumn's hand. "You did a fabulous job as my maid of honor *and* my stylist."

Autumn laughed softly. "I'm sad we lost touch. Sad I let Summer's absence push me away. Sad I didn't make an effort."

"I'm as guilty, but we're in touch now, Autumn." Spring squeezed and released her hand.

"I confess there are times—and I guess it's the latent scientist in me—I wonder if we could fix us. Be the Four Seasons again."

Oh, Autumn. If only. Spring shook her head. "I doubt it."

"It's too late? Too much time has gone by?" Autumn sipped from her refilled soda. "Friends do reunite all the time. Especially as they get older."

"The Four Seasons aren't just any ol' set of friends, Autumn. We were bonded for life. All for one, one for all. Until . . ."

Autumn looked away, eyes glistening. "I hate remembering."

"We were the perfect storm that summer." Spring sighed. "What would it take to bring us back together? The four corners of the square. *No one* can be missing, and you know as well as I do, *that* cannot be fixed."

Spring

'77

Spring lay in the dark, waiting, her heart thumping, the *thing* in her carefully stored haversack under her bunk.

She thought she heard Summer outside of Moonglow earlier, but when she looked out the window, the only light was the rental cops' firepit.

She rolled over and tapped the light button on her clock. Just after one. She'd wanted to head to the latrine an hour ago, but she couldn't make herself move.

"Spring?" Greta whispered from her top bunk. What was she doing awake? "I had fun with my grandparents, but I'm glad to be back at camp. They almost talked Lily into leaving me there."

"We'd have come for you, Greta. Never fear." She was so sweet. Spring loved her to pieces. "Now go to sleep. It's late." Please. She wanted no observers when she executed her predawn mission. "We'll swim tomorrow until the new Tumblers arrive, okay?"

"Spring, are you sad?" Greta said.

"What? No, sugar lump. I'm not sad. Do I look sad?" The girl was too observant.

"Sometimes."

"I guess everyone is sad sometimes. Now, go to sleep and dream of Moxie's French toast for breakfast."

Greta rolled over and whispered softly, "I love you."

The girl's tender vulnerability, her trust, almost overwhelmed her. Greta didn't know it, but Spring had let her down. She'd let everyone down.

She pressed her hand to her flat belly. Swear to goodness, if Summer asked one more time what she bought at the drugstore, she'd have blurted out, *"A pregnancy test, okay?"*

But Autumn's announcement about cosmetology school stole the show, and Spring could kiss her for it.

When the glowing hands of her clock hit two, Spring reached into the cupboard for her flashlight and then retrieved her small suitcase, where she'd hidden her haversack. She tiptoed past Greta's deep breathing and stepped outside.

Locking the door and leaving Greta alone was breaking all the rules, but what choice did she have? She'd be quick about it.

Jim and Cam talked by the fire. As she passed, she called out. "Jim, it's me, Spring. Just heading to the latrine."

"We'll keep an eye out."

"Th-thanks." Though now that she told them, she was embarrassed. What if the test thing took too long? She'd read the instructions ten times already, but still. Pee in a vial, wait two hours. Bada bing, bada boom. She'd not have said a word to them except announcing late-night movements was another one of Lily's rules.

"I don't want you to get your head blown off by accident."

This was turning out to be a really weird summer.

The cinder block latrine was cool and dark. Spring flipped on the lights and locked herself in the farthest stall from the door. She set a torn newspaper page on the floor and retrieved the e.p.t. kit.

In the claustrophobic space, she reviewed the instructions. *Put three drops of urine onto the test tube. Add contents from the plastic vial. Shake—*Shake?*—Set in the holder for two hours. Do not disturb.* The mirror on the bottom of the holder would reveal the results. If she saw a brown ring, the worst was true.

"Be kind to me, brown ring."

Wait . . . She needed a cup from which to retrieve her three drops. A stupid cup. Dang—

"Hello?"

She jumped at the masculine voice. Jim?

"Yes?" What did he want?

"You've been in here a while. Wanted to make sure you were okay."

She'd only been in here five minutes, if that, and no, she was not okay. "I'm fine. Thanks. Don't feel well."

"Do you want me to get Summer or Lily?"

"No!" Fake laugh. "No need, b-but thanks."

She could hear him announcing she was fine to the other deputy. "I told you she was fine, Cam." Could she just flush herself down the commode? Save her embarrassment? Please?

Eyes shut, she whispered something close to a prayer. She'd have to make a run to the kitchen for a cup. She dreaded the call to Jim.

I'm going to the kitchen.

What for?

Yeah, what for? Then she'd have to announce her return to the latrine, where she'd get the stupid test over with and stored somewhere—she had yet to cross that bridge—and go back to Starlight, where she'd shout out to the deputies one more time.

She might as well be a headline in the *Tumbleweed Gazette. Counselor at Camp Tumbleweed Taking a Pregnancy Test.* This whole affair was supposed to be private.

Know what? Forget it. She yanked up her haversack. She'd do this tomorrow. Or Monday. Or never. Unless . . . Spring stared at her hand, cupping it into a saucer. Would *that* work?

The latrine door creaked open, then clapped closed. Was Jim coming in? Spring sat up. "I said I was fine."

"Did you?" Moxie. "Good to know. Spring, what are you doing in here?"

What do you think? "Hey, Moxie, I, um, have a bit of an upset stomach." Shoot, shoot, shoot. The kit was on the floor. Visible beneath the door. Spring scooped her contraband to her lap.

Moxie's feet stopped at her stall. "Need help?"

"Um, can you get me a glass of water? I'm really thirsty."

"7-Up would be better for an upset tummy. You puking?"

Give her a minute. "No. But 7-Up is good. Thank you."

"Dry toast?"

For crying out loud. "No, thanks."

Moxie retreated, the latrine door clapping closed, and in the warm, stuffy stall, Spring shivered. All she wanted was to curl up in her bunk and dream of floating on white fluffy clouds.

After an eternity passed, Moxie returned with a glass of 7-Up. "Come on out. Let me check your temperature."

"Can't. Got the runs."

"Runs? From O'Sullivan's? Best let Tank know." Moxie passed the glass under the door, and Spring juggled her test kit as she reached for it, almost losing the instruction paper. "I'll wait. See how you're doing."

"That's okay. Y-you should go. Breakfast comes early." Spring chugged the soda, sneezing when the fizz went up her nose, but she had her glass . . . which was contaminated with sugar residue. Crudola.

"I can't have one of you sick. I should check to see if you have a fever."

"The 7-Up helped, thanks. I'll be all right."

"Want to give back the glass?"

Would you just go? "Still some left. I'll take it to the kitchen in the morning."

"If you're sure . . ."

"I am." *Now go!* But what did Moxie do? Step into a stall two doors down.

For the love of Pete!

Moxie did her business, washed her hands, and made a final call to Spring. "Knock on my cabin if you need me."

"Will do, Moxie."

When she was sure the coast was clear, Spring settled the newspaper and test kit back on the floor, darted from the stall to rinse the glass and dry it, and got down to business. She deposited three drops in the test tube, added the mixture, gave it a shake, and secured the vial in the holder.

Stuffing all evidence into the haversack, she looked for a place to hide the kit. Ah, the utility closet. Clicking on her flashlight, Spring nosed up to see beyond the bottles of Pine-Sol and Mr. Clean, and through the cobwebs, to shove the test-tube holder all the way back to the dark corner of the closet. Safe and sound.

"See you in two hours."

Clicking off the latrine lights, she headed back to Starlight. "Just me," she called to the deputies.

"Girl, we thought you'd fallen in." Jim's laughter chased her.

Shoot fire. How was she going to sneak back in two hours to see if that night with Mal produced a new human life? She'd just have to, that's all. Or bump Lily's stupid rules and sneak across without an announcement. Or just claim she was sick, which wouldn't be far from the truth.

But like Grandpa Duval always said, *"It's best to face a problem head-on."*

What would he think of her now? She felt ashamed. Undeserving of the name Duval.

Back in Starlight, Spring stretched out on her bunk and listened to Greta's deep sleep. She envied her. There was no need to set her alarm. Falling asleep was not an option. Not tonight.

17

Thanks
for the Memories

Summer

'97

After her night at the Broken Barrel, Summer didn't go to Nashville. She rebooked her room at Shady Rest and slept for three days, waking up for long hot showers and a large breakfast at the Sixty-Six Diner across the street.

On day four, when she felt something like the girl she used to be, she replaced the strings on her guitar, sat on the stoop outside her room, and sang old country songs until the stars started to shine.

Day five, she drove to the mall for clothes, shoes, whatever caught her eye. She booked a hair appointment at a mall salon, and on day six, the stylist trimmed her wild blond locks, then streaked them with golden highlights.

And every day, when she woke up, when she went to bed, and a thousand moments in between, she pictured Levi, reliving the look in his eyes, the taste of his kiss, and the feel of his body against hers.

The images morphed into a fantasy, one that had them married, living on Foley Ranch, waking up before dawn in the cold and heat, snow and rain, to wrangle cows.

She'd make him, and any cowboy who showed up in time, a grand breakfast of eggs, bacon, ham, homemade biscuits, pancakes, and hot coffee with cream.

She'd fix lunches and dinners, sing songs while she cleaned the house and bought the groceries. They'd make love every night to the music of the prairie.

They'd have two babies right away because, well, she was no spring chicken. A caboose baby would surprise them just after her forty-fifth birthday. She'd cry and wonder, *Why, God, why?* but the little munchkin, a girl, would be a mini Levi with his Irish-German features and bright blue eyes. She'd bring so much joy and sweetness to the family that they'd comment every day how they couldn't imagine life without her.

The Foleys would attend church on Sundays, and maybe she'd have answers to the mysterious music and tent from the summer of '77. To why God let bad things happen.

Once in a blue moon, she thought about that night on the dock with the Seasons where she'd called out to Him. *"Hey, God, where were you that night?"* Maybe it wasn't her business why the Girl Scouts had been murdered, but it sure was her business about the secrets and the events surrounding the big-top tent.

In her alternative universe, Summer would sing a Sunday morning special now and then but nothing more. Music was for the family and her own soul.

After church, they'd have a family lunch, rotating houses with Levi's brother and his parents. Summer would always invite any newcomers, singles, or elderly folks to join them.

Levi would sign up the kiddos for the Christmas pageant, and the night of the performance, her kiddos would break the fourth wall by waving to Daddy and Mama, Grandpa and Grandma Foley, the aunts and uncles, cousins—well, the whole Foley herd. Including G'ma Lily. Yes, she'd be there.

But too much of a good thing made a girl's heart sick. On the evening of day six, she called, "Cut!" to her fantasy. Such a life was not possible. Levi thought he wanted her, but he deserved a woman so much better than Summer Wilde.

She'd lost too much of herself on the wild side. Betrayed every value her parents instilled in her. Just like they'd betrayed her and the family they'd created.

On the seventh morning, she woke up feeling free. Like she didn't need Nashville to do what she loved. She only needed a guitar and a place to play. The front stoop outside her Shady Rest cottage was a grand stage.

On day eight, she checked out of the motel without a glimmer of a plan.

"I'll miss your evening songs." Bob was the front desk clerk from seven at night to seven in the morning. "The guests keep asking about you. Do you have any CDs?"

"Not anymore." The money from "The Preacher" funded all her record projects. All the CDs she had were in the minibus when the Sparrows drove off. "But you might be able to find some in a used record store."

After she paid her bill, he wished her luck and told her to come back. "And if you come across any of your CDs, send them my way. Happy to send money back."

His sincere compliment had her smiling all the way to the diner, where she ordered coffee and an apple fritter—okay, two apple fritters. After bidding the Sixty-Six staff good-bye, Summer pulled out a map and planned her route home.

Except for one thing. Where was home? Nashville? Tallahassee? She and Mom were on better terms, but she had yet to mend her fences with Dad. If she could even call him Dad.

"I am *your father, Summer."* He'd told her over and over. Yet he'd lied. For a very, very long time. He'd bamboozled her and Mom.

So, where to, Summer Girl? She shoved the map back inside the glove box and faced east, where the colors of the morning were starting to show.

Sitting on the truck tailgate, kicking her heels, she finished her first fritter, washed it down with coffee, wiped her fingers, and started on the second one. When she was done, she tossed her trash in the diner's can, then slipped behind the steering wheel.

With the engine idling, she shifted into reverse and backed out of the parking lot.

Don't think, just be.

This was the kind of thinking that got her into trouble. That landed her in the beds of men she barely knew. That ticked off her bandmates. That got her dropped from her second and third label. What was a girl to do? Stay quiet when they asked her to record songs she hated?

"It's bubble-gum country. I have a whole catalog of songs for you to choose from."

The kind of impulsive action Mom warned her about most of her teen years. When she trusted her heart and never consulted her head.

So, she aimed for Tumbleweed. Nashville had nothing for her. She'd moved out of her apartment before the tour, selling or giving away her furniture. The things she kept—some clothes, the dress she wore to the CMAs when "The Preacher" was nominated for Song of the Year, her grandmother's antique curio cabinet, her guitars and banjo, keyboard and boxes of music, and her computer—were stored in a friend's garage. If necessary, she could live without most of it.

"Fire, aim, ready" was her motto. One of these days, it just might work.

Tuning into an oldies country station, she sang along with Patsy,

Dolly, and Loretta, the miles turning back time until she was eighteen again, stepping off the Greyhound in Tulsa with Spring, who was not herself, Autumn, who brought cases of beauty supplies, and Snow, loaded down with her cameras.

For the first time in ages, the memory didn't sting. In fact, she found comfort in the old shades and shadows.

By the time she arrived in Tumbleweed, hankering once again for the Number Five for lunch, she thought she just might stay for a while. Take Clark's advice and rest.

She hit the brakes when she spotted a Realtor storefront. The agent behind the desk shook her hand and showed her the only thing he had for rent—a small cottage on the western edge of town.

"Do you rent by the month?" she said.

"We do."

"I'll take it."

She went straight there, unloaded her suitcases and guitars, then stood on the front porch facing Camp Tumbleweed. It was then she knew why she came.

For Levi? Not really. She still believed he could do better. To hide from the world? Quite possibly. To write a few songs? She never seemed to run out of melodies. Yet none of them were the true reason she'd returned to the little town on the Oklahoma prairie.

No, Summer Wilde came back to find herself.

Spring

'77

When Spring opened her eyes, daylight flooded the cabin. Shoot! What time was it? Still wearing her clothes from last night, she dashed past Greta's empty and made-up bunk out the door.

She'd overslept. *Overslept.* How? Shoot, shoot, shoot.

"Hey, Sleepyhead," Summer called. "We were just about to wake you up. We're going into town for breakfast. Moxie said the little café on the edge of town, Dottie's, has yummy omelets."

"Okay." But she didn't comprehend a word as she ran down the worn path toward the latrine. Why hadn't she set her alarm?

"Spring!" Man, Summer had a big mouth. "Tinkle fast. We're hungry."

In the latrine, she beelined to the utility closet and, on tiptoe, felt around for the wooden holder and vial.

Where was it? She stretched farther until her fingers hit the block wall. It wasn't there. *No, no, no.* She ran her hand along the shelf, wincing and shivering when she dusted a couple of dead cockroaches over the side. Where was the vial?

"Crap!" She dropped to her knees and searched the floor, the corners, the buckets. Gone.

"Is this what you're looking for?"

Moxie.

Spring looked up to see the ex-POW army nurse holding the pregnancy kit in her hand.

"You shouldn't have moved it." Spring dusted her knees as she stood, determined not to break, not to let Moxie in on her business.

"I saw the bottom of the vial. It was brown." Moxie set the kit on the edge of the nearest sink. "How far along?"

The tenderness in her voice broke Spring's resolve. "Not sure. I'm about three, maybe four weeks late. That's all I know."

Except she was pregnant. She knew that now.

"Morning sickness?"

"Yes, well, I did have it, but it's getting better."

"Lucky you."

"Lucky?" Spring shot her a look. "If I was lucky, I'd not be standing here with you as my confessor. Was the bottom of the vial really brown?" She angled around to see the mirror on the bottom of the holder.

"It was brown. But you didn't need a test kit, did you?"

173

"I kept hoping I was wrong."

"Have you told your parents?"

"I just now told myself. I thought being late and sick was from stress. After all, the Lincoln High prom queen was arrested for vandalism and shipped off to Oklahoma. And we ate a lot of junk food on the way out."

"Do you have a plan?"

Nope. She had a plan for everything except getting pregnant after one night of passion in Mal's car. Acting without thinking was supposed to be Summer's terrain.

"How did I let this happen, Moxie?" Spring covered her face with her hands. "I'm scandalizing my family. This will humiliate my parents. They may never talk to me again. And what about school? I've wanted to go to FSU since I was born. I'm supposed to room with Summer, Snow, and Autumn—though she put a kibosh on things last night 'cause she's going to cosmetology school. Unless her parents kill her, then I guess she won't be going anywhere. I'm supposed to rush my mom and grandma's sorority. I'm supposed to try out for cheerleading and be on the freshman homecoming court. What I'm not supposed to do is get pregnant." She peered at Moxie. "Do you think anyone would notice if I just wear baggy clothes? I may not show for a long time. Maybe I can do all that stuff, then . . ." An idea formed. Not a good one, but still. "Then I could get sick and drop out for three months."

"That's your plan?"

Okay, so it wasn't great. Give her a minute. It was then she remembered the ad she'd ripped from the *Tulsa World*.

"You might be able to hide for a while, this being your first pregnancy and all." Moxie waited for Spring's affirmation. Was it? *Well, of course!* "But six, seven months down the line . . . though I had a gal in the Philippines who succumbed to the charms of a handsome lieutenant, and when she went into labor, we thought she was dying. She hid it for nine months. Skinny thing too."

"Moxie, do you think I can do that? Do you? How'd she do it?"

"Spring." Moxie set her broad hands on Spring's sagging shoulders. "Let's not count on hiding a pregnancy. It's time for a real plan. What do *you* want to do?"

Spring regarded her for a moment, holding herself together for half a breath before crumpling into sobs and falling into Moxie's strong arms.

18

Saturday in the Park

Summer

'77

Another week of camp in the books. Summer was back at the laundromat, and the hot, narrow room was growing on her. If nothing else, Saturday laundry allowed them some freedom, even though Mom demanded their feet step on Camp Tumbleweed grounds by four. While in town folding linens and undies, a police officer or deputy checked on them every half hour. Ridiculous.

When she said so out loud, Autumn commented, "You know she's reporting our actions to the judge in Tallahassee."

"What?" Summer stopped the melody she picked on her guitar.

"I forgot that part." Spring looked up from where she fumbled with her haversack. "Remember, the judge asked for a personal report along with her filings with our parole officer?"

"Right, and I heard Lily tell the sergeant . . . Dover."

Snow had brought her camera this week and snapped a picture from Tumble Time's front door.

"You mean *overheard*. You were eavesdropping, Fall." Summer said.

"Can I help it her voice carries? I was outside her office, waiting to call home the day we heard about the murders."

"Mom's voice carries like a lead balloon."

"Leave her alone, Summer." Snow sat with Autumn on the folding table and took another round of photos. "Fall doesn't eavesdrop."

"She is if she's listening to a conversation uninvited."

Autumn made a face at Summer. "That's all I heard. About the judge."

"Next time, hear more." Summer grinned and ducked as Autumn's sneaker flew past her head. "Geez, if you're going to be a good Season, you have to be good at being clandestine and sneaky."

"We thought we'd leave all of that to you, Miss I-Sneak-Out-At-Midnight."

Camp Tumbleweed week three had been uneventful, except for the presumed element of danger that had Mom on fear alert. Summer barely recognized her mother. The single mom who finished college and landed a great guy like Dad, who helped found Wilde Engineering and did consulting on the side, had lost all reason.

On Thursday, Sergeant Dover had announced the boot prints she and Snow found didn't match the ones found in a cave by Locust Grove.

"So who was in our camp?" Mom said.

"We don't know. Could've been anyone."

"Anyone?" Mom turned whiter than the bedsheets. *"There could be a second or third killer on the loose?"*

"We don't think so, but—"

"Seasons, we're on double lockdown."

"How can we be on double lockdown?" Summer asked.

"I don't know, but we are. Be double vigilant. Double-check

locks. Double guard the Tumblers with your life. There may be someone else out there intending harm."

Yesterday, Mom caught a Tumbler, sweet Tootsie, running to the latrine by herself right before the play started, and darn near had a conniption. Read Tootsie the riot act in front of everyone until Summer intervened.

"Geez oh Pete, Mom, you sound like a crazy lady. Go on, Tootsie. . . . Hey, don't cry. Just take a buddy next time, okay?" Then to Mom. *"She's nine. Doesn't know anything about Camp Scott or stray boot prints. Right now, she's more terrified of the Camp Tumbleweed director than any lunatic carting her off to the woods."*

Mom relented and apologized to Tootsie after the play, but Summer felt sure she'd ruined the girl's entire camp experience. She'd never be back.

Taking up her guitar again, she played a slow melody with the hum of the washing machines as her rhythm section. Snow exchanged her SLR for her movie camera. When she zeroed in on Summer, Summer sang a bit of Joni Mitchell's "Both Sides Now," then glanced down the row of machines toward Autumn.

"Can we talk about it?"

"What?"

"You going to cosmetology school. Are you really going? Who's going to room with Snow?"

"Don't worry about me," Snow said.

"Your new roommate will affect Spring and me, Snowy. Who do you have in mind? What about my cousin Meg?"

"Or, God forbid, we make a new friend." This from Spring, who stared out the picture window, clutching her haversack against her side. She'd been more than weird this past week, starting Sunday morning, when she didn't go with them to eat at Dottie's.

"I'm sorry, am I missing something?" Summer said. "The plan was to go to college together, room together, the Four Seasons. Did y'all change without telling me?"

178

"I want the plan as much as you, Summer, but sometimes things happen that are out of our control." Spring glanced back at her. "If Autumn wants to go to beauty school, let her. She's our friend, and we should support her."

"Thanks, Spring," Autumn said. "I wasn't even sure I was going to apply until May."

"Then you should've told us." She looked at Snow. "Do you have any secrets?"

"No." But by the way she'd given all her attention to the camera, Summer figured she was lying. "Is Babs still selling the Camaro?"

"So she says."

Summer looked at Spring before turning back to Autumn. "What about you, Springroll? Any secrets?"

"If I did, you think I'd tell you now?"

"Summer, just play your guitar," Autumn said as a pink hue filled the gaps between her freckles.

That girl was definitely hiding more than cosmetology school. She'd looked like she had a sunburn their entire freshman year whenever Blaine Snowden walked into the room. The Seasons knew she crushed on him something fierce, but Blaine never noticed. She was his "other" little sister. But if they'd chivvied her into confessing, it would've made nights at Snow's house very awkward.

"I wonder if you're still in love with Blaine," Summer said. Her question stilled the room. Even the machines went into a low hum.

"Summer Wilde, gah, you can be such a jerk." Snow charged at her. "Why would you even . . . bring that . . . What, do you get up and say, 'How can I be mean today?' Maybe I should come at you about a few things."

"Me? Bring it, if you think you're woman enough." Summer slid off the washer. "What you got?"

"Stop. I'm sick of this." Spring stood in the laundromat doorway. "I'm going down the street. You think you can play nice until I get back?"

"Spring, you can't go alone." Autumn, their den mother.

"I'll be fine. Tumbleweed is crawling with shoppers and coppers."

"Where are you going?" Summer followed Spring out the door and down the steps. "Calling Mal?"

"Yes. . . . Yes, I'm calling Mal."

"Then why didn't you say that?"

Spring shrugged, still hugging her haversack close. "I'll be back." She headed down Main, away from O'Sullivan's. Away from the only phone booth in town.

Snow was ready for Summer when she went back inside. "What about you?" she said. "Any secrets?"

"Is this you coming at me? I'm disappointed."

"How about my brother? How you ignored him even though you knew he had a crush on you?"

"If you knew he had a crush on me, Snow, it's not a secret. And I didn't ignore him."

"Did you know Blaine liked you?" Autumn whispered.

"Maybe, but if I said anything, it would get all weird." Summer glanced back at her. "Just like if you admitted you liked him."

"So you're saying you *didn't* like him?" Snow pressed.

"Sure, I did. Everyone liked Blaine, but I didn't *like* like him."

"You had a huge crush on him in ninth grade."

"I got over it." Summer leaned against the doorframe. "And I knew Fall liked him."

"I-I, um, I didn't . . ." Yeah, there was nowhere to go with that one. "Do you like Levi?" Autumn said.

Nice deflection. "Yes, but that's not a secret." Summer stepped out of the laundromat to see if Levi had come to town. Pickups of all shapes and sizes lined the street, but not one was Levi's little red Chevy LUV.

She was about to go back to her machine and guitar when she spotted Spring entering the Rancher's Security Bank. "Hey, y'all, I'll be back."

"Wait, Summer, you can't go alone."

Too late. She snuck down the street and into the bank's beautiful, cool lobby. Glossy, ornate beams crisscrossed the ceiling, and the floors were black-and-white marble. Summer peeked through the etched glass of the interior double doors to see Spring at a teller window, accepting a wad of cash and placing it in her haversack. When she turned to go, Summer ducked down to sneak out the main doors and ran straight into Levi.

"Whoa, where you going, beautiful?" He held her so close she could breathe his skin, clean and fragrant with the open prairie.

"Let's go. I don't want Spring to see me." Now if her knees would stop wobbling, she could make a run for it.

Grabbing her hand, Levi pulled her around the side of the bank, where they watched Spring step off the curb to cross Main Street without checking both ways.

"What was that about?" Levi said.

"I'm not really sure. She's hiding something." Summer watched Spring until she disappeared inside O'Sullivan's, then turned to Levi. "I looked for your truck."

"I looked for you at Tumble Time. I wondered if y'all wanted a ride on the carousel."

"The park is closed."

"True, but . . ." Levi laced his fingers with hers. "I know a guy who knows a guy."

"Are you the guy?"

"I might be. What do you say?"

"I say let's get the laundry in the dryers first."

Levi helped as they moved five loads of bedsheets and towels to the dryers. Spring returned as he dropped dimes in the machines, and the rest of the Seasons sorted and started the next washer round.

"Hey, Levi," Spring said, still hugging her haversack. "Don't tell me Summer roped you into doing our laundry."

"He's arranged for us to ride the carousel," Summer said. "Where have you been?"

"I told you. I went to call Mal." Spring busied herself with her laundry, sorting the colors from the whites, then measuring out detergent. "Autumn, I need a couple of quarters."

With ten machines agitating and tumbling, the Seasons locked their things in the office—except for Spring's haversack—and made their way down a side street, through an alley, and past a row of craftsman cottages to the park.

"Can you really get us a ride?" Summer ran with Levi toward the carousel.

"Watch." He jumped up on the platform and addressed the older man standing by the inner panels, working the gears. "Milo, we good to go?"

"If I get in trouble for this, I'm going to need a whole side of beef as compensation." He looked at the Seasons. "I seen you girls before, ain't I?" Then to Levi. "Which one am I doing this for?"

Levi winked at Summer. "All of them."

He reached for her hand and led her to a pair of horses riding side by side. One white, one black.

The rest of the Seasons chose their trusty steeds, and after some gear grinding, along with a few choice words from Milo, the tinny music of the carousel played, and the ride started round and round, up and down.

"Can I say, 'Weeee!'" Summer kicked out her legs and laughed.

"Go ahead," Levi shouted, then chirruped to his ride and pretended to race.

Every word the Seasons had spat at each other back in the hot laundromat faded with the winsome atmosphere of the park and carousel.

This was quintessential "the best summer of our lives." Summer determined to write about it in her journal. She had to make at least one entry before the summer was over.

"Kids, I'm shutting 'er down," Milo said from inside the operating booth. "I want to be out of here before a bunch of kids come racing at us, wanting to hop on."

While there was no official ordinance against running the carousel, there was the ordinance of public opinion.

"Wait," Snow said. "I need pictures."

Levi schmoozed Milo for one more ride and sealed the deal with a handshake. When Milo said yes, Summer caught the very tip of green in his fist.

Levi, I just might fall in love with you.

Another trip around on the carousel, Summer didn't care a wit about missing Europe, the beach, and all the antics they'd planned for the best summer of their lives.

This was so much better.

Snow worked her photographer magic, then, miraculously, handed the camera to Levi so she could be in some of the shots.

"I've set the f-stop and aperture. Just point, focus, and shoot."

When Milo tried to call it quits again, Summer was the one who charmed him into another go-round. She challenged Autumn to a horse race, and Spring seemed to forget herself and started pratfalling all over the place like one of the Three Stooges, and Summer never laughed so hard.

Then Milo called, "Enough! I'm late for lunch."

"That was a blast."

"Thank you, Levi."

"I needed this so much."

"You're so welcome. *Psst*, Summer." Levi grabbed her hand. "Can you hang back a sec?"

Summer glanced at the departing Seasons, who talked eighty miles an hour in between laughing and singing. She needed to be in on the fun. "I should help fold." Then she looked into Levi's blue eyes. "But sure, I've got a minute. You want to come fold with us?"

"Yeah, but first, let's get some ice cream. Tops is the best."

"Ice cream?" What were the Seasons saying? She was missing the carousel recap. Or Spring confessing that her phone call was really a trip to the bank.

"Summer?"

She turned to Levi. "Lead the way." She slipped her hand into his. He was too kind and generous to turn down. And so very darn cute.

She ordered a cone with two large scoops of chocolate. Levi went with butter pecan. They sat at the stone tables and faced the wind coming off the prairie.

"You busy Fourth of July weekend?" He sat so close their arms touched.

"Got another group of campers coming. *But*, if I were home, I'd be helping with our family party. The Wildes throw the best and biggest Fourth bash and everyone comes." How was Dad going to throw the party without Mom and her clipboard? "Why? What are you doing?"

"I have tickets to Willie Nelson's Fourth of July picnic. A bunch of us are—"

"Get out." She slapped his arm. "You're inviting me to the picnic? The best concert of the year?"

"Can you go? It's on a Sunday, so the laundry will be done."

"Sunday? Right, well, I, um, I don't know." *Girl, what are you doing? Of course you can go!* "The new Tumblers arrive between two and four. And Mom's cuckoo for Cocoa Puffs about her lockdown."

"I heard about the boot print."

"Sergeant Dover said it doesn't match the one they found in Locust Gove, but that actually scared Mom even more, and now we're on double lockdown. She almost made a Tumbler pee herself when she caught her running to the bathroom alone."

"It's scary, though. This guy is out there, maybe killing again."

"I try not to think about it. I don't want to live in fear." But she felt a lot of it . . . fear. Not necessarily about a deranged murderer but about her parents.

"Then there's that Bundy guy in Colorado who's linked to murders of girls your age."

Summer's ice cream soured on her tongue. "Yeah, Mom mentioned him too." She shivered. "Creepy."

"Still," Levi said, "I have two tickets to the concert."

Summer sighed and caught a run of chocolate ice cream down her cone. "I'm not sure. Do you know I'm here because I got in trouble? All of us did. We dumped soap in the FSU pool."

"You what?"

"Sixty gallons of concentrated car wash soap."

Levi muffled his laugh with his fist. "You and those beauty queens you call friends?"

He looked impressed, which made her blush and feel all warm inside. With a bit of pride, she filled him in on the details, ending with how Mom asked the judge to let the Seasons' community service be at Camp Tumbleweed.

"I say lucky me." He nudged her, smiling, and yep, she melted a little. "I'll have to come to your supersized Fourth of July party next year."

"Really? You'd come all the way to Florida?"

Levi took a big, bold bite of his butter pecan. "I'd fly around the world to be with you."

His confession stole any attempt at a pithy reply and quite possibly all of her heart. How could he say that so sincerely? He barely knew her. She'd thought he was only flirting with her for the summer, but now her insides were even more fizzy and gooey, and she wanted him to kiss her.

"You're crazy," she said.

"For you."

She laughed. "Come on, be serious."

"Will your dad still have the party without you and your mom?"

"He says so, but—" She lowered her ice cream, lowered her gaze. *Don't cry. Don't cry.*

Levi scooted over to put his arm around her. "What's wrong?"

She shrugged, then took a big lick of her melting cone. "I miss my dad," she said softly. "He and Mom aren't getting along, and—" She looked up at him. "Dad adopted me when I was three, and sometimes I wonder if he really considers me his kid."

Levi brushed aside the lock of hair that blew over her face. "Sounds like a lie to me. Or fear."

"Maybe." Her ice cream continued to drip as they sat in the afternoon sun. "I mean, he's good to me and Mom. He says he loves me, and we're close but . . ."

The sharp memory of his comment from nine years ago joined them at the table. "I was nine when we had our first Fourth of July barbecue. Dad had just started his business, and all these important people came. At least I thought they were important. I hung around, helping him because I wanted him to be proud of me. Autumn's and Spring's fathers were always saying how proud they were of their grades or for doing their chores. My dad wasn't like that in the beginning."

"Mine's not touchy-feely either or easy with the 'atta boys,' but I know he loves me."

"Yeah, but did he adopt you?"

"You really think that makes a difference? You're his kid, Summer. He gave you his *name*."

"Then why did he call me 'Lily's kid'? That's what he said. To one of the important-looking men at the party. 'She's Lily's kid.'" The edges of his comment had dulled over time, but saying it out loud to Levi made the phrase sharp again.

"Why don't you just ask him?"

"Be real."

"I am. I mean, if it's bothering you—"

"We should go." Summer tossed the last of her cone in the trash, rinsed her sticky fingers in the water fountain, and wished for one of Autumn's hair ties. "The Seasons will string me up if I don't help."

"Blame me." Levi tossed the last of his cone and drew her close. "How could your dad not love you? You're so lovable."

For a second—and only a second—Summer wrapped her arms around him, rested her head against his chest, and let her burden go while accepting his compliment. It felt good to lean on him.

"Thanks. I mean it."

He wrapped his arms around her and held tight. "Anytime. I mean it."

He walked her back to Tumble Time, past the old movie theater, the Galaxy, where the marquee advertised *John Wayne at His Best in El Dorado*.

"Old Man Rafferty owns the place," Levi said. "He shows what he wants. The old Hollywood stuff. Believe me, you get desperate enough for a night out and a bucket of popcorn that you'll watch *El Dorado* for the thirty-ninth time." Levi laughed. "My brother and I know all the lines. But Mr. Rafferty is a good egg, and—"

She grabbed his shirt, pulled him down, and kissed him. The move was awkward and bumpy with her lips landing mostly on his cheek. But in that moment, her heart was his.

She broke away after a few seconds, hand over her mouth. "I can't believe I did that. In the middle of Main Street."

He said nothing but grabbed her hand and ducked between the theater and Robinson's Furniture. Gripping her waist, he pulled her in, kissing her, his entire being radiating heat. She'd been kissed before but not like this. Not in a way that made her extra glad to be a girl.

"Sh-shew," he said, lifting his head. "I'm so glad that's out of the way."

"Guess so." She grinned and kissed him again, quickly. This time hitting her mark. "I needed to correct my mistake."

Levi wrapped her in his arms for another kiss, lightly picking her up, which almost made her swoon.

"I like kissing you," he said.

"I like kissing you. But I'm desperately late to fold clothes."

"I'll help. And I'll buy everyone's lunch."

"You don't have to do that, Levi."

"Are you kidding? This is my day to impress you."

She leaned against his arm as their footsteps echoed in unison. "Is the invitation to Willie Nelson still on the table?"

"Absolutely."

187

19

California Dreamin'

Snow

JUNE '97
HOLLYWOOD HILLS

"The studio called, love. They're anxious to read the script."
Snow's husband, Loudon, took a seat in Paps' old wingback chair,
the one she'd shipped from Tallahassee when Mom got married.

"They called again?" She turned the screen so Loudon couldn't
see. "Good news, I'm nearly done." Not true but she *intended* to
be done. That had to count for something.

"Really?" He made the appropriate face of disbelief. "Just five
days ago, you complained about being stuck."

"Really, Loudon, why can't you be like most men and forget
what I say the moment I say it?"

"You knew when you married me I was no ordinary bloke."

True. Which was why she'd fallen hopelessly, unapologetically in love.

As for her writing? She was blocked for the first time in her writing life, and it terrified her.

She had shelves of old or partially completed romantic comedy screenplays. The ones she wrote and wrote and wrote during and after college.

Then it happened. She hit Hollywood magic. First, she met Loudon, a British actor, writer, and producer from a distinguished family with very deep pockets.

Looking to impress her, he'd invited Snow to a Sunday brunch at the home of Hollywood's up-and-coming director, Raymond Daschle. His wife, actress Rachel Hayes, was as beautiful as she was talented, and the fresh face of Hollywood films.

Loudon, being Loudon, with his aristocratic confidence and upper-crust accent, pitched Snow's screenplay, *Funny Is Always in Love*, to Raymond.

The calculating, reserved Snow Snowden fell in love that night. Not because he pitched her movie, but because he believed in her.

A year later, they married on the grounds of the historic Adamson House in Malibu, with the sunset blazing red, gold, and orange. A year and one month after their first anniversary, baby girl Olive completed their family.

What happened with *Funny Is Always in Love*? Raymond loved it. Called Snow at two in the morning, laughing. *"Let's make a rom-com."*

"Do you think I've lost it?" Snow stared out the window as she asked her question. "My mojo? My ability to write anything good?"

He grinned. "No, darling. Never. We started our production company last year because of your talent." He stretched forward to see her computer. "Do you have *anything* written?" He motioned to the bookshelves loaded with the old scripts. "Maybe you could—"

"No. Old scripts are a monster to rewrite and fix. I have the story idea. After all, Snowden Films pitched the treatment. It's just . . ."

"You're stuck."

"Stop saying that." She'd never concede to being stuck. Falling into a funk, maybe, but *never* stuck. "My problem is my husband keeps interrupting me. Aren't you supposed to pick up Olive this afternoon?" Their six-year-old had dance and gymnastic classes all summer.

"Yes, I'm off now." Loudon pushed up from the chair and kissed her cheek. "You can do this, Snow."

Did she have a choice? She *had* to do this.

This summer her usual funk around the anniversary of Blaine's death hit a bit early. Typically they'd be on vacation, but their fledgling production company demanded their attention.

Then she'd happened on an article about the twentieth anniversary of the Camp Scott murders, and the memories of that summer came flooding back.

Something happened on her thirty-eighth birthday too. She felt it. She missed her childhood. She missed the Four Seasons and the girl she'd been. If not for Spring, Summer, and Autumn, she would've been the shy kid in the back of the class, scribbling in her notebook, dreaming up stories.

If not for them, she'd have been a high school wallflower. If not for them, she'd have gone through Blaine's death alone. Though if not for one of them, he might still be alive.

If not for them, she'd not have gone to UCLA or written screenplay after screenplay. There'd be no Loudon or Raymond Daschle. No romantic comedy that won four Academy Awards. No Olive.

Snow glanced back at the fireplace mantel, where her golden statue sat in the shade.

Funny was a huge hit. Critics compared it to *It Happened One Night* and *Philadelphia Story*. The lead actress earned an Oscar nomination. Raymond won for directing, and Snow for best screenplay. One of the supporting actors also won.

Doors she never knew existed suddenly opened. Since then, she'd written, produced, and even directed three more hit rom-coms. She was on the fast track. Until now.

But the wall she hit wasn't just her birthday or the Camp Scott murders or even the twenty-second anniversary of Blaine's death.

The wall rose up when Mom drove out with her husband for their annual spring visit.

"We were cleaning out the guest room over the garage and came across your old photo albums, some old movies you took, yearbooks, and boxes of your black-and-white prints. You always had a good eye, Snowy."

Dad, as she'd started calling Jeff Wilde about ten years ago, hauled in Paps' old army trunk of memorabilia.

She'd started dreaming of the Seasons as they used to be— sisters, best friends, full of dreams and laughter. Last night, she dreamed they were going around and around the rink at Skate Inn East until the light from the disco ball transported them mysteriously to the Tumbleweed carousel. All while the Bee Gees sang "How Deep Is Your Love."

Ever since then, she'd felt . . . *homesick*. It's the only way to describe it. A few weeks ago, she spent an afternoon going through the photos in the trunk instead of writing.

"Darling?" Loudon strode back into her office. "The Daschles rang, invited us over for dinner. Ray's throwing some steaks on the grill."

"Not sure I have time. I really need to work." Sit up. Face the computer screen. Fingers on keyboard. Go! "Though Olive would love it. She thinks Kate and Chloe are her best friends."

The Daschles' young teenage daughters treated Olive like a little sister, taking her out to lunch and shopping, or to the beach.

"He's invited the Gondas too. It'd be good to connect with them. Jeremiah just started a film with Clive Boston, and Raymond said Laura's performance in *Field of Gold* will get her a Golden Globe, if not an Oscar."

"You're saying I should go then?"

Loudon leaned over her, compassion in his eyes. "Maybe a break will give you inspiration. You can always talk to Ray or Jer about being—"

"Don't say it." *Stuck.*

"—whatever it is you are."

Snow closed her document and shut off the computer screen. "The thing is, love, I don't know if I have a rom-com in me. I don't feel funny."

"It's about the Seasons, isn't it?" Loudon knelt next to her chair.

"Maybe. I don't know." She'd shared Season stories with her husband over the years. He'd gone as her boyfriend to Spring's wedding.

He'd joined her for an hour the afternoon she looked through the old photos and yearbooks, listening to her stories, laughing. Even so, Snow felt sure Loudon didn't really understand what it meant to be a Season. What it meant to lose her entire childhood.

"If your heart needs to talk about Summer, Autumn, and Spring by writing a script, then do it. We'll produce it. I'll find the right studio partnership."

"The queen of the rom-com telling a serious coming-of-age story? I'm not sure Tinsel Town is ready for that, love."

"Then they'll adjust. Give it some thought, Snow. You're a brilliant writer and—"

"Go get Olive. She hates to be the last one picked up." She kissed him softly. "I need to shower if we're going to the Daschles'."

Loudon left and Snow stood under a steady stream of hot water, trying to imagine the plot of a serious film. One about the Seasons.

She saw the beginning—the four of them becoming friends in kindergarten—followed by the middle: a coming-of-age journey that included the FSU pool debacle and the bus ride to Tumbleweed.

Then the black moment. The four of them yelling at each other that night on the dock.

And that's where the story ended. No overhaul or recovery. No healing for a happy ending.

Just a bunch of hurt and confusion.

And fade to black.

193

20

You Should
Be Dancing

Autumn

'77

There were moments when Summer Wilde demanded admiration. Okay, lots of moments, if Autumn was honest. Her brash bravado had inspired more fun than trouble while they were growing up.

She'd certainly brought her out of her shell, along with Snow. If memory served, Summer was the first to break the ice at Spring's birthday party, the one that kicked off their friendship. Right then and there, she became the perfect balance for the frilly and persnickety six-year-old Spring.

Why the current admiration? Summer was convincing Lily to let them have a barn dance. Her skill was unparalleled. Her negotiation was akin to watching Mozart compose an opera or Renoir paint a beach scene. There was an elegance to Summer's brashness.

Autumn focused on her argument, hoping to learn something.

"Mom, the town used to have a dance on the weekends until the murders. So why not have one here, with us?"

"If the town canceled, I don't see how we can start one up, Summer. We're showing respect. We have the play, that's enough."

"Showing respect or living in fear?" She looked to Moxie for help. "It'll be like the play. Just us. I didn't bring my record player and records to sit under my bunk. Come on." Summer grabbed her mother's hands and did a jig. "Please?"

"We'll draw too much attention." Lily pulled her hands away.

"Oh, good grief. Mom, take a chill pill. Have some fun. You and Moxie."

"Leave me out," Moxie said. "I had plenty of fun dances at your age. Yours too, Lily."

"See, she wants you to have fun. And what about Greta?" Summer snatched the edge of the girl's T-shirt and pulled her under her arm. "She needs to dance."

Autumn stepped up to help. "I agree. For Greta. This is her camp too. She's stuck here all summer and needs more fun than horseback riding on the weekends."

"Skip let me ride a minibike today," Greta said.

"And she had a whale of a time." Lily seemed resolved. No dance.

Summer patted Greta on the head. "No more talk of fun, Greta. Work with me here. I'm trying to get us a barn dance."

The girl flipped on a dime, facing Lily with the perfect eleven-year-old pout. "Please, Lily. I've never been to a dance."

Lily laughed and caved like a house of cards. "Fine, but no boys." She looked at Summer. "I mean it."

"Wouldn't even know where to find one at this point."

Autumn would bet her future cosmetology license Summer would invite Levi if at all possible. They were pretty cozy while riding the carousel, and later at Tumble Time.

"This is a Four Seasons dance, Mom," Summer said. "With and for this girl." She squeezed Greta close. "And of course, you and Moxie too. What about the deputies?"

"Well, I suppose we should invite the 'rent-a-fuzz,' as you say." Lily smiled as if the idea of a dance might break off her fear.

Well done, Summer.

Summer let go an ear-piercing whistle and rounded up the Seasons. Her dad taught her how to whistle with her fingers when they were in sixth grade, and for a year, she whistled at everything and everyone. Nearly got the four of them beat up when she sat behind high schoolers at a football game and whistled at some guy's girlfriend. He thought another dude was the culprit and . . . Autumn smiled, remembering how they ran when Summer was spotted.

She wished she'd never heard what Lily whispered to the sergeant. Maybe she'd dance so hard tonight it'd fall out of her head, instead of accidentally falling out of her mouth—like things did sometimes.

"The dance is on, Seasons!" Summer shouted.

Everyone went into motion, accepting assignments for food, lights, music, outfits, and Lily went to let the deputies on duty know.

Autumn changed into the only summer dress she'd brought and thought about Blaine. For her sixteenth birthday, all she'd wanted was a slow dance with him. But every time the DJ called for a couple's dance, he took Summer's hand.

Still, she hadn't given up. One day he'd notice her and realize she was his one true love. That day at the Springs, when he dove off the top platform, she'd been on her way to talk to him, attempt to flirt.

She saw and heard everything—Blaine, his lifeless body trapped underwater, unable to move.

For the past two years, she'd tried to forget what she saw, heard, and felt that day. The more she tried, the more the images wrapped her in fear. If one more person asked her why she wasn't swimming, she'd scream.

Maybe she'd dance even harder tonight and all the bad memories would fall out of her head.

But she wanted to keep her love for him. Even if he hadn't loved her back, he'd been one of her best friends.

Summer walked by, and Autumn wondered for the millionth time how she could not love him. He was the coolest. Smart and fun, desperately cute. Sweet and kind.

Because if Summer had loved him, Blaine Snowden would be alive today. Snow confided this to Autumn more than once in secret, and she believed it.

By the time Moxie rang the camp bell to officially start the dance, the barn glowed like something from the fairy tales Jenna and Janna loved. Skip had wired up a couple more fixtures for the play, and all the lights were blazing.

Up by the stage, Summer and Snow set up the record player and looked through Summer's records.

At her makeup chair, Autumn braided and pinned everyone's hair, brushed on mascara and a touch of lip gloss. Even Lily took a turn.

"Moxie? Saving the best for last." Autumn patted her chair.

"I don't do makeup, darling." Moxie patted her arm. "Never have."

"Just some lip gloss?" Autumn held up a new tube of nude. "Maybe some blush."

Moxie twisted up her expression. "Lip gloss. Nothing else." She sat for Autumn's ministrations, then looked approvingly in the mirror. "Well, that's not so bad, is it?"

"Never is." Autumn handed her the tube. "Keep it. It looks good on you."

To her surprise, the older woman teared up. "I never saw

myself as pretty growing up. I was a tomboy, and then joined the army. Didn't have time to mess with hair and makeup." She swallowed the choke in her words. "So, thank you, Autumn. I mean it."

She grabbed her in a tight hug. "You're welcome." See, this *was* what her heart longed to do.

Music suddenly filled the barn. Sergeant Dover and one rent-a-deputy leaned against the doorframe with amused smirks.

"Have a cookie." Summer pointed to a box on the props table.

"Come, join us." Autumn waved them toward the dance floor, even though no one was on it yet.

"I don't dance," said the older man. He reminded Autumn of her sweet grandpa in Indiana. "But I do eat cookies."

"It's looking like a party in here." Lily stood next to the sergeant. Even in her camp director outfit, with Autumn's light touches, she was beautiful. By the look on Sergeant Dover's face, he thought so too.

Lily had lost weight since camp started. The businesswoman with styled hair and perfect makeup was now tan and natural-looking, but with an ever-present worried look in her eyes. The murders? Camp Tumbleweed? Her marriage? Summer? All of the above?

Greta gave Lily a hug, who bent over and whispered something that made her laugh. She was a great camp director, giving so freely to the girls, especially Greta.

"Know what, y'all?" Summer moved into the center aisle, a record album in hand. "Greta is one of us. Spring, Snow, Autumn, how about if we induct her into our group as Baby Season?"

Greta's eyes popped wide, and she covered her mouth with her hand. "Really?"

"What a great idea," Autumn said. "Yes!"

"All in favor?" Summer said.

And the ayes had it. Greta was officially a Season.

"Thank you, thank you." She snatched each one of them in her lean, tan, and remarkably strong arms. No wonder she swam to the rock and back all the time. Autumn envied the girl's courage.

May you never learn to be afraid, Greta-girl.

Autumn held on to her a moment longer than the others, missing her own siblings, willing her love to protect this girl from harm for the rest of her life.

Lily squeezed Summer's hand—*Well done*—and laughed as Summer popped her mom a high five.

"Let's dance!" Summer's shout rattled the rafters, and the guitar rift of Fleetwood Mac's "Second Hand News" filled the old barn.

Snow grabbed the mic prop from the makeshift stage and danced down the aisle toward Autumn, singing at the top of her lungs.

Snowy, Snowy, I love you.

Underneath her winter exterior was a vibrant girl trying to find her way. Summer sashayed after her, dancing in a circle and waving her arms.

"Come on, y'all. 'I'm just second hand news . . .'"

Autumn grabbed Greta's hand and attempted to dance the Bump. Oops, a little too hard. She hip-butted Baby Season into one of the stalls.

"Let's try again." Autumn laughed as Greta gave her a monstrous bump, and that's when they found the beat.

Moxie and Spring arrived with pitchers of lemonade and bowls of popcorn and pretzels.

Lily danced a crazy version of the Charleston, but gosh, she was so graceful. Then Moxie, oh Moxie, get some rhythm, will you? By the time Summer spun a new record, Moxie had them all doing the jitterbug and the Lindy Hop.

Sergeant Dover and the grandpa rent-a-cop watched, laughing, then disappeared to do their rounds.

Summer went all bubble gum on the next song with Donny Osmond's "Puppy Love," then grabbed Greta for a dance.

"Autumn, remember when you were going to marry Donny Osmond?" Summer twirled Greta under her arm.

"And you were going to marry David Cassidy."

David was Summer's celebrity crush after Bobby Sherman. Thus the great debate of seventh grade: Who was cooler—Donny or David?

Autumn caught Spring's eye and moved over to where she sat on a hay bale. "Are you going to dance?"

"Sure. Waiting for the right song."

"Remember our first sock hop?"

"You and Snow sat on the bleachers until Blaine got his buddies to pull you out on the dance floor."

"He was a good dancer . . . Blaine."

Spring glanced at her. "You miss him, don't you?"

Ah, why did her eyes have to water? "We all do."

"You more than the rest of us?" Spring squeezed Autumn's hand. "I know Summer went after you at Tumble Time, but you don't have to defend how you felt about him."

"I was hoping he would eventually see me as more than a friend or little sister."

"You're too beautiful for him not to give in eventually."

"Naw, he was hot for Summer."

"Isn't every guy?" Spring said. "We roll into town and she picks up the foxiest cowboy."

"She doesn't even know how magnetic she is." Autumn slid off the hay bale to grab a handful of popcorn. "And you, so perfectly beautiful. Spring, are you okay? You look tired."

"I am a little. Camp life, you know?"

"Are you missing Mal? Do you think you'll survive being apart for four years?"

Spring looked away. "I'm not sure, but right now, we're missing the dance." She yanked Autumn to her feet and sent popcorn everywhere. Ah, who cares?

Summer spun the Jackson 5's "ABC" before really getting the party hopping with the rhythmic opening of "Listen to the Music."

"Everyone on the dance floor!" she shouted.

Lily, Moxie, Snow, Summer, Spring, Greta, Sergeant Dover, and even the grandpa, whose name was Dutch, juked and jived.

Who knew the old man with a badge and gun could swing those hips now.

"Soul Train Dance Line!" Autumn shouted over the music. The movement and laughter had chased away her shadows.

The Seasons, Moxie and Lily, and the deputies formed a tunnel in the center aisle. Summer was the first down, doing all sorts of moves. Then ol' Dutch hopped to the start of the line and did a funky little shuffle. Dang, Dutch. So cool. Now she missed her grandpa all the more.

Sergeant Dover grabbed Lily and jitterbugged from one end to the next. Hey, they were pretty good.

Next Greta stood at the beginning of the line, hesitating with a shy giggle. "I don't know what to do."

"Do what you've been doing. Move, dance, shimmy." Summer gave a shoulder shake.

"You can do it, Baby Season," Spring said, clapping and swaying.

Snow started the song again, and Greta took a step down the line with her arms wrapped around her waist. She took another step and swayed a little.

"Greta-girl, if you want to be a real Season," Autumn said, "let it *rip*!"

With a shy, perhaps impish, grin, Greta flung her arms wide and started to dance, juking and jiving, working a move that might have been the Hustle, Autumn wasn't quite sure. But sweet Baby Season had just blown up the night.

"Listen to the Music" faded to "China Grove," and the line dissipated. Everyone simply danced.

Long gone was their arrest, the appearance before the judge, and the never-ending bus ride to Tumbleweed. Tonight there was no lockdown or murderer on the loose. Forget the lost trip to Europe or parents who were four thousand miles away in Paris and

London. Forget beautiful boys who died much too young. Forget overheard confessions and secrets never to be revealed.

Autumn was one of the Four plus Baby Season. This was the last summer of their youth. The best friends from kindergarten to high school, from Starlight, Twilight, Moonglow, and Sunglow, were having the time of their lives.

21

Jesus Is Just All Right

Summer

'77

"I need some air." Summer exited the warm barn into the muggy Oklahoma night. A slight breeze came off the lake, and she lifted her hair to cool off.

The dancing, music, and laughter reminded her of the summer they were fifteen. They'd all landed jobs at Publix, and the bag boys and part-time stockers whistled and winked at them like they were the most beautiful girls on earth.

While she and Spring honed their flirting skills, Snow sharpened her sarcasm blade, and Autumn said things like, *"I have six siblings. If I go on a date, one of them has to go with me. House rule."*

Autumn hadn't wanted to date the cute boys at Publix since

she was in love with Blaine. Summer suspected he was one of the reasons Autumn was so close to Snow.

"It's hot in there." Autumn appeared next to Summer. "Greta's having a ball. She's so cute and kind of incredible, isn't she?"

"She's our Baby Season."

"We'll have to keep in touch with her. Hey, Summer, can I ask you something?"

Summer turned to her friend, who looked like Shelley Hack walking across the street in a Charlie perfume commercial. Lean, with an easy sophistication. "Shoot."

Autumn kicked at the dirt, then bent down to brush off the toe of her white Keds. "Um, what was your dad doing before he married your mom?"

"Why?" What a weird question.

Autumn shrugged and glanced toward the cabins. "No reason, just wondered. I don't think I ever heard what he did or where he lived." The light from the barn accented the tips of the tree branches and made Summer think of Christmas.

"He worked for the state for a while in city planning, then moved to Atlanta to work for a civil engineering company. He came back to Tallahassee to start his own company and met Mom."

"How'd they meet? I can't remember."

"At a party. Mutual friends. Autumn, why are you asking?"

"No reason, really. Filling in the gaps of my Season family knowledge."

Summer slipped her arm through Autumn's and leaned close. "Tell me if you know something. Do you? Is he having an affair? Is Mom? Is that why she's here?" Gasp. "That what you overheard?"

"What? No. An affair? Please, Jeff and Lily cheating on each other? Not in our lifetime."

Summer pinched her arm. "You promise you don't know anything?"

"Cross my heart, hope to die, stick a needle in my eye."

Summer laughed. "Let's not go overboard. No need for needles in eyes. And I certainly can't have you dead. The Four Seasons square would fall apart."

"Five now."

"True. Baby Season will probaby be the center that holds us all together."

"When we're old and fat."

"Can't walk or feed ourselves."

"Or drive."

They laughed and leaned on each other as the music changed from "Car Wash" to "Turn the Beat Around."

"Ooh, I love this song." Autumn headed inside but paused and pointed toward the clump of dark trees. "Is that your mom with the sergeant?"

Two silhouettes on the edge of light walked toward them. Were they holding hands? Summer moved around Autumn for a better look. What the—

But when they broke into the light emanating from the barn, Mom's hands were in her pockets and the sergeant was three paces behind her.

"I'm so glad you talked me into this, Summer," Mom said. "I needed a night of fun."

"Not too much fun," Summer said with an eye on Dover.

"Is there such a thing? Spring, Moxie, is there any more lemonade?" Mom started inside, then, "Cody? Want something to drink?"

"What were you two doing?" Summer followed Mom while shooting Cody a sharp eye. Dad had *Sandeee* and Mom had *Codeee*.

"Cody and Dutch were bringing me up to date on the Camp Scott investigation." Mom took the lemonade Moxie offered. "They found pictures of some women in a cave, but they—"

"—have no clue as to the whereabouts of Gene Hart. We need to be on the alert." Dover poured his own lemonade and grabbed a handful of pretzels.

The Mayes County sheriff claimed the murders were the work

of a prison escapee, Gene Hart, but so far, they had little to no evidence.

"Do they think he's near here?" Summer said.

"He's probably hiding in the caves or on an Indian reservation over in Mayes."

"Then we don't have to be on lockdown?" Summer turned to her mother even though not much would change if Mom miraculously ended the lockdown. The rigors of camp kept them busy and tired. But Summer could escape with Levi for the Willie Nelson picnic with a little less guilt.

"Nice try, Summer. We don't know the owner of our mystery boot prints, so we will remain on double lockdown for the duration of camp," Mom said. "I've pledged the utmost safety to the parents."

Locked down for a boot print of a man they didn't know or see.

"Let's forget all of that for tonight." Mom gulped down her drink and set the cup on the table. "I'm on the hunt for a dance partner. Greta-girl, let's dance."

The deputy paused by Summer, smiled with a nod, then made tracks for the dance floor. Summer snarled. What was that look? Did he *like* Mom?

"She's married, goofball." Her low words barely made it to her own ears, let alone Dover's.

Retreating outside to cool off only stoked her smoldering fear about her parents. She'd let her cares fade away between the carousel ride, ice cream with Levi, the barn dance.

Yet in the snap of a man's glance, her fears returned.

Autumn was right, though, wasn't she? Her parents were not the cheating type. So what bugged her? Why did Mom sign up for a summer away?

Nothing in life was sure. Who knew Blaine would hit his head and die at eighteen? Or that the Seasons would get swept up in mob mentality and vandalize the pool of their future university? Or that a murderer would claim the life of three little girls?

Who knew she'd meet Levi Foley? The cherry atop a pile of poop.

From the barn, Stevie Wonder's "Sir Duke" filled the air. "You can feel it all over . . ."

That's when Summer saw the bright light shooting through the trees. Startled, she hesitated, then moved toward it. Was there a fire? She sniffed the air. It smelled like the dew of night and the cooling prarie.

The flash of light gave way to a glow pressing through a dark clump of trees. Working her way toward the deputy's campfire, she found Dutch watching a small, contained flame.

"Oh, hey, Dutch, I thought I saw—" She did. There. Beyond the camp. Just like last week. "A light."

Dutch didn't respond. Just maintained his attention on the fire. "Dutch, do you see the light out there?" Summer pressed on and stopped at the edge of the camp.

The big top was back, along with the girl singing center stage.

"Don't tell me you can't see and hear that, Dutch," Summer called over her shoulder. "Dutch, hey." He wasn't hard of hearing when he shuffled down the dance line. "Dutch!"

Yet he lifted his head only to add more wood to the fire. Pulling a tin of tobacco from his pocket, he stuffed his cheek with a pinch, sat back down on the log, and looked right through Summer toward the lit tent. With a yawn, he rested against a tree and closed his eyes.

Impossible. He didn't see her or the tent.

What was going on? Summer anchored herself with a glance at the barn, where the light fell through the wide-open door along with the music of the Bee Gees.

Still, it was the happenings under the mysterious tent that captured her. Summer crossed the camp border into the meadow, ducked under the canvas, and stood on the sawdust floor.

The singer wore a white peasant blouse, bell-bottoms, and platform shoes. Her band was the same—a drummer with all the layers and flares in his hair, and an upright bass player sporting a crew cut.

"*Summer, come!*" The voice came from the tent. The one with the bright, vibrant tone.

She spun toward the campfire. "Dutch, hey, can't you—" The man was napping.

"*Summer! Go back.*" The other voice. The dark one she didn't like as much. Chills slipped down her arms, but she wasn't afraid.

She was curious. This was some strange Midwest version of *Brigadoon.* Maybe she should go back to the barn, to her friends and the dancing. Yet this tent . . . with the serene and pristine air.

She debated going forward against the merits of going back. Along with the music, sawdust floor, and mere existence of a tent magically popping up on the prairie, she couldn't make out why there were rows and rows of empty chairs. Where were the people?

The girl was talking to the band, and Summer *felt* as if she were talking to the band. This was nuts.

Just then the singer returned to the microphone, welcomed everyone—what everyone?—and started singing. "Put your hand in the hand of the man who stilled the water." Her voice floated loud and strong over the prairie.

"Welcome." Summer jumped as an older gentleman lightly touched her arm. "We're glad you're here."

"We? I'm the only one." Summer fixed on him a moment longer. He also looked, *felt*, familiar.

"The Preacher said you were enough." The tone of his voice seemed to fold her into the nearest chair, and after he'd handed her a Bible, he disappeared.

Now she was scared. Yet too terrified to run. Setting the Bible on the seat beside her, she hoped Mom didn't notice her absence. She'd freak out if she thought Summer was missing.

The singer circled through the chorus a second time, and Summer sang along. She had the Anne Murray record collection.

"Put your hand in the hand . . ."

What did that old man mean when he said, *"The Preacher said you were enough"*?

Let's see, there was an older couple up front in the middle, clapping offbeat but doing their darndest to keep up. On the far left, a young family looking a bit down on their luck took up half a row, and in the back, a rather rugged, too-long-on-the-trail cowpoke sat with his head down, shoulders shaking.

The singer ended the song with a happy chomp on the strings and a "hallelujah!" The drummer crashed the symbols, which made the old folks flinch, then laugh and wave their hands in the air.

The girl's next song was sweet and slow, about Jesus being bruised and scarred for "our iniquity" and being nailed to a rugged cross. Tears clung to Summer's lashes as an image of a bloodied, beaten man hanging on a cross by the thread of His skin filled her mind's eye.

She scrubbed her tears away with the back of her hand and wiped them on her shorts. She'd not get caught up in religious manipulation.

Sure, sure, she knew the stories from VBS and Sunday school with Spring. She'd listened to the felt-board stories of the man who walked on water and somehow magically fed thousands of people with a couple of fish and loaves of bread. She'd sung "Jesus Loves Me" so many times she woke up with it in her head now and then.

But this . . . what was happening here . . . was different. It was otherworldly, with a presence in the air, a weight of something divine.

The music lingered as the girl played a simple melody, her head back and eyes closed. The drummer followed with soft rim shots, and the bass player's fingers nimbly hummed up and down the tall fret.

The longer Summer sat and listened, the heavier the presence became until she just crumpled from her seat to the ground.

Facedown, weeping, the unfamiliar lyrics became her testimony.

She was sooty and stained, as if she'd run through the charred firewood and ashes of the deputies' firepit. She rubbed her hand down her arm, but her effort only seemed to spread the grime.

The music changed to a minor chord, and the girl's haunting voice beckoned. "I surrender, I surrender."

Sinking lower, her tears nonstop, Summer hid behind her hands. She wanted to run, to get back to the fun, laughter, and music of the barn, but her legs were married to the sawdust.

She knew the call was to Jesus, the invisible God who was somehow a man. But she didn't need God. Wasn't He for the poor, the weak, the broken?

Someone draped a blanket or something around her shoulders. Summer tried to shrug it off. It was too hot for a covering. But when she tried to see who stood behind her, she was alone.

The pressure of the blanket settled heavier and heavier. A sensation saturated her. And it was nothing like the haunting she'd experienced at Jenny Reed's slumber party séance. *That* scared the wits out of her. Cold. Dark. Ominous. Like the other voice in the camp's woods.

This presence was love. Overwhelming and pure. The breeze under the tent stirred and smelled like the prairie after a rain. Summer inhaled, fighting another wash of tears. Love, love, love spread to every part of her.

Was she loved? When she'd let everyone down? When she was so jealous of Spring she could scream? Or envious of Autumn and her big brain along with her crazy, loving family? Or Snow and her focus, her silent brilliance? She didn't think she was brilliant, but oh, Margaret Snowden was the most brilliant of them all.

Summer was the unwanted pregnancy whose real father abandoned them. Jeff Wilde adopted her so Mom would marry him. If they separated, would he still be her father?

Who was she made to be? She had so many dreams, yet none at all. Could she really be a singer, like the girl on the stage? Could she make a living with her silly songs and guitar? Why would the

God of the universe, who she could not see, want her, when the flesh-and-bone man who'd fathered her did not?

The more her thoughts tumbled, the more the presence enveloped her, pressing on her until she lay prostrate, confessing every sin from stealing candy from the Sing convenience store to almost *doing it* with Billy Crumpet last May before the bubble bath party. She'd not confessed that to anyone, not even Spring.

Thank goodness some frat brother knocked on the door, asking Billy if they could use his truck to get car wash soap. Summer was the first one out of the room. *"Cool. Let's go."*

"I'm sorry, so sorry." She wasn't even sure why she was sorry except the presence was so utterly pure. She had no goodness in her to match it, so the word just kept flowing from deep, deep down.

With sawdust clinging to her lips, she repeated her confessions. After the tenth or eleventh time, the words felt dull and flat, and the presence waned along with her tears.

Above her, a chair creaked, and when she sat up, hair in her face and sawdust sticking to her cheeks, a man with crystal eyes stared down at her with such love she felt emptied of herself and full of Him. She loved Him. Truly. Because somehow she knew He loved her. This was so outta sight.

Instantly, she knew she'd give everything for Him. To Him. She'd do whatever He asked. What did anything matter when His love was so consuming? This must be what the Jesus hippies talked about.

"He's the best high ever, man."

"You love me?" she whispered.

He smiled and swept her hair away from her eyes. "I love you." Then He offered His hand, pulled her from the sawdust. "Come, sing for Me."

Summer pulled her hand free. "Wait just a second. I've got a few questions."

He waited, listening.

"Okay, who the heck are You?"

"Who do you say I am?"

"I'm shooting in the dark here, but Jesus? Don't you live in heaven?"

The Preacher gave her such a fiery gaze that it burned up every fear, doubt, worry, and pain. "Come, follow Me."

Summer woke in her bed at the clang of the breakfast bell, still wearing her shirt, shorts, and sneakers from the night before.

She shot up. A dream. It was all a wild, crazy dream. What had Moxie put in the lemonade? She rubbed the sleep from her eyes— man, she'd slept like a rock—then raked her fingers through her hair. Pieces of sawdust peppered her legs.

Bursting from the cabin, Summer ran through the trees, still cloaked with the night's shadows, to the beginning of the meadow. There was no tent, no crushed prairie grass from a sawdust floor, no evidence of anything she'd experienced.

"Wha—" Was she in the wrong place? But no, the deputies' firepit was right behind her. The tent was right . . . *there*. . . .

She'd seen the lights, touched the chairs and sawdust, heard the music, talked to the man with eyes like liquid fire who smelled better than any cologne at the Gayfers counter. Summer slapped her hand over her pounding heart. Even now, a residue of the presence remained with her. She felt different. Clean.

"Summer Wilde, what in the world?" Mom charged toward her like a mama bear. "You scared the what's-it out of us last night, disappearing, not saying a word to anyone."

"I didn't disappear. I went to the tent meeting. Right over there."

"Summer, please." Mom sighed. "I don't want to play your games. Next time you want to go to bed early, tell us. We scoured the camp all the way down to the road and across the prairie. Cody called in extra men."

"What? When? Why didn't he ask Dutch? He saw me." *But did he?* "I walked right past him to the tent meeting."

"What tent meeting?"

"Well, it's gone now, but it was right over there." Of which there was zero evidence.

Was she losing her mind? She'd learned in her psych class that schizophrenia and other mental illnesses could strike teens and folks in their twenties but . . .

"Mom, I—" Summer knew what she saw, what she felt and heard. Last night she'd touched something more real than real. More true than the sun rising in the east or the tall grass beneath her feet.

Mom drew her into a crushing hug. "I love you, Summer, so much. I want the best for you. I'll die if anything happens to you."

"Sorry. I should've told you I was going to bed." She had no memory of going to bed. Only that she'd followed the Preacher to the stage. Summer rested her chin on Mom's shoulder. "I love you too."

"You are going to change the world, Summer." Mom angled back to see her face. "You just have to control your urge to do what you want when you want. You're so impulsive."

"Isn't that what makes me lovable?"

Mom's laugh sounded like her old self. "I know you're worried about Dad and me, but put it out of your head. We'll be all right. You focus on having the best summer of your life. Treasure your friends. You're lucky to have them. Life has a way of changing in a moment."

"Not for the Seasons, Mom. We'll be best friends for the rest of our lives."

"I know you will. Now come on. Moxie made pancakes and bacon." She hooked her arm around Summer's shoulder, made a funny face, and sniffed her hair. "Summie, darling, why on earth do you smell like sawdust?"

22

Fire and Rain

Autumn

'97
TALLAHASSEE

In her Lake Iamonia home, Autumn poured a small glass of wine, then stared out the window at the pool's quiet blue water.

She'd broken an unspoken rule by having lunch with Spring twice within a week. Now she yearned for what she'd lost. Her old friends. What was it Spring said?

"All for one, one for all. No one can be missing from the square, and . . . that cannot be fixed."

She'd never put words to it before, but Spring was right. The Four Seasons could not be fixed, and Autumn was the one who'd broken them.

Their teenage conversations lived in her memories. The mornings she piled into Spring's or Snow's car for school seemed like yesterday. Looking at her pool, she could almost hear the splashing and shouting at one of Summer's pool parties.

And sometimes, between appointments and doing the salon's books, she'd catch a sweet scent of that Oklahoma prairie.

Yet Autumn knew the trickery of memories. They melded together, creating emotions, images, ideas that never existed. Memories were often fueled by the power of suggestion.

Nevertheless, her memories of that night on the dock remained crystal clear. Autumn sipped her wine and asked herself for the millionth time, *Why did I open my big mouth?*

She had no answer other than that the weight of her secret finally broke her. Her secret? No, Lily's. One little, dynamite-packed secret. She wondered if her so-called forgiveness toward Summer's offenses over the course of their friendship wasn't actually the fuse that lit the dynamite.

Autumn watched as lives crumbled and changed over the years. Snow never returning from California. Jeff and Lily splitting up. Jeff marrying Babs. The shock of the '80s.

Summer hightailed it to Nashville. Who could blame her when her new sorority sisters were so cruelly murdered? And only seven months after the Camp Scott murders. Then her parents fell apart. Autumn wanted to reach out so many times but felt she'd be reaching for a rabid dog.

So she gave her heart and soul to her career. When she opened the Kitchen seven years ago, she'd worked hard to offer an elite salon experience, and she quickly built a solid clientele of business and city leaders, FSU professors, and college students who could afford something more than Supercuts.

Her success was more than she ever dreamed. As the Kitchen grew, she scoured the southeast for top stylists and paid them well. Every Kitchen client experienced a thirty-, sixty-, or ninety-minute escape from the world into Southern luxury. Opening a second shop, AC Style, would be more for the blue-hair set, busy moms and the guy who wanted a quick clip and buzz.

She could honestly say she was satisfied with life. Romance would be nice, but her family filled her heart well enough. For now.

She'd built a house with a pool believing her old fear of water was behind her. Then she threw a lavish housewarming party, bought a new swimsuit, ready to dive in, yet as her guests arrived, her old anxiety surfaced. She'd not been within ten feet of her beautiful pool in two years. Was this *still* about Blaine's death? Or something else?

Her primary care physician gently suggested, *"I think you're dealing with issues of the heart, Autumn."*

Which was why she'd just spent an hour navel-gazing—Autumn's takeaway—with a kind, bespectacled psychiatrist who really, *really* needed Autumn's hairstyling talent.

The woman's blunt cut with squared-off bangs did nothing for her angular face. At one point, she reminded Autumn of Mr. Ed, the talking horse. Once that image hit, she couldn't take the sincere doctor seriously. She proved to be a disappointing patient anyway, with no childhood drama or abuse to report.

"How about your parents? Were they good parents?"

"The best."

"The best? What does that mean?"

"Surely you know the definition of 'the best.' They were kind, loving, and available. I had a great childhood, so don't waste your time there."

"Fine. You're a hairstylist."

"I am."

"Did you do well in school?"

What kind of question . . . *"I was a National Merit Scholar."*

The doc almost looked impressed. *"Did you have friends in school?"*

Did she have friends? *"The best."*

"What do you mean, 'the best'?"

"I had three best friends. We called ourselves the Four Seasons. Spring, Summer, Autumn, and Snow."

"*Really?*" Once again, Autumn had stumped the good doctor. "*How very special. Are you still in touch?*"

"*No, not really.*"

"*Ah, I see.*" Jackpot. The doctor scribbled madly on her notepad.

The appointment ended fifty minutes later with Dr. Heavy-Bangs prescribing a weekly meeting and medication she called "happy pills."

Autumn dug the prescription from her handbag, looking up as the front door chime sounded. "Tabby?" She tossed the Rx paper back in her bag and leaned for a glimpse of her sister.

Baby sister had been living with her for the last two years, ever since Mom and Dad moved to Indiana.

"Tabs?" Autumn moved to the foyer, where a chandelier with three thousand crystals hung from the vaulted ceiling. She wondered now why she had wanted it so much, other than the pretty pattern it made on the ceiling and floor. And Tabitha had not come home.

Back in the kitchen, she stared toward the pool. *It's just water. Beautiful, cool, blue water.*

She'd managed her bouts with anxiety by counting Pi or reciting Tennyson poetry—Dad was a Tennyson man. For years, she thought she'd grown out of it. However, since the housewarming party, anxiety thought it had an open invitation.

There was absolutely no reason to be anxious. Her life was lovely. Throw in a hunky husband and a kid, it would be perfect. But when did fear and anxiety need a rhyme or reason? Last year, while driving down I-10, a nearly overwhelming panic fell on her and she wondered if she'd lose control of her wits and drive into oncoming traffic.

The pièce de résistance was when she woke up from a dead sleep feeling as if she were trapped in a watery grave and a prisoner of something she could not see.

Autumn moved from the pool doors, carrying her wine to the

family room. Surely there was a comedy rerun she could watch. *Cheers* or *M*A*S*H*.

She landed on *Cheers* and sat back, eyes closed, wine glass resting on her lap.

She prayed to God after the watery grave dream. One of her clients, a woman with a glow beyond her natural appearance, believed He was real, with a heart big enough to love Autumn.

"Talk to Him."

"God," she whispered now, "how do I get beyond this?"

Ridley and his family were coming for the Fourth. His kids *lived* in the water, and she wanted to join them when they called to her, *"Aunty A, come swim. Pulleeeaase."*

Just like the summer of '77, she watched the fun from a safe distance.

"A, you're home." Tabitha entered the kitchen from the back staircase. She was a first-year engineering grad student. It took a while, but Mom finally molded a child after her own heart.

"I didn't know you were here." Autumn muted the television. "There's wine in the fridge."

Tabby was ridiculously beautiful—Judith Duval had tried to get her on the pageant circuit. She was also a runner and a skilled pianist.

"I'm heading out to have dinner with friends." She plopped down on the sofa next to Autumn. "How'd the appointment go?"

Tabby knew about Autumn's "moments," but since she was the strong, in-charge big sister, she didn't share much.

"I shocked her with my healthy upbringing and friendships."

"I'm proud of you, A. You're not ignoring the issue like so many." Tabby glanced at her watch. "I'd better go, or I'll get stuck in traffic."

"Have fun tonight." Autumn rested her arm on the back of the couch, watching as Tabby slung her Gucci bag—a Christmas gift from Autumn—over her shoulder. "Are you tired of school yet?"

Tabby laughed. "Never."

"'Cause I have a chair waiting for you at the Kitchen."

"Your reputation would be ruined. My clients would be bald, with pieces of ear missing. You're the talented artist in this family." Tab's new cell phone rang from her bag, and she picked up the call. "Sonja, I'm heading out now. Yeah, okay, sounds good." She hung up and paused under the kitchen archway. "What are you doing tonight, A?"

"I don't know. Order a pizza, watch a movie."

"Chris said you had lunch with Spring again today."

Littlest brother had a big mouth. She'd only told him because he came in for a haircut right after and Autumn had needed to process. "She and I ran into each other at Publix. I don't think we'll make it a thing."

"Why not? You're becoming the family hermit. Don't let anxiety or fear or your lack of a love life hold you back. Get out there. Take a swing-dance class or go to LA and see Snow."

Autumn made a face. "If I'm not planning on seeing Spring, who lives five miles away, why would I fly across the country to see Snow?"

Tabby returned to the family room and perched on the back of the sofa. "I wish you'd tell me what happened to the Four Seasons. Y'all are like a mythological bedtime story. Every childhood story about you starts with 'Autumn and the Seasons . . .' Even my high school teachers talked about the Four Seasons. Spring lives in town, and I've only met her once. You know I'm dying to meet Snow Snowden and Summer Wilde. Y'all must've been something, Autumn. The Four Seasons grew up to be a movie producer, a country singer, a lawyer, and the best hairstylist in the Panhandle. Just what *were* you? The best of the best? The *Top Gun* of friendships?"

Autumn regarded her sister and sipped her wine, wishing she saw the Four Seasons through Tabby's eyes. "You're welcome to reach out on your own. They'd probably respond to you better than me."

Tabby's phone rang again, and she answered in a hurry. "Daniel, hey, let me call you back. . . . Yeah. . . . Five minutes." Daniel was her new beau. Autumn approved. He was handsome, courteous, and smart, which was more than she could say for the boys Tabby dated in high school.

"Autumn," Tabby said, "will you tell me about that night? I know about Camp Scott, but what happened at Camp Tumbleweed?"

"Not sure it's worth telling." Mostly because Autumn didn't want to walk that particular Memory Lane. She downed the last swallow of wine, then set the glass on the coffee table. "I can tell you this, though. I breathed life into smoldering ashes I didn't know existed and turned them into a flame."

23

Photograph

Snow

'77

On Sunday morning, Snow locked herself in the darkroom. She'd taken so many pictures in town, at the carousel, and then during the barn dance that she was anxious to see her work in print. As for the movie film, she'd have to send it off.

The Seasons had a blast yesterday at the carousel, like old times, falling into their best-friend rhythms. Snow hadn't laughed this much since before they stood in the judge's chambers and heard the fate of their summer.

She had shots from the laundromat, O'Sullivan's, and Tumbleweed's Main Street. Her growing collection of black-and-white photographs would require a new suitcase.

Not to mention all the candid color photos she took around camp of the Tumblers as well as the group shot, then cabin by cabin. Skip ran the film to a Photo Bug on the western side of Tulsa to be developed in an hour. On Saturdays, Lily created a display for the parents to review and place orders.

With her tongs, Snow pulled the latest black-and-white from the stop bath. It was of Autumn, looking straight ahead, completely unaware of the camera, lost in a world of her own. She was the deep color of their group. She could be as sober as Snow at times or as bright and lively as Spring.

But the second anniversary of Blaine's death was in a few weeks, and Snow wondered if she was already thinking of him. Last year, Autumn grieved almost as much as Snow. Though, in this picture, she hoped her friend was dreaming about cosmetology as much as missing Blaine. At some point, a girl had to look to her future.

"Hey, Snowbird." Summer rattled the door. "Can I come in?"

"Yeah." Snow hung up the photo to dry. What did she want?

"How'd the pictures from the carousel turn out?" Summer examined the drying shots. "Can I have this one of Levi?"

"This one is better." She pointed to the one of Levi laughing with Summer. "He's head over heels."

"I don't know." Summer squinted through the low light. "We leave in five weeks. Why start something I can't finish? But he is something else, isn't he?"

"He is." Finished with the first roll, Snow turned on the light and blinked at the brightness. "What time is it?"

"Lunchtime. We thought we'd go for a swim after we eat, before the new Tumblers arrive."

"Even Autumn?" Snow grinned at Summer, then felt guilty. She was on Autumn's side, and Summer didn't need any encouragement.

"I doubt it." Summer perched on the stool. "Spring's in a funk too. Been in her cabin all morning."

"Think she and Mal broke up?"

Summer shrugged. "He sent her a box of cookies last week."

"And she didn't share? She's so dead." Snow put the caps back on the developer bottles. "What about you? Everything okay with you besides the great question of your parents, which I think is all in your head?"

"Mom says there's nothing to worry about, so I have to believe her. Based on the amount of soap she made me eat as a kid for lying, I don't think she's going to take it up as an art form now."

Snow laughed. "Then don't worry about it. Your dad is terrific. If you didn't have a dad, trust me, you'd never complain about a few parental scuffles. Mr. Jeff is the bee's knees."

"If he and Mom *did* split . . ." Summer played with the wooden tongs. "What happens to me? But . . . hey, Dad really likes you too, Snow. He's said it to Mom a few times. Even said if anything happened to Babs, you could come live with us."

"Really?" That made her blush and feel warm all over.

Summer twisted the top from the developer bottle, leaned in for a whiff, then jerked back, making a face. "Why not? We're practically sisters."

Snow dumped the stop bath into the tiny sink in the corner, along with a bit of her resentment. Maybe it was time to stop blaming Summer for what happened to Blaine.

"Let's pray nothing happens to Babs, all right?" She looked back at her. "However, if I did live with you, I'd need my own room. And no wearing my clothes."

"Snow, Spring and I have been dressing you and Autumn for the past, I don't know, twelve years? I don't think your closet has any worries from me."

"Don't exaggerate. It's only been since junior high." Snow tossed the clean water in the bottom of the tray at Summer, who ducked.

"Hey, are you really okay with Autumn going to cosmetology school? Who will you room with?"

"I have to be okay. She's my friend and I support her. You will too when you think about it."

"I know, but the Four Seasons were supposed to stick together forever," Summer said. "Autumn will miss out on so much. We can't call her for every late-night food run or dance party."

"No, guess not." Maybe Snow wouldn't tell the Seasons about UCLA. She'd say she and Mom were road-tripping to California, and, oops, she decided to stay. "Did I tell you Mom and I are driving out to California when we get back?"

"Really? Why?"

"She's always wanted to go. Should be fun in Paps' big Mercedes."

"Hey, maybe we can all go with, cram into the backseat, and—"

"Kill each other along the way?"

"Salute." Summer slid off her stool and retrieved a couple of photos from the clothesline. "Can I have these?"

"Sure." Snow removed her apron as she closed up shop. "Can I ask you something?"

"Depends," Summer said, studying the images of the Seasons she'd selected, along with the one of her laughing with Levi.

"Why do you smell like sawdust?"

Summer

'77

Why *did* she smell like sawdust?

Lying on her bunk Sunday night, her new batch of Tumblers still whispering to one another, Summer stared at Moonglow's ceiling and considered Snow's question.

The strange encounter had somehow changed her, left its scent on her. Even after her morning shower and afternoon swim in the lake.

The smell was on her skin and hair, in her nostrils, reminding her of last night. Reminding her of the Preacher. Even the night breeze punching through the screens carried a hint of the tent floor.

Tonight, one of her new Tumblers propped against her during the evening campfire and whispered, "You smell like my Pawpaw's workshop."

Besides the sawdust perfume, she questioned the tent, the rows of empty chairs, the man who greeted her, the older couple up front worshipping, the singer and the band, the Preacher. Was it real? Would it happen again?

Summer rolled onto her side. Encountering a mysterious tent was one conundrum. Sneaking off with Levi to the Fourth of July picnic was another.

Her confidence waned when he'd come by right before the evening campfire to confirm the details. Mom would freak out when she turned up missing next Sunday.

She could tell her, but then Mom would probably have Sergeant Dover handcuff her to the hitching post by the barn. The Four Seasons would be furious, but they loved her and would overcome their angst. Covering for each other was core to their friendship.

However, Sunday afternoon was critical in getting to know the new Tumblers and helping them settle in. She might miss something important with one of her girls.

On the other hand, she'd go crazy if she didn't do something wild to make the summer memorable. Waylon and Willie was it. *Definitely* it. Shoot for the stars, right? Levi was a star.

She'd also be celebrating the Fourth of July. A Wilde family holiday. Mom may not want to commemorate it, and who knew what Dad was up to with Scumbag *Sandee*, but Summer would be at the Tulsa Fairgrounds with Levi singing "Blue Eyes Crying in the Rain" at the top of her lungs.

Yet her debate continued . . . Mom . . . Levi . . . Mom . . . Levi . . .

Summer clicked on the little lamp she'd bought in town a few Saturdays ago and fished her journal from under her bunk. The pages were still blank. She was too tired to write most nights.

Mom,

I'm with Levi at the Willie Nelson picnic at the Tulsa Fairgrounds. Don't worry. I'm sorry I didn't tell you, but I really wanted to go.

Love,
Summie

She shoved the journal under her bunk and tried to sleep. Tried not to let her thoughts wander, imagining what Dad would say when he found out.

Somewhere in a dreamless sleep, she heard, "Summer?" The small whisper was desperate. "Summer, it's me, Greta."

"Greta?" At the window over her bed, the girl tiptoed up to peek in. "Is everything okay? What's happened?"

Was he here? The murderer? Or the man who left the boot print?

Yet the camp was quiet and peaceful, filled with the scent of rain. They'd be in the Lodge most of the day, playing games, getting restless. Not a good start to week four.

"Spring's gone," Greta whispered.

"What do you mean she's gone?" Summer wiggled her feet into her once-white sneakers. "She's probably in the latrine. Let's go look."

"No, she's gone. Took the old army jeep and left."

24

Honesty

Spring

'77

"You in trouble, girl?" From behind the registration desk, the woman with the long dark braid, piercing black eyes, and a name-tag that said *Wind* leaned to see Spring's awkward left-handed signature. *Tammy Cronkite.*

"Not in the way you might think." She set down the pen by the registry and took the envelope of bills from her haversack. She'd cashed a check from her money market account for her needs today. When Dad handed it to her on the way to the bus station—for emergencies, he'd said—he'd never imagined this. "How much?"

She felt sick for sneaking out early on a Monday morning, but what choice did she have? The women's clinic was closed on

Sunday, and she couldn't muster the courage to sneak out on Saturday morning. She'd miss saying good-bye to her Tumblers.

"What do I think, Miss, um"—Wind looked at the registry—"Cronkite? The room's twenty dollars." The woman took the money and handed Spring a key to Bungalow Ten.

"You think I'm running from the law or my parents. Maybe a bad boyfriend." Spring tucked the key into her pocket. Twenty dollars for a cottage at the Shady Rest Motor Court on Route 66 was cheap.

"For most girls like you, them's the options." Wind showed a bit of compassion as she hit a button on the old cash register. A bell dinged as the drawer popped open. "You seem a bit more uppity than most gals on the run. So, are you?"

"If I am, it's only from myself." Who she could never really escape.

She'd left Camp Tumbleweed before dawn. She'd planned to steal the truck, but when she snuck into the kitchen for the key—without announcing her presence to the deputies—she'd knocked it off the hook and under the fridge. So she snatched the jeep key instead.

She'd stalled the Willys MB something fierce, making a horrible racket as she worked the clutch and gas, burping and jerking down the camp's long drive.

How she'd managed to get away without alerting the rental deputies had to be an act of God. She took it as a sign her decision to abort the baby *was* the right choice. Knots in her gut aside.

She'd escaped without detection. Except Greta. The fly in her ointment. Just as she'd snuck out, Baby Season had placed her tan hand on Spring's shoulder.

"Did the bell ring?"

"No, baby. I'm going to the latrine."

Greta sat up, her face so innocent in the moonlight leaking into the cabin. *"Really? Then why are you dressed? You have your haversack."*

Spring squeezed her hand. *"I'll be back. Take care of the new Tumblers for me."* She removed the cabin key from around her neck. *"You're in charge. Lock the door when I leave."*

Greta hung on to Spring's sleeve. *"Where are you going?"*

"To take care of something."

"Can I go with you? Will you really come back? My sister never did."

"What do you mean your sister never did?"

"She had a baby. Never came home."

"Ah, no, Greta." Spring's whisper trembled. *"It's nothing like that, so don't worry. Go back to sleep."*

"Shame about them girls at Camp Scott." Wind leveled a hard gaze at Spring. "The whole territory blew up with fear when the news broke. You wouldn't know anything about it, would you?"

What? *Good grief.* "No. Who do you think I am?"

"Tammy Cronkite with a sack full of money. Ain't that right?"

"Th-that's right. . . . Tammy Cronkite." Spring clutched her haversack and turned for the door. "Th-thank you."

"Interesting vehicle you got out there." The woman came around the desk and pulled back the curtain. "Don't see a lot of people traveling in army jeeps. That's an old Willys MB. Don't make them anymore." She looked Spring up and down. "Don't seem like your kind of ride."

"Just goes to show you can never judge a girl by her *ride.*" Spring reached for the door before the dark-haired, dark-eyed inspector shared another of her opinions. Before she ended up completely exposed.

Bungalow Ten was old, from some decade before one of the world wars, but it was neat and clean. Spring set her haversack on the twin bed farthest from the door and the backpack she'd borrowed from Summer—Spring was sure she wouldn't mind—on the scarred dresser. The furnishings, the wallpaper, the bathroom tile, and the clawfoot bathtub had to be original.

Spring sat on the side of the old tub. Granny had one at her cabin in Thomasville. The summer place, she called it. She'd filled it with hot water and bubbles when Spring was little.

Granny would be disappointed to know why Spring was at the Shady Rest Court. Why she'd taken the jeep. Why she had an appointment mid-morning at the Tulsa Women's Clinic.

Back in the room, Spring sat on the edge of the bed and stared out the window. Her stomach rumbled, but she wasn't going to answer the call until the deed was done.

She deserved to be hungry for what she was about to do. Yet she couldn't see any other way. She felt selfish and shallow almost as much as she was ashamed and embarrassed. They don't show this part of passionate, carefree sex in the movies.

Perspiration clung to her skin, so Spring opened the door, and the morning breeze tripped across the threshold, tasting of dust and motor oil. Spotting the AC unit under the window, she flipped the switch. The old thing shuddered and kicked, exhaling a puff of Freon-scented smoke.

Ha, the whole scene was a comment on her life. Stinky and weak.

For the rest of her natural days, she'd be *that* girl, the one who broke the rules. Who let herself down, and her parents and friends. Never mind Mal. Or God. What must He be thinking? Spring didn't want to know.

She moved to the door at the sound of a distant melody. Where was it coming from? The familiar tune was one she'd sung in church a hundred times.

"His eye is on the sparrow. . . ."

The wind gathered ominous rain clouds. Spring remained at her post by the door, hands in her shorts' pockets. A tornado or tsunami could roll through the Shady Rest, and she'd not move. She deserved an Oscar for her performance so far this summer, pretending everything was okay when she was dying inside.

". . . He watches me."

"Are you there, God? It's me, Spring."

A Dodge station wagon that had seen better days pulled into the parking lot. A woman emerged from the passenger side, complaining about driving all night and too many flat tires. Opening one of the passenger doors, she gathered a little boy into her arms and carried him to their bungalow.

The man retrieved a second child, a little girl with brown hair flying free from drooping pigtails. She started to fuss, but he patted her back and crooned, "Shhh, Daddy's got you. Everything's okay."

Spring slipped down the doorframe and sat on the short stoop, her bare feet restless against the dirt.

Everything was *not* okay. She was exhausted from pretending. Tears she could not feel spilled down her cheeks.

"God, if there's any way you care, if you see me at all, please, tell me what to do. Is this the right decision? If not, then what?"

The light from the family's bungalow made a square across the court's dirt. The father came out with a bucket for ice, pausing when he saw Spring.

"The rooms are hot, aren't they?"

"Yes," she said.

"Your AC work?"

"Not really."

"Ours either. I'll let Wind know."

"Thank you."

She missed Mal. She missed the girl she used to be. The one she'd never be again. A girl cannot be unpregnant. A girl can only be pregnant for the first time once. And she was ending hers.

In a few weeks, she'd go home, having served her community service in more ways than anyone could imagine. She'd shop for her fall wardrobe, move to campus, and begin sorority rush, pretending to be the Spring Duval from eight weeks ago. But she'd be lying.

The man returned from the motor court office. "She said she'd call the technician but it'd be a while." He paused at his door. "You all right?"

"I will be, yes. Your family is lovely."

"There's nothing I wouldn't do for them." He stared into the cottage, then looked back at Spring. "Horrible about those Girl Scouts. My wife and I talked about sending our daughter to camp one day, but now . . ." He sighed. "I hear camps are locked down tighter than a drum."

"I've heard that too."

"But you're all right, aren't you?"

"I am, yes." Which was true. At least in the way he meant.

The rain clouds blocking the morning sun clashed with a rumble, broke open, and poured buckets over them.

The man darted inside while Spring ran to the center of the court. A gust of wind brought more rain, and she welcomed the thick, cool drops on her hot, dusty skin.

She missed the lake. She wanted to run down the dock, leap from the edge, and dive in deep. Sinking, sinking, and leave her troubles on the bottom. Only without terrifying Greta.

The summer rain thickened and formed a puddle behind the jeep. Spring splashed through the muddy water, staining her legs. Another puddle collected by the family station wagon. She splashed through it.

Running, running, leaping, she landed in every collection of water in the Shady Rest Motor Court. Then she ran to the road and splashed along the berm, kicking up dry grass, dead leaves, and guilty stains.

"I've let you down, Malcolm." She kicked through a puddle under a tree. "I've let you down, Mom and Dad." She splashed through the water by the Willys MB again. "I've let you down, Spring Duval." She jumped in the deep puddle by the station wagon. "I let you down, Seasons."

Then as quickly as the rain came, the sun broke through the edge of the clouds. And seeing that the road was clear of cars, Spring took off running toward the light.

Summer

'97
TUMBLEWEED

Summer had fallen through the looking glass. Though not into a world of weird wonder but one of gentle breezes combing through the hot prairie grass.

Sitting at Greta's picnic table under two thick elms with heavy branches, Summer Wilde was at ease—a strange yet delightful sensation—and she wanted to hang on to it.

"Summer, do you want ice cream with your pie?" Greta poised the ice cream scooper over a gallon of vanilla. A slice of hot, cinnamon-spiced apple pie waited for Summer's decision.

"Triple scoop."

Greta wore a pink summer dress today and walked around barefoot through the thick grass with three dogs and a goat tagging along. No doubt she was a soft touch for scraps from the table.

Greta scooped a large serving, then passed the plate over. She may be an MD with a handsome husband and a sprawling, renovated farmhouse situated on a finger of Skiatook Lake, but to Summer she was still the innocent, sweet, wise eleven-year-old from twenty years ago.

Though her blondish-brown hair was now streaked with gold highlights, and her blue eyes were more peaceful and wiser, Summer suspected Greta Yeager was a force to be reckoned with. She envied her. Wanted what she had more than apple pie and ice cream. More than country music fame.

And while they'd only known each other for those eight weeks in '77, sitting with her now, Summer felt deeply connected.

"I want to be you when I grow up, Greta," she said.

Greta scoffed and offered pie and ice cream to Levi, which he accepted. "I always wanted to be you."

Summer's bite of pie and ice cream filled her with a warm and cool sweetness, canceling her snarky reply—about herself, not Greta.

The shoe was on the other foot, wasn't it? Greta had worked hard and made something of herself. Something respectable and honorable. Summer chased rainbows and sold her soul for a fictional pot of country music gold.

Greta's husband, Darrian, tossed the football just beyond the shady picnic area with a couple of boys they were fostering.

"Their parents are meth addicts," Greta had said to Summer and Levi when they arrived for dinner. *"Horrible living conditions. Wouldn't wish it on a roach."*

Across the table, eating his dessert, Levi gave Summer a blue-eyed wink.

"What are you looking at?" she said.

"Seems I'm looking at you."

Hmmm. *Seems I'm looking at you* had a nice ring to it. Could be a song title. Nope, that life was behind her. Country music was the rocky road of her demise.

"Foley, come QB with Jethro," Darrian called. "I'll QB with Archie."

Levi devoured a fortifying spoonful of pie and ice cream, kissed Summer *on the lips* in front of Baby Season, and hurried through the sunshine to the game.

"All right, Season girlfriend of mine, dish." Greta stored the ice cream in the outdoor kitchen freezer and joined Summer with her own plate of dessert. "I think that boy is head over heels in love. Are you going to break his heart?"

Summer glanced toward the game, where Levi's time in LA showed. His muscled frame wasn't cowboyed-up but Yuppied-up in khaki shorts, a Tommy Bahama pullover, and Adidas.

"He deserves better than me, Greta." She hated singing the same song, but truth was truth. Ever since she'd landed in Tumbleweed, she'd wrestled with regret over past decisions. If she knew then what she knew now . . .

A month had passed since she'd moved into her cottage, which she loved. With Levi's help, she'd planted a late vegetable garden, and painted every wall. Then today, just before heading to Greta's, she'd finished refurbishing the hardwood floors with a friend of Tank's. The delighted Realtor-owner, Murry, waived three months of her rent.

Three months? She'd be gone in one. Two, tops. She wanted to taste her tomatoes. But she couldn't stay in Tumbleweed for three more months, could she? Fixing up the house was just a fun, much-needed distraction.

She'd started cooking too. Shocker. She found a used copy of *The Joy of Cooking* from Second Read Books and started on page one. She'd broken three dishes and ignited one kitchen fire before she invited Levi to dinner. At a table set with a white linen cloth, white china, and crystal glasses of iced tea, they dined on baked chicken, roasted vegetables, and chocolate cake. None of it was as easy as writing a song.

At Foley Ranch, the Circle F, she'd ridden a horse twice, which was more than enough. But what kind of cowgirl doesn't ride? If Levi had his way, he'd make her a working cowpoke by the end of summer. *If* she was staying. Which she wasn't. Though it seemed a shame not to enjoy the refreshed cottage and the free rent.

As for Levi, he'd bought the ranch house from his parents and was in the middle of his own renovation. The kitchen was rustic with brick floors, a beamed ceiling, a gas range, and a deep, porcelain sink.

He'd surprised her with dinner a week into her stay. After a tour of the house, he opened the double French doors to a romantic table setting on the wide wraparound porch and served her a steak dinner as the sun set over the western meadows.

That night she felt like she'd actually found the pot at the end of the rainbow, and it terrified her. What kind of life, career, could she have in Tumbleweed, Oklahoma?

Yet the peace and quiet, the steadiness of sleeping in the same bed night after night, intoxicated her. In the evening, she sat on her little porch and serenaded the birds and bees as the sun whispered good-night. Many times she'd set her guitar aside and simply listened to the music of the wind harmonizing with the hum of the waving grass.

She called Mom once a week. Twice she'd driven to Camp Tumbleweed. The grounds were overgrown, and the clapboard cabins were falling into ruin, and the white paint of Starlight, Twilight, Sunglow, and Moonglow had all but disappeared.

The Lodge, however, stood strong and sturdy, sure to survive Armageddon.

Summer drove through the high grass and around fallen limbs to the edge of the camp where the tent had been. Where she'd experienced true love while facedown on the sawdust floor.

"I loved 'The Preacher,' Summer," Greta broke in. "I love all of your music. I play it in the office before we open."

"All my music? I only made two records, and I'm not sure how you got a hold of either one." Summer smiled and finished her pie. "I was lucky with 'The Preacher.'"

"Your mother sent them," Greta said with a smile. "And you weren't just lucky. 'The Preacher' is so heartfelt and true. Did you know it'd be a hit when you wrote it?"

A shout drew their attention. Levi had just thrown a touchdown to Jethro. He met the little guy in the end zone and lifted him off the ground in celebration.

"How old are they again?" Summer said.

"Nine and ten. They're small for their age. Horrible nutrition. Jethro used to dumpster-dive for food. We have them on supplements and are working on a decent bedtime. We read to them every night. Take them shopping. We're going to Six Flags in August.

Darrian wanted to put them in private school in Tulsa, but it's an hour away, and while we're flexible with the practice, it's too far to be involved. Their parents wouldn't let us anyway, and until their rights are terminated—"

"Are you trying to adopt?"

Greta watched the boys start a new game. "We can't give them back now. They call us Mom and Dad."

"I definitely want to be you when I grow up."

"Stop, you are amazing on your own."

"You say that because you want it to be true, but Greta, I'm nowhere close to amazing. I want to be, but that ship has sailed."

Greta spooned a big bite of her pie and leveled a knowing gaze at her. "You know your problem, Summer?"

She sat back at Greta's forthright question. *Okay, we're getting real.* "Only one?"

"Yes, one."

"Tell me." Summer rested her arms on the table and leaned in. She could use some honest insight. "You make it sound like the missing piece of the puzzle is in my hand."

"Because it is." Greta scraped her plate with her spoon to finish off her dessert. "We should get in this game." She collected her plate as well as Summer's and hollered to Darrian, "Babe, time for the girls to play, and do not tell me to *go long*."

"Greta, hey, wait, what about my problem? What puzzle piece?" Summer followed her to the football game. "What's in my hand? Tell me what you mean."

"Greta, you're with me. Summer, you're on Levi's team." Her heart flipped a little, even though Darrian's assignment was obvious. She wanted to be on Levi's team for more than a short game of backyard football. Like Greta, she wore a summer dress—hardly fitting for football—but she kicked off her flip-flops and joined the game.

"Look sharp, boys," Darrian said to Jethro and Archie. "Girls don't fight fair."

"We fight fair," Greta said, lining up for the play. "Just according to our rules, not yours."

"Levi?" Darrian pointed at him with the football. "No tackling your own teammate."

"Ah, come on, man, you are no fun."

"Is she your girlfriend?" Jethro peered at Summer with his big brown eyes. "She's pretty."

Levi bent down to his level. "You have good taste, little man. Now, let's win this game."

And they did. Team Levi twenty-one, Team Darrian sixteen. Darrian tackled Greta in the end zone and called it a safety and added two points to their two touchdowns. Levi argued he couldn't get two points for tackling his own teammate, but Darrian said it was his field, his wife, his rules. Okay, big deal, cheat away. Team Levi still won.

With a smile plastered to her heart, Summer helped Greta clean up dinner while the boys cared for the Yeager dogs, cats, goats, chickens, two horses, and three cows.

After they'd loaded the dishwasher, Summer cornered Greta. "What did you mean? The puzzle piece is in my hand?"

"Summer," she said, draping the wet dishtowel over the sink to dry. "'The Preacher.' It's in your own song. Every line of that song feels like your heart in words and melodies. That's why it is a big success. It's raw, it's real, it's personal. I feel it every time I listen to it, which is about a thousand times. Tracey and Aubrey's version." Greta sang one of the lines. "'You met me in that tent, when I was so unfit, facedown in the sawdust, you poured out your love.' I don't know exactly what that means, but it feels like a moment every soul craves."

"I'm still trying to figure it out myself."

"Spring told me once you saw a tent or something on the prairie the night of the barn dance. That's why you smelled like sawdust for a week."

Summer laughed softly. "And people say I have a big mouth. What else did she tell you?"

"That the fight on the dock toward the end of camp was about something Autumn said."

"Yes. And Snow . . ." Summer thought to end the conversation but instead asked, "So back to my problem?"

"Your problem is you know how to get what you want, but you don't do it."

"Excuse me. Greta, come on, I've done nothing but try to achieve what I want. Eighteen years on the road and a million miles, singing in honky-tonks, fairs, bars, private parties. You name a venue, I've sung at it." The cozy feelings from dinner and the football game faded.

"Okay, fine. Look me in the eye and tell me in your heart of hearts that you have no regrets and you'd do it all over again."

Now Summer wanted to end the conversation and moved to the double doors going out to the porch. Greta was reading her secrets as if they'd been tattooed on her skin. Could everyone see her so clearly?

Levi and Darrian walked toward the house with the boys on their shoulders.

"What about him?" Greta said.

"No, Levi cannot be one of my broken roads." Her eyes welled up as she thought of the men and music in the junkyard of her past. Did she have regrets? Some days she had nothing but.

"What about the Four Seasons?"

Summer whirled around to Greta, her heart burning with too much truth, on top of the pie and ice cream. "Dinner was lovely. We should probably go."

25

Both Sides Now

Autumn

'77

"Get up." Snow shook her awake. "Emergency."

Autumn roused from a dead sleep and shoved her hair from her eyes. "What emergency? Another boot print? A tornado? What?" She kicked away the covers, feeling a bit out of control, and looked out the window. There was no wind, and only a whisper of rain tapping the velvet dawn.

"Tornado? Fall, chill out. Spring is gone."

"Spring is gone? To where?"

"We don't know. Greta woke up Summer to tell her. Get your shoes. We're meeting in the Lodge."

"What? We can't leave our Tumblers."

"Lock up. I'll tell the rent-a-fuzz to keep an eye out."

"Okay, but we can't leave them long. What if there's a fire and they're locked in?"

"The deputies will come get us. Now come on."

What was up with the universe? Wasn't the moon in the seventh house and Jupiter aligned with Mars? Where was the peace?

Autumn tied on her sneakers and headed for the door. After that first week, she'd abandoned her pajamas and slept in shorts and a T-shirt, ready to run. From a storm. From a madman.

Wait, she forgot her lanyard. She turned back to retrieve it off the hook. She shouldn't leave her Tumblers at all, if she were honest, but *Spring* was gone.

One of her girls stirred. Cassie. Sweet thing. She was the youngest Tumbler this week but oh so fearless, running and diving into the lake for the swim test yesterday.

Autumn moved a lock of Cassie's hair from her warm face, feeling every bit like this little Mighty Mouse could protect the entire cabin.

Locking up Sunglow, she dropped the lanyard around her neck and made her way through a gentle rain to the Lodge.

This emergency, whatever it will be, rescued Autumn from the well she was drowning in. Her recurring nightmare had plunged her headlong into a dark well of endless water. Flailing about, she tried to grab something to keep her from being trapped on the bottom, but the smooth well walls gave her no help.

She was too grown, too smart for this nighttime drama. But she couldn't get the scene of the beautiful Blaine hitting the clear blue water face-first out of her mind.

Did a piece of her drown with Blaine? During the FSU pool party debacle, someone pushed her under and she truly thought she'd never surface.

The Lodge was dark except for the glow of the kitchen lights around the doors and the sound of Moxie starting breakfast.

"Autumn, up here," Summer said in a gruff whisper, leaning over the second-floor balcony.

Summer was on the couch with Baby Season. Snow sat in the overstuffed club chair, somber, jiggling her legs up and down. The old lamp of dull brass and fake Tiffany glass shot a golden light to the floor.

Autumn sat on the other side of Greta. "We're giving you a summer you'll never forget, aren't we?"

"Let's keep it down. Moxie's in the kitchen. Mom's not far behind." Summer looked to Greta. "What happened? What did Spring say? Any clues where she went?"

The girl grimaced and lowered her eyes. "I should've told you, but I wasn't sure." She shrugged.

"Told us what?" Summer brushed the flyaway chestnut locks forming a curtain around the girl's face.

"Well, I don't know. She, um, she's like my sister."

Summer peered at Snow then Autumn. "What do you mean?"

"Do you think she snuck off to meet Mal?" Snow said.

"Mal? Where? How? She can't drive a stick shift, so—"

"Yes, she can. Sort of. Not very good. I watched her go," Greta said. "In the jeep."

"Wait, let's not rush ahead," Autumn said. "Greta, how does Spring remind you of your sister?"

"She was sick a lot 'cause she was having a baby." Greta's sweet, small voice sucked the air from the room. "Spring had a bunch of crackers under her bunk."

"Your sister had a baby?" Snow knelt in front of her. "So you think Spring is having a baby?"

Summer guffawed. "Spring had sex? When? With who? Mal? Did he get Judy, Judy, Judy's permission?"

Autumn made a face with a nod toward Greta. *She's eleven.*

"Did Spring tell you she was having a baby?" Snow said.

"No, but I think she went away to have her baby like my sister."

"Greta, good job for coming to us." Autumn drew her into a hug. "You're very observant."

The girl twisted the end of her long ponytail into an even bigger knotted mess. How had Autumn missed Baby Season's personal care? This afternoon during free time, she'd wash and trim Greta's hair, paint her nails, remind her she was special. People said all sorts of things when their hair was being washed and their head massaged.

"Fall is right," Summer said. "You are the bravest girl I know, G."

"My dad got mad at my sister. I didn't want anyone mad at Spring."

"We aren't mad at Spring. We're worried." Autumn kissed the top of the girl's head. She could relate to holding back a big secret to protect others. "You did the right thing. Why don't you and I go back to Starlight while Summer and Snow figure out what to do next? You can be in charge of the Tumblers until Spring gets back."

Greta looked up at Autumn with large, wet eyes. "Will she be mad at me? I don't want her mad at me."

"No, she won't be mad, darling. She knows you love her. We all do." Autumn walked her toward the stairs with a glance back at the remaining Seasons. *Get a plan.*

"Are you sure? I don't want her mad at me."

"Trust me, she won't be mad at you. Hey, I've got some chocolate in my cabin. Want to share a Hershey's bar?"

"Before breakfast? Cool."

With her first bite of chocolate at, um, wow, six thirty in the morning, Autumn watched Greta's burden lift. She talked of the new Tumblers, how she really liked Cassie, and how she'd do her best to fill in for Spring.

Even Autumn's fears didn't seem so fierce as she sat on the stoop talking, eating chocolate, and watching the sunrise.

One day she'd reckon her fear of water and missing Blaine. But for now, she'd learn to live with one in order to preserve the other, because that's what love did.

Summer

'77

Summer and Snow batted around options. Comb through Spring's stuff looking for a clue? Knowing Spring, she'd have cleaned up any paper trail. Maybe she left a note in her journal. That's what Summer planned to do.

Snow suggested they take the truck and look for her. But where? Besides, they couldn't have two more counselors out of commission. It wouldn't be fair to the Tumblers.

Call Mal?

"What if he doesn't know?" Snow said.

"Know what? That she's pregnant? We're not even sure she's pregnant. I mean, Greta's a smart kid and all, but she is only eleven."

"We've been saying all summer something was up with her. This sort of makes sense, even though I find it hard to believe," Snow said. "But now all her weird moods and funny looks—and that time she ran off to the latrine when we were waiting to go to breakfast—make sense."

Summer debated a couple more options with Snow, but in the end, one remained.

"We have to tell Lily." Standing, she handed Snow her key lanyard. "You check on the Tumblers. Ring the bell at seven."

Their eyes met in the glow of the lamplight. Stuff was going to hit the fan.

"We'd be traveling around Europe right about now if we'd not dumped soap into the pool," Snow said. "You think Spring would've told us over there?"

"If she didn't tell us at Camp Tumbleweed, I doubt she'd have dropped the bomb at a London tea house or while touring the Louvre."

Summer started for the stairs, but Snow grabbed her arm. "Do you think she went to see a doctor? You know, to take care of *it*?"

"Can you think of another reason why she'd drive off in that crappy army jeep in the middle of the night?" Summer said. "I bet Sergeant Dover will have a few choice words for his rent-a-fuzz boys."

"Wouldn't want to be them." Snow gazed out over the balcony. "This is blowing my mind, Summer. Spring was the one who promised she'd never have sex before marriage."

"She and Mal love each other," Summer said. "Maybe they felt it was right."

Snow glanced at Summer. "What about you?"

"What about me?"

"Have you done the deed?"

No, but she liked having an air of mystery with the Seasons. "Snow, go check on the Tumblers. I'll get Mom."

"Do you think our mothers considered getting rid of us?" Snow followed Summer down the stairs. "Your dad took off, and mine died before I was born."

"Are you brave enough to ask Babs?" Summer said. "'Cause I'm not asking Lily."

Snow grinned. "Touché."

On the first floor, Mom's office light was on. "Here I go. If you hear a bloodcurdling scream, run, save yourself."

"Forget about me," Snow said in a low, mock yell. "*Saavvve yourselves.*"

Summer punched her arm but was grinning as she headed for Mom's office, where every ounce of humor evaporated the moment she knocked on the director's door. This was one messed-up summer. Spring Duval pregnant? Armageddon had begun.

"Mom, can I come in? We have a situation."

Spring

'77

Spring hovered against the truck's passenger door as Lily drove in silence back to Camp Tumbleweed, Moxie following behind in the MB.

She'd been lying awake on top of the bedspread, her rain-damp clothes nearly dry, staring at the one thread of light shining through the window from the center of the court when Lily knocked on her door.

"Spring? We know you're in there. Come on, open up."

Funny, it was as if she'd willed them to come. She fell into Moxie's arms, a blubbering ball of snot and tears.

"Thank God."

From the truck radio, Glen Campbell sang about the Wichita lineman. The haunting, whiny sound of the steel guitar resonated through Spring.

Another mile cutting through the afternoon shadows, and she couldn't take it any longer. She was sick of feeling sorry for herself. Sick of denying the truth. Sick of what she almost put herself through. She gathered the Spring Duval her parents raised and put on her big-girl britches.

"How mad are they?"

"The Seasons? Not very."

"I'd be livid if one of them did this. If they'd kept such a secret on Truth Night." Spring turned to Lily. "I'm sorry I caused trouble. Sorry I didn't tell you."

"I'm more angry Moxie didn't tell me."

"She asked me to tell her when I'd made a decision about, well, you know, but I thought I had to figure this out for myself."

"Which shocks me the most, Spring. You've been a part of four families all of your life and you thought you had to do this

246

on your own? What's the point of being a Season if you can't rely on each other? Right now, Baby Season is the glue holding y'all together."

"I didn't mean for her to bear my burden."

"She loves you, Spring. You need to let her know she did the right thing in telling the Seasons you'd gone."

"How did you find me?"

"Sergeant Dover put out an APB. Then we looked for clues in your cabin. Moxie found an ad for the Tulsa Women's Clinic buried in the latrine trash."

"I should've known she'd look there."

"The clinic said you'd canceled. We still didn't know where you were until the woman at the motor court called."

"Wind?"

"She didn't say, but apparently she listens to the police scanner in case anyone on the run ends up at the Shady Rest. Which she suspected of you."

"I couldn't do it." She glanced at Lily but not eye-to-eye. "I ran around in the rain after the dad one cottage over started talking to me about the Girl Scout murders, how he'd do anything for his kids. I guess I freaked out a little. I don't want to be a mom, Lily, but this kid—" she pressed her hand on her abdomen—"shouldn't pay for my sins."

"I know you want to go to FSU, join your mom's sorority, and do all the fun things available to a pretty college girl, but—"

"You're right, I want all those things. To room with Summer and Snow and go to football games and try out for cheerleading. What I didn't want was to be the high school prom queen who got preggers after a beach party."

"A beach party? Is that where—"

"Metaphor, Lily," Spring said. The truck motor hummed as Lily slowed and downshifted for a slow-turning tractor trailer. "I went to the women's clinic. When I walked in, there was no one at reception, so I sat down. I started wondering about the procedure.

Would I be awake? Would it hurt? Then I remembered Mrs. Crippen's biology class, where we learned a six-week-old baby has a heartbeat." Lily cleared the big semi, shifted back into high gear, and lowered the radio volume. "I thought, *No other tissue in my body has its own heartbeat.* I started getting nervous, so I picked through the old magazines, and under a battered *National Geographic* was the *Tulsa World* from the morning the Camp Scott girls were found." Spring ran her hands up and down her arms, against the chill inside.

"I couldn't stop looking at the picture of Lori Farmer and thinking how her life, and Michelle's and Denise's, were snatched from them without a thought to their purpose, their future, and I, um, I . . ." Her fresh tears watered the story. "Wasn't I doing the same thing? Making a decision about this child's life with no regard to her future? I threw up in the bathroom, left a note saying, *Spring Duval canceled.*" The confession filled her with relief. "Maybe this baby girl, or boy, could take the place of one of the Camp Scott girls. Sort of like a memorial to them. Is that stupid?" Spring rested her head against the seat, eyes closed, perspiration gathering on her forehead. The late afternoon wind blowing through the open window was thick and hot.

Lily grabbed her hand. "It's the exact opposite of stupid. It's kind and true."

"So now what, Lily? What about college? What about Judy and Mike? This will kill them. Mom was scandalized over Susan Buckwalter being pregnant. She was so proud that she and Dad raised me right, saying I'd never do such a thing."

"Does Mal know?"

"No, and he's not going to."

"You have to tell him, Spring. He is the father, isn't he?"

"He's off to college in six weeks. That's all he needs to know." That's all anyone needed to know.

Lily was silent for a long moment. "All right, we should come up with a plan, but first you need to call your parents. Give them some credit, Spring. They love you. I know Judith can be exasperating, but she's a good woman and a good mom. And your dad will probably defend you more than anyone."

"Maybe. Dad's pretty cool. But with Mom . . . I've broken the rules and that's a no-no."

"Is she so shallow and small?"

"Isn't she? You went to high school with her." An oncoming semi shook the truck as it sped past.

"Your mother was the most stuck-up, snobby, prissy girl in school. But she was also really sweet . . . when she wanted to be." There was a bit of humor in Lily's voice.

"Mom claims all the girls, especially you and Babs, were jealous of her because she was so popular *and* dated the star quarterback. Dad." Spring sensed a growing peace about her situation, about her decision to cancel her appointment. "Did you have a crush on him?"

"Every girl had a crush on your dad. He was *the* nicest guy in school. Didn't make sense he was so good-looking and athletic too. He worked hard to get ahead. School didn't come naturally to him like it did to your mom." Lily downshifted as she slowed behind another eighteen-wheeler making a hard left turn. Johnny Rodriguez sang "Desperado" through the speakers. "Everything came easy to your mom except Mike. She had to use all her charms to catch him. She hated me because your dad and I were good friends."

"Really?" Spring sat up a bit straighter. "You and Dad? Did you ever go out?"

"Seventh grade." Lily laughed. "He gave me his ID bracelet and called me on the phone a few times. But, you know, we were thirteen, too young to know what we were doing. My mom wasn't too keen on me going steady at such a young age and made me give the bracelet back."

"David Vest gave me his ID bracelet in sixth grade," Spring said. "I thought I'd died and gone to heaven."

"I remember. Summer was so jealous."

The history lesson faded as Dolly Parton's "Jolene" took over the radio. "I liked her on the *Porter Wagoner Show*," Lily said.

"Me too," Spring said. "Thanks, Lily, for everything. Not just for coming to get me but for fighting to make us your camp counselors. Except for being pregnant and all, I've had a blast."

Lily snapped off the radio. "If I tell you something, will you promise to keep it a secret?"

"Promise." The intimate moment demanded such a response, and Spring loved being invited in.

"I almost terminated Summer," Lily said, her voice low.

"What? Really?"

"I worked at Camp Tumbleweed the summer before my senior year at Agnus Scott. Met a handsome cowboy—"

"Like Levi."

"More charming. More nefarious. I fell madly in love. Thought he'd marry me. I stayed another month after camp just to be with him. We conceived Summer on a blanket under the stars. I knew I was pregnant the first week of school. I wrote about the surprising but joyous news to my *man* with idyllic notions of him riding his white steed up the campus drive to carry me away to happily ever after. Summer gets all her wild dreams from me."

"What happened?"

"He never wrote back. So I called him, and his mother informed me he was on his honeymoon. She gushed over how much he loved his 'darling wife,' whom he'd met at college. Then she said, 'What is your name again, sweetheart? Do you want me to give him a message?' I gave her a message all right, which I won't repeat, and hung up. I was devastated. I hated him, hated myself, and hated his child."

Suddenly Spring didn't feel so alone and confused.

"I told my parents. I was almost two months along, and after their initial shock, we talked about options. I didn't want to have a baby, so they found a doctor in Jacksonville."

Lily shivered. "An odious woman. Talked to me like I was

twelve." A second shiver. "On the drive over, I couldn't stop thinking about this being living inside me. What would she, or he, be like? How different would the world be—my world be—with her in it? At one point, I promise, I smelled baby powder.

"By the time we got to the doctor's office, I was a mess. Mom put her arms around me and said, 'Let's grab a bite to eat and figure this out.' It was hard, Spring, but we worked through it. Summer was a small baby, so most of my classmates didn't even notice I was pregnant. I went up a dress size and pretended to eat too much so my roommates thought I'd just gained weight. Classes ended, I graduated, moved home, and gave birth to Summer the first of June."

"Then you met Jeff."

"Three years later, yes. We'd met right after I had Summer, but he moved away for about a year. When he came back to Tallahassee, we reconnected. And once I saw how much he loved Summer, I let myself love him back."

"You know Summer has a hang-up about him. Something about how he doesn't really think of her as his kid."

"That girl . . . she feels what she wants to feel. It's going to get her into trouble one day."

"Are you going to warn her off Levi after your bad experience with an Oklahoma cowboy?"

"No, because it's not fair to Levi. Besides, if I say go left, she'll go right. Warning her will send her straight into his arms."

"What should I do?" Spring said. "Keep the baby or . . . ?"

"Nothing will be easy from here on out, Spring."

"I was hoping you'd lie to me about that."

"But before you decide anything, you should talk to your parents. And Mal."

Spring pillowed her head against the passenger-side window, feeling as if she could own the peace she felt. "First Autumn backs out of our plan. She's going to cosmetology school. Now I ruin things. Summer and Snow will have to room together."

Lily laughed. "I'm not sure you can put fire and ice in the same small space."

"No, probably not." Spring sighed. "Lily, I'm serious, I don't want Mal to know. I'm not telling anyone else he's the father. I'll say I cheated on him. He has to go to school. He's worked so hard to earn a scholarship and get into Duke. I can go to FSU next year."

"You really love him, don't you?"

"Yeah. I do."

The Camp Tumbleweed sign came into view, and Lily turned down the long, winding, tree-lined drive. When she parked by the Lodge, Summer, Snow, and Autumn came from various directions and enveloped Spring with hugs. That's when she really knew she could walk through this very unexpected season.

26

Good Hearted Woman

Summer

'77

The Willie Nelson picnic was far out. Far out *and* solid. As Summer stood in a crowd of thousands, with Levi's arm around her, singing at the top of their lungs, she made a cardinal error.

She looked at his watch. Five o'clock. The new Tumblers would be in the middle of their swim test, nervously watching their new friends swim the front crawl to where Snow sat on a raft. With a whistle blow, they'd tread water for a minute with Spring. Another whistle, and the girls were to swim to Summer, who tested their ability to float.

Only Summer wasn't there. She'd run away for the day. To have fun. With a boy.

Who was in the water making sure they could float? Autumn? Hardly.

Why Mom had allowed Autumn to neglect her duties in the water was a mystery. When Summer got back, if she was allowed to live, she determined to have it out with Autumn.

Why won't you swim? You're letting down the team.

Who was she kidding? Summer Wilde was letting the team down right now. More than Autumn. More than Spring.

She shifted away from Levi. As much she loved being in his arms, catching his kiss after one of his favorite songs, being here was wrong. Very wrong.

Queen of Selfishness right here, folks. Step up and pay homage.

Sneaking out was akin to lying. If Dad found out, he'd be so disappointed, and hadn't she disappointed him enough this summer?

"You're only as good as your word, as your character, Summer."

The lights, the music, the artists, the crowd yielded to the darkness mounting in her mind. She was a horrible, *horrible* person.

The song ended, and the crowded roared. Not Summer. Levi cupped his hands around his mouth and shouted, "Free Bird!" just as Lynyrd Skynyrd struck the opening chords.

That's when she remembered the man from the tent standing on the side of the road as she snuck along the camp perimeter before dawn to meet Levi. The Preacher. How, she didn't know, but His eyes met hers through the gray morning light, and her heart stood still.

"Sing for Me." Then Levi came around the bend and He was gone.

"Levi, I need to go." Summer pressed through the shoulder-to-shoulder crowd. "Excuse me, please. . . . Pardon me."

"Summer, hey, wait. Summer." By the time they arrived at his truck, she hated herself and halfway hated him.

On the ride to camp, she was surly and rude, shooting down his small talk and telling him just to drop her off at the end of the driveway when the Camp Tumbleweed sign came into view.

When he slowed to let her out, she grabbed her backpack and gripped the door handle, shoving herself out of the cab when he barely tapped the brakes. She uttered not a word of good-bye, thanks, or see you soon. She wanted to bury this day and never remember. At least Spring had a legitimate problem. What did Summer have? Nothing. Just a hankering to do whatever she wanted. Mom was right, she was impulsive. Acted first, then considered the consequences.

Tomorrow, she'd start over, if that was even possible, and be more kind and caring. Scarlett O'Hara seemed to think "tomorrow is another day" had merit.

She was hot, sweaty, and on edge as she tiptoed into Moonglow to find Mom sitting on her bed, reading.

Their eyes met in the early evening light coming through the screens.

"Where are the Tumblers?" Summer stayed put in the middle of the aisle, hanging on to her backpack.

"Their first play practice." Mom calmly closed the book. "If you ever do that again, Summer, you are on the first bus back to Tallahassee, and you'll be picking up trash off I-10 for the rest of the summer." She held her anger behind a drawn, pinched expression. "If you were even one or two years younger, I'd—"

"You and what army?" Now she was mad, swallowing the apology she'd prepared.

"What were you thinking?" Mom jumped to her feet. "We were frantic trying to figure out where you'd gone."

"I wrote you a note."

"Where?" Mom looked around, as if the note might magically appear.

"In my notebook."

"Fat lot of good it does me there, Summie."

"Chill out, Mom. You didn't get this upset when Spring took off."

"I was terrified. How could you sneak off a week later? I thought I'd lose my mind until two cowboys with long, determined strides walked into my office. One of them had the same vivid eyes as Levi, and I knew you'd gone off with him. To a concert, Summer?

Really? At least Spring could plead emotional distress. You are just selfish. And once again, the others had to double up, which risks everyone's safety."

"Mom, oh my word, when did you exchange fun for fear? You're a walking, talking fear machine. Levi invited me to go to the Willie Nelson picnic, and it seemed too good of an opportunity to pass up." Her rebellion talked over her regrets. "I'm eighteen—"

"And living under my total authority, not only as your mother but as your judge-ordered, Oklahoma parole officer. Until you've served your time, you go nowhere without my permission. Don't worry, I gave Spring the same talk after I got her home."

"What happened to you, Mom?" Summer edged close with her rising accusation. "Maybe Dad encouraged you to relaunch this camp so he could have some fun with Sandy."

The slap was quick and sharp, stinging all the way down to her fingertips. Tears flooded her eyes and spilled over before she could catch them. Her comment was angry and out of line, but so was the slap.

"Summer Elizabeth Wilde, you *will* respect me. Especially in matters of which you have absolutely no knowledge. Your arrogance is appalling." Mom started toward her cabin. "Campfire in thirty minutes. I expect you there with a smile and your guitar."

"Did Autumn at least put on her swimsuit and help out with the swim test? Huh? Why don't you make her get in the water, Mom?"

Mom didn't reply, unless Summer counted the slam of her cabin door.

Shaking and weak, she dropped her backpack, then burst out of the cabin to walk among the trees to cool off, to fight her tears. Mom's handprint still burned her cheek.

She passed the men on duty as they drank coffee around a smoldering fire, talking in low tones. Summer stopped where the tent lights had appeared on the meadow a week ago and wished she was there again, inhaling the scent of the sawdust floor with the love of the Preacher washing over her.

At first light, Summer grabbed the mirror she kept by the bed. Mom's hand imprint sat subtly on her tanned cheek.

She scooted down under the covers and tried to fall back to sleep, but her heart pounded. She'd avoided the Seasons last night, trying to get to know her Tumblers. Trying to hide her cheek. What would they say to her? Would they let her apologize today or sometime next week, or month, or year?

When the morning bell rang, Summer hopped up. Might as well face the music.

"Morning, y'all." She gently roused her Tumblers. "Let's have fun today. Hurry now, put on your shoes, then we'll line up for the latrine. Get your toiletries kit so you can comb your hair and brush your teeth. Anyone need help? What's your name? Goodness, look at your curls. Then we'll come back, put our things away, make our beds, and have a fun chat until the breakfast bell." She began the camp song. "Oh come and let us sing, the joy of Camp Tumbleweed . . ."

On her way to the latrine, Summer determined to make this *the most fun week* of their young lives. She'd give them her all.

Then she saw Autumn and the Sunglows. Their eyes met as Summer's Tumblers marched past. She fished for her practiced apology.

But before she formed a word, Autumn raised her hand to Summer's cheek. "I've got something that will cover that up."

Summer blinked back her tears. "It wasn't Levi."

"I know. I heard you and Lily."

"Gosh, did everyone?"

Summer turned as a gentle hand touched her shoulder. Spring, then Snow.

"Y'all, I'm so sor—"

"We know, we know." Spring grabbed her in a hug. "Growing up isn't as fun or as easy as we thought, is it?"

"No." Summer rested against her friend. "Also, your mama can still slap you into next week."

In one accord, they shouted, "Salute."

Spring

'97
TALLAHASSEE

"Babe?" Mal called as the front door shut behind him.

"In here." Spring stared at her computer screen, wondering if any of her words were good. Maybe she'd get the guts to send the first chapter to a sorority sister who was a *New York Times* bestselling author. She'd offer her legal services in exchange for feedback.

One of Spring's new writer buddies on AOL had just sold her first romance novel, and it put a little fire under her.

"How goes the life of a great novelist?" Malcolm kissed her with his warm, full lips and dropped into the Denman Scandinavian chair Spring just had to have for her writing space. She called it *inspiration.*

"I've written a thousand words, and I think a hundred of them are worth keeping."

"Then you're well on your way." Mal grinned as he sorted the mail. "When you get your first rejection letter, we'll celebrate your promotion to a full-fledged writer."

"Are you open to me still writing after the summer? Not going back to Case and Turner?"

"I'm open to you doing what you want to do." Mal handed her a couple of letters. One from Greta Yeager and the other from Mrs. Wyatt Stoneburner. Bless her heart, she was always after Spring to work with the Miss Florida pageant. She'd served in '84 and '85, after her year as Miss Florida.

"I love the law. It's just . . ." She stared out the window, where she could see the lawn crew pull in. They were late today. "I want to do something different. I don't know, maybe I'm restless."

"Babe," Mal began, "listen, if you don't want children, then—"

"What?" She swiveled in her chair to face him. "Where's this coming from?"

"I thought a lot about it today, and the evidence points to you not wanting children, Counselor. We've been married for ten years, and we've discussed children, what, a couple of times? First, you were building your career. Then I started the business with Dan."

"Mal, I know it seems like we've—"

"It's simple, Spring." He set the stack of mail on the table by the chair. "Do you want to try for a family or not? Dan said something interesting today—"

"Dan? You talked to your brother about this?"

"He's my brother, Spring. My best friend, next to you. He said, 'Spring changed when she worked the pro bono case,' and suddenly things started clicking for me. Like when I found you in the closet going through your photo albums. Then the picture from the other day, of the little girl."

Spring laughed. "Tree, door, dog, judge! This guy is the murderer. We must convict."

"What? Oh, I see. I'm cobbling together evidence to make my case."

"Exactly, Computer Man."

"Okay, fine. Tell me straight up, Spring. Why do you shut down any discussion about expanding our family? We said we wanted kids, but maybe that's changed for you. I want us to be settled on this, Spring. We're not getting any younger. This Computer Man needs to align his expectations. Our future is very different without children. Was there something about the pro bono case that bothered you? Made you change your mind? What about the picture I found? Was that from the case?"

Spring looked away, because if she met his gaze, she'd lose it. She'd imagined telling him the truth ever since their second first date twelve years ago. It just never seemed to be the right time. But ever since the pro bono case, the truth rumbled to be free. What seemed like a buried and forgotten issue now kept her awake at night. When she rehearsed her confession, she pictured his face and lost all courage.

"I want children," she said, her tone so low and flat she wasn't sure she believed it.

"Okay. When?"

"S-soon." She faced her computer and tried to distract herself with the words on the screen. Beyond the window, the riding mower roared past, and Spring imagined the scent of freshly cut grass.

"Soon? Not that merry-go-round again." Mal leaned to see out the window. "What's out there that's so interesting? Are you having an affair with the yard guy?"

She laughed. He'd better be kidding. "I can't believe you said that, Mal. Of course not. Geez."

"Then look at me, Spring." With his hands on the arms of her chair, he leaned to see her face. "When? Tonight? Next week? Next month? Let's nail this down."

She fixed on a smile and peered into his golden hazel eyes. "End of summer. Let me see if I can power out a novel. Let me scratch this itch."

"All right." Mal regarded her for one long second, then two, before standing back. "You'd tell me if there was anything else, wouldn't you?"

"Anything else? Like what?"

"You tell me." He had a way of looking at her, as if with a bright light, and she wondered if she had any secrets at all. Did he already know?

"Mal, you're my husband and best friend. I'm not hiding anything." Why not add another lie to the web she was weaving?

He kissed her sweetly, tenderly. "You know you're going to be an amazing mom."

As he turned to go, she grabbed his hand. "I love you, Mal. Always have."

"Always?" He squeezed her hand and arched his brow. "Only after I chased you down our senior year."

"Couldn't make it too easy for you, could I?" The mower sped past the window again. "Let me finish this scene and then I'll rustle up some dinner."

"I feel like a thick pork chop. I can run to Publix while you write, then fire up the grill. We had a few kinks in the project we're doing for Bezos, so we didn't break for lunch today." The first meeting with the Amazon dude had gone well, and Mal walked with a lot more confidence. "We're going to get Smith Technologies off the ground, babe. Which, by the way, Dan's having a Fourth of July party. I guess we're going."

"Of course. Dan throws a mean party." Almost as good as Jeff Wilde's back in the day.

"Oh, one more thing. I almost forgot now that I've got chops on my mind. We've written some search engine code, and I wondered if I could test a few things on your computer. See how it works for the average author working at her desk."

"You won't give it a virus, will you?" Mal made a *come on* face, and she laughed. "Okay, fine, you won't give it a virus. But please don't crash the hard drive."

"Now, that I can't promise, but I will back up your data to a floppy disk first." He gathered the mail, then paused at the office door. "Maybe when you're done here . . ." He tipped his head in the direction of their bedroom. "We could, um, practice baby-making."

"Go to Publix. I'll see you when you get back."

"And then maybe . . ." His smile, his sweet, sincere request, made her fall in love a little more. She'd not deny him.

"I thought you were hungry."

"Not *that* hungry."

"See you when you get back."

He rushed back to kiss her, then headed out, asking what she wanted with her pork chop. Salad, corn on the cob, or baked potato?

She wrote another paragraph to her story, then shut down her computer and sat in silence.

She had to tell him. The secret from the summer of '77 was starting to get in the way.

Lily had tried to convince her. *"He has a right to know."*

But her mother agreed it was best to let Mal go on with his plans.

"You'll be back on track next year, Spring. Let's not muddy the waters with Mal and his parents."

She'd convinced herself Mal would forget all about her once he arrived at Duke. She never counted on love coming back around.

27

You've Got a Friend

Summer

'97

Tank, the bighearted lug, set Summer up with a gig in the diner. Every Tuesday, Thursday, Friday, and Saturday, at eight and ten in the evening, she sang her songs on the tiny stage in the corner of O'Sullivan's, where the old phone booth used to be.

He'd said he was going to do it, and one day she walked in to see construction had started. He'd carted the phone booth to his repair shop. *"It's been falling apart since Ford was in office."*

Since everyone was line dancing over at the Boot Scootin' Barn, Tank wanted live music to "up his game." He leaned toward Summer with a wink. "We can bring back the two-step. Maybe even some slow dancing."

"Tank, you old romantic." If Tank had ever been in love, he'd kept it to himself. Seemed to her the diner, even the town of Tumbleweed, was his lover.

The Boot Scootin' Barn was one of the few new places in Tumbleweed. A DJ spun records six nights a week. They served beer and bar food, and at least once a night, a couple of cowboys got into it and threw each other out a window.

A familiar scene to Summer. Saw it a thousand times on the road. She was glad to be away from it. So, when Tank asked if she'd come and play a few nights, she hesitated. If she wanted to start a new life, shouldn't she leave music behind?

Tank upped his appeal with "You can bring a singer-songwriter vibe to the place."

"Oh, I can? What do you know about the singer-songwriter vibe?"

"I read the magazines, keep my ear to the ground. Now, you going to make my day or what?" He looked so sweet and contrite. "I built the stage for you, Summer."

"I'd love to" was her only possible reply.

No strings attached, though. She promised him the summer but no more. Tank produced a two-page contract and sealed the deal.

O'Sullivan's proved to be the perfect place for her to do what she loved. Sing her songs with little to no pressure or expectation.

After two weeks, a handful of songs were being requested.

The first time she played "Love Lassoed the Moon," which had been recorded by SongTunes artist Gina Allen to a modest reception, Summer nearly got a standing O. Honest.

She closed every set with "The Preacher." Invariably, someone would whisper to her as they dropped a few bills into the tip jar, "That's my favorite Tracey Blue song."

Why, thank you. I wrote it. But she never said it out loud. No one cared who wrote the song, only that the music, the lyrics, the singer's voice made them feel something that held them together as they danced in a slow sway.

Now, on this first Saturday in August, as she entered the diner through the kitchen door, Sooner greeted her with a Number Five sans the fries and chocolate shake. Tank waved a bank deposit slip at her.

"You're gold, girl. Business is booming."

"You get what you pay for, Tank." She winked at him, set her guitar down, and landed on a stool at the prep table. "Sooner, maybe just a few fries. Not a lot."

She did this every week. Saturday was her burger night, but since her jeans felt a bit snug, she nixed the fries and shake from her regular order.

Sooner served her burger on a bun with no mayo or ketchup (too much sugar), with a side salad and applesauce for dessert. But every week, without fail, she asked for a small side of fries. Sooner served them hot and crispy.

"I started this music thing 'cause you looked like you needed something to do," Tank said. "And I needed a boost to take out that old phone booth and drum up some business, but dang, girl, if you've not got the Midas touch." Tank slipped a check under her plate. "It ain't much, but I'm grateful."

"Tank, no, I can't take this." She shoved the check toward him without turning it over. "I get tips, and really, I'm doing all right with royalties on 'The Preacher' and a few other songs."

"Don't care what those songs earn you. I care what I earn you. A laborer is worthy of her hire, S. Wilde. Take it, or you ain't playing." He turned for the dining room door. "Buy some new jeans. Yours are a bit tight."

"Tank!"

His big laugh rumbled and rolled as he greeted the customers at the counter.

The trouble with playing four nights a week and Tank treating her like his own kid? Tumbleweed *was* becoming home. She liked it here. Maybe even loved it.

Her little cottage cocooned her. She slept well, ate well, played well. The love she'd lost for the simplicity of music returned. She'd written a few songs and didn't care one wit if anyone on Music Row heard them.

She had lunch with Greta once a week, and every Friday night, she and Darrian dined at O'Sullivan's and stayed for both shows.

Then there was Levi. She took a bite of her burger and pictured the muscular cowboy who sat on her porch Sunday and Wednesday nights after church, talking and sometimes just listening to the prairie. Sometimes she played, sometimes she didn't.

He had a reserved O'Sullivan's booth with Greta and Darrian on Friday nights but sat with family and friends on Saturdays.

Monday evening, he worked with the local 4-H club, teaching kids about ranch life, and she tended her garden. Things were starting to grow.

Last week, Levi got roped by a six-year-old girl. Had him down in the dirt, feet tied up before he could holler, "Hold on a sec."

Summer laughed and laughed as he recounted the story. One day she'd turn it into a song.

They didn't talk about their relationship or the future, or if she'd even be here come September, but his kisses spoke of a love she'd been craving her whole life.

She didn't deserve him—which she told him on a weekly basis, and he ignored. If he was plotting to get her to fall in love with him, it might be working.

Her phone buzzed as she washed down another bite of burger with a Diet Coke. Ah, it was Mom.

The quiet and routine of Tumbleweed gave her a different perspective of some things, and she'd been talking more to Mom. She owed some of that to Greta too.

"I keep in touch with your mom. In fact, Darrian and I are stopping in to see her on our way to Melbourne Beach for vacation."

Greta was a better daughter than Summer.

"Hey, Mom." Summer reached for a fry.

"I got a dog."

266

"A dog? What kind?"

"A mutt from the Humane Society. Harvey. He's six years old, very sweet. When I was signing the papers to take him home, he put his front paws on the counter and gave the worker a high five."

"Email me some pictures."

"I've already taken like a thousand," Mom said. "I'll send you the best." Mom loved computers, cell phones, and her newfangled digital camera.

"Don't send a thousand." Mom was brilliant, but taking pictures wasn't one of her more polished talents. Summer fully expected an email of blurry, off-center photos of Harvey either running away or toward the camera.

"Don't worry, a thousand would take forever to upload. I'll send a few. So, how are you?"

The conversation turned to Summer's singing and her small garden. Mom shared about her company, her new house, her friends, and life in general as a sixty-one-year-old career woman.

Dad gave her half the assets of Wilde Engineering when they split. Mom started her own firm, LW Consulting, and presented at conferences around the country on the core elements of entrepreneurship.

Her clientele included everyone from small business owners to Fortune 500 CEOs. Last year, she spent a month in Europe traveling to small villages, training men and women on how to launch mom-and-pop startups. Even Dad consulted with her. His engineering company was now one of the biggest in the South.

After the surface talk, the conversation fell silent. The real stuff was hard. Sooner eyed Summer's plate of remaining fries, and she motioned for him to take it.

"Are you going back to Nashville?" Mom said.

"I don't know. I really don't."

"Hey, I have someone here who wants to talk to you."

"Who?" Summer flipped through mental images of friends in

Tallahassee who might be at Mom's place. Spring, maybe? Autumn? But Mom knew better than to surprise her with a Season.

"Hello, Summer. H-how're you doing, kiddo?"

Dad? Mom, what the heck? "I'm not a kiddo."

"No, no, you're not." His forced chuckle echoed the laugh she remembered. "Lily says you're in Tumbleweed."

"Yep." Talking to Dad was the hardest. Painful. Summer equally loved and hated him. She missed him. Above all, she regretted the person she'd become trying to make him proud.

"Guess I'll cut to the chase," he said. "I'd like to see you sometime."

"I'm pretty busy."

"Name the time and place, I'll be there."

"I'm not sure where I'll be." Tank hovered nearby, so Summer slipped off her stool and moved to the back door.

"I'll fly to wherever you are, Summer. Are you going on the road again?"

"Dad, we hardly talk on the phone, so why would we—"

"Because you're my daughter. Look, I know things were rough after your mom and I split but—"

"Can we not do this, Dad?"

"It's been a long time since we've been together, Summie."

"You made your decision and I made mine, Dad. Never the two shall meet. Look, I've got to go. Say bye to Mom for me."

She was about to hang up when he squeezed in the final word. "I love you."

Summer fell against the wall, phone in her hand, tears rising. "I, um, know." Did she? If she took a lie detector test, would the needle go crazy?

He and Mom stole her childhood, and while she was working her way back to her mother, he was the one who kept the secret. The one Summer couldn't quite get over.

"Summer, you all right?" Tank spoke from his spot at the stove, where burgers sizzled over an open flame.

"You tell me." She tucked her phone into her bag and grabbed her guitar. "I'm thirty-eight years old, Tank. I should have some idea of who I am and what my life is about, but I'm more confused than ever. How did I get so lost?"

"If you feel lost, go back to the last place you felt found." Tank flipped a half-dozen burgers with his eyes still on Summer. "You know where that might be?"

He sounded like Greta. *"You know what to do. . . ."*

Summer returned her guitar to the case and grabbed her bag. "I'll be back."

"Where you going? You got a show to do."

"Camp Tumbleweed."

"Camp Tumble—Summer, girl, wait. You'll find more snakes and spiders than the meaning of life out there. It's a jungle."

"I know." She headed for the door, her bootheels thumping. "But that's the last place I felt real love."

28

Sing, Sing a Song

Spring

'77

Two weeks had gone by since Lily found Spring at the Shady Rest Motor Court. Two weeks being a camp counselor, loving on little girls so they had *the best summer*, even if their camp only lasted six days.

Two weeks of her personal reality. She was an unwed, pregnant teen. And a week since Summer ran off with Levi to the Fourth of July picnic.

So this was the best summer of their lives?

So far, the Seasons had left her and Summer alone, though everyone had to be bursting with questions. The next Truth Night would be a dilly.

As the last Tumbler drove away with her parents, Spring started gathering the linens from Starlight. That's when Lily knocked on her door.

"You ready?"

"As I'll ever be."

Spring had resisted calling her parents until Moxie showed her a book with pictures of an eight-week-old fetus, which looked more like a shrimp than a human, and Spring bubbled with tears. That little "fish" had its own heartbeat, its own life, and gave her the courage to face her parents. Give an account. Thanks to Moxie and Lily, she also had a plan.

Lily set Spring up in her office, then waited by the door with Moxie. "Do you want us to go?"

"Or stay. Help you talk it through." Moxie had been Spring's, well, *moxie*, ever since she found the pregnancy test kit in the latrine. "You're sure on your plan?"

"I'm sure. And I can talk to them by myself." Spring took Lily's seat behind the desk. "They're my parents and I'm their only child. We're nine hundred miles apart, so they can't kill me." She smiled. A real, genuine smile. "At least not yet."

Spring dialed collect as Lily and Moxie closed the door behind them. "Hey, Mom, it's me. I'm good. Is Dad there? Can he get on the other line? I have something to tell y'all. Hold on, I'll tell you in a sec. . . . No, not bad." *Well, sort of bad but in a good and unexpected way.* "Hey, Daddy. I miss you too. Yeah, we're having fun. No, we've not killed each other yet. The Seasons are the best. Summer? Of course, she's driving us all crazy, but she's our Sum-Sum. Sooo . . ."

For one lightning moment, Spring almost called for Lily. *You tell them.*

But she found her courage. "I'm calling because, well, um, Mom?" Her voice warbled with tears. "You'd better sit down."

Summer

'77

"Hey, *psst*." Levi stood on the edge of the lake's shoreline, his ball cap on backward, his jeans and boots dusty from a day's work on the ranch. "Got a sec?"

Summer scanned the Tumblers racing in and out of the water, kicking up sand and lake spray. How were they already at the end of week seven?

A tan and much happier-looking Spring stood on the dock, watching, twirling her whistle around her finger, no hint of her pregnancy showing.

Summer, Snow, and Autumn tried to busy themselves with gathering laundry the afternoon Spring called her folks. The phone call had been short, only thirty minutes, when she emerged from Mom's office with red-rimmed eyes and an air of peace.

The Seasons had a million questions. When did it happen, and where? What about FSU? Wait, was she getting married? What did Mal say? And, you know, was *it* . . . fun?

"Truth Night" was Spring's only answer. Such a Spring thing to do. Milk a moment for all it's worth.

Summer looked back at Levi just as little Mina Pierce, so cute in her pink swim cap and pink nose plugs, called out, "Summer, hey, Summer, look at me." She ran down the dock and leapt off the end in a teeny-tiny cannonball.

"Far out, Mina. You're a regular Mark Spitz!" Summer gave her two thumbs-up and her brightest smile. To Levi, she said, "I got one second."

It had been almost three weeks since she'd slammed his truck door and walked off. Her anger toward him faded as the days passed. It wasn't his fault. He'd invited her and she'd said yes. She knew the consequences.

During laundry day, when she didn't see him in town, she'd started missing him and remembering how her heart palpitated when he stood behind her as Willie sang "Crazy," holding her against his chest, his voice soft in her ear.

Levi had given her a glimpse of her greatest dream—to be in love, of course, but to be on a stage singing with the country greats. She was born to sing. She felt it in her bones. Now she understood more fully all the hours in her room listening to records, playing her guitar, and scribbling silly lyrics.

"You still mad at me?" He gave her a quick up-and-down as she walked toward him in her bathing suit, brown and muscled from a summer of chasing preteen girls. "I'm sorry I got you into trouble." He reached for her hand but didn't hang on. "My dad gave me a butt chewing."

Summer touched her cheek where Mom had left her mark. The imprint had faded, but the ice between them remained. The business of camp and the Tumblers were a sweet distraction.

"I'm not mad. It's not your fault I abandoned my post."

"You wouldn't have if I'd not asked."

"I wanted to go. Wanted to be with you." She smiled. "It should've been the highlight of my summer but—wait. I've not seen you on guard duty."

"Cody fired me. Probably your mom's doing." He shrugged. "Or my dad's. Guess I deserved it. They replaced me with one of my cousins."

"Not surprised. Mom is still vigilant. Still on double lockdown. Sergeant Dover told us the state investigators at Camp Scott are going back to Oklahoma City. He said the Mayes County sheriff's team is taking over the investigation."

"Yeah, the guy who did it is in the wind."

"I was hoping Mom would let up. It's exhausting taking thirty-six girls everywhere. Just when you return from taking a couple of them to the bathroom, another one is racing to the latrine."

Levi pulled her to him, this time not letting go. "Even though we both got an earful about the concert, I had a great time, Summer. Will you miss me when you go?"

"I'll forget all about you, Levi Foley."

"Fine. I'll forget you too."

She laughed and brushed a bit of dirt from his shoulder. "Did the cows win today?"

"Yeah, sorry." He stepped back to dust off his shirt and jeans. "We had to brand a couple of them." He leaned toward her. "Maybe we can go swimming and hang out for a day when camp is over."

"Can't. Mom has us washing all the linens that Saturday, then cleaning and packing up camp on Sunday. We catch the bus from Tulsa on Monday at eight in the morning."

"Could you go to the movies with me Saturday night? Mr. Rafferty is reopening this weekend. I can already smell the popcorn."

"The Seasons have a Truth Night Saturday." Though she'd like nothing more than to sit with him in a dark theater, holding hands. But she'd not miss this Truth Night for all the Levi kisses in the world. "Plus I'm on tenterhooks with Mom." She glanced toward the Tumblers when she heard a loud splash, but Spring remained on guard duty. Autumn had a group on the softball field, and Snow had taken a dozen girls on a photography hike. "The Seasons have been quiet about my escapade. They might lynch me if I duck out of Truth Night."

"Truth Night, huh?"

"Yeah, it's where we talk open and honest about anything and everything with no consequences. We can't get mad at each other or walk off. Can't stay mad. . . . Have to forgive and forget."

Levi made a face. "And that works?"

"So far." Summer laughed. "But ask me next week."

The clang of the dinner bell rippled through the air, and Spring whistled the girls from the lake, commanding them to line up.

Summer left Levi leaning against a tree to help her Tumblers find their lost thongs or flip-flops, depending on where the girl was from.

Greta moved among the Tumblers like a skilled counselor. She'd befriended the only girl her age this week, Betsy, and switched her from Autumn's cabin to Spring's without asking.

"Lacy, get your towel," Greta said. "Tumblers, dry off and hang up your wet things on the line."

Spring exchanged a look with Summer. "She may live with me, but she's a chip off the ol' Autumn."

"Salute." Summer was going to miss Baby Season.

"Hey, Levi," Spring said as she walked by.

"Hey, Spring," he said, waving at the girls who giggled behind their hands. "Guess I should go."

"I need to stay with the girls. Lily's rules." Summer started up the path from the beach, but Levi caught her hand before she could walk away.

"Just know, I'm kissing you in my mind right now with everything I've got."

She laughed and backed up the path. "Pretty corny, Foley." But he'd melted her with a look and a few words. How was she going, going, *gone* for him so quickly?

"Aren't you kissing me back?" he said. "In your mind?"

"With everything I've got." She caught up with Spring and Greta, who were wrangling the Starlight and Moonglow Tumblers.

Autumn crossed the camp with her happy, dusty, and red-faced campers. One of the girls held a bloody rag to her nose. Happened at least once a week. The ball took a funny bounce, or a girl who was new to the game didn't quite know how to catch. Or the girl was a competitor and didn't mind a bloody nose to score a run.

Snow hiked out from the meadow where Summer had seen the tent, camera around her neck, Twilight Tumblers carrying finds from the trail.

Summer paused in the small yard by the cabins, breathing in the scent of sunbaked grass. Where did the summer go? In a little over a week, they'd head home, and the realities they had yet to confront— Autumn going to cosmetology school, Spring having a baby.

Funny how she didn't want the summer to end.

The rent-a-coppers were changing shift. Two coming on. Two going off. They'd become as much a part of the Camp Tumbleweed backdrop as the trees and cabins, the lake and softball field.

They gave Sugar Daddy candies to the campers and made sure there was enough firewood for evening campfires. They were the only audience for the Friday night play, unless parents came in the night before, which happened last week. The actors were always so much better with an audience.

But of all the things she'd seen, touched, and experienced this summer, it was that tent pitched on the open prairie that resonated most.

"Sing for Me."

A whiff of hickory smoke drifted past and the voices of the Tumblers rose and fell around her.

"Summer, *help!*" That'd be Marylou. The girl could never get out of her wet swimsuit.

"Coming." Summer paused on the steps of Moonglow, hand on the screen door, and watched Levi's truck bounce out of the camp, then she glanced toward the meadow.

"I'll sing for you," she whispered, "if you tell me who you really are."

Snow

'77

Sweat trickled down her back as Snow moved a load of sheets from the dryer to one of the laundromat's wire push baskets. Two more loads to fold, and they'd be done. She was starved and ready to get out of the hothouse of Tumble Time.

Autumn worked alongside her, while Summer sat on her washing machine, reading magazines and singing along with the radio. "*Don't it make my brown eyes blue.*"

"Get up, lazybones." Snow threw a hot towel at Summer. "Or your blue eyes are going to be black."

"Take a chill pill." Summer laughed and retrieved the towel. "The *Midweek* magazine has an article about the murders."

The song ended, and the DJ came on with his fast talk. "You're listening to KVOO 1170 on your AM dial. That was Crystal Gayle, sister of the great Loretta Lynn. . . ."

"Anything different than what the deputy said?" The word *murder* made Snow's skin crawl. How could anyone—

"Only that a crime calling for no-holds-barred investigation and using all the latest technology, that has two hundred lawmen and four hundred volunteers, that has even offered a reward, still has no answers. It's almost the end of July."

Snow glanced toward the door when a ragged and tired-looking family peered inside. The husband muttered something, and they moved on.

"Hey—" Summer tossed the magazine aside and slid off the washer. "I've seen y'all . . . at the tent meeting."

Spring looked up from where she unloaded the last of the wet linens. "Tent meeting? What tent meeting?"

"Do you want to come in?" Summer said to the man, who looked like he'd walked out of a 1930 Dust Bowl photograph.

"We're good, thank you all the same. Come on, Maggie." He motioned to his wife and kids.

"Steel, couldn't we just—"

"We need to move on."

"Summie, what tent meeting?" Snow asked with a glance at Spring, who'd been quiet, almost solemn, the last few days. One week from today, camp ended and reality began.

Tonight was Truth Night, where Spring would spill her secrets. Snow planned to break her news tonight as well. A minor announcement compared to Spring's story.

"Nothing. Forget it." Summer watched the family from the large glass window.

Didn't look like nothing. But she'd wait for Truth Night—which would be one for the books. "Wait for Truth Night" had become their catchphrase the last few weeks.

"What happened when Levi stopped by?"

"Wait for Truth Night."

Snow snapped a sheet from the basket and started to fold. She was getting pretty good, if she did say so herself. She could even get a perfect tuck on a fitted sheet.

"Snow," Autumn said. "What do you want to do tonight for Blaine?"

Right . . . She'd been thinking about the anniversary of Blaine's death in between rehearsed confessions about UCLA.

Seasons, I'm going to UCLA. Love y'all. Good night.

"Maybe tell our favorite memory?" Snow glanced at Summer, who loaded her and Lily's clothes in the washer.

"I made bark boats during arts and crafts this week," Spring said. "I'll get some candles from the Five and Dime." Her voice was softer than usual. "We'll light the candle, say something we loved about Blaine, then set the boats on the water."

Snow's eyes watered. "Th-thank you. I love that idea."

"Remember tonight is *Truth* Night." Summer emphasized the word as she pushed a wire basket to a buzzing dryer.

"What *truth* are you going to tell, Summer?" Snow said.

Summie flashed that grin of hers, the one Blaine loved. "I don't know. I'll have to hear yours first."

"Maybe I don't have one."

"Maybe I don't either," Summer said.

"Two words," Autumn said. "Levi Foley."

"Salute!"

Summer turned up the laundromat's radio, and the girls sang to the latest country hits as they finished their second-to-last Saturday at Tumble Time.

278

"I'm going to miss this place," Snow said as they carried the laundry bags to the truck.

"Has it been a fun summer?" Autumn leaned against the truck and peered down Main Street. "Has it been the best?"

"It's been interesting. Lots of surprises." Summer hoisted her laundry sack into the truck with a glance at Spring. "What do you say?"

Snow caught the glisten in Spring's eyes as she turned back to the laundromat. "I'll make sure we got everything."

"Way to go, Summer," Snow said. "You have to push and prod, don't you?"

"What? Aren't we asking if the summer was good?"

"You know what she's going through, yet you still poke her."

"No, I don't know what she's going through 'cause she's not said one word to any of us." Summer started down the sidewalk toward the park. "I'll be back. Order me a Number Five."

"Where are you going?" Autumn said. "You can't go—"

"Alone?" Summer raised her arms, gesturing to the busy shoppers. "Look around, Autumn. We couldn't be any safer. I choose freedom."

"Leave her be, Fall. Everyone knows Summer Wilde does what she wants."

Summer whipped around to stand nose-to-nose with Snow. "What is your problem? You got something to say?"

"I thought you might want to support your friend. She's going through something and—"

"I've been supporting her. Going to see the carousel doesn't change that."

"Stop." Autumn stepped between them. "Let's not fight. Y'all are best friends, and our last week at camp should be about making the best Four Season memories ever! Not nipping at each other."

Snow glanced between Summer and Autumn. She was right.

"Apologize." Autumn was really annoying when she launched into big-sister mode.

"Sorry, Summie." Snow tried to sound like she meant it.

"Me too," Summer said. "And before I forget, your idea to do a play this summer was terrific. It made camp so much fun, and I'd love more copies of your photos."

How'd she do it? Instantly go all nice and sweet on her with a dollop of sincerity on top? This was and always would be her struggle with Summer Wilde. One minute she'd be in your face, the next offering to do your homework. Snow, on the other hand, liked to stay mad for a while, thank you very much.

That's why they were fire and ice.

"Summer, maybe we can listen to *Best of the Doobie Brothers* when we get back." Snow smiled and meant it. "Blaine and I used to listen to it when we played rummy."

"You got it, Snowy."

Watching Summer hurry down the street, Snow tried to image Blaine alive, married to Summer, which would make her an honest-to-goodness sister, and the pain over her silent accusation—*You're the reason Blaine is dead*—faded away.

Tonight, she'd remember her brother with her "sister," Summer, then head for UCLA with the sadness of the past two years wrapped in the memories of the best summer of her life.

As Snow headed to O'Sullivan's with Spring and Autumn, she could've sworn she heard Blaine whisper, *"Salute."*

29

Reflections

Spring

'77

Lily found Spring in the craft room, setting up the bark boats for Blaine's vigil, fitting the slim pieces of wood Skip had sanded down for her with a small votive candle.

"Your mom is on the phone."

"Tell her I'm busy."

"Spring—"

Boy oh boy, Judith Duval was fighting fit. She'd overcome the shock of Spring's news, holstered her previous compassion, and unleashed on her daughter like an Oklahoma tornado.

"You're going to live with Irene, one of my sorority sisters, in Montana. She's a nurse and can—"

"Montana? Mom, I'm not going to Montana."

"—help you find the best doctor and adoption agency. In fact,

I've already set up a few appointments. I've even reviewed a couple of potential parents. Money talks when you want to speed things up."

"Let's go back to 'I'm not going to Montana.'" Spring didn't have many cards to play, but she'd play the ones she had with gusto.

Gearing up for Truth Night brought her emotions, her courage, to the surface.

"We're going to keep this quiet, Spring. No one will *ever* know. Just Dad and me. I trust you can swear the Seasons to secrecy for the sake of your friendship. It's a risk we have to take."

"You just have it all planned out, don't you? What about when people ask why I'm not in school? We've talked of nothing else since first grade!"

"The story is you went to Oklahoma for the summer and decided you wanted a bit more *adventure* before the rigors of college. I'll say a friend of mine offered you a place in the Wild West of Montana and you thought it exciting."

"Who will believe it? Maybe the family, but my friends? My Lincoln High classmates? Never in a million years. Everyone knows the Seasons are going to college together. Period. End of sentence."

Never mind Autumn already bailed, but that could be explained. Shoot, probably everyone but her best friends could see she was more interested in hair than periodic tables. Even though she could name the elements in her sleep.

"I'll say you took my advice to expand your horizons, visit new places, make new friends. You'll have to think of something for Mal. He'll be harder to convince. Dad and I think it's best not to tell him about, well, you know. Let him go on to school." Mom actually paused for a breath. "He is the father, Spring, isn't he?"

Spring slumped down in Lily's chair. That was the one detail she'd left unclear during their long conversation. The less said, the better. She didn't want Dad to get worked up about honor and integrity and demand Mal "do the right thing" and marry her.

"Goodness gracious," Mom said. "Spring Tuttle Duval, for the life of me I cannot imagine what you were thinking. I'll tell Irene to get you a VD test."

"Mom!"

"You can never be too careful. Which I taught you, but I guess that went out the window." Choo, choo, another ride on the guilt train. "Either way, break up with Mal. He goes to Duke a bit brokenhearted, but some cute, southern darling will catch his eye. The south is full of gorgeous women. Spring? You still there?"

"Yeah," she whispered, on the verge of tears. "Mom, I *know* I disappointed you and Dad. I disappointed myself. I do remember things you taught me, don't worry. I already told you I'm breaking up with Mal. I already thought of what to say to him. None of this was *ever* the plan, but I'm not—"

"Going to Montana? Then what, Spring? What is your grand plan?"

"I told you. I'm staying here with—" She turned at a soft knock on the door. Moxie peered in with *Everything okay?* written on her expression.

"Moxie. She's an army nurse and ex-POW, and every bit as competent as Irene, whoever she is."

"Please do not tell me keeping it is an option."

"Mom, it's a baby. Your first grandchild. Stop talking like it's a bad haircut or mangy dog." Which she'd keep. The dog, not the haircut.

And so it began. The roller coaster, the merry-go-round. Two hours later, two *turbulent* hours, Spring finally said, "Mom, I have to go."

She walked into Starlight, and Moxie came in after her. She sat next to Spring, who collapsed on her shoulder and cried. She knew her mom loved her, but she'd never felt more alone.

"Greta's parents showed up this afternoon," Moxie said, tugging a handkerchief from her pocket.

"Really?"

"They wanted to take her home, but she flat refused. Said she was a Season and was not leaving until y'all did."

"She's the best." Spring wiped her tears. "Were her parents nice?"

"I know we made them out to be selfish prigs, but yes, they were. Seemed to really miss her. They took her to her grandparents for the weekend, but she made them sign a piece of paper agreeing to bring her back tomorrow." Moxie pointed to Greta's bunk. "It's under her pillow."

Spring laughed. "I need a little more Greta in me." She peered at Moxie with watery eyes. "Mom wants me to go to Montana. Stay with a friend of hers."

"When we get settled at my place outside of Ponca City, we can invite them to visit. They'll feel better. I got lots of land and privacy."

"She'd like that," Spring said. "She doesn't want me to keep the baby."

"Don't be too hard on your mother, Spring. She wants what's best for you. But what do you want?"

"I want her, or him, to have the best chance in life. I wish that was with me, but I'm not ready, Moxie. I want to go to college, maybe law school, live in an apartment with one or all of the Seasons, travel. And even if I don't do those things, I know I don't want to be a mom right now."

"What if I told you I know a lovely couple looking to adopt?"

If she didn't know Moxie was the one to walk her through this when she found her e.p.t. test vial, Spring knew it now.

———

Summer

'77

"I say we have Truth Night first," Summer said from the center of the dock, waiting for Spring to come down the path.

"Do we have to sit on the dock?" Autumn stood on the grassy part of the shore.

"I won't throw you in, Fall." She'd regretted tossing her in all summer. Autumn deserved better from her. But sometimes she just got so riled up. "Hey, Snow, sorry about this afternoon—"

"Forget it." Snow aimed her camera at Summer. "Me too. Here, Autumn, take our picture." She ran down the dock and pressed her cheek against Summer's. "Autumn, come closer. Summer won't throw you in."

In Summer's mind, Camp Tumbleweed made the Seasons more like sisters than ever. They fought like sisters. Loved like sisters.

Spring arrived with four bark boats in her hand and sat cross-legged on the dock.

"Spring, these are really cool." Summer examined the smooth slab of wood with the candle. "Autumn, come on, it's safe out here. Spring, you want to go first?"

"Might as well. But let's not spoil Blaine's memorial by fighting, okay?" She glanced at Autumn. "You coming?"

The fall Season made a face, ducked her head, made her way to the circle, and squeezed in between Snow and Spring.

Summer settled into the familiar cocoon of her friends, into the quiet of the lake, and waited for Spring's story.

"I'm pregnant, which you all know." Her blue eyes brimmed with tears. "Mom called today and told me I was going to Montana to stay with a friend of hers, give the baby up for adoption, and no one would ever know. She trusts y'all won't tell anyone. You won't, will you?"

"No."

"Your secret is our secret."

"Is Mal the father?" Summer liked to cut to the chase.

Spring sighed and went on with her story. "I'm going to stay with Moxie on her farm about an hour away."

"Are you going to keep the baby?" Autumn said. "They're a lot of work, trust me."

"Moxie knows a family who wants to adopt. She can arrange it with the adoption agency." Spring wiped away her tears. "It's cool Moxie knows these people. The baby will have a good home." Spring peered at each one of them. "I messed up, y'all. How could I do this?"

"What about Mal?" Summer said. "Are you going to tell him?"

"No." Spring sat up, pushed back her shoulders. "He . . . he's not the father."

A chorus in three-part harmony—"*What?*"—echoed across the water.

"Then who?" Summer sucked in a deep breath. "The dude from the Kappa Alpha party?"

"Yes." Spring slumped down, shaking her head. "No. I'm lying. Mal's the father, but you can never tell him. Never, ever."

"Why not? He's as responsible as you." The junior feminist in Summer pulled up a chair.

"Because if he gets involved, his parents get involved. The dads will decide we should get married. Mal won't go to Duke, he'll go to junior college. He'll stock shelves at Publix nights and weekends, which is a fine job, but not what he wants to do. Dad will find me a state job, and all the while we're playing house, I'll know, Mal will know, we're not ready to be parents. I want to go to FSU and be *that* girl, you know? Mary Tyler Moore and Marlo Thomas."

"Salute."

All the questions Summer had been dying to ask faded away. Spring had poured out her heart, and they had a lifetime of friendship to tell the rest.

Then Autumn leaned toward Spring and whispered, "Well, how was it? Sex?"

Summer burst out laughing, which got the rest of them going, including Spring and the crickets.

"Not like the movies," she said.

"Nothing ever is." Summer slapped her a high five.

"Will y'all be there for me? Write me? Call me? I'll be home by next June. I want to lose the baby weight before I go back. I can't convince people I've had an adventure in Oklahoma if I come home fat. I know it sounds all buttoned-up, but it's not, and I'm sad and scared."

Summer scooted over and linked her arm through Spring's. "We're here for you. If anyone can get through this, it's the great Spring Duval with her Seasons. I'll keep FSU warm for you."

"I won't be at FSU." Autumn stretched forward to place her hand on Spring's knee. "But I'll be in Tallahassee, waiting for you. Snow and I will double team to keep Summer out of trouble."

"I'm going to UCLA." Snow blurted the news with an exhale, like she'd been holding in the words for a long time. "Yeah, next month. So, um, that's my truth tonight."

"Come again?" Summer said. "UCLA?"

"Crazy, huh? Blaine and I used to talk about it all the time. Mom encouraged me to apply. I got accepted."

"You're just now telling us?" Spring said. "How long have you known?"

"Since April."

"Unbelievable." Summer launched to her feet. "First Autumn drops out, then Spring gets knocked up—"

"Hey!"

"Well, it's true. Now you're going to UCLA and I'm going to FSU *by myself*? And when—*when*—did you and Blaine *ever* talk about UCLA? All the nights we spent at your house . . . You never said a word. Is that your so-called California vacation?"

Snow coughed up the whole story. UCLA. Tuition paid for by a benefactor. Driving out in her grandfather's Mercedes.

"I don't know what to say." Summer examined each one as she towered over them. "I'm stunned. I thought we were best friends. Thought we told each other everything. I thought we were honest. But now, six weeks from our freshman year of college, the truth comes out. We're not good friends at all. We're not sisters. We're liars." Her voice faded.

"Summer, sit down." Spring tugged on her shorts. "If we love each other, we'll stand by each other. This is what growing up is all about."

"Truth Night is over." Summer snatched up one of the bark boats. "Let's just remember Blaine and go to bed. Last week of camp starts tomorrow."

She wanted to get this over with so she could go to the meadow, cry, scream, and kick the long grass. Maybe the tent and Preacher would show up again.

"Summer, don't be mad," Spring said. "Come on, none of us planned this. It just happened."

"You may not have planned it, but those two did." She flicked the lighter to her candle, then raised her bark boat. "To you, Blaine, wherever you are and whatever you're doing. Wish you were here because everyone is abandoning me."

30

That's the Way
of the World

Summer

'97

Twenty years after Camp Tumbleweed, Summer didn't expect to
find anything like a tent meeting in the meadow, but she was disappointed all the same.

How many blades of grass and flowers had lived and died on
the ground where she'd met the Preacher? The memory of that
night seemed more like a dream than a reality.

Yet as she stepped through the tallgrass, milkweed, and an array
of purple, white, and yellow flowers, something in her shifted.
Raising her face to the orange and red sky, Summer breathed in
and tried to let go of the many weights she carried.

Glancing at the stand of trees behind the dilapidated Twilight,

Starlight, Moonglow, and Sunglow cabins, she listened for her name.

She'd given into fear the first time she saw the tent, but the second time, the night of the barn dance, she'd had to go. Had to see, hear, even feel what was going on with the lights and the music.

Facing where the tent had been pitched, she said, "Are you there, God? It's me, Summer Wilde." She'd made a promise to Him all those years ago, and if He was listening, if He cared despite the life she'd lived, she'd like to start over. "You said, 'Sing for Me,' and I said to tell me who you are."

Summer exhaled a bit of the pain stirred by Mom's phone call. The fresh resonance of Dad's voice lingered in her as she drove to the camp.

"I love you."

She'd rehearsed a thousand conversations with him. She'd given him more pieces of her mind than she had to spare, yet never said anything to him. The few times they'd talked since she started a life of touring didn't leave room for it.

Today, hearing his voice, she really missed him. Missed his laugh, the glint in his eye when he teased her, or the way he hovered over his drafting table in the evenings, muttering to himself in numbers and measurements, then saying, *"Summer, come here. Let me show you what we're doing in Orlando."*

The divorce made her feel like she had no right to her childhood because she wasn't really his daughter, was she?

"So, God or Preacher, tell me who you are." It occurred to her the better question might be, *"Tell me who I am."*

The July sun burned hot, cooking the meadow, while the stiff breeze stirred a sweet fragrance. Birds in the trees called to the prairie hens warbling through the grass.

"You feel like you've been in a desert, don't you?"

She turned at the sound of His voice. The Preacher walked toward her, smiling, His eyes like blue fire. He wore the same Oxford button-down, wide blue tie, and bell-bottom jeans he wore twenty years ago.

"Yes." She collapsed against Him without reservation. "A dry, hot desert."

"There was always going to be a desert, Summer. Just a different desert than the one you chose, but you're here now, where you were meant to be."

She shoved away from Him. "What? Why? Why was there always going to be a desert?"

"Because of Lily and Jeff, and the Seasons. Part of your journey to draw you to Me."

"Then why didn't you tell me that night in the tent? All you said was 'Sing for Me.' I don't even know what that means." Was she screaming? She felt like she was screaming. "Why did You let me go through all of that crap? All my stupid mistakes? I don't get you."

"What do you remember of the tent?"

"What do I—" She glanced behind her, looking between the light and shadows for a memory. "Lights, sawdust floor, a stage with a singer and a band. You."

"And the chairs?"

She glanced at Him. "Yeah, the chairs. They were, um, empty. Except for the cowboy in the back, the older couple in the front, and the family down on their luck."

"Hundreds of empty chairs, waiting for the hurting, the sick and the lost, the broken to come."

"But they didn't." She felt a shift in her understanding. She'd come, more broken, wounded, and hurting than she imagined. "Did the others see the tent or the lights?"

"Everyone has a chance to see the light, to see Me, Summer," He said, looking down at her. "Now you will sing for Me. This is your time."

His words burned in her soul. "I'm not sure I understand, but—"

The Preacher put his arm around her. "Summer, your desert is finally in bloom."

Autumn

'77

"I see him." Autumn's voice was so low she almost didn't hear her own confession. "Blaine, buried in the water, facedown, not moving." Summer and Snow stopped arguing and gaped at her. "If I think about it, I can't breathe. Ever since that day, I panic if water covers my head. I have nightmares where I'm stuck under a rock or down a well and can't get free. I have to breathe, but I'm underwater. I wake up gasping for air. I can't stop thinking about Blaine, if he tried to breathe or call for help."

"That's why you don't swim?" Summer sat next to her, holding her bark boat on her knee. "Why didn't you say something?"

She shrugged. "I wanted it to go away. Mom said I was just grieving because we were close, and because Snow is my best friend, but I can't get it out of my mind that he might have called out for someone to save him. If he'd been rescued in time, he might have lived."

"I don't think so, Autumn," Spring said. "He was dead before he hit the water."

"Stop, just stop." Snow paced back and forth. "I don't want to relive it, please."

"Sorry, Snow," Autumn said. "But Summer's been poking me all camp about why I don't swim. There it is. I hate the water."

"But you jumped into the FSU pool," Spring said.

"I wanted to fit in. I was tired of being afraid, so I jumped. Then some bonehead pushed me down, and honest to Pete, I thought I was going to die." The flame of Summer's bark boat flickered

292

against the night. "You'd better blow that out or you won't have a light for the memorial, Summie."

Summer hesitated, then blew out her candle with a huff. "Know what my truth is tonight? We hide things. We lie to each other. Blaine's been dead two years, Autumn, and you're just now telling us—"

"Fine. You want the truth, Summer?" Confession was good for the soul, right? "Sometimes I hated you because I loved Blaine and—"

"Not this again."

"Yes, this again. Ever since he and his friends crashed my fourteenth birthday party with shaving cream, I wanted to marry him. I don't know why or how I knew, but he was my future. Yet he only had eyes for you."

Summer

'77

"He never said a word to me." Why was it her fault Blaine only saw Autumn as a friend?

"But you knew, didn't you?" Snow stopped pacing and leaned over Summer's shoulder. "You knew Autumn liked him too, but you still flirted and consumed his attention."

"Okay, okay, Snow, come on, that's not fair. Let's not say things we'll regret." Spring retrieved Summer's bark boat and lined it up with the others. "I thought Truth Night was going to be all about me but seems like y'all have some things to say."

"I said my piece. Y'all are liars," Summer said.

"Like you're not a liar?" Snow bumped Summer's shoulder, bringing her to her feet. "You lie like a rug, sneaking out, not telling us where you were going with Levi."

"So what? We've covered for each other before. Spring didn't tell us about her little trip either."

"Y'all, stop. Stop." Autumn reached for one of the boats. "I'm sorry I said anything. This is Truth Night, not fight night. Spring, give me the lighter. Let's just move on to remembering Blaine."

"Fine." Summer retrieved her boat and candle. "I wish everyone would stop accusing me of hurting Blaine." She took the lighter from Autumn and relit her candle. "I loved him as a brother."

Spring stood next to her to light her candle. "No one is accusing you, Summer."

"Could've fooled me. Fall, what are you going to do about your fear of water?"

"Watch me." Slowly, she moved to the edge of the dock with her boat, the small flame of the candle flickering large against the dusk, and lay prostrate.

Snow lined up on the other side and Spring passed down the lighter. In a flick of a Bic, all four boats were ready for the "sea."

Summer lay on her belly next to Spring, still fuming on the inside. She *was* going to apologize tonight for sneaking off to the concert, but now . . . Forget it.

"Salute, Blaine," Autumn said. "We miss you. Snow, why don't you go first? Say a few words, then put your boat in the water."

Summer's ire faded as Snow lowered her boat to the water and gave it a gentle push.

"I miss you every day, big brother." The emotion in her voice tugged at Summer. "I'm going to make you proud out at UCLA. Tell Paps and Dad hello for me, okay?"

Tears slipped down Summer's cheeks, and she swiped them away before anyone could see. She was suddenly homesick, missing her dad.

"I'll go next." Autumn hesitated, then stretched out over the water. Snow whispered, "You're okay, I got you. Summer can't reach you from here."

"Come on, y'all, I'm not going to—" Never mind. Let it go.

294

"I loved his smile," Autumn said. "He reminded me of James Dean. He also had great hair, like John Travolta." Autumn loved *Welcome Back, Kotter* just for John's hair. "It was so dark and shiny, with a bit of curl in the layers. He was funny. Had good taste in music. Sometimes he seemed larger than life." She gave her boat a little push. "I wanted to be in his life for all of mine."

Snow squeezed her arm. "Blaine loved you, Autumn. He thought you were the coolest. One day he would've realized just *how* cool."

"Are you aiming that at me, Snow?" Summer said.

"If the shoe fits—"

"You got something else to say, come over here and say it."

"Hush up. It's my turn." Spring's boat sailed after the others. "Sometimes I hear his laugh. And you're right, Autumn, he was larger than life. My best memory of him is how we begged him to take us to Skate Inn East, and he'd say, 'Roller skating is for kids,' but he'd take us anyway, and he became the best skater. Mom used to say, 'Be nice to Blaine, say thank you, because not many brothers would drive around their little sister and her friends.' She'd give me ten dollars to help with gas, but he always gave it back to me." Spring laughed. "Mom never knew. I bought my Aigner purse by saving up that gas money."

"Well, Blaine would have driven us to Timbuktu if Summer was going along," Snow said.

Summer was about to snark back when Spring lightly touched her arm. *Shhhh.*

"He'd pick me up from the Northwood Mall Publix when I worked until eleven," Snow said. "Never got mad when I slept in his Keep On Truckin T-shirt."

"He'd pick me up so I could spend the night with you." Autumn's voice faded. "Nothing is the same without you, Blaine."

The votive boats began in the same direction as the wind shifted the water, cutting a bright light through the darkness.

One more to go. Summer's. "I loved when he was on the football field. He was so . . . confident, even cocky, but in a cool way. He was a good cook. I loved his spaghetti."

"Now I want spaghetti," Spring said.

"He was a daredevil." Summer continued her reminiscing. "I can still see him sitting on the goalposts after the homecoming win his senior year. Climbing to the high platform at Wakulla Springs was so like him. He—"

"Don't say another word." Snow sat up, her petite frame silhouetted in the thin light of the moon. "He wasn't a daredevil. He only did stupid things like climbing goalposts and jumping off thirty-three-foot platforms to get *your* stupid attention."

"His chocolate chip cookies," Spring said, "were the best."

"Shut up, Spring." Summer's and Snow's voices collided.

"I'd love one right now." Autumn interjected her big-sister vibe. "We should make a batch tonight in his honor." She pushed to her feet. "I'll ask Moxie if she has the ingredients."

"Hold up, Autumn," Summer said, turning back to Snow. "You're part of this. So, Miss UCLA, you got something to say? Cough it up. You've been daggering me all night. Really, you've been taking shots at me ever since Blaine died. What gives?"

"I don't have to tell you anything, Summer Wilde."

"Yeah, you do, Margaret Snowden. This is Truth Night." Using her given name was throwing down the gauntlet. "You're not a Season if you lie on Truth Night."

"Ha, that's rich. You just said we all lied. And I'm every bit a Season. More than you!"

"Hey, y'all, look." Spring stood on the edge of the dock. "The votives are drifting apart."

"How fitting." Snow's tone mocked. "Guess Blaine is telling us it's time to go our separate ways."

"Will you just stop?" Autumn cut between Summer and Snow. "You're ruining Blaine's memorial."

"Sorry, Fall," Summer countered. "Tell your friend Snow to spit out her truth."

Out on the lake, one of the candles flickered and died. Only three remained.

"You want the truth, you blond bimbo?" Snow pushed Summer back a step. "Blaine was in love with you. He wanted to marry you." She turned to Autumn. "Sorry, but that's what he used to tell me."

"I know," Autumn said. "He said it to me too. I still hoped one day he'd choose me."

"Love me? Marry me? He was eighteen, I was sixteen when he died. I don't want to get married for at least a decade. And he never told me of this grand plan."

"He would wait until the cows came home to marry you."

"How does that make me the bad guy?"

"'Cause you teased him, flirted with him, and—"

"Summer flirts with everyone, Snow," Spring said. "You can't hold that against her."

"So this is gang-up-on-Summer night? If that's the case, I'm leaving. Y'all gossip about me by yourselves."

"Come on, Summer, you know what I meant," Spring said. "I've said it to you before."

Summer whirled around to the remaining Seasons. "Yeah, but never like I was some villain because our friend liked me and died before anything came of it. I loved Blaine, but he wasn't for me. I'm sorry. Autumn, I wanted him to notice you, trust me. Blaine, he . . . he would've suffocated me."

"Suffocated." Snow morphed into a wintery storm. "That's rich. Because *you* suffocated *him*. He's dead because of you. Face-down in that water. Unable to breathe."

"Snow, stop." Autumn's command carried no authority.

"You, you killed him." Snow charged Summer with a growl, knocking her down on the dock. "He wanted your attention at Wakulla Springs, but you were *too* busy flirting with every guy in the place. We tried to get you to watch, but you didn't even turn around, so he did something stupid, a back flip, and died. For what? Nothing. You are *nothing*, Summer Wilde, and I hate you."

Summer launched to her feet. "Back at you, Margaret. I hate you more."

"Stop, stop, stop." Autumn's voice was the shrill wind of a hurricane. "You can't hate each other. You're sisters! Don't you know? You're sisters?"

What was Autumn shouting? Summer shoved past Snow. "She's not my sister anymore. The Seasons are through."

"Not the Seasons. But Jeff." Autumn's voice quavered as she stepped backward toward camp. "Jeff Wilde is Snow's real father. You're *real* sisters."

"What? You're crazy."

"I'm not, Summer. That's what I heard. . . outside Lily's office." Autumn covered her mouth and whispered through her fingers. "Jeff is Snow's dad."

31

Your Song

Summer

'97

"Evening, everyone. Welcome to O'Sullivan's." Summer strummed her guitar, did a bit of tuning, and winced when the microphone squealed.

Tank had purchased a little secondhand soundboard and now doubled as Summer's sound man. He was still learning the ropes, but she'd known worse.

Two weeks had gone by since she'd encountered the Preacher in the meadow and, without making any sort of fanfare, she felt changed, rested, delighted with her little stage at O'Sullivan's and sweet cottage on the edge of town. Though she'd not voice it out loud, she was falling in love with Levi.

"I've got a new song for y'all tonight." She played a few chords, eliciting applause, then paused again to tune her guitar. "I call it 'August in Tumbleweed.'"

The melody was in C with several minor chords to create a mood. She'd worked on the song in the evenings as Levi sat on the edge of the porch, whittling. *Whittling*. Like they lived in another era. Like a scene from Walton's Mountain. And now he was teaching her to shape things from wood.

O'Sullivan's was packed tonight. Tank had added three more tables and hired a third server, but pretty soon he'd be turning people away. There was a rumor going around about a chain drugstore popping up on the outskirts of town, so Tank talked of taking over the drugstore side and expanding the diner.

> August in Tumbleweed
> Is where my heart leads me.
> I'm lost, but found, dead but alive,
> I see myself when I look in your eyes.
> I've been a tumbleweed most of my life.
> Going here, going there, going nowhere.
> Never sure of anything,
> No rest, no home for this old tumbleweed.
> Then in a meadow, under a tent of lights, I found love.
> Alone among the masses no more, I'm finally home
>   with you.
> My August in Tumbleweed.
> No place like you I need.
> August in Tumbleweed,
> It's like heaven on earth to me.

When the last note rang out, a hush fell over the diner. "'August in Tumbleweed,'" she said, startled when a heady applause broke out. "Wow, thank you." She was used to applause, but not like this—resounding, heartfelt, and honest.

Levi sat at his usual table by the front door with Greta and Darrian, and even through the heads and table candles, she could see the light in his eyes, feel his love. He'd made no concrete declarations. Not even said, "I love you," but the radiance of it existed between them.

There were still a lot of shadows in her, hiding from love's light. For one, she'd not confided her past to him. Not the nitty-gritty of it. Then, Sunday night, as he'd helped her carry in the dishes she'd taken to the church potluck, he said, *"We all have a past, Summer. I think my love is enough to cover yours."*

Their eyes met, and, in a flash, Summer was back in the meadow, standing with the Preacher. If He loved her and Levi loved her, why couldn't she love herself?

Tank's new server, Oaklee, brought her a Diet Coke. Summer thanked her with a smile, took a sip, then chatted with the crowd.

"Who's not from Tumbleweed?" Half the hands went up. "Wow, O'Sullivan's is getting famous, Tank. Where are y'all from?"

"Oklahoma City."

"Tulsa."

"Missouri."

"Kansas."

"Hey, Oklahoma City." She started the chords of a song she wrote during her first tour. "Your names wouldn't happen to be Steel and Maggie, would they?"

The couple laughed, shaking their heads.

"I met a Steel and Maggie in Oklahoma City years ago. They reminded me of a couple I saw at an old tent meeting." She played through the melody, pulling the lyrics from the back of her mind. "Anyway, Steel and Maggie came to a show, and afterward told me my songs gave them hope. During a songwriting session, I hit on a melody that sounded like them, penned the lyrics that afternoon. 'Steel and Maggie.'"

The melody, the lyrics of a hardened man down on his luck with a beautiful, strong woman at his side, shifted the diner's atmosphere. It was a song of love and commitment.

In the back, a man entered and leaned against the old phone

booth. He wore the look of a Music Row exec with his slick hair and expensive-looking suit. Despite the low, ambient light, Summer recognized him immediately. What was he doing here?

The door opened again, and one of the servers told the new arrivals to try the second show.

> He's a rambling man with a heart of gold,
> Down on his luck with nowhere to go,
> He's got a woman of steel with a heart like a rose.

She sang song after song before closing the set with "The Preacher."

> A man like one I'd never known
> Dressed like any other Cowboy Joe
> His eyes bluer than a California sky
> With fiery light to break away the night.
>
> Down on my face, my tears on the ground
> I met the Preacher man, by love He was bound.
> Years go by and I think of that night.
> How He came for me, what have I done to make it right?
>
> Oh Preacher man, you will make it right.
> Oh Preacher man, who came to me in the night.
> You took my burden and filled me with light.
> Oh take my burden and fill me with your light.

With set one in the books, Summer slid into the booth with Levi, Greta, and Darrian and reached for one of Levi's fries, the melody of the Preacher clinging to her. She tried not to observe the diner customers, one after another, dropping tips into her jar.

"Fries are cold," Levi said.

She dropped the fry and signaled Oaklee.

"How you are not all over country radio is the world's greatest wonder," Greta said. "You've got to get some of your CDs to sell here."

"You and Tank say the same thing, Greta. I'm not investing in CDs when I'm not sure what my future holds." She glanced at Levi. What was she saying? That she wasn't going back to Nashville? If the Preacher was right, her desert season was over. How could she not try again?

"Stay forever," Greta said. "You could turn Tumbleweed into Nashville West. Or a southern Branson."

"I do love my little house. I heard Tracey Blue just put out a greatest hits album with 'The Preacher' on it. I could live off the royalties from that and the goodies from my garden." She nudged Levi. "This guy makes sure I don't kill everything we plant."

"She's a natural." Levi rubbed his hand down her back, making her feel warm and wanted.

"Summer," Tank said as he passed by with plates in hand, "we are *hopping* tonight. Anyway, someone's here to see you. He's out back. Here you go." He set the food down at the table behind them.

"Was he wearing a fancy suit?"

"That's the fella."

With a glance at Levi, Summer headed for the kitchen by way of the tip jar. She set it on the corner table with her guitar case.

Sooner and his new sous chef, Rip, battered chicken breasts and dropped them into the fry basket. The servers, Tondra, Oaklee, and Eva, were opening new ketchup and mustard bottles and re-filling the salt and pepper.

The kitchen was a symphony all its own.

Summer grabbed a wad of bills from her tip jar and stuffed them in Tank's back pocket. "Got to take care of my sound man."

He protested as usual, and she ignored him, as usual.

"Where's this man you spoke of?"

Tank tipped his head toward the door, his attention otherwise fixed on flipping a dozen burgers.

"Hello?" Summer stepped into the warm, humid night. "Rob Gallagher?"

The hot day had faded into a cool night, and for a moment, Summer sensed the fragrance of fall.

Fall. Winter. Spring. Summer. She couldn't go through any season without remembering the Four Seasons. Life on the road didn't allow for much sentiment or reminiscing, but memories of her former best friends remained close to her heart.

"Summer Wilde, hello." The man in the suit stepped out of a black sedan. "I'm Rob Gallagher from SongTunes Records." He offered Summer his card.

"I saw you in the back of the diner." She was suddenly nervous, even though he appeared rather thin and ghostly under the diner's bright corner spotlight. "We met a couple of years ago." She didn't reach for the card. "Why on earth are you in Tumbleweed?"

"I've been at an event in Stillwater with Kathy Fox." Another one of their new artists, along with Davis Hayes.

"She's really blowing up the charts. SongTunes must be rolling."

"We are, but I'm not here to talk about her. I want to talk about you. What I heard tonight, what I saw. You're a star, Summer."

She laughed. "Five years ago you said I was ordinary. Two years ago, you said, 'Love her, don't know what to do with her.' Hardly star quality, Mr. Gallagher."

"You never came to us alone before. You always had a band."

"So?"

"They dulled your shine. You're the singer, the songwriter, the talent, *the show*. I watched those people in there. You had them in the palm of your hand. The big guy in the chef smock must love you. I know we do, Summer. We're looking for someone like you. An artist with a storytelling voice like Dolly, Loretta, and Emmylou."

Summer lowered her defenses. "What are you saying?"

"We want to sign you. I was just on the phone with your manager, Clark." He held up his cell phone. "He'll be calling you."

"Oh, he will? Did he tell you he was my *former* manager?"

"At least hear what he has to say."

Sure enough, Tank stuck his head out the kitchen door. "Some fella named Clark on the phone for you."

"I'll call him back," Summer said. "Look, Mr. SongTunes, I'm thirty-eight years old and spent the better part of eighteen years on the road trying to build a career while Music Row folk like you shut the door in my face. My songs have been cut by Aubrey James and Tracey Blue. 'The Preacher' is on its way to becoming a classic. Still, no one has ever wanted to sign me as a solo artist."

"Let's change that, Summer. I can have a contract faxed to Clark by next week, and we can begin talks."

"How did you even hear about me? Tumbleweed isn't exactly a metropolis."

"A friend of mine lives in these parts. He ate at O'Sullivan's a couple of months ago. He asked if I knew you. I did some digging, made some calls. Someone sent me a story about you in the *Tumbleweed Tribune*."

"You're serious."

"One hundred percent. Summer, this isn't Music Row 'Hey baby, give us a call' mumbo jumbo. We're ready to talk business. With what I heard tonight . . . you have enough to go straight into the studio. I'm sure Tracey Blue and Aubrey James would love to sit in on a song or two. I'll reach out to them. I think a spring release followed by a summer tour will make you a household name. A luxury tour, by the way. Nothing like you've been on before, I'm sure."

In that bright, white light, the thin, ghostly looking Rob Gallagher morphed into a giant, wish-granting Music Row genie. Summer turned to putty as he flashed his big, white, record-exec smile and said, "Welcome to SongTunes, Summer Wilde."

32

Baby I'm-a Want You

Spring

'97

If this was the author life, Spring might not survive. Sitting on the office floor in a stream of July sunlight, a stack of spiral notebooks next to her, she flipped through the pages of her past for inspiration. Also known as procrastination.

> *July 5, 1975*
>
> *Had a blast yesterday at the Wildes' 4th party. I was the champ of the tube. I could knock anyone off. Even dad. So much fun. Summer tried to be the tube champ, then Snow, but those wimps were no match.*
>
> *Lying on my bed, I'm laughing, thinking of all the fun times I've had with Summie, Autumn, and Snow. Can you believe we met in kindergarten and stayed friends this long? Mom tries to say it's because of her. She knew Lily and Babs at Leon High, but buttinsky Judy, Judy, Judy has nothing to*

do with our friendship. We make up the Four Seasons and no one else. We'll be friends4life.

We're going to FSU together and everything. Mom wants us to rush Phi Mu. We'll see. . . . She's so bossy. Lily has an aunt who was a Chi Omega. She wants Summer to rush them. We've agreed, though, all for one, one for all.

Snow just called! Blaine's organizing the gang to go to Wakulla Springs in two weeks. He's trying to "get it on the calendar." Oh brother, who says that? My dad, that's who.

Guess I'll sleep. Nite.

P.S. I can't believe I'm so lucky to have my friends.

P.P.S. How could I forget this? Snow got a car! A '69 Camaro with an 8-track player! It's so tuff. Snow doesn't know who it's from, but gee whiz, how cool.

Spring warmed with reminiscing, and for a split second, she was sixteen again, enveloped in a world of innocence.

If she knew then what she knew now . . . But that wasn't the point, was it? Life couldn't be lived in perfection. Mistakes and disappointments were what carved out our existence. Made us who we were meant to be. Trials made folks seek God. Which made her think He was with her long before she knew.

Even though she was raised in church, Spring was late to the faith game. But little by little, she learned God's ways. He was all about relationship. Following God was remarkably simple, all while being oh so difficult.

How did Mal put it? *"Difficult in its simplicity."*

Reaching for a tissue, Spring wiped her eyes and flipped through the diary. A crumpled napkin, scrawled with her handwriting, fell from between the pages.

July 22, 1975

We're at Snow's, along with a million other people. I can't believe I'm writing these words, but BLAINE IS DEAD. He hit

his head on the third platform at Wakulla Springs. We are sick,
just sick. I'm in the den with Summie and Fall. Snow is with
Babs in her room. I don't think any of us will ever sleep again.
    I heard him hit and—

She'd just stopped writing at this point. She had no words.
Snow ended up sleeping with the Seasons in the den. They talked
until three, only to awake early to a very different life, one without
Blaine Snowden.

Spring replaced the napkin in the diary and set it aside for one
marked 1978 with KEEP OUT written in black block letters across
the green cover.

She flipped through the pages to February.

February 10, 1978
    She was born six days ago. She's with her parents who
love her. I'm happy for them. I honestly and truly am.
    Moxie said they're going to call her Joy. I shouldn't know,
but I begged her to tell me. She also snuck me a baby picture.
The mother wanted me to have it. I've not looked at it yet.
I'm not sure I ever will.
    I guess part of me is sad because my first child now be-
longs to someone else. But I know this is right. If I think of
keeping her, I hyperventilate!
    Guess I'm relieved. It's over and done. Fat and homesick.
    I think of the Seasons a lot. I miss them. Moxie treats
me like a queen, but I'm lonely and sort of confused about
my life right now.
    Since camp, I've only heard from Summer once or twice.
She's left FSU and moved to Nashville and even Lily doesn't
know how to contact her!
    Snow is loving UCLA. She's two hours behind me, and if
she calls, it's at midnight. I haven't heard from her all winter.
I called her dorm, but they said she was out.

Autumn is "in the wind" as Starsky and Hutch would say. I've written her, but she doesn't write back. That night at the dock . . . I still think about it and cry. Moxie says it's hormones, but I say my heart is broken.

Summer really tore into sweet, sensitive Autumn, and I'm wondering if the Seasons will ever recover. One day they were in my life and the next, boom! They weren't!

Dare I write it? The Four Seasons are no longer all for one, one for all.

In other news, Mom's here. She wants me to go home with her, but I'm staying until June. Maybe July. Lily said I could be her assistant director at Camp Tumbleweed. But I can't go back there, not to camp or Tumbleweed, ever again.

Spring closed the notebook but remained on the page, in the story, for a moment longer. Going through that alone with Moxie changed her. Possibly for the better. Made her grow up.

Still, falling in love, weddings, babies . . . those monumental moments were to be with the Four Seasons. *Salute.*

This morning, on a sentimental whim, she'd emailed Moxie with a short, coded note.

"How's it going?" Translation: *"How's Joy?"*

Spring knew the basics. Joy had just finished her freshman year at Oklahoma State, tentatively majoring in political science, considering a career in journalism or the law.

Spring looked up when a first-floor door opened and closed. Scrambling off the floor, she called over the balcony, "Lorraine?" Her cleaning lady usually came on Friday. "Did you lose half the week, sugar? It's only Tuesday." She waited, listening. "Hello?"

Someone was definitely in the house. Quietly, Spring crept down the stairs, circled through the kitchen for a wooden spoon—hey, it was better than nothing—and inched toward her office, where the door sat slightly ajar.

Someone sat at her computer. Taking a deep breath, Spring shoved the door open, wooden spoon at the ready.

"What are you—Mal." She lowered her weapon, trembling, exhaling. "You scared me. I thought someone broke in." She dropped to the Denman chair and laughed. "Look, I even brought a weapon." She whipped the spoon through the air. "I was going to stir the intruder to death."

"Mal?" He wasn't looking at her. Only the computer screen.

"Spring," he said, his voice low and controlled, if not a bit confused. "You have a daughter?"

"What?" Was it possible to go numb instantly? "W-what are you—" She leaned forward to see her computer. Her private email. Which he was reading. Oh no, no, no . . .

"You have a different email account? A secret one?"

No, no, no. She was always so careful to switch back from her LostInSpace@aol.com account to MalSpringSmith@aol.com.

"Um, Mal, I, um—" *Good grief, Spring, just tell him. He knows!* Surely some portion of the hundred speeches she'd practiced hovered near the surface.

"Moxie just wrote you." He pushed back from her desk. "Said Joy is doing great at Oklahoma State. She also said, let's see." He fixed on the screen. "'You should see her now. Just gorgeous. She has your eyes and smile. She could be Miss Oklahoma if she wasn't such a cowgirl. That girl can rope and ride.'" He stepped back. "Apparently her mother said she's curious about her birth parents. She wonders if you'd be interested in opening a dialogue. There's no pressure or obligation."

Spring stared out the window, wishing the lawn crew was filling the air with their motor sounds and the fragrance of cut grass.

"Spring, you have a daughter?" Mal exploded from the chair, his expression taut.

She flipped a switch and stood to meet his challenge. "Get out of my office and stop reading my email. It's none of your business." She pushed him toward the door. "We might be married, but I have a right to privacy." She sat in the seat warmed by the man she loved most in the world. He didn't deserve her ire, but he was getting it. "What are you even doing home?"

"I told you that Dan and I were testing some code on home computers. I brought an .EXE file to load on your PC. But I was going to save your data first." He waved a floppy disk at her.

"You should've told me you were here."

"I telephoned and left a message. I also called out when I walked in. 'Babe,' I said, 'I'm testing something on your computer.' You didn't answer, so I thought you were in the shower or out for a walk."

"A walk? At ten a.m.? In August? It's ninety degrees with a hundred percent humidity and no breeze."

Mal stared down at her. "You never answered my question. Do you—did you—have a daughter?" Spring looked out the window again, her attention on the tree limb where the neighborhood cardinal usually took his morning nap. "Spring?"

Say it. He knows! But the words would *not* come. She'd locked the truth inside for so long it'd become a part of her. Telling him meant ripping herself apart.

"All right, let's do some math. We've been married ten years, together for twelve. So that takes us back to '85. Before that, you were at FSU, winning the Miss Florida pageant and entering law school. This Moxie character mentioned Oklahoma, so I assume you met her when you were out there with the Seasons. Your email address is LostInSpace, which gives me no clue other than you trying to be obtuse."

Spring tensed as Mal expertly reasoned the facts.

"Around August of that year—I remember because I'd just returned from the fishing trip to Canada with my dad and I couldn't wait to see you—I got a Dear John letter. You said you were staying in Oklahoma because you wanted a year off from school. You thought we needed to be free to date other people."

She could see his reflection in the glass as he stood behind her. "Spring, did you cheat on me? I guess I can't say much now as it's been twenty years, but did you? Did you get pregnant? Why didn't you tell me any of this?"

She maneuvered the cursor to close her AOL account, then powered off the screen.

"Spring?" He didn't say the words, but she could hear *I'm waiting* in his tone.

"I was pregnant—" Her voice was so faint she couldn't hear herself. She breathed in and started again. "I was pregnant when I got on the Greyhound bus to Oklahoma. I stayed to have the baby. Moxie took me in, helped me find a family to adopt her. In February of '78, a lovely couple named Nancy and John Millhouse adopted her and named her Joy. I stayed with Moxie until July."

"February of '78. That means—"

"You're the father, Mal. From that one time . . . in your car." If she knew then what she knew now, she'd have never climbed into the back seat. If she knew then what she knew now, she'd have told him the truth the summer of '77.

"And you're just now . . ." His exhale felt like fire.

Then he was gone, the office door slamming behind him. Spring shuddered with regret. After a moment, Mal returned.

"Why? Why didn't you tell me? I feel like an idiot."

"I didn't want you to know. Didn't want to mess up your plans. Mom agreed with me and—"

"Well of course the great Judith Duval would not want me to know. Not want the world to know her family wasn't perfect. Her precious, perfect, pretty daughter."

Spring pushed to her feet. "That's not fair. She wanted to spare me embarrassment. She wanted you to go to school, earn your degree, set yourself up for a good life. She cared about you, Mal."

"I can't believe this. . . . So you postponed college to have a baby while I headed off to Duke? Why were my plans more important than yours?"

"Because you weren't pregnant, Mal. Besides, it wasn't your fault. It was mine."

"I can't believe my 1997 ears. You're seriously telling me getting pregnant twenty years ago was all your fault? I was there, Spring. I participated. It takes two to tango. If you had to put off your life for a year, why didn't I?"

"Because our dads would've decided we had to do the stand-up thing and get married. You'd have agreed and traded Duke for Tallahassee Community College and—"

"TCC is a good school."

"But not the school for you. Not the route you wanted to take. I didn't want to marry you because you felt responsible or guilty. Even if we didn't get married, what were you going to do, sit around and hold my hand for six months? You'd have driven me crazy. If we got married, I wanted it to be because you were madly in love with me and wanted to build a life with me. We were eighteen. What did we know?"

"My parents weren't much older. My grandparents were sixteen when they got married."

"They're from a different era. Either way, Mal, it's done. I put her up for adoption and went to college." Spring shuffled the papers on her desk. Just a distraction from the knife twisting in her chest.

"Is she the reason you've put me off about having kids? Hiding behind your career and now your novel? Because somehow having a baby would . . . what? I don't know." He started pacing again. The house phone rang, as if calling a time-out, but Mal said not to answer it. "It's probably Dan wanting to know if I ran the test."

"I knew once we got pregnant I'd have to tell you. There's no way I could say this was our first child when it wasn't. I felt trapped by it all. I know you love me, but keeping such a big truth hidden . . . I honestly thought it would break us. Maybe not divorce, but it would change how you saw me, and I couldn't bear it."

"I'm trying to wrap my head around the fact that in the last ten years, you never found a way to tell me. Unbelievable."

"You don't know, Mal. You weren't in my shoes. And didn't

you hear me? I was afraid it would change us, change how you saw me. I love us. I love how we are together."

"Why would it change how I saw you?"

"I don't know. Call it intuition."

"I call it Judith Duval."

She almost laughed. He had a point.

They retreated to their respective corners. Mal sat in the wicker chair Spring kept from her college days, and she continued to straighten her already-organized desk.

"You know what really gets me?" Her stoic, even-keeled husband broke, emotion leaking from his voice. "You went through it alone. Without me or the Seasons. Was your mom there?"

"She came out right before the baby was born. I was upstairs just now, reading my diary from that year. I'd forgotten how hard and lonely it was, how sad." She glanced at Mal. "I'm sorry I didn't tell you. I'd messed up my life. I didn't see the point in messing up yours too."

"You wouldn't have messed up my life, Spring. I could've gone to college a year late. Or I could've gone to college like planned and visited you at Christmas. Come out after the baby was born and supported you."

"You really think you would've done that? And tell your parents what?"

"The truth."

"Right, then they'd want to be a part of the decisions. Their friends would know, and by Halloween the whole town would be talking behind our backs."

"Fine, that explains 1977. But what about now? What about the last decade? You really think it would've changed how I see you or our relationship? I disagree—"

"Mal, it's changing us as we speak. Put yourself in my place. How does a woman say to the man she loves with all her heart that he has a child? 'Hey, babe, how was work? Want pizza for dinner? Oh, ha, funny thing, we conceived a child at Bobby Pearce's birthday party. Remember how we drank too much and shagged in the back seat of your car by Alligator Point?'"

"Minus the sarcasm, you've got yourself a story." He stood and stared out the window, hands anchored on his belt, his blue shirt still as crisp as when he put it on this morning. "At the end of the day, you don't trust me."

"Mal, babe, I do trust you. I absolutely trust you."

"Not about this, something so personal. Something that touches the core of your heart." He sighed. "Well, it's nice to know where I stand with you, Spring. I know plenty of married couples who keep secrets. I just never thought we'd be one of them."

The front door clicked closed as Mal exited the house. Spring moved to the window and watched him bypass his car and disappear around the corner, never breaking his long, even stride.

Summer

'77

Dad was Snow's *real* father? Summer slipped on a film of mud as she walked off the dock. She caught herself and whipped around to the stunned three standing where she left them.

In the distance, only two of the bark boat votives still flickered.

"What were you thinking, Autumn?" She jumped back onto the dry gray boards. "You don't just blurt—gah, you're supposed to be the smart one."

"Summer, come on. She didn't mean to—"

"Do I look like I care, Spring?"

Autumn wrung her hands and looked as if she were about to cry. "I didn't do it on purpose. You and Snow were fighting, and—"

"We always fight. But this . . ." Summer pointed at each one of them. "Too, too much. I'm through with y'all." She pointed back to Autumn. "Especially you. Why don't you go jump in the lake? Stop being a scaredy cat."

"Summer, you jerk. Chill out." Spring stepped forward. "Autumn said she didn't mean to do it. If you're mad at anyone, it should be your parents. Don't shoot the messenger."

Summer made a pistol with her thumb and finger. "Bam." She pretended to blow away the smoke, backed off the dock, and jumped over the muddy ground, beelining past Twilight, Starlight, Moonglow, and Sunglow for Mom's cabin.

As she approached, a small light edged the curtained window. Sergeant Dover's RMP was parked outside.

Summer entered without knocking and walked into the hum of the wall AC unit and tension between Mom and the law officer. She looked frazzled in her director's uniform—khaki shorts, a Camp Tumbleweed T-shirt, and frizzy hair. Her pink robe, which looked more like it belonged in a room at the Ritz-Carlton than a rustic, creaky cabin on the Oklahoma prairie, hung on a peg in the corner.

She had her back to the door when Summer entered. "It's not that simple, Cody. I can't—"

"Is Dad Snow's father?" Might as well cut to the chase.

Mom whirled around with a look of surprise. Maybe terror. "What?"

"You heard me. Is Dad Snow's father?"

"Well, um, Summer." She pressed her hand to her chest and tried to smile. "What makes you—"

"I told you that Autumn heard us, Lily," the sergeant said.

"How could she? We were whispering."

"She heard you, Mom."

Mom drew a long, deep breath and motioned for Summer to sit in the rocking chair while she remained standing. "Dad is Snow's biological father."

"How long have you known?"

"A few months. Since March. He'd written a couple of large

checks from a private account I didn't know about, and the company accountant called to verify the amounts. Then she congratulated me on your admittance into UCLA."

"Did he buy Snow's car?"

"I don't know for sure, but possibly."

"I don't understand." Summer sank down to the nearest chair. The truth knocked a bit of the fire out of her. "Why didn't he tell us? Why didn't he tell Snow? She practically grew up at our house. How long has he known?"

"He's always known. He met Babs shortly after Jack was killed, and she found *comfort* in his arms. It was a one-night affair. Nothing more. So for the sake of Blaine, Babs decided to make Snow Jack's daughter. She and Blaine moved to Montgomery for the next five years, coming back to Tallahassee just in time to put Snow in kindergarten. In the meantime, Jeff and I met, fell in love, and got married. He was fine with Babs' story about Snow. It was what she wanted. He agreed it made for a more cohesive family. Then Snow got sick when she was in first grade. Do you remember that?"

"Barely."

"Babs reached out to Jeff for help. Your dad, being your dad, set up an account to funnel money through, should she ever need help again."

"What? Did he think that'd make him a stand-up guy?"

Mom made a face. "Doesn't it? Even though Babs didn't want him in Snow's life, he set aside money to support her."

Summer shivered. After months of heat and humidity, the air-conditioned room felt like an icebox to her.

"I-is that why you were fighting?" Summer peeked at Dover, wishing he'd get a clue and excuse himself. This was a private conversation.

"Partly, though things have not been good between us for a while. We've been trying to work it out. When he told me about Snow, how he'd kept it from me for over fifteen years, how he built up a bank account for her and supported her . . . I admit I felt betrayed. It brought up my own hurts from the past related to your biological father, how he abandoned me."

"What does this mean for me?" Now it all made sense . . . Dad's affection for Snow. Not because she was the only Season without a father. But because *he* was her father.

"Nothing changes for you, Summer. Your father loves you very much. You're his girl." Mom's expression hardened. "This is why we decided not to tell you. Dad didn't want you to feel insecure. He's your father and always will be. When I confronted him, the first thing he said was 'Summer is my priority.'"

Insecure? Priority? Her whole life was a lie. Every insecurity she'd ever felt or tried to ignore had just become a reality. Dad had a *real* daughter. Margaret "Snow" Snowden.

She wasn't just Babs' daughter. She was *his* daughter.

"Gee, why would I feel insecure, Mom? Because Snow is his real daughter and I'm the kid who came with the woman he wanted to marry? Who he is now fighting with behind closed doors?"

"Our struggle has no bearing on you." Mom lowered her head, as if the conversation exhausted her. Sergeant Dover remained a statue against the wall. "I'm guessing if you know then Snow knows? Which Babs never wanted."

"Autumn just told all of us."

"Where is she now?"

"Snow? I'm not sure. Probably in your office making a long-distance call. This news is why you're in Tumbleweed, isn't it?"

"I thought your father and I needed some space." She sighed. "Look, Summer, sweetie, I'm sorry you found out this way, but this changes nothing. We are still a family and—"

"Mom, this changes *everything*. This is not the *Brady Bunch* where we're one big happy family hugging and kissing at the end of an episode."

"Why not? Snow is one of your best friends. She is practically a sister already."

318

"You mean the girl who just blamed me for Blaine's death? I hate her."

"She what? Surely not. How can she pin Blaine's death on you?"

"He was showing off for me or something. Did that stupid dive off the third platform. She says he loved me. Wanted to marry me."

"Poor Autumn."

"Mom, focus. Don't you see? Snow has a dad now. The dad she always wanted. *My* dad, who is paying her college tuition."

"He's paying your college tuition too. I'm telling you, none of this changes our family."

"How do you make that out? Our family is now you, Dad, and me, *and* Babs and Snow."

"There is no Babs and Snow."

"There's definitely a Snow and Dad. The cat's out of the bag." The more Summer spoke, the more she painted the picture of their future. "Mom, Snow lost her Paps five years ago and her brother two years ago. She just found out she has a father. Do you think she's going to let it go?"

"Maybe not, but don't believe the lie that Jeff isn't *your* father or that he doesn't love you."

"It all makes sense now," Summer said. "Why Dad told his buddy at the cookout I was 'Lily's kid.'"

"What are you talking about? When did he say that?"

"When I was nine. At the first Fourth party. He was grilling burgers and one of his friends said, 'Summer's a sweet girl, Jeff,' and Dad said, 'Well, she's Lily's kid.'"

"He simply meant you're like me. He says that all the time."

"Because it's impossible to be like him."

"Ho ho, missy. Don't look now but you're acting *just* like him."

"What about my biological dad? Where's he? Who is he?" Summer glanced at the sergeant. "You? Are you my daddy?"

"Summer!"

"What are you doing here anyway? In Mom's cabin?"

"Just updating her on the Camp Scott case. Making sure you all are okay." Sergeant Dover left his spot against the wall. "Summer, I'm not your father. But I was around when your mom dated Alec. He was a piece of work."

"But I couldn't see it." Mom sat on the edge of her bunk. "Cody says Alec is on his third marriage and has several children he's not claimed."

"I have more siblings?"

"Somewhere in the world, yes. Look, Summer, Jeff is *your* dad. He's a good man. He was a godsend, so don't let this news change the truth. He loves you. You're a Wilde through and through." Mom started for the door. "I should find Snow."

Sergeant Dover walked out first, then Mom paused to look back at Summer. "Stay here tonight. We'll talk."

"What else is there to say, Mom? Our lives changed tonight and there's no going back."

33

I Fall to Pieces

Snow

'77

Lily's office was locked, so she couldn't get to the phone. She pulled and pushed, kicked, hammered, and screamed at the door, then jerked the Willys MB keys from the hook in the kitchen to head to town, grinding the gears and stalling down the camp driveway.

Then, a mile down the road, Snow crashed nose-first in a ditch, abandoned the jeep, left the keys in the ignition, and ran blindly toward town.

Jeff Wilde was her father?

No, no, no. Autumn heard wrong. She . . . she . . . *must've* heard wrong or misunderstood or something. How was that even possible? Her father was Jack Snowden, same as Blaine's. They both looked like him. Mom said so. All the time.

Snow stumbled when her foot hit the edge of the asphalt, but she kept going. The dark road was nothing to the darkness of the lies.

What was true? Who was Blaine's father? Was he really a pilot who died in a training accident? What else had Babs kept hidden? Was Paps her true Paps?

Snow's foot crashed into something, a moving animal of some kind, but her bloodcurdling scream provided a good defense, and she kept running, pushing past the burn in her lungs and the ache in her legs. She had to call Mom. She had to hear the truth.

By the time she hit Main Street, she was a sweaty mess and out of breath. Spots flashed before her eyes. Streetlamps gave the town an eerie glow and . . . were those tumbleweeds drifting down the brick street?

Every shop was dark except for O'Sullivan's. Snow ran between the parked cars in front of the diner and burst through the door, aiming for the phone booth, bumping into the first table. The man had just taken a sip of his soda.

"Hey, watch it."

"Sorry." Her reply used her last breath. She dropped to one knee, head down, perspiration burning her eyes and dripping from her chin. Her lungs expanded with each inhale of the diner's cool air.

"Here, here. Snow, youngin, what's going on?" Tank's big hands raised her up, and she leaned against him as he walked her to the counter. "Sit, Snow. Lurlene, get her a tall glass of water, room temp."

"Phone," Snow said when she caught her breath and had taken a long, long drink. "I need to use the phone."

The diner's wall phone rang, the shrill sound making her jerk. "Tank," Lurlene said. "It's for her. Are you Snow?" She handed him the receiver, stretching the long, coiled cord.

Snow reached for the receiver. "Hello?" She expected to hear Lily's or Moxie's voice.

"Baby, it's Mom."

She slumped down to the counter and rested her head on her arm. "Is it true?"

Mom didn't answer at first. "Lily called, told me what happened. She said you'd taken some Willys thingamabob and gave me this number."

"This is the diner phone, Mom. I can't tie it up. I'll call you collect from the pay phone, okay?"

Sitting up, she wiped the sweat from her arm and the counter with the edge of her sweaty T-shirt and handed the phone to Tank. "Thank you."

"Can I get you a soda or something?" he asked.

"I don't have any money."

"This one's on me."

"A Coke, please."

Tank pulled out a tall, cold glass and set it in front of her. He leaned on the counter and said in a low, tender voice, "Want to talk about it?"

Her tears mingled with the sweat still on her cheeks. "Why do parents lie, Tank?"

"Ah, ain't no simple answer, Snow. Parents are human. They make mistakes. Sometimes they're hiding their own pain. Other times, they're trying to protect you. Sometimes, I hate to say, they're just liars." He yanked a wad of napkins from the tin dispenser. "Dry your face. It'll work out."

"Parents also say that too. Doesn't make it true."

"No, but nine times out of ten, things look different as time passes. Sometimes talking it out makes a situation better and you realize it's not as big a deal as it seems. Now, can I get you something to eat? Fried catfish tonight. Best in the state."

"You say that about everything on the menu." She took a long sip of her Coke. "My mom lied to me about my father."

Tank's eyes went wide. "I see."

"Lily's husband, who adopted Summer, is my real dad. All my life, I thought my dad was a pilot who died in a training accident."

"Ah, the plot thickens." He took the towel from his shoulder and started wiping the counter. "So, you and Summer grew up together but never knew the truth?"

"Nope." Snow tore at the sweat-soaked napkin, leaving shreds on the counter. "Just a few weeks ago I confessed to Summer that if I ever had a dad, I'd want him to be like Jeff Wilde."

"Does Summer know?"

"Yep, and she burned rubber all the way to Lily's cabin. Wouldn't want to be Lily." Snow slumped over the counter. "This is the second-worst summer of my life."

Losing Blaine was the first worst.

The diner's wall phone rang again. Lurlene answered, "O'Sullivan's. . . . Hold on. Snow, your mama wants to know if you're going to call. She *really* wants to talk to you."

"In a minute."

Lurlene relayed the message. "She said in a minute, ma'am. She's talking to Tank. Whatever it is, it's upset her pretty good. We'll see ya." She slapped down the receiver. "Bossy, that one."

"Is it so bad to know?" Tank said.

"You don't know Summer, Tank. She won't want to share her dad. She's kind of insecure about their relationship, though heaven knows why. He adores her. That's why I like him so much." She slurped the last of her soda. "What's worse is he probably bought my car, and dollars to donuts, he paid my UCLA tuition. So if he's doing all of that, why didn't he and Mom tell me? Does he not want to be my dad? How long has he even known about me?"

"Mercy. How'd you come by all this secret information, 007?"

"Autumn overheard Lily telling Sergeant Dover about it."

"Tumbleweed's Sergeant Dover?"

"Yep. I have no idea how he fits into the picture, but Autumn swears she heard it."

"Snow, look. I know it seems bleak on a hot Oklahoma night when all you've got in you is a Coke, but it seems to me this man is trying to step up, even if he abandoned his post as your daddy.

324

This must mean a great deal to you, otherwise you'd have not run to town like a bat out of hell, showing up here all out of breath, red-faced, looking to call home. Lur, another Coke for our girl and tonight's special. She needs to eat." Tank patted her on the arm. "Then you call home. Ain't no good to dive into a story like this on an empty stomach. I'll call your mama, let her know."

He was right; the catfish was far out. He was also right about a full stomach making her feel stronger, ready for an emotional conversation.

The phone hadn't even rung when Mom answered. "You took time to eat first? Who was that man who called? I don't care for him."

"That's how you answer the phone? Chewing *me* out? Try 'I'm sorry, Snow, for lying to you for eighteen years.'"

"I didn't lie. I just didn't tell the truth."

"As I recall, I got grounded one time for an answer like that when I was twelve." Deep-fried catfish made good fighting food.

"Well, what do you know? And how did you find out?"

"Jeff Wilde is my biological father. Autumn overheard Lily talking to some local sheriff's sergeant. Though I'm not sure why she told him. Jeff paid my UCLA tuition, didn't he? Did he buy the Camaro?"

"I see."

"I see? That's it? Mom, I'm nine hundred miles away and just found out my father is alive. He's actually a man I know and love. Should I go talk to Lily? She's probably already told Summer everything."

Mom's sigh was long and heavy. "No one was supposed to know, Snowy. Jeff and I agreed."

"The ship has left the port, so dish."

Another long, heavy sigh. "I meet Jeff right after Jack died. He was handsome, kind, generous, and, well, he comforted me one night."

"Good grief, Mom."

She detailed her very brief relationship with Jeff Wilde, how she still loved Jack, how she and Jeff parted ways. "Then I found out about you. Your grandparents were livid. Especially Paps. Wasn't it enough, he said, to lose Jack and have Blaine to raise on my own . . ."

The image of Paps letting Mom have it almost made Snow smile.

"Anyway," Mom said, "your grandparents and I talked it out, and I decided you were Jack's baby. He'd only been gone a month when I met Jeff, so it wasn't much of a stretch to say I was pregnant when he died. I moved to Montgomery to live with Aunt Hilly, got a job, and built a life. Then Mom died and Paps asked me to move back. I never imagined you'd meet Summer, let alone become her best friend. Paps wanted to move to a different part of town so you'd be in a different school, but you were so happy and settled. So was Blaine. You found this unique set of friends at such a young age, and I couldn't bear to rip you from it. We'd had enough change and death for a lifetime."

"When did he know about me? Jeff."

"From the start. But once I told him my plan, he agreed it was for the best."

"He's known all along that I'm his daughter? All the nights I stayed at Summer's? All the parties and holidays and birthdays, my dad was there?"

Silence.

"And he said nothing?"

"We agreed. No one was to ever know. How did Lily find out?"

"Not sure."

"Well, anyway . . ." Snow listened as Babs explained how she had to swallow her pride and call Jeff for help when she was sick, how he set up an account for her, all the while keeping the secret.

"So what about now? Does he want me to know?"

"Does it matter? In the past, he just wanted to keep the apple cart upright. I suppose it's all sorts of turned over now. You're eighteen. If you want to talk to him, go ahead."

"No, I don't think I will. Tell him to keep his guilt money. I'd rather he'd been my actual dad, even if it was awkward, than just a sugar daddy. Too little, too late."

"Snow, he's paying. He wants to pay. We need him to pay."

"We don't *need* him, Mom."

"Fine. Then I hope you're resigned to going to FSU. 'Cause I can't afford UCLA without his help. No film school for you. No future of making movies to change the world with your stories."

"I never said I wanted to change the world with my stories."

"You changed my world, Snow. I can't imagine life without you. I have no regrets. Only that you found out this way. I *am* sorry."

"I'd better go. I left the army jeep in the ditch."

"I love you, Snowbird."

Snow startled when someone knocked on the phone booth glass. Lily and Moxie peered in at her.

"Mom, I got to go."

34

Haven't Got Time for the Pain

Spring

'97

"You should've seen the look on his face, Autumn." Spring sat at the large white-and-blue island in Autumn's airy kitchen. "Shock. Hurt. Maybe disgust."

"What did you expect?" Autumn handed her a bottle of water, then took a seat at the end of the island. "Mal just found out he had a daughter."

"He shouldn't have read my email." Spring sounded more like a lawyer than a broken woman with a secret.

"Why'd you leave your private email account open?" Autumn countered. "So, now Mal knows. What are you going to do?"

"What can I do? She's a nineteen-year-old college sophomore

with a life of her own." Spring twisted the cap from the water bottle with a glance at Autumn. "You're dressed for work. I'm sorry. I didn't even consider it's the middle of the day."

"You're fine. I'm only doing office work this morning. My first client isn't until two." She twisted the cap from her own dewy water bottle. "I am curious why you drove to my house instead of your mother's. We've had lunch twice in the past month, but before that we'd not talked in, what, two years? It's not like we're confidants, members of each other's inner circle. Not anymore."

"I've been wondering the same thing," she said, "about coming here. Yet the moment he confronted me with the truth, you were the only person I wanted to talk to. You knew me then. You knew Mal. Who else could I talk to without an hour of preamble and explanation?"

And I still love you, my friend.

"So, Mal's gone, but you don't know where?" Autumn said.

"His brother called looking for him, so he didn't go back to work. I called his cell phone, but it rang from the kitchen." Spring walked around the island to the French doors overlooking the pool. "Your place is marvelous, Autumn. Your hard work has paid off."

"Cosmetology has been good to me. I make more than a nuclear physicist or a college professor, and my hours are much better. I'm not sure I'm contributing much to the human condition. Mom always wanted me to discover something amazing like the cure to cancer, or if the universe was truly expanding or contracting."

"Tall order." Spring liked the cool dew of the water bottle against her palm. "But you love what you do?"

"More than I could've imagined. This is a secret, so don't tell, but I'm working on a hair color line. I've done some research and talked to some labs." She shrugged. "We'll see. Jenna has a degree in marketing. I could tap her for help on the back end if the products ever launch."

"I'm impressed. Not surprised either. You were voted *Most Likely to Invent Something Great* by the class of '77. Every woman knows a hair color that doesn't fry her hair is something great." She walked along the fireplace built-ins where Autumn had framed images of the Childe family. Ridley and his wife and kids. Jenna and Janna with their families. Autumn with Chris and Tabby, and one with Devon and his buddies at the Eiffel Tower.

Spring checked out the porch off the family room. "A four seasons room?" She turned back to Autumn.

"The irony is not lost on me."

Spring returned to the island. "What happened to us, Fall? Friends since kindergarten and we didn't survive the so-called best summer of our lives."

"You know what happened. You were there," Autumn said. "That last week of camp was awful. The temperature was near one hundred. Humidity out the wazoo. No breeze. The lake felt like bathwater. The tension was so thick between us Seasons the Tumblers steered clear. Greta called her parents and told them to come get her."

"Those poor Tumblers of week eight. We weren't present for them. And Lily never relaxed her lockdown rules. Those girls were prisoners with ticked-off wardens."

"Everything we said we were going to do for the next four years—for the rest of our lives as friends, *sisters*—collapsed before our eyes." Autumn moved to the family room, carrying a bowl of pretzels.

"We didn't do the play the final week, did we?" Spring tried to place the barn and players, but in her memory the stage was empty. "Snow didn't take any photographs. Moxie roped us in for the group shot and that was it."

"Which I'm not in," Autumn said.

"That's right." Spring searched the mental images she'd draped in black and locked away. "You left with your folks Friday morning."

When her father told her mother how distressed she was over the fight between the Seasons, Shirl insisted they drive to Oklahoma. All of them.

Spring's parents flew out the week after to help her settle in with Moxie and confirm the plan. She'd begun to loathe the word *plan*.

"Do you regret any of it, Spring? Giving her up for adoption?" Autumn motioned for Spring to move to the large overstuffed sofa and set the bowl of pretzels between them. "You walked through that alone. Mal wasn't with you. We weren't with you. Not in heart, mind, or body."

"Moxie filled a lot of the cracks. She allowed me to wallow, then kicked me back into play when I wallowed too long. She said if I was going to act like a grown-up then I had to endure grown-up consequences. The hardest was everyone else. Granny was the most compassionate, if you can believe it. My stiff, upper-crust, prim and proper, southern church-lady Granny. 'Simmer down, Judith,' she'd say. 'It's not the end of the world. Just a detour. A precious new life is coming into the world, and by George, God is still on the throne.'"

"Say what you want, but your best friends had abandoned you."

"We abandoned each other. I didn't stick up for you enough when Summer tore into you. I probably thought she had a right to do it."

"I've debated that question for twenty years." Autumn held her pretzels in her hand. "Did I say it on purpose, or did it just slip out? I don't know, Spring. The more time goes by, the more I can't discern anything about that night. All I know is there was a hurricane, nor'easter, blizzard, and tornado in the camp the rest of the week." She reached over to squeeze Spring's hand. "I'm sorry I wasn't there for you."

"Same, same, Fall." The midmorning sunlight streaming through the French doors gave the room a magical feel and broke the tension Spring carried from her argument with Mal. "But we found our way back to each other and I'm grateful. I grew up the summer of '77 and maybe that makes it the best summer of my life, I don't know."

"Didn't we all?" Autumn munched contemplatively on a pretzel. "Maybe that was our mistake. The Four Seasons focused so much on the best summer of our lives that we forgot the reality of being four young women on the brink of adulthood. We didn't need backpacking through Europe or spending every possible moment in the pursuit of fun. We needed to grow up."

"Twelve years, though, Autumn . . . Twelve years of friendship and camaraderie shredded the moment we were really tested."

"I'm not sure we could've ever been ready for that kind of testing. Pregnancy, secrets, truths about fathers."

"Now look at us," Spring said. "You're a successful businesswoman. I made partner at my law firm in record time. Snow makes movies."

"Oscar-winning movies!"

"Summer is, well, Summer."

"She had a hit song."

"'The Preacher.'" Spring wanted to love the song, but every time she heard it, all she felt was loss. "I'm sad we've not shared all our moments with each other."

"What say you and I do better?" Autumn said. "Let's not wait another two years to have lunch. Let's make it a regular thing. Get two of the Seasons back on track."

"I say, let's try." But Spring knew the debris on their old road of friendship would take time to clear.

"To be honest, Spring, I don't think the Four Seasons will ever be together again. At one time I believed we'd find our way back. Then Jeff and Lily divorced. I knew it would be hard for Summer to come to Tallahassee, but I had hope. Then Jeff married Babs and that was the nail in the coffin for Summer and Snow, thus the Four Seasons."

"Jeff and Babs were a twist in the plot no one imagined."

Lily and Jeff divorced in the early '80s. A few years later Jeff and Babs flew to LA for a movie premiere on which Snow was assistant director. They became friends. Started dining together. Going to movies. Fell in love. Surprised everyone who knew them.

"We could invite in Baby Season." Spring reached for a couple of pretzels. "But she lives in Tumbleweed, and I'm not too keen on—"

"Maybe that's what we need, Spring, to go back to Tumbleweed. Back to where it all fell apart." Autumn got up to refill the pretzel bowl. "Didn't you say Joy is asking about her birth parents?"

"She lives in Ponca City when she's not at college," Spring said. "I'd have to talk to Mal. Now that he knows, I want him involved with everything going forward—assuming he wants to be."

"Give him time to wrap his head around all of this, Spring."

The conversation faded for a moment, and Spring finished off her water and set the bottle in the recycle bin. "I should find my husband and fix the Hindenburg-sized hole in our marriage." She grabbed her bag from the island. "How about lunch or dinner next Thursday?"

"We could do a movie night." Autumn set the empty pretzel bowl in the sink. "Watch *Funny Is Always in Love*? It's Tabby's favorite. By the way, she doesn't believe I ever had a best friend, let alone Snow Snowden, Summer Wilde, and Miss Florida, you."

"We'll have to prove her wrong."

Autumn walked Spring to the door. "Thank you for coming over, Spring. It means the world. More than I imagined."

"Thanks for opening the door. See you next Thursday." She stood in the threshold between the light of Autumn's foyer chandelier and the muggy heat of a northwest Florida day. "Do you think if you and I start mending fences, maybe we could draw in Snow and then—"

"Maybe. But we'll need a force more powerful than a tornado, hurricane, nor'easter, and blizzard."

Spring headed down the stone steps to her car. "I'm not sure such a force exists."

35

If You Leave Me Now

Summer

'97

"So that's it? You're leaving?" Levi stood under the elm where he'd hung a bench swing three weeks ago—wide enough for the both of them to sit—and watched her carry her bags to the truck. "You're breaking your lease? Never mind your agreement with Tank."

And me. He didn't say the words, but she felt them.

"I'm all paid up on the house, and Tank knew from the get-go I wasn't staying." She tossed her suitcase and duffel bag into the truck bed, then slid her guitars along the bench seat.

Behind her, the house contained more items than she thought she'd acquired in the two months she'd been in Tumbleweed. Dishes. Clothes. Linens. Pots, pans. Food. The kind you cook, not merely heat up in the microwave. She had a quarter of beef in the freezer. She owned a lawn mower, for crying out loud!

Tumbleweed had lured her in for a long summer's nap. But her dream woke her up.

"What about your stuff?"

"Take the food and beef, and anything else you want. I'll tell Murry he can keep the rest. The pots and pans are from Made In. All the linens are Peacock Alley, and the furniture is Williams Sonoma." She glanced back at him. "I hate cheap stuff."

"Especially Tumbleweed. We're all cheap stuff to you, aren't we?" Levi's voice shot through her as she slammed the truck door. "Just country bumpkins, ranchers and farmers, small town, small minded. Easy to leave when the big time calls."

"Stop putting words in my mouth. I never said those things. I don't even think them. My biggest fans are that lot." Summer stepped closer to Levi, ready to stick to her guns. Yet one look in his eyes almost made her crumble. "Levi, don't you get it? *This* is my last chance. A real shot at music." As for his unspoken *What about me?* she'd been very clear on the fact he could do better. Which she was proving right now. She was a rolling stone. "Did you really think we were going to get married, settle down, and have a couple of kids?"

"Yes!" Any other time, any other man, his insistent reply would've made her laugh. But not Levi. Nothing about this was funny. He wanted her, sincerely wanted her. Warts, cracks, mistakes, selfishness, and all. And the power of such a lure was almost too much to resist. *Almost.*

"You can do music anywhere, Summer, if it's music you love. You're making a difference to people around here. When you live in a small town you sometimes feel like no one sees or cares. It's Whoville all the time. Good talent, good art, good music passes you by for the big cities. But the word is getting out. . . . You have a unique opportunity to make something all your own and not become a cookie-cutter Nashville artist—and you *know* that will happen. Because the music business is about fame and fortune."

"Yes, Levi. Absolutely. So what? I've spent eighteen years living on crappy tour buses and sleeping in cheap motels, crisscrossing the country to sing my songs, often to people too drunk to realize I'm not Trisha Yearwood, and finally—*finally*—it paid off. Seven weeks ago, not knowing why, I came to Tumbleweed. To find some lost piece of myself? Maybe. But *this* is *why* I came. I know it now."

"I thought you came to keep your promise to the Preacher." In the shade, with his thumbs hooked through his belt loops, his ball cap backward with a thick tuft of his dark hair curled through the closure, he looked like he belonged on a Hunky Cowboys of the West calendar. His tanned high cheeks and angular jaw, and the expression in his sky-blue eyes, made her feel lucky to have known him, let alone be loved by him.

And to love him back. Yes, she loved him. More than anything. But . . .

"Don't you see, Levi? This is what the Preacher meant. He brought me back here by some divine providence so I could rest, find myself, find my muse. Then, wonder of wonders, Rob Gallagher takes a detour to *Tumbleweed*. I don't have to tell you something like this rarely, if *ever*, happens. I'm Lana Turner sitting on a stool in a Hollywood malt shop. I think the Preacher did this. I do."

She had to make him see. Understand. Their love must submit to her need to share her songs with the world.

"Seems to me the Preacher's opponent is at work here."

Summer laughed. "The devil? *Please*. He's far too busy corrupting world leaders to bother with me."

"You could say the same of the Preacher. He's far too busy saving the world to bother with you, yet He pitched a tent in the meadow and appeared to you twenty years ago. As far as I know, He didn't appear to anyone else. You're not Lana Turner. You're the woman at the well."

"One of these days I'm going to have to look up what that means, but for now, Levi, I have to finish what I started. If this opportunity didn't come from the Preacher, then who? Either way, it's here, and if I don't go, I know I'll always wonder. Did I miss out on anything? Did I miss my chance? What if, what if, what if?"

"What about the things you started here? What if you let yourself love me? What if you have a couple of kids who help heal your heart? What if you bless ol' Tank, who's tirelessly manned that diner for forty years? What if people needing a night on the town come in to hear you, and some lyric or note in your song breaks open their hardened hearts? How many Steel and Maggies are there—"

"Very poetical, Levi Foley. You should pen a song." She smiled, but he did not. "You know you're making my point. Through SongTunes I can reach millions. Not tens or hundreds."

"What if Nashville is nothing more than the knockout round of the fight?"

Okay, enough. "Are you done? 'Cause it would be rude to walk away from such an encouraging pep talk."

"I know artists, Summer. I lived in LA. I worked with aspiring singers, musicians, and actors. Your drive is unique. Most would've quit years ago. But not you. Eighteen long years and still ticking."

Summer turned for the driver-side door. She'd listen to no more of this. Her mind was made up.

"I wonder if all you need is a better offer," Levi said, and when she glanced back, he slowly bent to one knee, a ring box in hand. "I started looking the moment you came to town."

Summer stumbled backward against the truck and grabbed the door handle. "I, um—" Her eyes filled. *Do not, Levi. Do not say, "Will you marry me?" Not from you.* Not when she knew she'd turn him down. "Gotta go."

He opened the box, right there, in front of her little house where they dined on the porch at sunset, watched movies, cuddled on the couch, made out until he pushed away, declaring, *"I'll carry you upstairs right now if I don't go. But I made a commitment to God and myself when I left LA that my next lover would be my for-real wife. You are killing every desire to keep my word."*

337

Of course, that only made her fall in love with him even more. No man she'd ever so much as flirted with honored her that way.

"I love you, Summer Wilde. Will you marry me?" The question hit in the air with the fragrance of the flowers and night-blooming jasmine.

"Levi . . . what in the . . ." She started to climb into the truck, then whipped around to him. "Are you kidding me right now?" She kept her gaze well above the diamond's enormous sparkle. "A proposal? When you know I'm leaving? I'm thirty-eight, Levi, a dinosaur in the music business. The fact I'm being offered a record deal at all is nothing short of a miracle. Can't you see I have to try?" She was a broken record.

"You took the words out of my mouth."

Her attention dropped to the ring. Oh, that diamond . . . like a full moon against a black velvet night. Apparently, he hated cheap stuff too.

"I've always loved you, Summer. I can't offer you fame or fortune, but I can offer you all of my heart. I can offer you a life that lasts well beyond the adoration of fans or the whims of a record label. I'm offering you a home, not just a house. I'm offering stability. Commitment. Children, if you want. In fifty years, I'll still be by your side. Will this record label?"

"How should I know? I'm not a fortune teller." Her blunt, stupid answer was no match for the sincerity and heart of his proposal. "I don't know how long it will last, or if the fans will stick with me, but in fifty years, at least I can look back and say I took my shot."

"You have two shots here, Summer. Me or Music Row." Levi tucked the ring box into his pocket. "I can guarantee you'll regret one of them."

"That's not fair, Levi. After seven weeks with you, you dare me to give up the last eighteen years in Nashville? Why? Why are you doing this? Why can't I have both? You and music?"

"I'm all for that, Summer. I want you to do music. I also want you to marry me." He stood, taking her hand in his. "We're right together. I know you love me."

I do! "Come with me. To Nashville." Her invitation sounded pleading, with a lace of anger. Truth? She was scared. He was challenging her, and she didn't like it. Even worse, he was ninety percent right. She pulled out her well-worn self-deprecation card. "You shouldn't want to marry me, anyway. You know how many lovers I've had?"

"Don't care as long as I'm the last."

"I've dumped men like cold hotcakes, Levi. I've never had a man in my life for more than six months. I walked out on my parents. Shoot, I walked away from the Seasons. I was supposed to be Spring's maid of honor. I didn't even go to the wedding because Dad had started dating Babs. I don't think I've talked to Autumn or Snow since I walked off the dock the night all the truths came out. What makes you think I'd keep any commitment to you?"

She shuddered with tears, resenting his confidence and her weakness. "Even if I accept you, I'll leave you. One day you'll wake up, and I'll be gone. Too selfish, too restless to stay." Yet hadn't Tumbleweed proved to be home, a place of peace and rest?

"You're a coward, Summer."

"Excuse me?" Coward? She was a lot of things, but a *coward* was not one of them.

"You heard me. I didn't stutter. You won't give anything or anyone a chance beyond what you can control. In your stubborn mind, the only way you can sing your songs, do music, is through the Nashville system that would as soon crush you as build you up. You can't open your heart and mind, your imagination enough to see out of the box. But it's not about music, is it? It's about that day on the dock, that day all your fears came true. You weren't your dad's special girl anymore, at least in your mind, and now you have to control—"

"Stop, Levi, just stop." She pressed her hands to her ears. He was strumming her pain with his words.

"Then your parents divorced, and you decided your dad divorced you too." How in the deep blue did he know all of this? Was she so easy to read? "You came with your mom into the marriage, so the opposite must be true if the marriage ended. Then you saw your dad with Snow at some pizza place."

"Barnaby's." She'd written Dad right after that happened, told him to leave her alone, that he wasn't her father. She regretted it the moment she dropped the letter in the mailbox. When he called her a few days later, she said she meant it and hung up.

"And you left FSU for Nashville."

"Ted Bundy killed my sorority sisters. I had to go. Too much death and loss. Too close to the Camp Scott murders." But he was nailing her to the wall. The picture he painted brought her life into full view. Had the last twenty years merely been rebellion against her dad?

Levi walked to his truck, opened the passenger door, and returned with a stack of letters. "I reread these last night. There's a tenderness in some of them you don't have anymore."

No surprise. Summer stared at the pile of letters in his hand, tied with a piece of twine. "Y-you kept my letters?" She'd thrown his letters away when she downsized a few years ago to spend more time on a tour bus.

"I was going to toss them when I moved home, but Mom got a hold of them. Tied them up with this twine. Said I might need them some day." He offered them to Summer. "But I think you need them more than me."

She refused his offering. "Burn them if you want. They're yours." Tears stung the back of her eyes. "I've already lived that life. No use living it again."

"Can I just say one more thing before you go?" Levi tossed the letters back into his truck. "If the Preacher asked you to sing for Him, don't you think He has a plan?"

"Levi. Hello, McFly, this *is* His plan." Summer glanced between the tree and the cottage and quelled the sense she was falling apart. "Otherwise, what would I do? Sing in church on Sunday?"

Levi laughed. "Boy, you don't think much of someone who has the name Almighty, do you? I think He's a bit more creative than Sunday morning for twenty or thirty minutes, Summer. He gifted you. He called you. He'll make a way for you. Yet you think you're the only one who can hold the reins. You won't trust Him because He might be a liar like your dad, or not love you like He claimed.

"You know," Levi went on, "if a horse and rider get into a tug-of-war over who's controlling the reins, the rider has to train the horse to know that he's the boss. The horse fights the reins, but the rider holds on, only giving in when the horse yields. You've been fighting the Preacher for control of your reins for a long time. He's only going to hold on until you trust Him. Or maybe He'll just let go until you mess up so bad you realize He's your only hope."

She could spit in his eye for how his words cut through to her secrets, to the fears she'd buried.

"You don't have to marry me, Summer. But speaking to you as a friend, as a guy who tried to do it his way for more years than I care to admit, this is your chance to do it His way. Maybe it is Nashville, but give Him time to prove Himself to you. I like the prodigal son story. You know it?"

"Sort of." *Look up the prodigal son story.*

"Kid asked for his inheritance, so his pop gave it to him. He squandered it all on gambling, women, carousing, and ended up living with pigs. One day, he came to his senses and returned to his father's place." Levi leaned into her. "*Came to his senses.* Come to your senses, Summer. I sure wish I'd come to mine a long time ago."

"Why can't that be me coming to my senses?"

"Is it? Summer, I see you with the people at O'Sullivan's. You're doing way more for a crowd of fifty than fifty thousand. Why? 'Cause you're there with them, singing *their* songs, the ones they'd write if they could. You're one of them. Not some icon on a stage they forget about the next day. Folks come to see you every week. 'Wouldn't miss one of Summer's sets,' they say. You're impacting them. And I think there are songs in you that will release people from their loneliness and pain."

"Levi, oh my gosh, you're relentless. You don't get it, do you? I have to do *something* great and grand because Snow won a freaking Oscar when she was thirty-three. An *Oscar*!"

There. She'd said it. What she'd never confessed to anyone. Happy now?

"What? You think . . . Whoa, Summer—" Levi stepped toward her, but she moved back. "You can't believe that makes your dad love her more. That she's better than you."

Doesn't it? She's his blood. I'm a name on a piece of paper. "I should go."

"I wish you'd stay and talk about this."

"There's nothing more to say."

He surrendered his hands. "Then I hope it works like you want, Summer. I do." Levi backed toward his truck. "Good luck."

"Levi." He was leaving and . . . wait . . . wait. "Didn't you *just* propose?" She'd never formally answered him.

"You turned me down."

"Did I?" She began to tremble as he slid behind the wheel of the truck. "I thought this wild conversation was some kind of negotiation."

He stood on the truck's runner and peered at her over the top of the door. "Do you love me?" His blue eyes demanded the truth.

Yes, I love you. But . . .

"I know you do," he said. "Just not more than a record deal." He fired up the big diesel engine, shifted into gear, and pulled alongside her. "Good luck, Summer. I mean it."

She watched him go through a pool of tears and the rhythm of *Go after him* drumming in her head. But she didn't move. Nashville, her tough old lover for eighteen years, *wanted* her. Why couldn't he see that?

342

Locking the front door of the house, she tucked the key into an envelope with a note to Murry.

Ten minutes later, she drove through downtown Tumbleweed, where nearly all the angled parking spots were full and the sidewalks bustled with business. Levi's dad talked to the mayor in front of his insurance company. O'Sullivan's *Open* sign flashed above the script on the glass declaring *Live Music with Summer Wilde*.

So sorry, Tank. But she'd promised him she'd be back. Tumbleweed was her base now. A pilgrimage home would be an annual thing if for no other reason than to stay connected to the magic.

She called Greta to say good-bye. "I'm so grateful for all you did for me, Baby Season." Dr. Yeager was quiet, if not too quiet. But it was okay, you know? Summer didn't need any weepy good-byes.

The door of Tumble Time was propped open. The new owner, Ralph, had installed a wall unit air conditioner, but the place was still hotter than blazes. She parked at the Murry Gaylord Real Estate office and left the envelope with his assistant.

The next stop? Tumbleweed's one and only traffic light, then Nashville or bust.

Summer waited at the red light with a nervous energy in her bones. She turned the radio up, then down, glanced in the rearview mirror to see the town she'd grown to love behind her. Her cute cottage, her garden, her corner stage at O'Sullivan's, Levi . . . all the things that brought her peace.

Leaving Tumbleweed now, on a high note of hope, healed a bit of the past. How she lit into Autumn after she dropped the "sister" bomb. How she'd told the lot of them, *"We're through."*

She'd written songs about the healing of friends, but it would take more than four chords and kitschy lyrics to reunite the Four Seasons. Time and distance had created an even wider canyon between them.

The light flashed green, and Summer hit the gas. As she approached the edge of town, past the park and the carousel, she saw a hitchhiker on the side of the road.

Nearer and nearer, she realized he wasn't thumbing for a ride but looking right at her. It was the Preacher in His hippie bell-bottoms, wide tie, and blue Oxford button-down.

What is He doing out here?

Summer gunned the gas and purposed not to look at Him. She gripped the wheel and sped around the bend. *Made it.* But there He was again, on the other side of the road, and His voice filled the truck cab with thunder.

"You promised, Summer. Sing for Me."

36

I'll Be There

Snow

'97

The script was done, but Snow wasn't happy with it. But as August rolled around, she didn't have time to doubt herself.

She emailed a soft copy to Loudon and to the studio. Then she printed four copies, slipped them into manila envelopes, and mailed one to the studio, one to Aaron Heinley, who was another newcomer with buckets of talent, one to Jeremiah Gonda, the new director who was sprinkled with gold dust, and one to Raymond Daschle.

Her cover letter had one word. *Notes?*

Once she got their feedback, she'd roll up her sleeves and re-write. Now that July had passed, she'd go into August and the fall more focused.

She'd written in the early mornings and late evenings to free her days to be with Olive. They'd gone to the beach, to Disneyland, up to the mountains. They'd hosted cookouts and parties, attended many of the same. Snow was exhausted. She'd miss her girl when school started, but how she yearned to hear the school bell clang.

Being busy in July proved cathartic. She'd healed a lot over the years, but she remembered every detail of Blaine's dive, his head hitting the platform, and the splash of his lifeless body.

Over time, that memory had bonded with the night at Camp Tumbleweed, when they floated their memorial bark boats over Skiatook Lake. The tension. The arguments. How she'd tried not to blurt out, "He died because of you, Summer," but the relief she felt when she did.

Then Autumn . . . oh, Autumn. The peacemaker Season was only trying for peace when she declared, "You're sisters!" The price she paid, that they all paid . . .

She could still *feel* the flicker of the last bark boat, sailing alone toward the rock, a metaphor for the days ahead.

Then it too went out.

"Babe, just got your email." Loudon peered into her office. "Can't wait to read it. Is it a summer rom-com? The studio said they preferred summer over a holiday film."

"It's a fall rom-com. The scenery is prettier, and we can have a cozy fireplace scene."

"Yeah, love, but no chance for a muscled chap in swimming togs or a sexy lass in a bikini."

She threw her pen at him. "Get out of my office."

Loudon ducked, his big grin full of mischief. "By the way, I sent a car to pick up your folks. Didn't know if you'd finish in time."

"Good idea." Snow shut down her computer. "I'll start dinner, have it ready when they walk in."

Her parents' visits always brought on a bit of reminiscing. She missed her friends, and try as she might, she could never forget that Summer was also Jeff Wilde's daughter.

"Olive is so excited." Loudon made his way to the chair beside her desk. "Forget about the script for now and relax."

"I'm not thinking about the script. I'm thinking about what used to be." She leaned toward the light coming through the large-paned window. "Me, the Four Seasons. Watching Olive and her friends reminds me of how we used to be. Makes me miss everyone. Then there's Jeff—Dad. I've spent the past twenty years getting to know him while Summer spent twenty years running away. She had him the first quarter of her life, and I had him for the next quarter. But shouldn't we both be his daughters?"

"Love, Summer has to sort out the issue her way."

"Her way stinks. And she's wasting time. Dad isn't getting any younger. He'll be sixty-four this fall."

"You could always reach out to her."

Snow gaped at her husband. "Do you love me at all? Or do you want to see me curled in a ball in the corner of our room, weeping, calling for my mommy? Loudon, that girl has a two-edged sword for a tongue. Besides, what would I say? 'Dad loves you. Grow up, you freak.'"

"Never doubt the double edge of your own verbal sword." He grinned. "I'd leave off the freak part, but yeah, say something like that, only in your nice Snow Snowden director voice. 'Darling, great scene, but do you think you could, I don't know, add some emotion? You're so good at emotion. That's why I cast you. I believe in you.'"

"I mean it when I talk to the actors. I'm not sure I'd mean it if I talked to her. I'd like to kick her in the knee and the other knee."

"Then why are you even giving her a second thought? Admit it, you love her, and, my darling, you miss her."

"Go read my script." She rose to kiss him. "I'm going to cook dinner."

"Darling, one last thing about Summer. Has it occurred to you that your success only fuels the fire? Her music hasn't taken off, and you won an Oscar for your first movie."

"Maybe."

Constance came in with the mail and handed it to Loudon. "Olive is still in the pool with her friends. Should I get her out for a snack? A bit of a rest?"

"Only if she wants," Snow said. "She's a strong swimmer and knows when she needs a break. Why don't you put out some snacks? Let them grab them when they want." Loudon passed a letter to Snow. "You know, I think I have time for a run, and a good sweat, in the park before I start dinner."

Snow glanced at the postmark on the letter as she jogged up the curved staircase to the bedroom. *OK. Oklahoma?*

Pausing on the landing, she tore open the flap and pulled out a notecard with *Greta Yeager, MD* imprinted on the bottom. The handwritten note was short and shocking.

"Snow?" Loudon looked up at her from the bottom of the stairs. "Who's the letter from?"

"Greta. Baby Season. Summer's in Tumbleweed."

Spring

'97

The truth will set you free. It will also cause pain, riffs, and sorrow. But for Spring Duval Smith, she lost a hundred invisible pounds when Mal found out about the baby girl named Joy.

She came home from Autumn's to find him waiting for her, full of compassion and questions. They'd talked until shadows crossed the living room walls. At the end of it all, the one reverberating word was "Sorry."

Now, dining on the lanai with the evening sunset glinting off the pool's blue surface, enjoying a dinner of salad, grilled salmon, and sparkling water, Spring believed she was truly ready for their future.

"I've always kind of regretted that night, Spring," Mal said out of a moment of silence. "What a rotten way to ask the girl I loved to lose her virginity."

"If you'd not suggested that back seat, I would have."

"The next day I woke up in a panic, wondering if you could get pregnant. I was too scared to ask, but that's why we, um, never did it again. I wanted to, but, man, between health class and Coach Truman's bare-knuckle lectures about sex and birth control, I could just see Duke being flushed down the drain and—"

"Mal." Spring set down her water goblet with a clank. "That's why I didn't tell you. You're making my case. You wanted Duke so bad you could taste it. I knew I'd put the baby up for adoption and go to FSU. Autumn had diverted from the great plan to go to cosmetology school, and then Snow declared she was off to UCLA, so what if I diverted too? Saying I wanted a year off was an easy story to tell. Summer wasn't too thrilled to go it alone, but she didn't even last winter quarter."

"The Chi O murders were tragic. Trina was good friends with Lisa Levy." Trina was Mal's big sister. "She couldn't sleep for months after it happened."

"Know what Summer said when she called me to tell me she was leaving? 'On top of *all* this, Elvis is dead.'"

Mal spewed his water. "Elvis? What does he have to do with—"

"Nothing. It was just her way of dealing with the world's brutality."

He reached for his napkin to wipe water from his chin. "I'm surprised not one of the Seasons told me about the baby."

"We may have gone our separate ways, but our loyalty ran deep."

"No kidding. You went to the movies with Craig Emmitt during senior year spring break, and not one of the Seasons broke ranks. I went to Summer's, Autumn's, and Snow's looking for you, and all I got was a Sergeant Schultz 'I know *nothing*.' Though for a moment I thought Summer would give you up, but she was just messing with me."

"You had to know she'd mess with you, Mal. Teasing, goading, sarcasm was her art form. Did I tell you how she freaked out Snow when we arrived at Camp Tumbleweed? The cabins were so run-down. They did look like something from a horror flick. 'Look,' she said, 'The Texas Chainsaw Massacre Slept Here is carved on the side of a cabin?' She knew Snow *hated* that movie, and it freaked her out. It's no surprise she writes rom-coms now."

Spring laughed softly. "Anyway, she was starting to freak out Autumn a bit too—we were so punchy from the bus trip—when we heard a chainsaw revving, and this massive man with a bandana over his nose and mouth comes from behind one of the cabins—Starlight, which was my cabin. Anyway, there he is with his chainsaw raised. Autumn or Snow, I can't remember, yelled, 'Leatherface!' and Summer started screaming for us to run, but her shoelace was caught on something, and she couldn't get out of the truck bed, so she lamented, 'Forget about me, *saavvve* yourselves.' Oh my gosh, we laughed so hard." The dormant residual laughter stirred in her. "Turns out it was the maintenance man, Skip, who was really a gentle giant."

"Say what you will, but you miss her, Spring."

"Maybe, I don't know. Sometimes you can't go back, Mal. Autumn and I talked about the Seasons today. I don't think there is a force strong enough to bring us together. And, I might add, you should be grateful I went out with Craig. That date proved what a great boyfriend you were."

"What about the Kappa Alpha party?"

"Never mind." She smiled. "Don't tell me you didn't kiss a few girls at some of the graduation parties we went to that year. None of your football buddies gave you up either, mister."

"Ah yes, Jenny Reed. Man, she was—"

Spring tossed her napkin at him. "Hush."

"—nothing compared to you."

"More like it."

They'd found their rhythm again, a deeper rhythm now that she carried no secrets. He did see her differently, and to her surprise, it was with greater love and respect.

The kitchen phone jingled, and Mal rose to answer it. "Dan was working on a new interface when I left work."

Spring started stacking the dishes, wondering if a midnight swim with Mal might be a pleasant way to end the evening. Without the weight of her secret, she felt a greater freedom to love—her husband and their soon-to-be child, if God so blessed.

"Babe, it's for you. Autumn." Mal stood in the doorway with a gallon of ice cream in one hand and portable phone in the other. "You know," he whispered, "I think she'd hit it off with Lucas. He's smart, funny, plays a mean game of golf."

Lucas was Mal's best friend from college, and one of the new partners in the firm. He was too handsome for his own good.

"She doesn't do blind dates, and she hates golf." Spring took the phone. "Autumn, hey, what's up? Greta? I don't know . . ." Spring headed inside, scanning the island for the mail. "How do you feel about blind dates and golf?" She laughed. "As I thought. No reason. She what? You're kidding. Hold on, I'm looking." Spring shuffled through the mail, and there on the bottom was a note postmarked *OK*. She pulled out the card to see the exact same words Autumn had just read to her.

Spring,

Summer is in Tumbleweed. Been here since June. One word comes to mind. Reconcile. I may be the Baby Season, but I've been to medical school, so I know stuff. Summer misses the Four Seasons. She hurts over that summer. I can see it in her eyes if anyone brings up Camp Tumbleweed. Won't you come visit? Labor Day weekend. Darrian and I have a big place on Skiatook Lake. You can stay with us.

There's also a lovely, modern B&B in town. Bring your family. Yes, I'm writing to Autumn and Snow as well. I love you all so much, but this rift must end.

> *Yours always,*
> *Greta*

Summer

'77

No one could ever tell Summer that God didn't have a sense of humor. Not while she stood in her Bryant Hall dorm room overlooking the FSU pool.

The very pool where she was arrested for vandalism and trespassing.

If the summer had gone as planned, she'd be laughing about this irony with the Four Seasons over a can of Miller Lite. They'd brag about their antics to the various sorority houses they rushed. They'd regale fellow rushees, new friends, and classmates with how they attempted to fill the great pool with bubbles. *Soap bubbles in the Westcott Fountain is for amateurs.*

But the summer of '77 wrote a very different story.

"We need to black out this window." Summer's declaration to her new roommate left no room for rebuttal. "I hate all the light."

"What? I love the light. I'm not living in the dark, Summer." Teri leaned against the glass. "I love seeing the pool. I'm on the swim team, you know."

"Then find a roommate on the swim team."

Nothing, nothing was right in Summer Wilde's world. She hoped diving into school, *doing* the plan she'd talked about for years, would make her feel some sense of normalcy. She'd tried to room with her cousin, but it was too late. So, Summer went with the luck of the draw. Teri was nice enough. From Miami. Pretty. Very neat. But she wasn't a Season.

When was it that Summer realized nothing—*nothing*—plugged all the holes in her heart? The day she left Camp Tumbleweed? The day she arrived home, or the day after? The day she moved on campus? All of the above?

The biggest cavern was the truth about her parents' marriage. They'd lied to her. Things were *not* good.

Her best friends had secrets. Spring's pregnancy was one thing, but Snow and Autumn didn't even *hint* at wanting to go a different way. Where was the love? The trust?

Maybe she could've managed those things, given time. But what she couldn't get over was Dad had a *real* daughter. Bone of his bone, flesh of his flesh. Summer was "Lily's kid."

His *real* daughter was Snow. How many nights had she spent at Summer's house? How many pool Saturdays, barbecues, birthdays, Christmas and spring break vacations had they shared? All the while Dad knew. Boo on Babs for keeping it all a secret. A million boos on Autumn for blurting it out like a ref throwing a flag on the football field.

What did it matter? Summer didn't have a father. Not a real one. The guy who contributed to her existence was a skank. A playboy who scattered his seed everywhere.

After camp, Dad assured her, *"Nothing changes between you and me, Summer. You are my daughter."* Maybe he meant it, but every weekend he carved out time with Snow before she and Babs drove out to California.

Suddenly Snow was Cinderella, and Summer an ugly stepsister.

"Summer, did you hear me?"

She turned to Teri. "No, what?"

"If you're going to be like this all quarter, I will find a new roommate."

Summer shrugged. "Go ahead."

Teri snatched up her suede fringed purse. "I thought we were going to be friends."

"We were never going to be friends."

Summer didn't have a space for friends. No one could replace the friends she'd just lost. Besides, she couldn't bear the idea of getting close to someone only to lose them.

She'd kept Levi at arm's length the night before she departed Tumbleweed. They sat on the dock, feet kicking through the lake water, and said pithy things like, *"It was cool to meet you"* and *"Will you write me?"*

When he kissed her good-bye, she wanted to let go, give in, love away the pain, but he was smarter than she realized.

"You're hurting over your dad, Summer."

The knock on the dorm door startled her. "Who is it?"

Billy Crumpet peered inside. "Me, unless you're going to throw something at me."

"I should. You escaped community service." Summer glanced around. Everything was still in boxes, except for the keys to the '69 VW Bug convertible Dad and Mom bought for her.

"It was in the plan long before the pool party," Mom said. *"This is not because of, well, what happened at camp with Snow."*

"I heard you and the Seasons had a sweet deal in Tornado Alley." Billy entered the room, leaving the door open.

"We did. Until we didn't." Billy's expression turned into a big question mark, so she moved on. "What's up?"

"Some of the guys are going to lunch. Want to come?"

"What guys? None of your Kappa Alpha brothers, I hope."

"Guys from the team. Do you remember the dude I was with when you first came on campus?"

"Tall, good-looking guy with lots of hair?"

"Yeah, Wally Woodham."

"No, I didn't notice."

Crumpet had a cool laugh. "Yeah, right. Anyway, he's our QB. Well, one of our QBs."

"I know who he is, Billy."

"Good, 'cause he wants to meet you."

Really? "Why would I want to meet him?"

"He's nice, cool. It's just lunch, Summer, not a marriage proposal." She threw her keys at him, which he caught in midair. "Besides, I owe you lunch and then some."

"And then some is right, bucko." She took her keys back.

"So, your summer as camp counselors in Kansas or wherever went well?"

"Oklahoma." Summer pulled out her ponytail holder and fluffed her hair with her fingers. "If you want to go to lunch, let's go. I'm starved."

Billy waited by the door. "I haven't seen Spring on campus yet. I looked for all y'all during rush. A bunch of us went to sorority row to whistle at the rushees. Didn't see any of the Seasons."

"Spring decided to take a year off."

His eyes popped wide. "No way. Did she hit her head on a rock or something?"

Or something. "She'll be here next year. She'll be homecoming queen, you watch." It was the Spring Duval way.

"What about Autumn and Snow? What are they—"

"Autumn's at cosmetology school."

Billy laughed out loud.

"Snow went to film school at UCLA."

Summer grabbed some cash from an envelope her so-called Dad handed her that morning and stuck it in her shorts pocket, along with her dorm key. "Are we going or what?"

Billy grabbed her hand as she passed by. "Hey, I'm *really* sorry about the pool party. And about what happened in my room."

"Forget it. So we made out for a few minutes. We were all pretty toasted." She started toward the stairs, passing Teri, who walked and whispered with another girl.

"Is it weird being here without the Seasons?"

"Not really," she lied. "We're moving on. A couple of us aren't even friends anymore."

"What the heck happened in Oklahoma?" Billy's low whistle echoed in the stairwell. "I'm not sure the world will stay on its axis if the Four Seasons aren't together."

"Well, then, hold on to your hat."

Summer didn't know about the rest of the world, but hers was definitely off its axis, and she had nothing to hold on to. Not even a hat.

37

That's the Power of Love

Summer

'97

Sitting at the prep table in O'Sullivan's kitchen, she ate a grilled chicken salad with a Diet Coke and a propped-open copy of *The Thorn Birds*, a book she'd always wanted to read but never took the time.

Since she was *confronted* by the Preacher two weeks ago as she headed out of town, she'd found peace. Not the temporary, shallow kind she was used to after a good show, but a real, true, deep-down, didn't-know-this-existed peace. It was clean, pure, and without end.

As August ended and Labor Day crept up on the calendar, she barely recognized herself as the roughed-up, worn-out, down-on-herself girl who drove into Tumbleweed three months ago.

These days, she slept in. Read books—something she'd always mocked Snow and Autumn about. Finally, she got it. Books were transformative.

She harvested vegetables from her garden and used them in *Joy of Cooking* recipes. Mrs. Foley was teaching her how to can.

Another bite of her salad and she turned the page, looking up as Sooner casually walked by and slid a plate of hot, golden, fresh-from-the-vat fries toward her.

"Sooner," she said with a chuckle, "I told you, no more fries. I must be getting old or something 'cause if I eat fries, I burp through the first set."

"Yeah? Then how come you eat almost all of them every week? Eat half and you won't burp so much." He slapped the bell sitting in the service window. "Oaklee, table one up."

"Hey, babe." Levi planted a full-lipped, warm kiss on her cheek and reached for a fry. "The cabinets came for your kitchen. Asa and I can install them next week."

"You are the best boyfriend ever." She pulled him to her for another kiss. "I still can't believe Murry sold me the house."

"Why not, when you offered him twenty grand over appraisal?" Levi sat on the other stool and flashed three fingers to Sooner. His favorite. Number Three, the Cowboy-Up Cheeseburger.

He'd not presented the engagement ring to her again since her about-face and return to Tumbleweed. In fact, she didn't tell him or Tank she was back for over a week. She and the Preacher had some work to do.

Then Levi ran into Murry, who said, *"Just sold the house to Summer. I thought she was leaving, but I guess not."* Ten minutes later, Levi knocked on her door.

When she put her head on the pillow at night, she felt the thickness of his chest where she'd fallen against him, weeping, relaying the story of the Preacher on the side of the road between sobs, and how He sat with her on the porch as she played her guitar. Only not in person anymore, but in Spirit.

Levi declared his love, and nothing else was said about the afternoon she left.

He snatched a piece of chicken from her salad as his new cell phone went off. He peeked at the screen, then walked toward a back corner, about the only place his cellular worked in the diner. Ho, that boy looked good coming or going.

She'd say yes to him the moment he proposed again. Yet she knew the journey to marriage would take some months. They both realized she had more work to do with the Preacher, unpacking His truths to eradicate her lies and fears and pain. She also needed more info on *"Sing for Me."*

She'd spent a lot of time facedown weeping the week she was alone at the cottage. She was a sweet mess. She grieved the loss of Nashville, and in some crazy way, she knew He grieved with her.

"I know, I know, but what I have for you . . ."

Clark nearly burst an artery when she told him she wasn't signing with SongTunes. *"Are you kidding me? Summer, this is what we've wanted—worked for—and now you're telling me no joy?"* He cussed a bit more and hung up on her before she could ask, *"Who's we, Batman?"*

She'd talked to Mom a lot more, and Dad? He was flying out in two weeks. Levi invited him to the Circle F, and Summer was okay with it. This meeting was long overdue, and she finally found the courage to admit she missed him.

Levi was still on the phone when Sooner set down his dinner. "Babe," Summer said. "Get it while it's hot."

Summer eyed her fry plate. Empty. Had she really eaten all the fries? Good grief.

She'd written three new songs. One about starting over and one about Levi. Lyrics and melodies were just flowing out of her. Then, Monday night while Levi was at 4-H, she wrote a song about the friends she loved and lost.

She laughed and cried through every iteration of the lyrics and chords. The melody was Beatles meets Tim McGraw, with a touch of the Bangles cleverness, until the chorus, where the simple truth took over.

Maybe, in some way, she hoped the wind would carry the song to Spring, Autumn, and Snow. She'd played it for Baby Season, whose eyes filled with big tears.

"Please reconcile, Summer."

"I don't think they want to, Greta. I said some pretty harsh things that night on the dock. Now there's too much water under the bridge."

"It's shallow water. You can cross, I know it."

How Summer loved that girl. She was a remnant of the Seasons and carried everything they'd been.

Levi returned to the prep table and fixed on his dinner plate, setting his phone aside.

"A rancher in Texas is selling his stock," he said. "I'm trying to figure out if we need to buy one of his bulls. I might run down there next week."

"Monday's Labor Day. Does your family celebrate? I'm not working. I could go with you."

"Um, yeah, sure." Levi bit into his burger. "Won't be much fun."

"Look, cowboy, if you don't want my company—"

"I always want your company."

"Then I'll go with. However, you can do the ranching and I'll do the musicking." Was the melody she just sang from *Oklahoma* or *Cinderella*? Hmmm. Hard to tell.

He laughed, covering his full mouth with the back of his hand.

"Sum, you singing or what?" Tank poked his head around the kitchen door. "Full house tonight, girl. I feel like a parrot, telling everyone you ain't got no CDs. We need to get your new stuff recorded."

Summer shrugged and reached for her guitar. She remained in no hurry to track her songs. She loved singing them for those in the room and was perfectly fine with letting the words and melodies go with them.

She took her seat on the stage, and Oaklee hurried to the soundboard. Poor thing was pulling double duty tonight because Richie Cantwell, Tank's new busboy and soundman, had football camp. Summer would share extra tips from the jar with her.

"Evening, all. Happy Labor Day weekend."

"Evening, Summer." The crowd, with one voice, in between the clank of forks and knives on their plates.

She strummed and tuned her guitar, chatting about the updates to her sweet cottage and how next week she might be learning how to discern a good bull.

"An actual bull. *Moo.* Not whether you're telling me a big fat lie or not." That drew a good laugh. "Eighteen years on the road out of Nashville, I can smell the manure before you open your mouth."

She finished tuning, sipped her water, and started one of her new songs. It wasn't first on the set list. In fact, she wasn't sure she was ready to sing it for anyone. But she'd played through the chords while tuning.

"This is a new song," she said. "Can't decide if it's any good or not, so I'll leave it to y'all." She smiled, looking through the dimly lit diner, and was about to signal to Oaklee that the sound was perfect when her gaze stopped on a familiar face.

The Preacher stood against the wall in His usual garb. But instead of His presence filling her with a big fat question mark, she felt like He'd come to hear her sing. *For Him.*

He smiled and gave her a solitary nod, and in doing so, released something from heaven in the room.

Summer started the song from the top. The room's hush felt weighty. Profound. Her voice sounded clear and pure, even to her tired ears, as she sang her ode of apology.

> When I last saw you, I said some things I regret.
> Fire and ice that can't be unsaid.
> And though time heals all wounds,
> The years have not built a bridge back to you.

Her voice broke, and she breathed in to steady the next lyric. *Help me, Preacher.* Eyes closed, she sensed another shift in the atmosphere, and a warm tear slipped down her cheek.

> I still hold dear the memories of your face,
> The way we laughed, the way we passed summer days
> I miss you, old friend, your heart connected to mine,
> I miss you every single day, with every tick of time.
> I don't know how to come back to you
> Seems the years have stolen the will and the way
> Yet I walk incomplete until I see you again.
> My friend, oh my faithful friend.
>
> We were little girls together, grown into women
> Holding hands through life's corridor
> I still can't believe that we are no more
> My friend and me, my friend and me.
>
> I said a few things that I regret
> I can't take back, the pain I said
> Our broken hearts did heal somehow
> But oh, my friend, I'm sorry now, so sorry now
> How I long to see your face,
> Now I know God's amazing grace,
> I send you all my love, I give you all my love,
> My friend, oh my faithful friend.

Lost in the song, in the prayer between the lyrics, Summer sang the last word and played the last chord, resting in the truth of her tribute. It didn't matter if they liked it; the lyrics were her freedom anthem.

After a moment, she inhaled and opened her eyes to see her song *literally* standing in front of her.

Spring, Autumn, and Snow.

Summer's guitar hit the stage with a resounding thump-clank as she scrambled to the floor, tripping over mic and speaker cables to shoot into Autumn's arms.

"I'm sorry. So, so sorry." She wrapped her up, squeezing her as if to deposit her joy and apology into her friend. "I'm sorry. Please, please forgive me. Please."

"It's okay, it's okay, me too. Me too." They rocked side to side, weeping, in the witness of every eye in the diner. "All's forgiven, all's forgiven."

"Let me in here." Spring fell into the hug. Still clinging to Autumn, Summer roped her in. "Man, I've missed you, girl. So, so, so much."

Wait. Snow, where was Snow? She stood off next to a handsome man, hands pressed to her damp cheeks.

"Hey," Summer said, looking around Spring and Autumn. "Y-you're here."

"This guy dragged me . . . onto . . ." Her eyes misted, and her speech wavered. "Um, onto . . . the, the, you know . . ." She made airplane wings. "Airplane."

"Go," Spring whispered, pushing Summer forward.

The sounds and life of the diner froze as Summer and Snow fell into each other's arms.

"I love you, I do. I do, and I'm so, so, so sorry." Summer had been storing up that word for far too long. "You're my sister, and—"

"No, you're *my* sister."

She had a sister. With whom she'd actually had a childhood. Maybe not in the traditional sense, but in every other way.

"I love you, Snow."

"Oh, Summer, I love you too. More than you'll ever know, you irritating ball of fire."

"Back at you, you beautiful block of wintery ice."

The tears gave way to laughter. To healing. Spring and Autumn piled back into the hug, and Tank, with his booming voice, announced, "Friends, we're witnessing the return of the Four Seasons and something akin to a miracle."

The customers cheered and applauded, no doubt feeling the love in the diner.

"How?" Summer said, drying her cheeks with the napkins some-one passed her. "W-what? Why?"

"Baby Season." Spring pointed to Greta, who waited on the edge of their reunion, hands clasped under her chin, her teary expression full of joy.

"Used her doctor credentials to lecture us." Autumn reached for Dr. Yeager. "She said we had to reconcile, and she was right."

"I knew y'all still loved each other." Greta fell into the Seasons with a low laugh-cry. "I never thought I'd see this day, though. I love you all so much. The summer of '77 was the best summer of my life. It changed me."

"Because you were a doctor in Snow's play seven times." Summer roped her arm around Greta, still wiping her happy tears. "Y'all want to stay for the set?"

"Are you kidding?"

"Just try and kick us out."

Greta pointed to Levi, who was tucked against the wall at his usual table. "To be honest, though, he started it. He knew Summer needed y'all. He asked me to reach out."

Levi waved, and for the first time since she'd known him, looked embarrassed. She motioned for him to join them, kissing him as her heart brimmed.

"Thank you, Sneaky Cowboy." How she loved him.

"I loved you too much to see you hurting."

"There it is, Spring. Right there, that's it," Autumn said. "The force more powerful than a tornado, hurricane, nor'easter, and blizzard."

Spring wiped her cheeks. "Love! Of course, Fall, of course. Love."

Autumn

'97

Her season was coming. Autumn sensed it in the way a fall fragrance accented the final weeks of summer. What was next for her?

Something extraordinary happened in O'Sullivan's last night. Something beyond her five senses. A love she'd never sensed before filled the diner, and she wanted more.

This Saturday afternoon, Autumn Childe and the Five Seasons lay head-to-head in the shade and sun, creating a sunflower on the refurbished Camp Tumbleweed dock, chatting and catching up on the last twenty years.

She was warm, content, and peaceful, listening to her friends' conversation, drifting in and out, the residue of last night still with her.

"Levi fixed up the cabins and dock for us," Summer said. "I had no idea."

"Mal and I are trying for a baby." Spring. "We're so excited."

"Darrian and I are too," Greta said.

Summer and Snow sat up with an excited "Yay!" But Autumn only raised her hand and waited for someone to slap her a high five. She was just too relaxed to move.

". . . come to my movie premiere next year. I'll send you the dates as soon as I know."

". . . Summer's wedding . . . can't collide."

"He's not even asked me yet . . . say yes . . . heartbeat."

Good, so, so good. Why had she wasted so many years in fear and anxiety? Wonder what Dr. Heavy-Bangs would have to say about this?

Autumn drifted into a warm, cozy sleep, then popped awake as Summer talked about the Preacher. What preacher? A preacher?

The Preacher? Her song? No, what was she saying about a tent on the prairie in '77?

Spring, Snow, and Greta said things like, "Wow" and "Really?" then peppered her with questions. Spring knew this Preacher but not from the tent. Where was Autumn during all of this? Ah, who cared? Today was one with the outdoors, the dock, the voices of friends and nature, with the love and peace she hoped would never end.

"I'll catch you." Autumn bolted up, glancing around. The deep, resonating, masculine voice made her pulse surge. Who said that? She'd *heard* a man's voice. Yet no man was on the premises.

"Did y'all hear something?" she said.

"Just the wind in the trees and the birds singing."

"Just Summer going on and on about Levi. He best propose soon, or she'll explode."

"Shut up, I will not."

Autumn smiled. The laughter of the Five Seasons was infectious.

"We owe Greta for—"

Yes, they owed Greta a debt that couldn't be paid.

"I'll catch you." The voice startled her. Even more because she knew what it meant.

Autumn gazed toward the water. Diving in was her final hurdle. To truly be free of the past. To thumb her nose at her fears.

Jump.

She hesitated, then stood with legs trembling. It was time. If not now, when? She'd been trapped in some sort of anxiety about death and water for twenty-two years. Blaine was long gone. He was free. Yet she was a prisoner.

She started for the front of the dock.

"Autumn, where're you going?" Snow said.

"In there." She pointed to Skiatook Lake with only an ounce of confidence.

"Wait, really?" Snow jumped up, then Spring, Summer, and Greta.

Yes, really. And it was now or never. Autumn backed up for some running room, and without another moment of hesitation, she took off, her feet hammering the new golden boards—*don't stop, don't stop, don't stop*—and pushed off the edge, drawing her legs to her chest, and splashed through the surface.

Down, down, down, she exhaled fear, anxiety, her limitations. Exhaling, exhaling, exhaling. When she came up for air, the Seasons stood on the shore, shouting to kingdom come.

"Autumn, you did it!"

"Way to go!"

"Biggest splash ever." Greta waved her towel like a banner.

A smiling Autumn walked out of the water and back to the dock. "I'm going to do that again. It was fun."

"I'll go with you," Spring said.

"Okay, but who is that talking to Summer and Snow?" A man with gorgeous golden-brown hair, wearing bell-bottoms and a 1970s wide tie.

He laughed and touched Snow's arm. Autumn felt the vibration of His sound, and it meshed with the feelings she carried from last night. When He looked her way, she instantly knew His was the voice. *"I'll catch you."*

"Autumn." Summer waved her over. "This guy showed up the moment you jumped in the lake. Come, I'd like you to meet my friend, the Preacher."

Author Note

One morning, during the writing of this book, I was in the prayer room at church. I went out to do something, and as I passed the sanctuary doors, I felt drawn to go inside. Immediately, I ran into the Lord's presence. It was as if He'd been waiting for me.

"We've spent a lot of time in this room together, haven't we?" He said.

I dropped to my knees in tears. "Yes, we have."

So many hours of prayer, worship, potlucks, youth church, Sunday morning church, fellowshipping with His "other kids" at parties.

He began to talk to me about Summer and the Preacher, and the scene where she realizes she cannot go back to Nashville. I sat on the floor, weeping, while the Lord talked to me about the desert seasons.

"There was always going to be a desert season," He said. "Your choice was if it was with Me or without Me."

In His love and mercy, by His great leadership, He brought Summer, aka you and me, back to where He wanted us all along. Summer is a fictional character, yet the Lord used her to make a point with me about trials and wilderness seasons. We all go through them. It's our choice if we go with Him or without Him. She chose the rough road for her desert season, yet He never left her. Never gave up on her.

The year 2021 was a season of trial for me. There were moments when I thought, "Will this ever end?" Yet as I determined to seek the Lord, to lean all the more to prayer and the Word—praying it, singing it, declaring it, writing it, you-name-it—He met me. He was with me! And that trial season did come to an end. While I hated some aspects of the journey, it marked me, and I am so grateful for what He did in my heart.

If you're in a hard season, lean into Jesus. Trust me, He is with you. Lean into prayer and the truth of His Word.

Grace and peace,
Rachel

Acknowledgments

Every book is a journey. This one is no exception. I mused over this idea for a couple of years. I had a title and a seedling of an idea, but no characters or plot.

In the spring of 2020, I started walking and praying every evening, and it was in those times, Summer, Spring, Autumn, and Snow came alive. As a teenager myself in '77, I remember the anticipation of discovering my life and who I'd become.

I had no real theme when I started this story, but as I wrote and edited, the love of our greatest friend, Jesus, became evident. His love is the force more powerful than a hurricane, tornado, nor'easter, or blizzard to discover truth and heal broken hearts, relationships, and disappointments. First John 4:18 says, "Perfect love drives out all fear." Jesus is that perfect love.

While helping me research an external event to drive the secrets from my characters, my husband discovered the Camp Scott murders. While it wasn't my goal to write in detail about the event of June 1977, I wanted to honor and remember Lori Farmer, Denise Milner, and Michelle Guse in this story. You are not forgotten.

I owe my gratitude to those who helped form this story. Let's start with my cousins, who talked me through a weird time during our family vacation the summer of '21 when I decided to face my fears and jump into the lake from a twenty-two-foot-high cliff. Rebekah, my sweet and funny sister, jumped twice without me— yep, I left her hanging. Thanks for climbing back up one last time. Morgan's "I'm coming, Rachel!" lives in my heart forever. Keri, for listening and offering sound advice. Julie, for being a source of love and encouragement. Kim, my floating-on-the-lake buddy. I love you all! See you in June!

Let's see, there's my amazing agent Chip MacGregor. Thank you!

From Bethany House, the fab Dave Long, who kept "asking." Thank you. Fifteen years after first reading your blogs, when every author buzzed about writing for you, here we are!

My lovely editors Jennifer Veilleux and Hannah Ahlfield. Much appreciation for your help and insights and for reading this manuscript who knows how many times. Thank you to Raela Schoenherr and her marketing team.

Gratitude and hugs to Beth Vogt, who answered my Facetime calls when I wanted to talk through the nitty-gritty details.

To Susie May Warren, for the breakfast conversations at Beachside Cafe.

To Eddie Tucker, friend and worshipper extraordinaire. Thank you for "Let It Burn." I started listening to the advanced release of your album *Oracles* the summer of '21, and while all the songs are great, "Let It Burn" ministered to me in ways I'm not sure I totally comprehend. As of this writing, I've listened to the song well over a thousand times. It was the soundtrack to which I wrote, rewrote, and edited *The Best Summer of Our Lives*. If Hubs was downstairs in his office and heard "Let It Burn," he'd say, "Time to write?" Yep. Eddie, you are a friend, a brother, a mentor, and worshipper of the highest regard. I am permanently marked with your worship and friendship with Jesus. To all the readers, check out *Oracles* on your favorite music platform!

To Scott Stradley, Jeanne and Danny Leininger, and Meg Callahan James who helped me remember Tallahassee "back in the day" and answered questions about Tallahassee and FSU in 1977. Meg gave me tidbits on the FSU pool. Jeanne and her sister Luanne reminded me about the Melting Pot. If I couldn't find the information I needed, I went with the best possible source or did what authors do—make it up!

I lived in Tulsa and Haskell, Oklahoma, as a girl, but the fictitious Tumbleweed is a place I just made up.

Shout out to my big brother Danny Hayes and my friend Kathy Fox who pointed me in the right direction for Tallahassee in the '90s. My memories of Tally end in the late '80s. Any and all mistakes are mine. Or just stuff I made up.

Thank you to all the people who post weird and unusual things on the internet. I found the instructions for the first e.p.t. pregnancy kit on eBay. Believe it or not, the information was invaluable.

My appreciation to the hubster, Tony, who is a gift from God. Thank you to Jesus for everything. And I do mean everything!

Above all, thank you to the readers! I mean it. Your notes and letters mean so much to me. Even if you don't write to me, thank you for spending some time with this story. Or any one of my stories. You're why I do this. In fact, books don't happen without you. God has used you to encourage me on the hardest days. Let's keep doing this for years to come.

Discussion Questions

1. Summer, Spring, Autumn, and Snow have a unique relationship. Growing up, I remember how the dynamics between three or four friends could get messy sometimes. What do you think makes friendships special?

2. Friendships can wound as much as heal. Was there a time in your life when a friend let you down? How did you move on? How did you heal the relationship?

3. Fear is a real factor in today's world. When Lily learned of the Camp Scott murders, she feared for the Tumblers in her charge. How can we be aware of dangers, yet not live in fear? How do we keep fear from being a stronghold?

4. Summer struggles to feel accepted by her father. Was it in her imagination, or was it a real truth? How can we confront the lies we believe of ourselves or others and overcome them?

5. The Four Seasons go to Camp Tumbleweed with secrets. Were they right to hold in those tidbits? Should they have shared? Why do you think Autumn didn't confess she wanted to go to cosmetology school, or Snow to UCLA? Why do you think Spring wouldn't want the support of

her friends if she believed she was pregnant? Are there limits to friendships? What factors keep us from confessing our secrets or plans to our friends?

6. The Preacher calls Summer to "sing for Him," but she doesn't understand and enters a desert season. Have you been through a desert season? Are you in one now?

7. Have you ever blurted something you didn't mean to, like Autumn did? How did you respond? How did the hearer respond?

8. At what lengths do we shield our children from the truth about their parentage or past? Was Babs right to hide the truth from Snow?

9. How have you confronted the lies you believe? Your fears or worries? What is your "jump in the lake" moment?

10. Who is your favorite character and why? Talk about how Jesus is a friend to all.

Rachel Hauck is a *New York Times*, *USA Today*, and *Wall Street Journal* bestselling author. She is a double RITA finalist, and a Christy and Carol Award winner. Rachel was awarded the prestigious Career Achievement Award for her body of original work by *Romantic Times* Book Reviews. Her book *Once Upon a Prince*, first in the ROYAL WEDDING series, was filmed for an Original Hallmark movie.

A graduate of Ohio State University (Go Bucks!) with a degree in Journalism, Rachel is a former sorority girl and a devoted Ohio State football fan. Her bucket list is to stand on the sidelines with Ryan Day.

Rachel lives in sunny central Florida with her husband and ornery cat.

Sign Up for Rachel's Newsletter

Keep up to date with Rachel's latest news on book releases and events by signing up for her email list at the link below.

FOLLOW RACHEL ON SOCIAL MEDIA!

Rachel Hauck   @rachelhauck   @RachelHauck

RachelHauck.com